THE DYING BREED:
HUNTERS

By

TJ Lombardi

A Product of:

Warrior Publishing

https://warriorpub.wordpress.com

THE GOD KING EMMANUEL SAGA

THE DYING BREED:
HUNTERS

BOOK 1

TJ LOMBARDI

The Dying Breed: Hunters

A work of Warrior Publishing LLC

Copyright © 2023 by: Warrior Publishing and TJ Lombardi

ISBN 978-1-960408-00-6 (print)

ISBN 978-1-960408-01-3 (ebook)

CONTENTS

"The only thing required for evil to succeed, is for good men and women to do nothing."

- Unknown Author

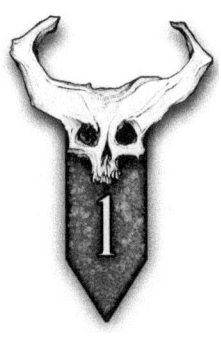

DESTINY

The wind howled in Liam's ears so loudly, he could have sworn the spirit of a wolf was intertwined with it. The temperature grew colder with every passing minute. Liam had told himself to wait until morning, but he couldn't contain his zeal any longer. He had hiked for days in search of this cliff, and when he stood at its base and looked up … he simply grabbed the first handhold he saw. His body began to tremble and he did everything he could not to look down at the valley floor below, but he couldn't fight his natural instincts. His rough guess was that he had climbed close to 400 feet.

He found a small notch in the rock face where he was barely able to sit down. His legs dangling over the edge, he let out a long breath. He could faintly make out the outline of the mountain range. The Valley of Jardak—the meaning of the name seemed to have been lost long ago. He'd asked numerous people about it on his travels, but no one could recall its significance.

Reaching up to a chest pocket that was sewn into his vest, he grabbed a small cloth sack which contained some smoked deer meat he bought earlier that day. Tearing a piece of the jerky off and chewing on it brought a sense of peace to his weary body. *Why didn't I just wait until morning?* he asked himself, though he already knew why. He'd set out on this adventure to find, meet, and witness for himself the warrior Codgarak, a figure that his father Judah had described as a legend. He couldn't wait till morning, not after his travels had informed him this mountain was where Codgarak could be found. The path wasn't easy, though, for the higher he climbed up the cliff face, the heavier the rolling fog became. The mist, carried by the howling wind, created a light sheen of ice over the coarse granite.

Liam tore another piece of the jerky off. This time, though, it had a new flavor; a hint of blood. He snapped his fingers and twisted his free hand in the quick motion of a simple flame-summoning spell. A tiny blue flame leapt upward and danced in the night long enough for him to see the small cuts on his hands. When he looked down, he saw droplets of blood on the rocks. An eerie sensation came over him; the red essence of life seemed like it had returned to a home it once knew. The cliff had begun to cut open his bare hands, but the cold of the night numbed them to the point that he couldn't feel it.

He lowered his hand and enjoyed the dancing of the flame for a few seconds before the next gust of wind extinguished it. His face was pummeled by a wall of mist that blanketed him and left him shivering. The wind didn't just howl this time but seemed to roar. He turned his face into the wind and gazed east towards the Forest of Zareel. It seemed as if the forest itself had launched an attack on the mountain, throwing its hatred at it out of malice for a long and forgotten past.

He placed the last piece of meat in his mouth and struggled to his feet, trying his best to see in the darkness. The frosted cliff shimmered enough for him to find his next handhold. He reached out and gripped the rock. Leaning on his right leg, he transferred his weight and began to lurch upward. Suddenly the rock gave way and his body dangled above the valley. Panicking, he tried to find a new footing as his legs slid up and down the cliff. Time seemed to slow as his fondest memories were brought back to life. Running through the fields with his sister. Sitting with his best friend, laughing at the common folk passing through the town square. Hunting with his father and hearing the calming voice of his mother as she sang while they sat around the campfire. He started to believe he had met his end.

His heart was pounding and he did his best to control his breathing after he miraculously found his footing on a stone ledge. "You're so stupid!" he bellowed at himself. He took a few more deep breaths in gratitude, appreciating the crisp cool air for a moment before he continued his ascent. His right hand was shaking. The strain from his slip had exhausted him to a dangerous level. "Is this truly worth it? Really, Liam? You just couldn't wait until morning … you had to seek out the story of some legend that you are not sure even exists anymore! You're now on a cliffside on the literal edge of death … *you idiot!*" He had opened the doorway for fear and doubt to enter his mind. "You abandoned your home, left everything you've ever known behind … and what are you going to do if you don't find him? *What then? And! What are you going to do after you meet him? Did you even think this through?*" The more he tormented himself, the more his spirit sent waves outward to those who lived and traveled through that realm. Unbeknownst to him, those waves didn't go unheard.

A cold shiver came over him. "And why does it have to be so damn cold?" Unknown to the common traveler, the hatred that had raged between the dark elves and the minotaurs at the beginning of the Age of Magic had never left the valley. The spirits of the dark elves had infused the landscape upon their deaths, transforming it into an eternally cold and desolate tomb.

The war had finished 884 years ago, but Liam didn't know that Thitra Kningol and a select group of his dark elf knights had not died during the war but were still lingering in the crevices of the mountains. The dark elves may have departed their physical bodies, but the dark magic they had utilized to try and win the war had preserved them after death and left them as wraiths.

The wind pushed against Liam, and he braced himself as best he could while reaching upward to the next crack in the rock. Shoving his hand deep inside and finding a hold, he repositioned himself just as he heard the faintest of whispers. "You're not going to make it, Liam."

His brow tightened and he squinted his eyes, trying to discern what he had just heard. *Was that me?* he asked himself. His fatigue had reached the point where he didn't know which thoughts were his own and which sprang from the howling wind that had begun to torment his mind and spirit. Huffing aloud, "This is insane," he used what little energy he still had to shake his head in disbelief and hoist himself to the next hold. "This is what you really want, huh? *'I want to follow my destiny!'*" Liam mocked himself in a whiny voice.

"Death is your only destiny." The whisper returned. Liam's whole body tensed up this time. *That wasn't me … was it?* He second-guessed himself yet again.

Liam fostered a slight glimmer of hope as he climbed up onto the point of a ledge. A giant circular cave had once cut into the cliff here, but it had caved in and been sealed up. A charred and burnt appearance coated the rocks that closed it. "Damn it!" he cursed, shoving his hands into his armpits to try and warm them. He followed the edge of the shape and noticed that the rocks seemed to show an old path that had been lost to the cliff long ago. As he leaned out to get a better look, he speculated that the mountain had been reshaped over time, and he was convinced an old pathway continued upward.

"I've come all this way. I might as well finish it!" Liam let out in a disgruntled yet determined tone.

"There's nothing to finish … is there?" Liam now began to think that his mind was playing tricks on him. *Why is my mind acting this way?* he thought. "Why is your mind acting this way, Liam?" the whisper echoed.

He had made his way another sixty feet from the former cave when, stretching out his arm, he grabbed hold of the rocks and felt it. The only way he could describe it was like a cold blanket wrapping itself around him. The feeling of something weighing him down and latching onto him.

He began to pull on the next rock, but it gave way and launched itself out of his hand and tumbled down the mountain. Thankfully he remained calm and collected, but he had a good secure footing this time, so it didn't actually affect him. "Why keep climbing? The only thing that awaits you is death." The whisper seemed to have a crackle in its voice at the end.

That … isn't … me. His eyes began to widen in fear. He now realized, it wasn't his mind playing tricks on him. He wasn't alone on this mountain. His heart began to thump, getting louder until it turned to a pounding in his chest. His breathing got faster, and the feeling of urgency to get off the cliff as quickly as possible came over him.

"To hell with this!" he shouted as he launched himself with his legs and began to claw upwards as if he were channeling the spirit of a mountain leopard. He charged upward as fast as he could. The weight wrapped around him now felt like it was trying to pull on him. *"Get off me!"* he yelled, and his body tensed further as the cold shroud tightened its grasp around him. He tried to block out the pain and exhaustion, internally pleading with his body for more energy and the strength to reach the top of the cliff and hopefully escape what he believed was a demon.

"Get off you?" It didn't hide its presence any longer. The scratchy voice was terrifying to hear in its true tone. "You're as good as dead, boy!" The voice crackled and sent out a bone-chilling scream, as he felt a blow to his face. The force didn't glance off him however, the feeling of an energy which entered him, grabbed hold and tried to tear this internal essence free from his physical body. The wind, seemingly on command, picked up its intensity as it screamed around him.

Liam was determined not to give in, and he continued to fight against the forces committed to preventing his progress. Every gust of wind tore across the cliff in an attempt to rip him off its surface. The demonic voice that haunted him began to scream out into the night. A beaconing cry calling out for others to home in on. He gazed upward and was hastily planning his next steps when a dark figure appeared above him. The wind and fog contoured around its shape, and a new screeching voice rang out as it dived straight towards him.

He reached out for the next handhold and felt pain tearing down his arm as claws dug into his hand. They were dragged down his arm and finally broke free at his shoulder. The screeching of metal pierced his ears. Whatever had just clawed him had left an imprint on the light armor that protected his shoulders and neck.

He couldn't control his heart, his breathing, and his mind screamed internally in fear. *I'm not going to make it!* echoed in his mind. "YOU'RE MINE, CHILD," the voice cried out as the second voice echoed from below. "DORMAGYN FOL WHOL UNS'AA!" Liam didn't know what it was, but … *That doesn't sound good!* He heard what sounded like claws tearing on the rocks. The second spirit was in pursuit of him as the first one still clung around his upper torso, doing its best to pull him off the cliffside.

As he sensed the second spirit come closer, Liam steadied himself. He grabbed the hilt of his father's sword, which was fastened to his belt, but with so little to cling to on the cliff face, he decided against it. He readied his dagger in his hand instead and shoved it backward as the screaming spirit flung itself past and took another swipe with its claws. The voices began to laugh. "Your pathetic knife can't hurt us, you stupid child!"

Liam didn't waste any time as he leapt and propelled his way upward. *There!* His eyes focused on a dim light that radiated from somewhere above him. *A cave!* The thick fog had stopped the light from escaping until he got within closer range. *"I … I … I can't make that!"* Liam shouted as he struggled for air and strength. The spirit screamed in anger, and he felt it pulling against him the fiercest it had yet. The second spirit came soaring down upon him. This time its claws caught his face and sent him falling backwards, bashing his head against the rock. "Owww!," Liam slowly exhaled. Though he could barely see in the darkness, he felt like he was spinning in circles. A sharp stinging pain ran through his head as he did everything he could to regain his composure and awareness.

His foothold had been deep enough when the wraith hit him from above, it sent him straight backwards, but his foot was wedged so tightly that it held the weight of his body. He couldn't feel it yet, but his ankle had broken under the strain. His dagger had left his grip and was probably clanging against the valley floor by now. He grabbed his head and touched his face, quickly realizing he was hanging upside down. For a few seconds, he thought this was finally the end. *It isn't worth it … let death take you.* He exhaled painfully. *It is everyone's destiny to die …* Before he finished the thought, however, his vision cleared enough for him to see a glimmer of light coming from the cave above. It glowed brighter as a torch pierced the fog. A low, forceful voice echoed out so the entire valley could hear it over the wind. "KHEL, ATHIYK, QUORTEK, DORN RUSVANAR DOS MAL'RAK MZILD!"

Liam heard the screeching of the spirits rise past him up the cliff, seeming to head towards the figure holding the torch. He ignored the pain in his ankle and surprisingly didn't have too much trouble regaining his footing. Looking up at the light, he listened.

"SSUSSUN DE' DRO, SSUSSUN DE' ELGHINN
SSUSSUN DE' DRO, SSUSSUN DE' ELGHINN!"

All Liam could see was a blinding streak of light cutting through the fog. Two vertical lines blazed in unison like scorching iron ripped directly from a forge.

"ELGG LIL' OLOTH, NACTA LIL' ISTO!"

As the spell was completed, two horizontal lines appeared and crossed paths with the vertical lines. The valley was immediately illuminated in deep orange with an overlay of fierce red. Just as Liam was able to take in the grand scale of the power he was witnessing, he saw the horizontal lines cut across the sky in a beam. As they did so, he saw two figures appear out of thin air, and he could also make out their bodies being severed in two by the beams of light. The vertical rays of light simultaneously angled downward and snapped with ferocity onto the bisected creatures. They burst into flames and the voice which had been haunting him could be heard being snuffed out. As they became engulfed in flames, Liam realized they were the shapes of elves and not what he'd always imagined demons to look like, with horns and distorted muscles.

After the elves had been consumed, the figure on the cliff faded back into darkness. Surprisingly, the fog seemed to evaporate, and the moonlight shone upon the cliff and revealed a pathway to the cave.

It took him another two hours to climb the remaining part, his ankle slowing him down the whole way. As he crested the edge of the cliff near the entrance to the cave, he fell to his stomach. Crawling with his final ounce of strength, Liam entered the cave and collapsed. He didn't know what or who the figure was that had exited the cave, but it had destroyed the two figures that had haunted him halfway up the cliff. His only hope was "the enemy of my enemy is my friend," and with that belief, he felt he had temporarily found safety. As he faded out of consciousness, Liam's final thought was *It is everyone's destiny to die ... but today is not my day.*

THE CLIFF

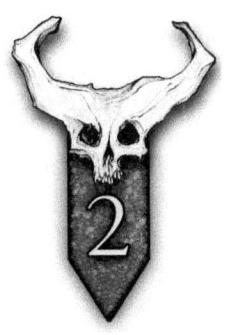

THE LEGEND

Liam's hearing began to return before his eyes opened.

He didn't need to see in order to feel the pain raging throughout his body, though. It seemed to surge from his ankle all the way to his head. He simply grunted. Finally, he attempted to move. Bringing his hand up, he grabbed his head, the belief that holding his head would bring some sort of comfort to his agony. "This is my luck," he muttered.

He still hadn't opened his eyes, but it wouldn't have mattered. Before he knew it, an added jolt came shooting upward as the handle of a battle-ax was jabbed into his gut. Liam couldn't contain his natural outburst. "Owww!" His muscles flared with what little energy they still contained as his body instinctively curled up to protect the area that had just been struck.

"The boy has chosen to live, I see." A deep voice said. He stood at the opening of the cave, a carved stone pipe protruding from his mouth as he exhaled the smoke from his last drag of his favorite Conocetico shade tobacco leaf. "I will miss this. One must not take such moments for granted." The sun had just set, and the clouds lingering overhead glowed with a golden radiance, reflecting the sun's rays. Liam's savior turned and walked back into the cave, past his injured body.

Liam still couldn't find the strength to open his eyes. All he could manage was the thought that whoever this was, they'd chosen not to kill him … at least for now. He heard some noise in the distance but couldn't determine exactly what it was; all he could tell was that footsteps were approaching him. He felt a giant hand grab his shoulder, repositioning his body against his will. He strained for a moment as he was forced to lie on his back. He began to moan and grimace. "Be still," The voice instructed him. Liam then felt a knife blade under his shirt and heard the fabric being cut until his chest was exposed. What felt like a large rock was placed on his chest. Soon afterwards, a pulse was emitted directly into his chest and reverberated all the way to the ends of his limbs and head. This wave of energy felt amazing! It instantly began to ease his pain, and before he could think of anything else, he passed out again.

Liam awoke to the sound of crackling flames. He began to blink slowly in an attempt to bring his surroundings into focus. A cool breeze hit his feet and drifted lightly over him, but could also feel a radiating heat behind him that countered the cold draft. His vision started to come back into focus and he realized it was either late in the evening or early morning, long before sunrise. A giant blanket had been placed over him, but the rock he remembered feeling earlier on his chest was gone. He took a deep breath and began to stretch. A smile appeared on his face and grew bigger as the realization set in: *I'm not in pain!* He continued to stretch, allowing his body to embrace its renewed vigor.

"You have respawned, I see." The deep voice carried through the cave from behind Liam. He sat up slightly and braced himself on his elbow as he twisted around to look behind him. All he could see, however, was the dancing flames of the campfire. Pictures were carved into the stone walls, complemented by words written in a language he had not seen before.

He felt confident that he wouldn't be attacked. He had, after all, been brought back to life by this stranger. "Yes … all thanks to you," he replied to the depth of the cave.

Liam got to his feet. He checked to ensure his father's sword was still strapped to his side, he then tightened the blanket—which appeared similar to a poncho—around his upper torso, and when he felt he presented a strong, confident image, he moved towards the campfire.

From the black depths of the cave came a long exhale. The force of it kicked up the dirt floor, the dust reflecting the light of the fire, and Liam noticed his rescuer wasn't far away from him. "What brings you to my cave?" The deep, yet curious voice asked.

Adventure leaping off his tongue, Liam proclaimed excitedly, "I have been on a journey to find a warrior of old. The legend that my father spoke of in his stories. He fought alongside him in battles and, in his words, 'would never have lived' if it weren't for him intervening on several occasions." Liam took a quick pause in his explanation but only received another dust cloud in response. "My father once said, 'I would follow him to the gates of hell and beyond, for I knew if I were to die, it'd be next to the greatest warrior I had ever witnessed, or he would ensure I would return to my family. I trusted him more than any other in the land.'"

Liam raised his chin and let out his own exhale, proud to tell of the lasting impression his father had imparted to him.

Another pause left Liam heavy with anticipation. "You haven't spoken this warrior's name," The voice asked and continued, "What does this warrior look like?"

Liam's eyes widened slightly as he realized he had missed the opportunity to convey those important details. "Ahh, yes. Cod-gar-ak." He pronounced it slowly in an attempt to make sure he honored the name his father had shared. His excitement quickly returned as he continued eagerly. "My father said to picture a warrior twice my size, twice as wide, with a confident stride that stood firm like tree roots! Strength to lift any size boulder you could find! A tactician of war and wisdom that matched the greatest wizards and mages!"

A smile broke across Liam's face this time. One could see that he had daydreamed of battles involving his father, this magnificent warrior, and himself throughout his childhood. As a young boy, he'd found the "stick of power" in the forest and filled his days fighting off the evil armies and monsters of his imagination. The young lad had dreamed of adventures, battles, and wars in a glorified mindscape, but he had never experienced them or seen their true nature.

The Voice interrupted Liam's memories with "You have not given me your names." Liam again felt he had failed slightly. He wanted to portray himself as someone who knew what destiny awaited him, yet he couldn't even produce the proper details in his presentation. *You're an idiot!* he thought.

"My father is Judah and I am Liam. From Artho."

The response was much quicker this time. "Judah and Liam of Artho."

Another pause filled the cave. Liam, growing impatient, finally lifted his hand to block the light of the campfire from his eyes, and as he did so, a large shuffling took place. He watched the giant figure beyond the fire rise from a seated position, stand erect, and take a forceful step forward into the light. Liam watched as a monstrous minotaur came into view. Fear immediately raced through his body. The beast towering over Liam, as he was twice as tall and twice as wide, but it wasn't just his size that terrified Liam. It was the minotaur's eyes.

It leaned over and brought his head lower so his eyes were level with Liam's. Liam was frozen with fear, and with his eyes ever widening, his brain was immersed in analyzing the details. The minotaur's cheeks were slightly sunken, highlighting his chiseled and refined features. Scars covered his face from wounds received in many battles and wars past. His horns projected the terrifying dominance of an experienced warrior who had survived at a time when many die young. His eyes glowed like a blacksmith's forge, but they had an active swirl that left Liam with the feeling that this beast standing before him fed on death and destruction.

Liam's fear was pierced when an outstretched hand appeared. Liam gazed upon this massive hand, which was capped with giant claws and custom metal armor that protected the back of the hand and proceeded up the forearm. "I am Codgarak, young Liam of Artho." Liam, finally able to break free of his terror, reached out his hand and met Codgarak's greeting.

His hand was barely half the size of Codgarak's. It felt a little odd shaking his hand, but his fear slowly departed as he grew slightly more comfortable with the giant beast. "Hungry?" asked Codgarak. Liam realized it must have been at least a full day since he had passed out. His stomach quickly followed suit and began to moan and churn.

"Yes, I am quite hungry."

Codgarak directed Liam with his hand toward an etched stone seat close to the fire. "Come and sit." He turned and proceeded past the flames into a large recess further inside the cavern. Liam's eyes adapted to the light of the fire, and he was now able to see further into the cavern. He noticed it was quite large.

"Is this your home, Sir Codgarak?" he asked, not wanting to make any assumptions.

Codgarak gave a huff. "There is no 'sir.' Codgarak will do." The clanging of utensils and dishes could be heard just off to the side. "This was my family's home. My grandfather and grandmother settled here with their tribes many years ago. My father and mother remained and raised my brothers, my sister, and me within these walls."

Liam was happy to learn more about his childhood hero but also didn't want to impose himself. His father had been very adamant that Liam must know his manners and always be a gentleman. "Ahh, I see! Will they be joining us soon? Or … I don't want to intrude." Codgarak returned as Liam finished speaking. In his hand was a large black iron pot that he placed over the fire on a tripod. The three metal legs established its base while the tops merged together; a chain dangled down with a hook, and the pot handle hung from it. Codgarak placed two bowls and spoons on the ground next to the fire.

"No, they will not." he said as he disappeared around the corner again and quickly reemerged with two carved stone cups. "Here." He handed one of the cups to Liam, who took it and brought it closer to him. Looking down, he saw a red color marbled with what appeared to be tiny green flakes.

Codgarak lifted his cup in salute. "To surviving your first wraith encounter," he proclaimed. Liam was a little stunned but felt pride in the fact that Codgarak wanted to recognize the occasion.

"Thanks!" he said with a slight chuckle, knowing full well that he wouldn't have survived if it hadn't been for this legendary fighter rescuing him from certain death. Was there really that much cause for celebration? *Maybe I'm just overthinking it.*

Clinking the cups together, they both took a sip of the red drink. Flavor burst in Liam's mouth. "This is delicious! What is it?"

Codgarak smirked at his question. "Alavaro berries."

Liam took another sip from his cup, savoring every drop. "I have not heard of these berries before."

Codgarak gave a slight nod. "Few ever have. They have only been found a few miles deep into the mountains and are high up in the alpine range. There is only a two-week period when you can harvest them." The marbled red juice was rich and creamy; it coated your mouth and tongue so you could enjoy the flavor long after you had swallowed. The sweetness was perfectly balanced with a tarty kick, but it also had a calming aromatic scent with a slight earthy spice when you brought it close to your nose and mouth.

"There seems to be something else in the juice," Liam said.

Codgarak smacked his lips after taking another drink. "My family perfected the recipe over a hundred years ago. My grandmother added leaves from the celloo flower and ground pieces of the happer herb." Liam nodded as if this made complete sense. Who wouldn't add leaves and pieces of the celloo flower and happer herb? Though he had never heard of these plants before, he couldn't fight his youth. He desperately wanted to feel connected to Codgarak, and his body language openly portrayed this. "You know these two, do you?" Codgarak already knew the answer to his question, but he gave Liam the benefit of a doubt. Liam had still been slightly nodding until he finally adjusted course and moved his head from side to side.

"Umm … no … I don't, actually," he said with a slight sigh of admission.

Codgarak smirked in return, his suspicions confirmed. "I assume you know what vanilla is? And the plant it comes from?"

"Yes. I used to pick it for my mother. She would bake vanilla sweetbread and sell it at market and to our neighbors."

Codgarak nodded. "The celloo flower looks almost identical but has orange and light-blue circles on the flower petals."

"Ahh, I see." Liam's head began to nod in agreement once again.

Codgarak continued. "The happer herb looks similar in shape and size to the herb sage. But the scent is that of charred wood and blackberries. The leaf is also very rough and coarse, similar to how granite feels to the touch."

He was normally a beast of few words, but he felt obligated to entertain his old friend's son and figured that he would only have to endure his company for a short while longer. As he looked down at the boy, an image flashed into his mind of a camp hand he'd grown to know during the War of the Circolitch Islands. Liam's spirit matched his, but he struggled to remember his name ... Samcha! That was it. A spirit filled with adventure and an optimism about the future. Yet the only future Codgarak had witnessed was his death at too young an age. It was so much easier to ignore the youthful, motivated fighters who joined the ranks of the army that he would aid from time to time. Why dedicate time to someone who was statistically predicted to die in the next battle they entered?

His mind almost continued down this rabbit hole until Liam interrupted. "And ... what does the celloo and happer aid with?" he asked.

Codgarak shook his mind off the old memories and focused on the current moment. "Flavor, for one." Liam chuckled at the obvious answer to the simple question. Codgarak glanced over at him and saw the smile on the boy's face. "The celloo flower helps open up your lungs and allows you to breathe easier in the higher elevations of the mountains. It allows you to basically double your distance and stamina. The happer herb strengthens your immune system but is also a direct energy source for your muscles." Liam was on the edge of his seat, listening intently to every word that came from Codgarak. "Your muscles are strengthened by eating meat. Cow, deer, squirrel, bear, rabbit, fish." Liam nodded along with every word. "The happer herb attaches itself to your muscles.

As soon you begin to utilize your strength—chopping wood, carrying stone—your muscles look for energy to restore them from exhaustion. The happer herb immediately fuels your muscles and delivers a source of energy to sustain your strength."

Liam's mouth was slightly open. Though he had heard of "academies" where people would go and learn a specific field of study, he had never experienced them firsthand. Academies were in the other realms, such as Februe or Portford. It would take hundreds of years for his small village of Artho to even come close to developing a large enough population to have an academy. At this moment, though, Liam felt like he had a front row seat to the warrior professor himself!

CODGARAK

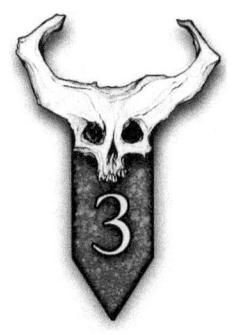

THE MESSAGE

He took another sip of his drink, not taking a single drop for granted with his newfound appreciation for all the goodness it contained. Codgarak leaned over and opened the lid of the pot, exposing a simmering stew. Eagerly receiving his bowl of stew, Liam looked down and saw lumps of meat and a few pieces of potato. Looking at Codgarak starting to enjoy the meal, he took his first few bites. "Deer, bacon, garlic, salt … and pepper?" he inquired. Codgarak nodded. "The pepper isn't black pepper, though, and it doesn't seem to be red pepper either …"

"It is purple pepper from the Asandee riverbed."

Liam was excited for lesson two of the night. "And what does that do?"

He slurped up the stew in excitement, but his joy was quickly snuffed out. "Nothing but flavor, boy. Not everything has to have mystical benefits … some things just taste good and that's all there is to it." Codgarak realized his response may have come off a little harsh. *The boy didn't deserve that; all he has ever known is Artho and the stories told by his father.* He, on the other hand, felt he had seen the vast majority of the corners of the world. So, for him, such simple questions were answered long before Liam was even born.

In an attempt to lighten the mood, he said, "Tell me of your father now. How is Judah these days, and what is he doing in these later years?" Codgarak felt this would be a good way to alleviate the negative tone he had just set.

Liam was staring down at his bowl of stew when the question landed. He glanced up at Codgarak and their eyes locked for half a second. "That's why I'm here." Liam moved his gaze to the fire, and his eyes followed the enchanted path of the dancing flames. "My father is gone … dead. His light has been extinguished."

Damn it, Codgarak thought. *That doesn't improve the mood.* "How did he die?"

Liam hesitated as his spirit sank down into the dark memory he had been trying to escape. "He was poisoned … but accidentally."

Codgarak tilted his head slightly. "How is one accidentally poisoned?" He let out a long but quiet sigh.

"My father grew ill—a sickness that kept him in bed for many, many months. No one in the village knew what to make of it. The healers did their best with herbs and medicines, but nothing seemed to work." The fire crackled and sparked as the wood popped under the pressure. "We had run out of meat two days prior. The deer had been scared off and pressed higher into the hills. I went off to hunt one. While I was gone, my little sister Audriana went to gather mushrooms and vegetables to make a soup for her and Father. I believe she went to an area she was not familiar with. I can only assume that she misidentified the nacoa mushroom as an apraiuh mushroom. Mother commonly used apraiuh mushrooms in her soups and taught Audriana how to identify them. As you are probably aware, though, apraiuhs and nacoas are very similar in color, texture, and smell."

He looked over at Codgarak to see him gazing at him and listening intently. He turned back to the fire. "Upon my return, I found Audriana and Father cuddled together in his bed. Both were dead. There were two bowls with a little soup left in them on the bench by his bed. I found some small shavings of nacoa mushrooms on the cutting board by the soup pot. I had almost taken a few spoonfuls of it myself, but thankfully I went searching for Audriana before I did, otherwise …" He wiped his face with his hand and then placed it on his neck and braced his elbow on his leg. "This may seem wrong and out of place … but I am at peace that my father is gone." Liam hoped the beast who sat next to him would understand. "He was suffering for months, living in pain every day … though he never said out loud that he hoped to die, his eyes told me his will to live had been shattered long ago." A pause filled the cave.

"I am happy that he is not suffering any longer. My father once mentioned the Valley of Haivan, where warriors lie in eternal rest, at peace physically, but their souls and spirits live together in harmony with past warriors. I hope he is there."

Codgarak didn't have the heart to tell Liam the exact details of the Valley of Haivan. The inscription at the gateway to the valley said that only those who died in battle or were buried in the valley would dine with their fellow warriors. It was the dream all soldiers held on to in their dying moments. Those who were in their last days of life would sell everything they owned to try and pay for the trip there to be buried, but most never made it in time. No … it was better to let the young boy hold on to hope and peace. Codgarak had seen the look a thousand times. A man's soul was forever lost when he watched his family ripped out of this world. He knew the boy's soul had been changed forever.

"I just don't see why my sister, though … she didn't deserve to die … she was of pure heart, and … and … fuck! Life isn't fair!"

Liam had taken his hand off his neck and clenched his fist. Codgarak could see the boy's eyes start to glisten as he fought back tears.

Codgarak attempted to shift the focus but failed. "I can imagine that your mother must be suffering through this loss, and to add on the fact that you ventured off to find me?"

Liam couldn't fight it any longer. He felt the tears well in his eyes and they gently overflowed. A few drops ran down his face and landed on the dirt floor. "She died a month before my father and Audriana. I had taken some items to market, doing my best to help provide for the family. Mother had gone foraging for berries that day. She was bitten by a green night viper. The venom stole my mother away from me." Codgarak felt sorry for the boy. Forced into manhood and providing for a family. "I never got to say goodbye … to any of them," Liam said with a slight tremble in his voice. The pain and sorrow was still fresh in his mind and spirit.

This story was one that Codgarak had heard all too often. He had witnessed child after child become motherless and fatherless after the many wars, battles, and evils that plagued the land—many of those warriors and battles he himself he had been a part of. What do you tell a child who has had their world destroyed in front of their eyes? How do you comfort a heart that hasn't just been shattered but ripped out? What can you replace the pain with?

The warrior had run over these questions in his mind many times before, but he'd certainly never thought he'd have to consider them on this night when a young boy from Artho climbed up the cliff and entered his home. "I understand," he told Liam. It was the only thing he could think of … and it was the truth. He knew exactly what the young boy was feeling and knew that Liam didn't have a choice; for the rest of his life he'd have only himself to rely on. The minotaur could only imagine how much the boy was fighting against despair within his heart and soul. Who could blame the boy if he chose to drink his sorrows away and arrive at an early grave? Yet here he was on a journey that had purpose for him.

Codgarak thought of another way he could help take Liam's mind off the pain he was feeling. "You said Judah shared with you stories of the battles we fought."

Liam wiped his eyes and pressed his lips together before trying to reply in a firm voice. "Yes … he did."

"Out of those, which would you say you enjoyed the most?"

Codgarak could see a little glimmer in Liam's eyes as he smiled. "I always enjoyed the Battle of Root."

Codgarak sighed and shook his head. "What a shitpile of a battle. Of all the stories your father told you, that is the one you enjoyed?"

Liam became defensive. "Well, yeah! The way my father told it, it sounded like everything that could go wrong did go wrong. You were outnumbered and had terrible ground and position, yet somehow your army was victorious."

Codgarak laughed. "Ha! That's how all battles go!" Nothing ever goes according to plan!"

Liam watched the wall of the cave begin to illuminate as soon as Codgarak finished saying the spell: "Ussta shar tlu." At first, images of gigantic trees came into view. The scale of them left Liam in awe, for there was still so much of the world he had yet to experience. "It was called the Battle of Root because it was held at the base of the giant root system of a celtagoff tree." As he finished, the images faded and a map appeared in their place. A small wisp of light formed

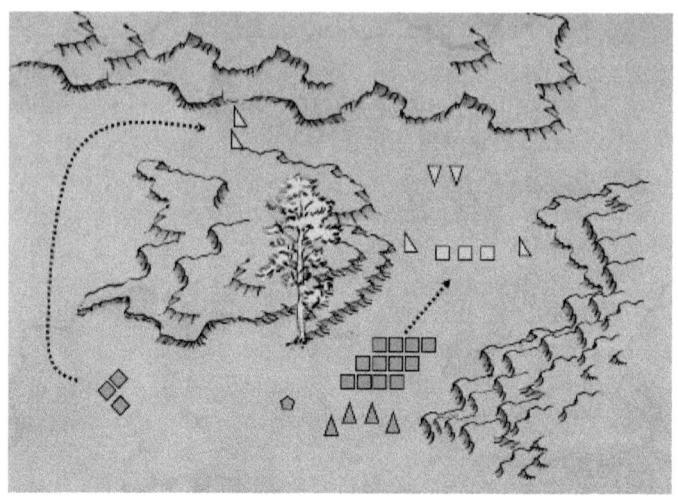

as Codgarak brought his thumb together with his ring and pinky finger and held his index and middle finger together. As he moved his hand, the wisp danced in front of the map.

"The orcs outnumbered us by at least two to one. They brought twelve gasts of foot soldiers, three ruffs of horseman, four links of archers, and one giant frog-looking thing that I think was supposed to be a mage." Codgarak's head tilted a little as he finished, still baffled to this day as to what exactly he'd seen.

Liam's sorrow quickly began to leave him, for this was everything he had hoped would happen upon meeting the legend. "How many orcs are in a gast? Did they have light armor? Were there actually horses or did they ride tamed milguards?" Codgarak turned his head, gazed into his eyes, and snorted. "Sorry! Please continue."

"The lord of the battle was ... Richard the Lionheart." As soon as the words left his mouth, he paused. Liam raised his eyebrows in anticipation. "No, wait ... that sounds stupid. That couldn't have been his name." Liam's gaze went back to the map and he chuckled lightly at the wisp of light, which was going round and round in a circle as Codgarak moved his hand out of habit while he went through a list of names, trying to recall. "Sir Robert the Fierce, Lord Geguilt the Great, King Cardco the Killer, Emperor Ezgerald, Irelo the Mad, Frank …"

Liam interjected in confusion. "Wait—you fought for a leader and his name was simply Frank?"

"Yes."

"Just Frank … nothing else?"

"Yes."

"Oh … okay … sorry for interrupting again."

"Come to think of it, Frank wasn't a bad leader. He wasn't anything you'd write about in a book, but I've certainly fought for far worse."

Liam nodded slightly in agreement. He had no reason to, but it felt like the right thing to do. "Forget it. It doesn't really matter what his name was. He died in the first wave of battle anyways." The wisp returned to the top left corner. "We placed two units of pikemen in the back valley of the root cliffs, predicting that the orcs would send their horsemen that way. We then placed two more units of pikemen in front of our main line, thinking that if the orcs changed tactics and sent the horsemen down the hill and into the main line, they'd be forced into the center, which was where our main warriors waited." The wisp glided across the green main line. "Though we only had two links of archers, they were quite skilled, and I did not worry about whether they would be able to sustain us with waves of supporting volleys.

"Sure enough, those giant frog bastards came bumbling down the hill in a frenzy—no organization, no tactics, just pure blunt aggression and the will to die in battle. Their stench hit us long before their swords did. The first clash went as expected. The men started to scatter in fear and the line weakened considerably."

Codgarak took a long pause from his story. Though the legend had contained the memory deep within his mind, the horrors seen in battle can never fully be contained. Reliving the moment when he first saw the front line of the army buckle and break as the orc weapons slashed through the poorly crafted armor. The minotaur began to tremble in anger as his memories forced themselves upon him.

His gaze peering out over the fire, but rather than seeing the cave wall, the site of the orc charging towards him on top of the milguard was the only he saw. The severed body of one the boys forced into the army was bouncing and flopping as the milguard dragged the body behind it during the charge. The body spraying blood outward with every impact it made on the ground. The only song sung that day was of the boys screaming and crying out for their mothers.

Codgarak finally pulling himself free from the trance of the memory, blinked and reoriented with his surroundings as he noticed Liam was leaning towards him, realizing something was wrong. A quick glance towards his guest left him seeing the innocence in his eyes, the ignorance of youth and the dreamer who sought a grand story. He chose not to go in depth with the horrors of war, but watered it down to the simple details he desired.

"The horsemen did what we thought and went around to the back valley. About twenty horsemen came charging the line just because I think they were too stupid to realize they needed to follow the others. Damn it, anyways … we thought the pikemen were more experienced. We were told they had fought in the War of Skilvage, but it was actually their fathers that had fought in the war, and these *boys* were merely your size!" Codgarak flicked Liam's shoulder, lightly breaking his trance.

"I'm listening! Just picturing it all."

36

Codgarak snorted. "Well, picture a large group of boys your size, with makeshift gear that didn't fit them because their king chose to order scraps from another realm instead of creating quality armor in his own." Liam could see Codgarak's eyes boiling with anger. He rolled his shoulders and cracked his neck, regaining his composure.

"Those boys never stood a chance and were cut down without hesitation! Before we knew it, the horsemen sliced behind our lines and immediately took out our archers before they came crashing down on us! Aibek did his best to keep some of the archers alive by summoning a giant storm that shot ice and rain down upon the orcs. The ice crashed down like arrows and formed giant shields that gave us precious seconds to fend off the horsemen one by one. The rain brought with it earth-shaking thunder and lightning that tried to tear the sky apart. Those green frogs must have never seen anything like it, because I swear their will to fight immediately left them. Mala immediately realized this and began to summon every type of lightning magic spell he knew."

Though Liam wanted to interrupt with more questions, he was able to maintain his self-discipline as Codgarak continued. "The valley was all rocks, and in that region it rained continuously throughout the season, so moss blanketed the ground. As soon as the rain fell, it made the ground as slick as ice. The second and third line of the orcs' foot soldiers fell right into each other, and some even fought one another instead of us. Once that happened, it was easy, because they were a blubbering mess of terrified frogs, and we just walked up the hill, slaying them as we went! Mala and I tried to see who could kick them the furthest."

Liam was now really confused. "Wait, what?"

Codgarak took a quick moment to enjoy another sip of alavaro juice. "Mala said, 'I bet I can kick one of these frogs farther than you can!' and with that, he took a three-step stride and straight-up kicked the fucking frog all the way to the other side of the valley. So of course I accepted the challenge."

"Well …?" Liam had a smirk on his face as if he already knew the answer.

"What do you think? Of course I won! I kicked one of those damn frogs so hard he bounced off the roots and went all the way to the other side of the valley." Codgarak let out a laugh and shook his head. "Those giant frogs can be kind of squishy, but they sure do bounce if you kick them just right!" Liam started to chuckle, a smile on his face as he was finally able to let his mind be still and enjoy the story. This was—

A deep red flame burst out of the ground in a circle. The flame began to split and inner circles were created; as intersecting lines created intricut patterns which formed inside the main circle. Liam leapt to his feet in fear. Trembling, he reached down to his waist for his father's sword. Finding its hilt, he drew it and brought both hands together in what he felt was a strong defensive stance.

As the circle completed itself, a deep red beam of magical energy shot upward and formed a portal. In an instant, a giant white tiger with light gray stripes stood in front of Liam. His size was only a few inches shorter than Codgarak and almost the same width as the minotaur. He could barely maintain his grip on the sword, his body trembled so violently from being startled. "Oh, come now, son of man, you won't be needing that." Mala snapped his fingers and Liam's eyes widened in shock as his father's sword disintegrated into particles of metallic dust. His jaw dropped and he gasped.

"Since when did you get a new toy?" Mala teased as he pushed Liam aside and walked past them into the cave. The white tiger striding about the cave. Liam taken back as he watched the tiger walk and move as a human would, but left him with the impression that the tiger could run on all fours as he naturally should. A mutation which showed parts that appeared like a man, but still bore true to that of a natural tiger. Codgarak just shook his head. Returning, Mala took a drink from the cup he had retrieved. He stared at Liam, who was frozen in disbelief. One of the few items that remained from his father was now a pile of dust.

"Son of man, you can stop pretending to be a statue. You may not realize this, but the minotaur sitting here before you is quite capable of defending himself." Liam turned his head and glared at Mala.

"Liam." Liam met Codgarak's eyes before he returned his gaze to Mala. "Why did you draw your sword?"

"Yes, son of man, I would love to know why you drew your sword."

Liam took a deep gulp and cleared his throat. "I thought he was some kind of bad guy."

Mala interrupted. "Ahh, yes, of course. Except what gave you that impression, son of a *stupid* man?"

Liam's anger started to build inside him. "I don't know! Maybe because this deep red flame just burst out of the ground, carved a circle … line … shape thing, and then, *bam*—in walks a damn cat through a magical portal!"

"Ah, yes, of course!" Mala said without missing a beat. "I should have known the son of man would be sensitive. Here, son of man, is this better?" The deep red flame instantly returned, but the light pulsated through shades of green, then white, and finally Mala stopped it at blue. "There. Does that make you all warm and fuzzy, son of man?"

Codgarak lifted his hands up in judgement, "Why must you always cause a scene?"

Mala looked down at the sitting beast. "I'm a cat. It's in my nature." And with that, he swiped his tail around and purposely pushed Codgarak's cup over, spilling his drink on the ground as he walked behind him. "Oopsie." Codgarak rolled his eyes and shook his head. "So, son of man, tell me … how did you come to be here, and what were you doing with my dear old friend?"

"Codgarak was just telling me the story of the Battle of Root."

Mala interrupted with a gale of laughter. "Codgarak! Tell a story? You must be joking, son of man!" Liam shook his head. "There was one year when Codgarak only spoke two—*two*—sentences. Everything else was huffs, puffs, snorts, and shaking his head up, down, side to side … and of course the occasional eye roll." Mala smiled as he finished, patting Codgarak on the shoulder. "It's okay, good friend. I still love your company. So, tell me, son of man, though I still find it hard to believe, but why would Codgarak tell you of all people a story?"

Liam spoke through clenched teeth. "I am the son of Judah of Artho."

Mala actually showed some compassion; his demeanor instantly changed. "Oh … you're *that* Liam."

"I am."

"I see. How is your father? It has been …" Mala looked down at Codgarak as he gathered his thoughts. "Four years now. Not since the Battle of GoGax." Codgarak nodded in agreement.

"He's dead." Liam was still clenching his teeth.

"Well … that actually does explain a lot. He was a good fighter, Liam. He fought bravely and was someone you could depend on."

"Thank you." Though this was the only nice thing Mala had said up to now, his words still stung as if he had insulted him.

"Well … no time to waste. Cod, old buddy, old pal … I need to talk to you." Mala plopped down right where Liam had previously been sitting, which added to the anger building inside him. As Mala continued, Codgarak motioned for him to sit on the other seat opposite Mala. Embarrassingly, he was still holding his father's sword hilt. He didn't know what to do with it, but he certainly didn't want to just put it on the ground.

"First thing … Aibek is missing." Codgarak didn't flinch. "We think it's connected to the second thing, which is that a dark energy has been felt in the Realm of Delco. Messages have stopped coming. There are rumors that magical runes have appeared that are blocking all outside magic from being utilized. No one has been able to teleport into that area at all. Aibek was going to travel in and scout through the northern region of Delco to see what he could discover, but then … nothing." Codgarak crossed his arms as he took it all in. "Cashmes and I believe everyone should return and discuss the information and see if the situation is more serious than we currently assume. I have to say, I can't recall the last time I've seen Cashmes so disturbed."

Codgarak's demeanor didn't change. He remained calm and collected, which was reassuring to Liam, but he something inside him still sensed that there was some cause for concern. "I will meet you there," Codgarak said.

"Right … well, I've delivered the message, and now I'm off to find Dhather and Edha."

Mala stood up and walked back to the area where he had teleported in. "Well, son of Judah, I bid you safe travels back to Artho." He stopped and, while he was looking at Liam, the teleportation circle reappeared, this time in blue. "Oh, wait! I forgot! Don't want to scare Mr. Sensitivity." The blue circle changed to a rainbow union of swirling colors, and magical butterflies began to flutter away from the portal. Liam's blood was boiling by the time Mala had vanished.

"Mala!" Codgarak yelled. As soon as he did so, the portal reappeared in a much smaller size. Mala's arm popped through, but you could hear his voice coming through from the other side.

"All right! *All right!*" He snapped his fingers and metal particles rose from the pile they lay in and flew over to Liam's hilt. Judah's sword reappeared in his hand. The portal closed and Mala was gone again.

"Thank you. You didn't say much," Liam said sheepishly.

"There's no need to talk when Mala does it all for you." Codgarak didn't take his eyes off the fire, but he knew exactly how Liam was feeling. "He may not seem like it, but he is by far one of the greatest warriors you'll ever meet."

Liam respected Codgarak, but his anger convinced him that there was no way this could be accurate. He tried to change the subject—anything to get off the topic of Mala. "What of this Realm of Delco? Do you think there is anything to be afraid of?"

Codgarak finally met Liam's gaze. "The Realm of Delco shouldn't be afraid …" His voice was low, forceful, and unwavering. "They should be terrified."

MALA

NO MERCY

The king's hall was full of people when the messenger came rushing up to the huge doors, the guards outstretched their hands towards him. "Stop!" He keeled over, out of breath, his clothes soaked in sweat and his face drenched; he could barely keep his eyes open, as the salt stung them constantly. "It's … urgent! An … army … marches … on us now!" The guards opened the doors without further delay and announced him to all standing within.

The messenger clamored as he staggered forward in the crowd, "Please … out … of my … way!" The people inside still hesitated until he pleaded with them, and they noticed his distasteful appearance. The man stumbled forward until he practically collapsed in front of the king, for he lost his balance when he tried to kneel at such high speed.

"My Lord … I was one that you assigned to the Link Mountains in the east. I have come to inform you that Lithram has fallen to an enemy force. They seem to have settled there, but they sent an army forward in advance, and it would appear they are marching on a path straight for us!" Gasps filled the room, as the vast majority of those present had never experienced a war. Lithram … Lithram had defended the realm for as long as anyone could remember. The Realm of Delco was one of the more peaceful realms that was unified through treaties, trade, and cooperation in securing its borders from outside threats.

The king sitting upon his throne just stared out of the stained-glass windows as the group awaited his response. "My Lord?" the messenger inquired. There was dead silence within the room. The crowd began to turn and look at one another, goosebumps and frightened chills quickly possessing them. The messenger made another attempt. "My Lord?"

The king balled his hand into a fist. *"Captain!"* he screamed.

The captain's armor clanked as he rushed to the king's side. "Yes, my king?"

The king opened his mouth but quickly realized he had a large audience. Attempting to recover from his slight pause, he yelled, *"Out! Everyone out!"* Guards quickly stepped forward and began to motivate the crowd to leave quickly, as they shoved the slow movers towards the exit. As the doors of the chamber thudded shut, the king contemplated his thoughts.

He rose from his throne and walked over to the window. A loud screech resounded as he shoved the metal frame open, exposing the room to the crisp breeze that flooded in. Turning to look back at the messenger, he said, "Tell us about this army."

"My Lord, I didn't stay long enough to gather many details on their strength. I counted at least seven thousand head strong before I departed. I do know there were more behind them that I had not yet counted."

The captain interrupted the answer with his own question. "Did they have banners? Markings? What kingdom were they from?"

The messenger tilted his head slightly as he ran back over the memory in his mind. "No … I don't remember banners of any kind."

The captain looked over at the king. They both felt lost without more details. "Since when does an army march without banners?" the king declared.

"It was quite strange, sire …"

The king was curious. "Why do you say that?"

"As you know, sire, Lithram is a great city, and being one of the main border cities in the realm, they are a respectable force. Their defenses have never been beaten till now … at least that I know of." The king looked over at the captain, who nodded in agreement. "I don't know the size of their army, but it is quite large …"

The king was growing impatient. "Get to the *point!*"

The messenger worked to retrieve his tongue after his fierce scolding. "My king … the army marching towards us was spotless."

The captain didn't hesitate. "You stupid twat! The fuck does that even mean?"

The messenger gesticulated nervously. "They were spotless. Not a single drop of blood on their armor … not a spot of dirt. Their armor was pure white." He let the information settle within their minds for a moment. "They sacked one of the greatest cities in our realm and walked out of there without a scratch on them. How is this possible?"

The king looked up and glared into the messenger's eyes. "That will be all." The messenger bowed and walked out. The doors thudded closed once again.

"Do you believe what he says or has he gone mad?" the king asked his captain, who shook his head in disbelief.

"I can't wrap my head around it, sire. It doesn't make any sense to me."

"How many men do we have ready in garrison to defend us?"

The captain cleared his throat. "Three thousand in garrison. We do have another one and a half thousand north in Wilpog conducting their annual training. If we sent a pigeon, it'd take a day or two … another day to decamp, then a five-day march … maybe four if they pushed the men … seven or eight days for their full return."

"Send for your best knights. Have them meet this army in the field and escort them here to discuss a truce. Our army isn't ready to defend Ashfurgoth. It would appear diplomacy may be the best option."

The captain was shocked, but he didn't show it. "Yes, sire." The captain left the room and the king went back and slouched in his throne. He grasped his face and tried to control his new thoughts of dispair.

When the first of Emmanuel's army appeared at the gates of Lithram they were welcomed with ceremony. The citizens of Lithram lined the streets to watch as the parade of soldiers marched forward. Their armorer was a pristine white, their entire bodies covered from head to toe as even their helmets face shields were covered. Gold interwoven and etched into the armor presented a grand scene of superiority from their commanding presence.

Marching in unison, their feet stomping into the ground as the noises echoed throughout the area. It was all a part of the deception, for the hair on the back of their necks began to tingle to life with uneasiness as the army began to change. What the citizens didn't realize was they were gazing upon an army gifted from hell itself.

They began to question what they were seeing as Emmanuel's machine knights proceeded next. The on lookers could tell there were at least three different kinds marching. One of them hissing as it marched. Steam spouting out of it as tubes and gears ground forward in their operations. The second group also had tubes that intersected and protruded in and out of their bodies. These tubes glowed with colors though, green, purple, and blue solutions seeping inside them as they marched behind their counter parts. The third group appeared as if they desired their own deaths. The skin old and decaying, but their eyes were nothing but glowing in either white or red light. Their bodies trapped to a plane they no longer desired to be a part of.

It was too late now. Emmanuel had assembled a joint army unlike any other at that point in their history. The army's vast size marching within their own walls carried so far back that the people hadn't even laid their eyes on the gnolls or the reptacrepts that had joined Emmanuel's campaign. What the crowd believed to be a parade was now the beginning of their slaughter as the command soon rang out, and the massacre was unleashed on them.

The halls of Lithram were now lined with metal machine knights and half-dead soldiers. When the dawn of the Age of Magic began, Emmanuel was one of the first mages to learn how to wield it and distort its use. Though Emmanuel's kingdom of Grenssoc was on the map and others knew of its existence, no one would be able to tell you any details regarding it. Emmanuel was very cunning at ensuring his empire remained in the shadows. While the world continued to turn and operate, Emmanuel worked to gain further insight into the five planes. Through his late mentor Klipkoshek, he began to learn how the future could be powered through machines. After years of developing this new technology, he marched his combined army forward into the realm his late mentor had desired. Emmanuel wanting to fulfill the destiny once desired and looked forward to the promises he was given years ago.

"HERE! TAKE HER!" The Grenssoc machine knight had to yell through the face covering which provided the steam for his internal mechanics. He was holding the royal princess by her ankle and dragging her behind him as he reached the main hall. His metal armor was stained with the blood of the victims he had butchered throughout the day. The ivory lace undergarment of the princess did little to absorb her blood as it slowly pooled beneath her. The half-dead soldier in the hallway looked down at her, following the orders just given him, he grabbed her by the ankles, and dragged her lifeless body down the main hallway. Its magnificent blue-and-silver embroidered carpet was now forever stained by the blood of the royalty it once represented. The soldier's chain mail clanked and swung back and forth as he trudged down the hallway.

After dragging the princess through the courtyard, down the main streets, and towards the outer walls, he finally arrived at the machicolation of the main gate. A machine knight overseeing the display directed the soldier: "Put that bitch on that spike." The machicolation had been modified with spikes set above it. The entire royal family, who had been found hiding in the castle, were brought up and impaled on the spikes. The soldiers stripped the nightdress off the princess and forced her body onto the spike. The blood draining out of the royal family flowed down in a stream that fell to the entrance below. The fresh blood was a feast for the demons that had just arrived and were walking into the city; lifting their heads and opening their mouths, they roared in delight as they tasted the victims' blood. The demon soldiers were also given to Emmanuel as a gift by Marduk. Though Marduk didn't want to commit any more of his army to Emmanuel, he did so as a sincere gesture to his brother Set, who convinced him it'd be worth the investment in the long term. The demon's shoved the half dead soldiers around as if they were a lower life-form not deserving of respect.

Emmanuel gazing out and admiring the massacre from the royal stained glass windows as it continued on. The sobbing was almost uncontrollable. "You said you would show us mercy ... that you would bring a new era to our lands if we trusted you!" The king brought his hands away from his face. The tears pouring out of his eyes mixed with the bruises and blood resulting from his beating. "You fucking half-dead corpse!" the king spat at Emmanuel.

Emmanuel looked down with no emotion on his face. "I am showing you mercy. I'm letting my men kill your family quickly."

A tortured soul screamed from down the hall. "And what of that?"

Emmanuel turned his head slightly. Hearing the laughter coming from his gifted demons, who were inflicting torment on new victims, he concluded, "Ahh, yes! Well, those are the demons. I couldn't promise that they wouldn't have their fill. You see, they enjoy certain ... pleasures." He put on the smile everyone has when they know they have purposely deceived you.

"You disgraceful lying piece of undead shit!"

Emmanuel drew his sword and, swinging, made a perfectly angled slice that ripped the king's lower jaw right off his face. The king coughed from the impact, which sent the gurgling blood jetting onto the ground. *"I didn't lie!"* Emmanuel shouted in a rage. Recomposing himself, he said, "This is a new era for your lands—the era of Grenssoc!" He smiled as the king dropped to the ground. "Take him to the spikes," he said, looking at two of his machine soldiers.

They dragged the king's corpse away as Emmanuel made his way from the window out and onto the king's balcony. Emmanuel watched Set walking towards him to join him. He greeted his visitor "It has been too long since my eyes have seen such beautiful carnage." Set merely chuckled as the screams of tortured souls rang out from below.

EMMANUEL

SACRIFICE

The sun rose in the east and the radiating light projected itself on the mountains across the valley. Liam lay on the ground and watched through the mouth of the cave as the orange glow slowly traversed downward, forcing the blue hues of the morning light back to their slumber until the evening.

The clanging of pots made him feel guilty for staying in his makeshift bed. Early mornings were not foreign to him, but after his travels and almost being ripped off the cliffside, he appreciated the chance to just let his body rest. The familiar sound of bacon sizzling in a skillet started, and the smell was the perfect motivation to begin the day.

"You awaken when the food begins but are nowhere to be found when the dishes need tending." Liam pressed his lips together bashfully, guilty as charged.

"You're right. I'm sorry." Liam looked around the cave, not wanting to make eye contact with his host. He let out a giant yawn and stretched as if he were already an old man living out his last days. "Sleep struggled to find me last night," he admitted. The minotaur didn't reply. He already knew the reason.

Liam stood by the fire, but his attention was directed outside to the mountain range. The thought of war and conflict ran rampant in his mind based on what Codgarak had said the previous night. "Your spirit will not find peace until you calm your mind from itself." The warrior's wisdom allowed his anxiety to rest for a brief moment. A slight nudge on his arm made him aware of a plate of bacon, eggs, and flatbread. "Thank you, Codgarak."

The giant beast nodded in response as Liam sat down and enjoyed the meal. "We might as well enjoy what little remains."

Liam looked over at him. "You make it sound as if you don't plan to return."

Standing and carrying the dishes back into the cave, Codgarak replied, "I will not be returning."

Liam's anxiety started to awaken. "Do you think whatever evil is affecting Delco will be the … end of us?"

Codgarak sighed as he walked back. "Trust in the Ancient One with all your heart; do not rely on your understanding. Seek the Ancient One's will for your life with every action you take, for the Ancient One will guide you on your path." Liam stared blankly ahead with a dumbfounded look as Codgarak turned and walked back into the cave and started to pack for the journey that awaited.

What does that mean? He challenged the response bluntly. "You didn't answer the question, Codgarak."

Codgarak paced around the cave, ensuring he didn't leave any stone or cubby unchecked. Not answering the inquiry, he walked over to a specific part of the wall. Large squares had been carved into the mountain. Bold black lettering was etched above each square, and at their centers were distinct carvings of emblems, unique to each square. He placed his hand upon the wall, closed his eyes, and tilted his head down as if he were saying a prayer.

Though he tried to speak softly and quietly, Liam could still make out his words, although he didn't understand them. "Xal dos satiir uns'aa nin tangis' wun elghinn. Xal dos zuch zhaun dos phuul naut zho'aminth. Xal does tlu a tre'as'anto amongst lil' slyannen. Xal usstan tlu a gre'as'anto zil usstan z'hin ulu ussta xuz."

Liam stood there nervously, not really knowing what to do with himself. *You don't want to get in the way, but you feel guilty for not helping, so you just stand around like an anxiety-riddled dog needing reassurance.* . "I just—" Codgarak finished his prayer and turned his head, his eyes flaring with a fiery blaze. Liam got the hint and shut his mouth.

Codgarak returned to his packing. He watched as Liam began to clean up his bedding area and rearrange his pack, inventorying what items he had. The minotaur noticed the actions of the small human, but he didn't say anything. That Liam would broach the argument soon enough as to why he should join him, and why he didn't want that to happen.

As Liam grabbed his things, he went to the mouth of the cave, and plopped down on the edge of the cliff where he had climbed up. He looked out to the horizon in the morning sun and appreciated the beauty of the valley. He flicked his wrist again and again as he summoned the simple flame spell he had used on his climb. It was a way to pass the time and keep his mind occupied.

He could feel the reverberating thumps of the minotaur's steps as he approached. "You should head out soon—cover more ground before the night sets in."

Liam was afraid to ask the question, but he knew this would be his only chance. "I can't go home. There is nothing for me there." Codgarak didn't say anything but turned his head away to look into the distance. "Let me come with you."

He watched the minotaur's face. It looked disdainful. "Do you know how many times boys like you have asked that question?"

"I know, but—"

"*There are no buts!* You're a boy … you have no training! This is the oldest story of time, and I will not have any part in it."

Liam's zeal began to awaken in him. "I am *not* a boy! I'm *sixteen*! I should be married by now—have gone to *war* by now!"

Codgarak showed his beastlike rage. He brought his face eye to eye with Liam and his eyes flamed with anger. "And why *aren't* you married? Why are you fleeing your home? Why do you seek the horror of war that plagues the living and the dead?"

Liam didn't know how to respond at first. He clenched his jaw tighter. Instead of trying to defend himself, he decided to attack his idol. "Oh! And who are you? Where is your family? Where is your home? You scorn me for wanting to help and yet you don't live out the same words you speak!"

Rearing his head back, Codgarak cried out, grabbed Liam by the arm, and dragged him into the cave. Liam tried to struggle, but it was no use; the minotaur could do as he pleased with him. Bringing him to the carved squares on the cave wall, he shouted, "*Here!* Here is my family! Here lies what is left of my tribe! When this valley was nothing but a battlefield, the War of Subalpine was fought by my grandfather … fighting the dark elf Thitra Kningol as he tried to invade from the Forest of Zareel! You almost died from the wraiths that still plague this land. You know nothing of what you seek!" He tossed Liam across the cavern, where he bounced off the opposite wall.

Codgarak turned and faced Liam, contorting his fingers into a spell. Words appeared on the wall above the tombs of his family. "XAL DOS SATIIR UNS'AA NIN TANGIS' WUN ELGHINN," the beast proclaimed. "Do you know what that means?"

55

Liam braced himself and leaned forward. *"You know I don't know what it means!"*

A large exhale flowed from the beast as he began to take long, steady, deep breaths. Smoke seemed to rise from Codgarak as his anger visibly increased. "May you feel me now, even in death." The minotaur continued, "Xal dos zuch zhaun dos phuul naut zho'aminth. It means 'May you always know you are not forgotten.'" The words continued to magically inscribe themselves upon the stone as he spoke. "Xal does tlu a tre'as'anto amongst lil' slyannen. May you be at peace amongst the stars." Liam's anger began to settle as the prayer rested within his mind. "Xal usstan tlu a gre'as'anto zil usstan z'hin ulu ussta xuz. May I be at peace as I walk to my end."

Liam was finally finding his calm again. "Why are you a warrior?" Codgarak didn't want to answer the question. He had made up his mind long before Liam had posed the question. All he wanted was for the discussion to end.

Liam finally continued. "My father was a fighter … fought to defend others, those who couldn't defend themselves. Fought to provide for my mother, sister, and me. Fought because he knew he was given gifts that others were not. I don't have a home to return to, a family that awaits me, a future amongst the stars. All I have is myself." The two kept their gazes locked together as Liam continued. "Are you born a warrior? No—you choose to be one when you refuse to stay seated as evil approaches your walls. You choose to be a warrior when you refuse to back down regardless of the enemy standing before you. You choose to be a warrior when you stand back up after darkness does its best to beat you down. You choose to be a warrior, because if not you … then who?"

The eyes of the minotaur squinted as he looked at the human intently. He didn't speak of it, but he could see a slight aura enveloping Liam. It was an effect he had only seen a handful of times.

Perhaps this is the young warrior's destiny. Codgarak reached over and placed his hand on the cave wall. He spoke a few words and a dark gem appeared, forming on the rough, stout wall. Liam's attention was drawn to it. "Is that a hematite?" Codgarak nodded as he pulled it off and placed it in a small pouch attached to his belt.

The cave was heavy with emotion as both man and beast propelled their energy into the conversation. "If you choose to live by the sword, then you will surely perish by the sword."

Liam, feeling more confident than before, replied, "It is everyone's destiny to die."

Codgarak nodded. "You're right … but you are speaking of physical death. I am not."

Liam was caught off guard and tried to wrap his head around what the legendary warrior had shared. He didn't understand exactly what he meant, but the words clenched deep within him.

"You want to be a warrior, fine!. I will show you the sacrifice you're so eager to embrace."

Codgarak strapped his bag onto his back, grabbed his battle-ax, and looked directly at Liam. "Are you ready?"

A smile formed on Liam's face. "Hell, yes!" He raised an eyebrow. "Wait—how do we get down from here? We're not taking the cliff, are we?"

Codgarak tilted his head. "I've been meaning to ask you about that. Why did you climb the cliff to get to me?"

Liam shook his head. "Wait … how should I have gotten here?"

The beast walked Liam to the cave entrance and pointed. "The pathway is normally what I'd recommend." Liam's jaw dropped as he saw, plain as day, a pathway wrapped tightly against the right side of the cave entrance. It went up the side of the cliff and finished on the top of the mountain. Perfectly cut steps made the journey a breeze for anyone who knew of the path's existence. "I have only known of one other who has climbed the cliff to get to me, and that was Agos. But that was because he was a little drunk one night and bet Mala he could beat him up it in a race."

Liam looked at the beast. "Who won?"

The minotaur snorted. "Well, I can't really say Mala won, because he tricked Agos into thinking he was racing him, but in reality, Mala just teleported to the top. To this day I don't think Agos has figured it out." Codgarak chuckled and Liam laughed at the simple trick.

Full of excitement to start this new journey, he said, "All right! I'll take the lead." With that, Liam started up the pathway with a double-quick step.

"Stop!" Codgarak snapped.

Liam retreated the few steps he had gone. "What's the problem?"

Codgarak shook his head. "I don't like stairs." Liam blinked with a blank stare. The beast began to wave his arm in a circle, and a black spike shot up from the ground and engulfed the pair. The two were teleported instantly down to the valley floor. "This way." Codgarak turned to the south and took the lead, proceeding down a slightly worn path, cutting through a meadow.

Liam looked back at the mouth of the cave as it slowly started to fade behind them. "This is way better than those stairs."

LIAM

VOW

The two had walked for miles after the midday sun had peaked in the sky. Liam was enjoying every stride he took in step with the giant warrior in front of him, but he couldn't deny that the long journey was starting to get to his stomach. The grumble in his belly, though noticeable, was mostly drowned out by the joyful chirping of the birds that flew through the valley. There is nothing quite like a gentle mountain breeze gliding across your face. The sweet and rich scent of the pine trees filled the air and brought a peaceful comfort to his spirit.

As Codgarak carried on, Liam's pace slowed. He closed his eyes and allowed his mind to be still within the moment. Grand mountains shot towards the sky on both sides of the valley. It would be amazing to simply stay right here, not a worry of evil or battle flooding in, just elegant tranquility …

"What are you doing?" Liam jumped, startled. He opened his eyes and saw the minotaur's face directly in front of his.

Composing himself, he said, "I was just … taking a moment to enjoy … well … the moment."

The beast ground his teeth. Clearly his travel companion didn't grasp the seriousness of the situation. "Daydreaming will get you killed. Tell me, what is beyond the bend?" He turned and pointed his battle-ax towards a spot where the trail curved around a clump of trees.

"I … I … don't know," said Liam sheepishly.

"Exactly!" The beast snorted and shook his head like a disappointed teacher at his simple-minded student. "You are not at home. You are in a place where evil and danger could be lurking around any corner. Your enemy is out there, just waiting for this moment when you let your guard down and …" Codgarak laid his hand flat, then hissed as he sent it flying sideways towards Liam. *"Ssshhhow!"* The hand moved as fast as an arrow, and when it passed the side of Liam's head, Codgarak clipped his ear and then slapped the back of his head with a *thwop*.

"Ahhh!" Liam let out a yell of pain.

"Trust me, an arrow hurts worse!" Liam rubbed the back of his head. "If you want to daydream, go back home. If I remember correctly, somebody told me they wanted to become a warrior—that they were willing to make the sacrifices required. Well, guess what? Daydreaming is a part of that sacrifice." Codgarak didn't wait for a response but turned and began walking down the trail. "Come, son-of-man," he said over his shoulder. The legendary fighter knew Liam hadn't moved from his position yet. The boy scolded himself. *You're an idiot. Way to go, Liam.*

He shut his mouth and carried on, doing his best to ensure he didn't fall any further behind so the warrior wouldn't take back his decision to let him tag along. The beauty of the mountains faded from his mind, and now, depressingly, he looked at them as if they were just obstacles they would have to traverse.

The trail carried them further through the forest-filled valley even later in the afternoon. Liam finally said his first words for hours. "Codgarak, where is this trail leading us to?"

"Mortagolff. We will have a meal there and then press onward to Fort Patton." Liam's excitement sparked inside, as he remembered his father telling him he had received his first military training at Fort Patton. *Sounds good*, he thought sheepishly. His confidence was at an all-time low; he was walking on eggshells with every question he asked the short-tempered beast.

A little while later, he noticed that the valley was coming to an opening. The massive granite mountains had now faded behind them. Ahead he could see the smoke of a village rising into the air. Eventually he also saw a scattering of livestock, fields of tall corn with squash vines sprawling out from their roots, and damp mounds of potatoes—the major food sources for the villagers. Step by step they came closer to the village. The locals were clearly dedicated to increasing their commerce and trade. Workers were laboring away at a large stone wall, as the buildings were starting to encroach upon the existing wooden defensive wall.

Approaching the wooden gate, Codgarak took a slight angle and headed to the left of it; he was so tall that his head cleared the wall and he glared happily down at the guards, who trembled in fear. They had never experienced trouble in their homeland. They had barely had any training, for that matter. Though the guards on duty that day had heard of minotaurs coming and going every once in a while, they had never seen one for themselves.

The gate guard looked up in terror as the massive beast gazed down at him. "H-h-hello," he greeted. A simple snort was all that came from the minotaur. "Wh-wh-what business do … do you have in Mortagolff?" The other two guards standing with the greeter clenched their spears with blazing white knuckles. Their grips couldn't have got any tighter.

The minotaur stared down at the three men. He brought up his enormous hand with its razor-sharp claws and rested it on the wall. Liam interjected, "We're just looking for a meal and a little rest before we head out this evening."

The guards were caught by surprise. They hadn't noticed the small human traveling with the giant. The second guard gulped loudly, his voice cracking as he responded, "J-just a meal … not sp-sp-spending the night?" His eyes danced between Liam and Codgarak.

"That's right." Liam lifted his hands outward to show a pure intention of peace. He noticed he still wore the poncho-like blanket that Codgarak had given him after slicing his cloak open in order to heal the damage from the wraith attack. "And … perhaps a new shirt."

The first guard returned to the conversation. "It is a fee of ten coin daily to trade in the city." Codgarak snorted even more loudly and deliberately stretched the wooden planks of the wall apart just enough for the guards to hear the withered timber squeak and squawk under the pressure.

The second guard, acting upon his authority, said, "But … I believe that won't be necessary in exchange of good faith that there will be no trouble from either of you." Codgarak simply nodded with a grunt. "Very well … then … open the gates, Karl." The second guard looked at the third, who was standing by the wooden brace keeping the gates secure.

"Don't you think, Sergeant—?"

"Shut up, Karl, and open the damn gate!" the other two guards said in unison.

The wooden gate creaked and shuddered as the brace was removed and it swung open. The pair made their way in. "Thanks," Liam said as they passed the guards, still hearing the rattle of their makeshift armor.

A stone road led from the gate down through the village to the main square in the center—a standard village setup during the Age of Magic. The village square was an open area where traders, religious zealots, cooks, and travelers gathered throughout the day.

As the two approached the main square, the villagers gasped in surprise at the sight of Codgarak. Though minotaurs were still present in the realm, many were killed in the War of Subalpine, others had died off for unknown reasons in recent generations. The view remained however of a mixture between celebrity and villain. Though the minotaurs had won the war when they'd defeated the dark elf Lord Thitra Kningol and claimed the region as theirs, they had never ruled over or barred newcomers from the land.

As minotaurs sought more war and conflict, their numbers began to dwindle from inbreeding. The humans that settled in the land eventually became the majority thanks to their faster reproductive rate. A legendary minotaur warrior like Codgarak, however, could potentially destroy the entire settlement and everyone inside by himself. Their immense power coupled with an abundance of grace made his kind celebrities, but throughout recent history minotaurs had been hired by evil nations and empires for their massive brute strength and their reputation for turning the tides of entire wars. For this reason people associated villainhood with them—that and the stories from those who had survived minotaur encounters in battle.

The two arrived at the town square as people went about their business, but everyone certainly made sure they knew where Codgarak was and what he was doing. "Go find a shirt," he said to Liam. "You can't be wearing that rag the whole trip."

Liam looked up at him and nodded. "What of you?"

Codgarak looked down a side street that was only partially paved with stone. "I will return here shortly after I tend to a matter." He said no more and walked off, the crowd making sure to clear a path for him. Liam began to look for a clothing merchant as he slowly made his way through the square.

The noise of trade and life quickly returned to what Liam believed was normal as Codgarak faded into the distance. Men and woman greeted one another, bargaining for the best deal or, here and there, chastising a child who interrupted proceedings. The thatched houses, a mixture of stone and wooden structures, seemed very creative to Liam. They were very different from the small huts and farmhouses that were prevalent in Artho. He had felt lost, for he had never been to a clothing merchant before; his mother was the one who bought or made the fabric and then dressed the family. He finally made his way to a table that appeared to have what he needed, where he found a few different types of shirts available. They were subtle colors: dark green, brown, rawhide tan, rust red. Anything would be better than the poncho he was currently wearing.

Liam took off his blanket and placed it on the shop's table. Standing bare-chested, he was reaching for the dark green shirt to try it on when he felt the soft scratch of fingernails gliding across his back. He jumped out of his skin, startled by the touch. "There's no need to be scared, hun … I don't mean you any harm but am simply enjoying the view and your soft skin." A beautiful woman came into view. Her hand finished gliding across his back and came to rest upon his shoulder, stroking his arm lightly. His eyebrows rose and his eyes traveled slowly from the top of her head all the way down her perfectly curved body.

He took in every fine detail. Her black hair looked as smooth as silk; her eyes were bright blue and she had soft, inviting pink lips that shone as if she had glossed them. She was wearing a snug rhodamine-red leather dress with a lacy blue top over it. The light reflecting off the glossy surface ensured every curve of her body was noticeable. She wore a black cloak, allowing her to be as discreet as she pleased but also flaunt the mystery of whatever else she was withholding. "I haven't seen you here before … I think I would notice such a delightful sight as you." Her voice was soft and brought a feeling of calm into his chest.

Swallowing the massive pool of saliva that had formed in his mouth, Liam said, "I just arrived. I've never seen a village as established as this … it is a lot to take in."

The woman chuckled. "You're cute. This tiny village is nothing grand to behold, I assure you." She smirked and raised an eyebrow as his smile followed.

He cleared his throat. "Excuse me …" He began to work the shirt into a position where he could put it on. As he did so, her hand grabbed his side.

"I don't mind if you leave that off. I mean, I appreciate what I'm currently seeing." His gaze moved from her eyes to the breasts pressed against her dress before returning to her eyes.

"I could say the same … my lady."

She smiled and laughed under her breath. "How long are you going to bless me with your presence?"

His eyes widened at the question. "I … uhh …" He didn't know how to answer, but he knew he wasn't the one who would determine his departure time. "I'm just here for a meal and some rest and will be continuing before dark sets in."

She frowned and batted her eyelashes at him. "I just found what I've been looking for and you tell me I can't keep it but a simple moment?"

Liam tried to recover his composure. "The moment is one I will not easily forget."

He took a slight step forward. Her eyes entranced him; he increasingly wanted to stay longer with her. "I know a place that could give you the rest you desperately need," she said, raising her eyebrows and ensuring her flirtatious smile was refreshed by a lick of the tongue.

Holy shit, he thought. He cleared his throat again and checked from left to right but was completely oblivious to anything else around him. "Umm, I need to stay here in the square and—"

She cut him off before he'd finished. "My quarters are right over there." She had shortened the distance between them to just a few inches. Her hand stayed on his torso and the other pointed to a small door nearby. She leaned close to his ear. "Come, let's make this short moment last as long as it can." She grabbed his hand and began to pull him out of the shop.

"Uhhh, okay ..." Liam retrieved two coins from his pocket and dropped them into the merchant's hands as they walked briskly out.

As they emerged—*thwop!* Codgarak's giant claw landed on Liam's head and held him in place. Both of them spun around to receive facefuls of smoke as Codgarak exhaled a big cloud from a drag on his tobacco pipe. "And what are we up to, Lorelaylee?"

Her expression immediately changed to one of disgust. "Cod." Her nostrils flared and she raised one eyebrow. "I haven't seen you around here in years. Didn't know this was one of your little lambs." Liam was now the one raising an eyebrow. *Little lamb?*

Codgarak turned his hand, causing Liam to tilt his head in sync with the motion. "This little lamb is not one of mine, but he is off limits to your clutches. You'll have to find another soul to devour today."

Lorelaylee grabbed the bottom of her dress and tugged to readjust it. "Fine ..." She turned her gaze to Liam for half a second. "Sorry, kid." She flicked her dark, silky hair in the breeze, turned, and made her way back into the busy square.

"Why?" Liam cried out. "Didn't you see what I was about to 'indulge in'?"

The minotaur moved his hand from the top of Liam's head to the back of his neck. In one smooth motion he picked him up and held him at eye level. "You have already started down a path that leads to death. Trust me, her path also leads to death, but it is a death that will remain with you forever."

Liam started to squirm and flail until Codgarak dropped him. He grabbed his neck and massaged it. "What the hell does that even mean? I'm already on a path that leads to death, but she also leads to death? I mean … that … *ughhh!* It was just going be for a moment."

"Come." The minotaur walked over to a small stone wall on the edge of the square. He sat down on it while Liam found some wooden crates to stack up so he could climb up and sit beside him. Codgarak reached into a small brown sack that Liam hadn't noticed until now. He grabbed a handful of cooked chicken and handed some to Liam to go with a portion of bread he had ripped off a loaf within the sack as well. He was gazing down at the ground as he began to consume his meal.

"Can you still see her?"

Without hesitation, Liam said, "Yes! She's at the tavern tables."

"Good. And the man she's with now?"

His lips pressed together in jealousy. "Yes …" Envy clung to his response.

"Tell me, what do you see?"

His head tilted in frustration at the waste of time. "She has her hand on his arm and is leaning in close to him."

Liam lowered his head but readjusted himself again as soon as he was corrected. "Keep watching." Lorelaylee and the stranger finally stood up from the table and began walking over to the door she claimed was her quarters. *Why not me?*, Liam thought jealously.

"Now what's happening?"

His face contorted in anger. "I don't know, *Cod* … I can't see through walls."

A giant claw pointed directly into his face. "Call me that one more time and this will be the last village you will ever see, for no form of magic or medicine will ever heal your shattered legs."

A slight tremble came into Liam's voice. "Sorry."

The claw lowered. "You're allowing your emotions to blind your observation."

Liam was curious now. "Okay then, what am I missing?" He didn't get his answer but decided to rescan the crowded square. He noticed something out of place. A woman began to make her way slowly towards the door of Lorelaylee's quarters and stood a respectable distance away. She had two children at her side. Liam guessed they were about seven and five years of age. The older appeared to be a boy who stood with his head down, while the younger one was a girl who clung tightly to her mother. "I think there—"

Codgarak cut him off. "Keep watching." A few moments later, the door opened and the man came walking out. His clothing was clearly disturbed and there was a smile on his face as he looked up at the sky, but when he lowered his head, he caught sight of the woman and children. He began to cry and started to speak to the woman.

As he did so, three cloaked individuals stood up around the town square. They had blended into the environment and not drawn attention to themselves. Lying in wait, they acted when it was their moment. Two of the cloaked figures approached the man from either side. He didn't notice them until they were already within striking distance. Two clubs, introduced from the concealment of their cloaks, struck both sides of the man's legs. He crumpled to the ground as the two men beat him mercilessly. His cries tore through the market. Some villagers paused and watched, others continued with their day, trying not to notice the ordeal.

The man screamed and pleaded with the woman. Liam grabbed hold of his sword hilt, but he felt Codgarak's hand land on his shoulder. "Don't." The two cloaked men continued beating the man until all the fight had been struck out of him. The children and their mother were wailing. The cloaked vigilantes stopped their attack. After standing over their adversary for a few seconds, they made their way behind the woman. The boy walked over to the man and spit on him before quickly turning and walking back. One of the cloaked men put his arm around the boy to comfort him. The woman handed her daughter to the other cloaked man and made her way over to the bloodied body. Liam could tell that she said something to the man, but all he saw was her wiping the tears from her eyes and placing her fingers on his lips before she rose and returned to her children. She never turned around but walked with her escort out of the square.

"That man made a vow to another. He made a vow to a family. He made a vow to his children. He broke that vow. He didn't break it today; he did it long ago … today was simply the day he was finally caught." Liam gazed at the barely alive sack of shit lying on the ground while Codgarak spoke.

"Words have meaning, Liam. Today that man brought dishonor to himself, dishonor to his wife, dishonor to his children, dishonor to his family, dishonor to her family. Where is she to go now? Those children will forever be reminded of the adulterer their father is. He will not be trusted in the village. He abandoned them for his desires. Her brothers you saw here today will now become fathers to those children. They will carry the burden, because their mother will more than likely not have another husband. Men will ask, 'What is wrong with her? Why did her husband run to the arms of another woman?' It is not her fault. She did nothing wrong. The fault solely rests on him, but others will not see it that way."

Codgarak's words brought a great weight with them that landed on Liam's shoulders. "Lorelaylee's path leads only to death. You now see that the path is not a physical death but an emotional death, the death of one's soul and spirit. The death of what a beautiful family could have been. She will whisper words of honey in your ears but will give you poison through her kiss." Liam looked up at

Codgarak and met his gaze. "Words have meaning. If you make a vow to another, you best not break it. The last touch that man felt from his wife was her tears being placed upon his lips. He will forever taste her scorn and the guilt of what he has done to them."

The minotaur dropped down from the stone wall. "Come. It is best we depart." Liam followed suit and got in step with his guide. As they turned to leave, he looked back. As he did so, Lorelaylee's door opened. Resting her shoulder on the door frame, she waved tauntingly to Liam in goodbye. *Well, shit* ... he thought. *That certainly wasn't the afternoon I expected to have.*

As they approached the gate, the guards noticed them and made sure it was open by the time they arrived, ensuring the guests didn't hesitate in their departure. "Codgarak, you said I was already on a path towards my death ... and you said Lorelaylee's path also led to death. So ... what path am I on that will lead to my death?"

It didn't take long to receive his answer. "You already know the answer to your question." Liam tilted his head and rotated it towards the sky as he rolled his eyes. He noticed a pinecone on the ground and launched it into a nearby field with a swift kick. *Great. This is going to be a long trip.*

Codgarak looked at him. "What are the lessons to learn here today?"

Liam reassessed everything that had just happened. "Well ... clearly it is not to break one's vow ... but I'm confused. I don't foresee getting married, so I don't need to worry about such things yet, right?"

Codgarak looked at him with a serious demeanor. "You may not have made a vow yet, but one day you will. One day you will vow to another in some form, and on that day, know the importance of what you speak, for should you break that vow, your fate will be far worse than that of the shell of a man who lay before you."

LORELAYLEE

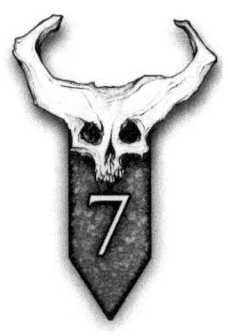

PAY NOW

The sun had set above them a few hours back. Scattered clouds placed golden oranges and romantic pinks upon the royal blue sky. *This realm is nothing but an enchantment,* Liam thought. His mind was filled with anticipation and curiosity about what Fort Patton would be like. He didn't understand why they were heading there, Codgarak being a minotaur of few words except for select moments. Even when he did speak, he didn't always explain the "why" behind his words but left them open to the young fighter's interpretation.

A glow could be seen up ahead. *We must be getting close to the fort,* thought Liam. "At ease. We come seeking your instructor." Codgarak launched his voice into the night, startling Liam and catapulting his senses to a heightened level. He glanced at the tree line but didn't see anything. *Wait—was that a pair of glowing eyes I saw dashing over there? I swear there was a glint of reflective light over there.* His heart rate climbed and his perception of danger amplified. He was unable to control his fear of the unknown.

He stayed in step with his leader, and it wasn't much longer before the fort was finally in view. A large wooden wall was set on the perimeter, with wooden platform towers in each corner. The tops of tall tents could be seen above the walls. Campfires were alight throughout the fort, and laughter, songs, and music peacefully filled the night. Now that he was able to lay his eyes on it, it didn't seem like a bad place at all.

The guards at the entrance seemed to be about Liam's age. They stood stoically to attention. "Welcome, warrior. How may we assist you?"

Codgarak respectfully replied, "We have come seeking Master Jack."

The guard nodded in understanding. "HUA, I will lead you to Master Jack," he snapped without hesitation and pivoted on his feet, leading them through the fort in a processional march and out the back through another gate.

"Master Jack is not within the fort?" Codgarak inquired.

"No, sir warrior. He is currently at Thunder Rock, just a little outside the fort. It is his select training grounds. He normally stays there instead of the fort." Liam watched but didn't respond; as they followed the guard without question.

The three were soon walking up a small hillside. A short distance from where they had originally arrived at the forts gate. Liam took in and analyzed Thunder Rock upon their arrival. The floor was a solid sheet of granite in the shape of a circular area that Liam guessed could be filled with a hundred soldiers training simultaneously. Stone pillars shaped like massive dragons' teeth were set around the circle. At the back of the circle, close to a sheer stone wall, was a crackling fire with a cloaked figure standing next to it. As they came closer to the fire, Liam could see a man of average height. Though he wore a cloak, it was clear he had a stout upper torso and resolute legs. He could clearly see his muscular outline and had the odd thought that the master standing before him was best described as a mountain man. He had a thick but trimmed bronzed beard and spice-brown eyes.

The master glanced over at the approaching party. "Now here is a sight I didn't expect." A large smile appeared on his face. He stretched out his arm and he and Codgarak clasped each other's forearms in an embrace.

"Master Jack."

He let out a sarcastic sigh. "Right …" A smirk appeared on his face at the warrior's compliment and he glanced at Liam and the guard. "That is all. Guard, you can take post at the entrance."

"Yes, Master Jack." The guard conducted a military about-face movement and marched to the entrance of Thunder Rock.

Letting go of Codgarak, Jack reached over and grabbed a clear glass bottle of amber liquid. "Join me?"

The minotaur chuckled. "Of course."

Jack turned to Liam. "And you, lad?"

Before he could answer, Codgarak interrupted. "It's best he didn't."

"I wouldn't mind joining; however …" Liam countered.

Codgarak and Jack looked at each other as if they spoke without words. "Sorry, kid; if Codgarak says it's not best, then his word stands." Liam didn't respond outwardly, but his heart was heavy with disappointment.

"One must earn one's spot at the table, and you have not even started," Codgarak said.

"You're right …" Liam couldn't deny there was a little bit of resentment for not getting to partake, but recognized the reasoning.

"Why don't you take watch with the guard at the entrance and allow us some time between old friends?" Master Jack instructed.

"Okay," Liam replied, but he was quickly reprimanded.

"'Yes, Master Jack' is the correct answer," Codgarak informed him.

"Yes, Master Jack," came the quickly corrected response, as he wandered over to the guard.

Master Jack watched Liam walk away before asking, "What's with the sidekick?"

The half bull, half man raised his arms in a "where do I begin?" gesture. "He is the son of Judah of Artho … I fought alongside his father in a few battles. He just appeared at my cave, seeking me out in a belief it is his fate or destiny or … I dunno."

Jack handed Codgarak a glass of the amber liquid and they both took sips from their cups. Jack thought aloud. "Recalling our battles together, I would assume I have walked past his father at some point, but I cannot recall this name."

"His father was a brave, solid fighter. Out of the hundreds of fighters I have met, his father is at least a name and face I can recall."

Master Jack tilted his head. "That says a lot."

Codgarak pointed to the fort. "His father received his military training here. If the boy chooses to continue down this path, he must at least survive here first. His body is able, but it is his soul and spirit I am most curious about."

Master Jack went from watching the fire to gazing at Liam and the guard standing at the entrance. "You brought him to the right place for that. I shall have him join the newest class tomorrow. Master DC and Master Fry will break him down and test his worth."

"Thunder Rock, huh? You are now the master."

The compliment was quickly met with humility. "I am just trying to bestow the lessons taught to me on a new generation. Warriors and masters far greater than I have filled this training circle before me. I can only attempt to honor them by maintaining the standard they set forth."

The minotaur smiled at his old friend. "A potter can only produce the finest of products if the clay is of significant quality. Though you were instructed by masters, it was your inner qualities that allowed you to be molded into the master you are today."

Jack gave a smile and nod of appreciation to the warrior. "To humble masters, then." They raised their glasses in salute and both enjoyed another sip.

After Master Jack and Codgarak had sent Liam away, he received an unwelcome greeting from the guard that took him by surprise. "Hey, I'm Liam," he said as he strolled up.

"Don't speak to me, FNG!"

The sharp verbal attack stung him. "What?" he asked in complete confusion.

"FNG. Fucking new guy!" A blank stare was all Liam could produce in response. "Wow, you really are an FNG, aren't you? Listen here, bitch, you're nothing to me. I'm a four-tiered troop. You shouldn't even be speaking to me right now!"

Liam was taken aback by this new information. "I don't think you understand ... I'm not here to join you."

The guard broke his composure and shifted his weight to one side. "Look, man ... you think you're something special because your friend is friends with Master Jack?"

"No, that isn't what I meant ... I just think you're confused, because I'm not here to—"

The guard interrupted him. "To what? Become a recruit? Look, bitch, if you were truly a fighter, then you and your cow-man hybrid wouldn't be here. I could tell from the moment you walked up that you haven't seen battle, let alone training!"

Liam started to get defensive. "My training is none of your concern."

The guardsman was laughing now. "You're right. It ain't my concern at all. Cause you're going to get your pathetic ass handed to you tomorrow by the masters!"

Liam did his best to bite his tongue. "Perhaps I should save myself the time, then!" He grabbed the hilt of his sword and pulled it free a few inches to show his intentions.

"You sure you wanna fucking do that, new guy? I'd hate to show Master Jack and your friend just how much of a bitch you are on your first night here!" The guardsman laughed louder.

By now Master Jack and Codgarak had noticed the commotion. "Damn it, now what?" Codgarak said, but Master Jack simply smiled.

"I kinda forsaw this happening."

The beast eyed Liam as they started to walk towards the two. "I figured it was a matter of time—just hoped it wouldn't be tonight."

The sword flew clean out of its sheath as Liam brought it upward at a 45-degree angle. The guard braced his spear on the ground and angled it to block Liam's sword. A clang rang out as it hit the spear shaft and, with perfect timing, the guard kicked the spear past Liam's foot, swiping towards his center of gravity. He knocked Liam off balance and executed a perfect roundhouse kick to his thigh that sent him down to the ground on his back. Liam looked up at the spear head, which was resting on his cheek.

"I see you have chosen to begin your training early, Liam," Master Jack said when the two arrived at the joust.

"Master, he thought he would be able to launch a surprise attack. I just acted in self-defense," the guard proclaimed.

"Unprovoked, I'm sure ..." The guard gave a blank stare but returned to his at-rest stance in an attempt to deflect the accusation. "In all my years of instructing, I've never heard of a higher-tiered trainee provoking a less-disciplined recruit with their words and gestures, have you, Codgarak?" The beast simply answered Master Jack's question with a huff.

"Get up, Liam," Master Jack instructed. "Guard, take Liam to the new recruits' tent without further escalation of force or speech." He continued, "Liam, if this is the path you wish to take, then we'd like to see your worth. You will begin training with Master DC in the morning." Liam wanted to protest, or at least ask a multitude of questions, but he maintained his composure and nodded in acceptance.

The guard didn't say anything else as he led Liam to the tent. Upon arrival, though, he said, "Good luck, trainee. I'll be looking forward to when you ring the quitters' bell and walk back to your trash pile of a home!" Liam's jaw locked with rage. He so desperately wanted a rematch. His father had taught him how to fight and spent time working with him, but Liam didn't train every day as these soldiers and recruits did. In the latter months of his father's life, Liam had spent his time dedicated to maintaining the homestead and providing food for the family while his father was ill. Though one may have the strength to wield a weapon, that is very different from having the articulate skill to tactically employ it. His skills had atrophied, and he was in desperate need of training.

The tent wasn't much to take in—four canvas walls with an open flap door, a pitched roof, and four cot beds. "Well, isn't this cozy?" He dropped his backpack on the ground and leaned his sword against one of the cots. He had just lain down on it and taken a few deep breaths when a calm voice intruded. "Welcome, sir. Do you need any assistance, or is there something I can get for you this evening?"

The voice was peaceful in its delivery. Liam sat up on the cot and saw a man slightly younger in appearance than Master Jack with a pleasant smile standing at the entrance to the tent. He wore white and gray robes with a light gray belt, and he had a clean-shaven face with a serene expression. He inquired again, "I believe this is your first night at Fort Patton, and I wanted to ensure I checked to see if you needed anything."

Liam appreciated the gesture. "Thank you. Yes—if the cook has any food remaining from supper, I will take that. A pitcher of water and a blanket will do."

The man nodded and put his hands behind his back. "Of course. I will be but a moment." Liam watched his figure disappeared down the inner pathway of the camp before he lay back down on the cot.

It really was just a few minutes before the man returned. "Unfortunately, there wasn't much left from supper," he said as he handed Liam a quarter loaf of bread, a few strips of bacon, and an apple. He placed a pitcher of water at the corner of the cot with a small cup and then produced a woolen blanket.

"Please." Liam gestured towards the cot. The man sat down as he continued. "How long have you been the camp servant?"

The man looked at him and then turned his head to look out at the tents lined up outside. "Oh, a few years it has been now."

"I see. They treat you well here?"

He smiled more widely. "Yes ... I am beyond blessed with my treatment here. There is nothing better than serving others."

Taking another bite and wiping his mouth, Liam continued. "And what of the training here? My father went through training many years ago and spoke highly of this fort. Is it still the same quality of instruction?" His curiosity overshadowed his discernment, for he didn't realize his questions could be interpreted as condescending.

The man maintained his smile but let out a slight exhale. "I believe the words of Master Jack put it best: 'Pay now or pay later.'" Liam tensed his eyebrows as he contemplated the motto. The servant, reading his body language, continued. "Too often, we see students who want to rush through their training in order to get to the fight faster. Or they want to sacrifice the dedication it requires to master one's skills in wielding the tools of war. The fact remains, pay now—dedicate yourself now, perfect your training regimen now. If you don't 'pay now,' you will certainly 'pay later' with your death, the death of your fellow warrior, the death of your family because you failed them. Your training and preparation for war should never be short changed."

The man's words took Liam by surprise. He sat back slightly as he reflected on the seriousness of what he had asked Codgarak for and his intention to truly pursue the path of a warrior. "In other words, your time here at Fort Patton is dependent on solely one thing: how much you dedicate to learning. The more you put in, the more you will receive. It is that simple."

Liam had just finished the food provided for him and taken a small sip of the water when a female figure came over to the tent and entered it. "Good evening, Master DC," the man said. Both he and Liam stood up.

Master DC nodded to the servant and then turned her gaze to Liam. "In four hours, when the morning bell rings, be at the training grounds and get in formation with class Echo-Core." She pointed with her right hand as she announced the instruction. "Any questions?" Her voice was stern and direct.

"No questions," Liam said.

"Best get some sleep," she suggested as she turned and left the tent briskly.

"It was nice meeting you, sir. I recommend you take Master DC's advice, however, and get some rest." The servant nodded as Liam thanked him before he departed for the night.

Liam lay back down on his cot and wrapped the woolen blanket around him. The night temperatures dropped low, and a crisp chill covered the fort, just cold enough that he could see his breath. He tried his best to sleep, but his mind would not allow it. The "what ifs" and the unknown kept his anxiety and anticipation at an all-time high. He lay restlessly in his cot for what must have been a few hours. His eyes had shut for what seemed like only a few minutes when *ring-ring-ring-ring-ring-ring* came blaring through the camp. A jolt of urgency surged through his body as he jumped up. As groups of soldiers went jogging past his tent towards the training grounds, he raced out to follow them. "Here we go…" He said under his breathe.

MASTER JACK

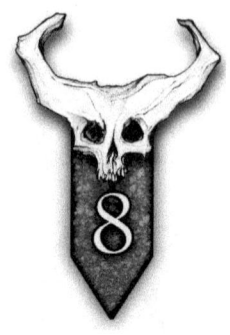

SWEAT AND BLOOD

Bodies bounced from side to side as the group of soldiers ran in a line. They made their way past all the tents and eventually the grounds opened onto a large field of short grass with three figures standing in the center. *"Fall in!"* came bellowing across the field like a verbal anvil pounding at Liam's ears. The trainees dispersed to imaginary squares on the ground and aligned themselves with the soldiers on each side and in front of them.

Where do I go? Do I go left or right? Liam's mind raced with anxiety. *Don't fuck up, don't fuck up, don't—* His thoughts were interrupted by Master Jack as the razor edge of an open hand shot towards his face. "Why are you here?" Liam's eyes widened. He hadn't expected to see Master Jack this morning, nor the forceful tone he had breached his thoughts with. Liam looked directly at him. *"Don't look at me!"* He snapped his head round to look in front of him. "You look forward! You are not distracted! You are focused solely on the formation!"

"*Fall in!* Five, four, three …" The instructions bellowed yet again across the training field as the soldiers and trainees moved at a pace that wasn't up to par with the master's wishes. "Two, one! On your face!" Liam hesitated to follow the instruction. He watched the soldiers all drop to the ground, landing on their chests. His delay of half a second was all it took for the master to gaze upon the poor sap. "You had better learn, and learn quick!" Master Jack warned, standing over Liam. When he began to walk off, Liam thought he was in the clear until—"Oh, we don't want to move with a sense of urgency?"—the other master's voice hit him like an arrow.

I hope that wasn't directed at m— Liam moved his head just an inch, but that was all it took for him to see the slender figure marching towards him and the few others in his area. The instruction resounded across the grounds. "Back on your feet!" The large group all regained their feet. "On your faces!" Again, the formation returned to the ground. Liam did his best to quicken his pace to match that of the other troops, but … *"Sleepy face!"* As the articulate description began, he noticed the highly polished boots arriving right next to his face as the penetrating tone of the master pummeled his eardrums from above. "'I want to be a fighter, but I'll do it when it's convenient for me! We'll train when I choose to!' *Re-cov-errr!*"

Again, the group rose to their feet. Liam noticed it was now Master DC standing in front of him, but he found yet another knifelike hand moving towards him, it came so fast, he couldn't focus. Master DC's hand was in front of his face, the fingers flat, the thumb slightly tucked in so that the knuckle protruded. The hand was used in a chopping motion, stabbing motion, slicing motion—hell, the masters could come up with some creative ways to execute these moves. The entire time it was happening to him, he watched this hand that looks like a knife about to stab his face as the master's nonstop yelling cut deep as if to his soul with whatever corrective instruction was being given at that moment.

Liam certainly didn't dare try to reposition his head to see what else was going on around him. Master Jack's earlier instruction had done its job as Master DC was now inside his personal space—*don't look anywhere else but forward*. "I don't know who you think you are, but I assure you, you're a clown!" Immediately his thoughts went on a mental tangent. *Why a clown? Am I funny? That is what I am compared to?* "Why are you here?" His thoughts were interrupted yet again.

"I ... am here ... uhh ..."

"Your hesitation will get us killed, clown! *Re-cov-errr!*" The whole group returned to their feet.

As Master DC stood uncomfortably close and dedicating a high level of attention of detail towards him, he heard Master Jack's instructions cut across the grounds. "In place! *March!*"

The entire group began to march in unison—the entire group except Liam, that is, who didn't grasp the obvious fact that you had to pick up your left leg first and then alternate in time with one another. Master DC tore into him with every infraction of the instructions she could find. "You sure you're at the right training fort? I believe the court jester training camp is in Misovaga! You might as well quit now and go ring the bell and save us all some time! We can't train because of you! Our time is wasted because of you!"

Master Jack called over, "Master DC ... apparently this trainee believes they can do a better job at correcting your trainee than you!"

Master DC's head snapped away from Liam and, like a shark smelling blood in the water, she streaked across the training grounds and pounced on the master's latest victim. "You trying to do my job, I see!" The tirade continued as Liam exhaled. *Master DC ... she seems pleasant ... at least I get a break for once ...*

His thoughts delayed him from reacting to the instructions yet again. *"On your feet!"* Master Jack corrected him from behind.

"If you can't handle the training and keep pace, then you best go ring that bell now and head back to your home ... *you will not be given any breaks, young Liam!*" Liam noticed Master Jack's boots walking away. *What have I gotten myself into? ...*

The masters didn't let up on him. For hours, the entire group suffered. Nothing was ever good enough. Liam was the main focal point, and the masters ensured that the entire group knew of his existence and the reason behind the punishment. *"Re ...cov ... errrrr!"* Master Jack bellowed across the training grounds. All the trainees were covered in sweat. "Everyone to the chow tent ... *move!*" The instruction was echoed as the trainees returned the command. *"Move!"*

The group immediately turned into a swarm of mountain deer that all rushed in the direction of the chow tent. Liam was the victim of multiple knocks and blows, trainees and soldiers taking advantage of the chaos to get a cheap shot in when they had an opportunity.

They arrived shortly at the chow tent, where Liam was given a bowl with what appeared to be some type of grain ... mush ... stuff. All he knew was that it was warm and helped offset the cold morning, at least for a few moments. It didn't taste bad, but it certainly didn't taste great either; it was simply sustenance. His mind wandered as he began to worry that another soldier might come and knock his bowl out of his hands, spit in his food, or maybe even take it for themselves, and he would be left to fend for himself. But that didn't happen. He was called over to the table of another group of trainees. He thought he would receive some type of welcome, since he'd been invited over, but it wasn't the case. "Hey, hey, hey, boys … look here at the fucking new guy!"

"You finally realize which leg is your left and right?"

"Hey, shitbird, do you think you could pull your head out of the horse's ass you have it shoved up? You know … so we can all stop getting our shit kicked in by the masters?"

A chuckle came over the group. He tried to avoid eye contact and just let the volley of insults fly at him.

"Hey, yo … this one right here …" The trainee pointed at Liam while calling loudly to everyone around. "This fucking guy … he's a reincarnation! Because there's no way someone can be this fucking stupid within one lifetime!" The group around him laughed.

"Yeah, shitpile! None of this is difficult! It's not like Master DC asked you to eat a crate of apples and shit out a fruit salad!"

Liam grinding his teeth with a clenched jaw was all the group needed to seize their opportunity. "Ohh, look here, lads! Baby boy cracking under the pressure! Hey, baby boy … you trying to tell the realm you're a fighter, yet you can't even face the heat of words? *Get the fuck outta here!*"

The next man teed off on the opportunity. "How you suppose to fight orcs, gnolls, reptacrepts, yet you can't even handle this?"

"He ain't a baby boy, chaps, he a baby back bitch! *Gonna ring the bell soon, this one!*"

The roaring voice of Master DC cut through the noise. "FALL IN!" The group stood up and ran in unison towards the training grounds. Liam made sure he wasn't the last to get into place this time. The line of trainees flowing through the camp found a bottleneck at one of the passageways. He waited for his turn to burst through and carry on to the training grounds, but during the three-second break, he noticed out of the corner of his eye that he was being watched by someone standing across the way. He quickly glanced over to see the camp servant in his white and gray robes with his arms still behind his back. "Face the fire and rise ... otherwise this path is not your destiny."

For hours they practiced marching drills. There was no stopping, no breaks, again and again. The only thing that rescued them was some trainees collapsing while standing to attention. "This is what you're going to do?" Master DC chastised. "You will march for miles to the battle, to rescue your army, and then you must stand battle ready to face the onslaught that awaits you ... and this is what you're going to do?" Her words cut through everyone's pride and ego. Every man thought they were the toughest, yet everyone struggled equally.

Some poor stupid soul decided he would challenge her. "We are ready to fight! Present to me the enemy and they will not prevail!" Liam was grateful, for earlier in the day he'd been questioning it, but he finally realized there was someone there who was dumber than him. The training ground was dead silent. Everybody kept their gaze forward and dared not look around to see what would happen next.

Out of the corner of his eye, Liam saw Master DC march from left to right, eventually ending up in front of the formation of soldiers in which the challenger stood. She glided across the ground without making a sound, as a leopard stalks its prey. Liam finally had the chance to really gaze upon the master as she walked by. She wore a Shaolin-rimmed metal hat, and the sun reflected a beam of light off its razor-sharp edge. Her beige olive skin beautifully complemented her deep brown eyes. She never smiled but always kept a scowl upon her face. A vein on her neck looked as if it was about to burst and her jaw muscles flared from being clenched so tightly.

She wore a heavy earth-brown sleeveless vest. Its V-neck exposed her upper chest, while her arms were expertly chiseled. A red sash belt tied snugly around her trim waist held up black pants that followed the contours of her physique. Her high brown leather boots were a shade lighter than her vest, but blessings upon the parents who made her, because she was a sight to behold.

That was, of course, what Liam thought until she unleashed the caged demon inside her upon the poor soldier. *"You are what?"* Her knife hand sliced at the face of the soldier as she happily accepted the challenge.

The second time around, his confidence had withered. "We are ready to fight …"

Her skin began to glow with red-hot intensity. *"You … are… not … ready!"*

The soldier, breaking his disciplinary bearing, turned his head and glared into her eyes. "Yes … we … are!"

Liam swore he saw an aura of orange waves wrap around her as if she were charging up with energy. She stood back and turned. *"Those of you ready to fight, remain … all others, fall out to the edge line!"*

No one hesitated; the vast majority immediately fell back en masse to the training grounds' edge. Everyone huddled down and watched in anticipation. A scattered group of soldiers remained on the training grounds. Whispers started. "I got thirty-six." "What? I counted forty-nine!" Liam's only thought was *Well, we're certainly fucked if we can't even count accurately.* He took his own rough count and found it to be forty-six … well, either way, he didn't see how one person, even if they were a master, could defeat forty-six people single-handedly.

Master DC walked over to a metal tube. Reaching behind it, she grabbed hold of a large mallet. She smashed it down, sending forth a ground-rumbling blast. "You might want to take control of your force!" she shouted at the trainee who had challenged her. The soldier stepped away from the few in his direct group, who stayed behind. "All right, boys! Rally up!" The group broke formation and ran over to him. *"V formation!"* They formed a giant inverted V, the two open ends facing Master DC and the base furthest away. This formation was commonly utilized to encircle a small force, especially if that force was backed up against a cliffside or wall that wouldn't allow them an opportunity to escape. The soldiers stood ready in formation. Though they weren't sure what would happen next, they hadn't expected to be fighting more than one master.

At the back of the training grounds was an entrance from the wooden wall of the fort. Codgarak and Master Jack entered and made their way over to Master DC. They conversed amongst each other, but no one could tell what they were saying. Whispers and assumptions danced from one ear to the next.

Master Jack then added a new dynamic to the mystery. "Master Fry!" Liam was startled to see the man he had thought was the camp servant step forward from behind the trainees gathered around the outer edge and make his way to the other masters.

"That's Master Fry?" Liam asked those around him, shocked.

"Yeah, new guy! Everyone knows that!" *Everyone … except for the new guy known as Liam.* A pit formed in his stomach. He felt terrible for treating one of the masters like a simple servant. Master Fry reached the group and joined the discussion.

The observers watched in anticipation as Codgarak and Master Jack left the group and walked to the back of the training grounds. "Oh shit!" a voice said behind him. *Twenty-three to one … this is crazy!* Liam thought. "Bet you ten coins the masters don't survive," one trainee said to another.

"Make it fifteen!"

"Done!" More added to the betting going on, whereas Liam stayed attuned to the movements of the masters and the formation of the trainees.

Master Fry walked over to a weapons rack and grabbed a large wooden staff, whereas Master DC fetched two small swords. Liam was curious, as she didn't hold them in a traditional stance but rather grabbed the hilts and held them upside down. She then extended her arms downward, which placed the sword blades against her triceps and the backs of her shoulders. Master Fry and Master DC made their way back onto the training grounds and stood back to back. Master Fry held his staff out in front of him. *"Forward … march!"* The formation pounded forward, drawing their swords from their sheaths.

"They're going to try and encircle them!" one trainee blurted out.

The formation drew closer to the two masters as they held their ground, but not for long. The lead trainee started to call out the command to wrap around and create a circle but was cut off by Master DC launching her attack. She darted forward and started slashing her way through the recruits. Liam watched in amazement as she executed precise strikes and slashes with her swords. Spinning, turning, pivoting, it was all a synced sequence of movements. It wasn't a dance of motion, but it could easily have been mistaken for one, for it seemed as if she never stood still.

Clang, clang, slash!

The metal singing to the rhythm of her combat sequence. The entire song playing out for them to hear as they watched her intently.

She was so mesmerizing that he completely forgot about Master Fry, who had been making calculated progress behind Master DC. After she'd sliced her way forward into the inner pocket of the V formation, she suddenly turned back, ducked, and spun over to the opposite side as Master Fry came leaping over her in perfect harmony. He brought his staff down in a powerful strike that the poor bastard trainee wasn't ready for. The trainee tried to bring his sword upwards to block it but wasn't fast enough. The *CRACK* resonated across the training grounds, and everyone saw a blast of blood shoot up like a geyser from the victim's skull.

Master Fry's staff never let up its attack as he whipped it back and forth, from side to side, and relentlessly kept on the offensive. His staff spinning around in a fury of strikes landing upon them. *Crack, crack, pop-pop-thud.*

The staff thrashing into the trainee's and soldiers as you could hear the breaking of bones. The sickening crunches followed up by painful screams of agony while their bodies fell to the ground. For all their efforts, they didn't stand a chance. "They're breaking!" a spectator yelled as the formation began backpedaling.

Their counterparts weren't just falling physically; their spirits, confidence, and will to fight were too. The few who remained broke ranks and sprinted away as best as they could, their "leader" in tow. *"The hell you are, coward!"* Master DC yelled. She grabbed her hat, leapt upward in a forward-spinning motion, and as she landed back upon the ground, she hurled it at the retreating leader. It soared through the air and sliced through his neck at an angle, lopping his head clear off. His decapitated body fell to the ground and his head rolled away. The remaining six trainees made it to the edge of the training grounds and leapt over the sitting spectators as if they were now safe from the onslaught.

Master DC retrieved her hat from where it lay near the final victim's body. Master Fry held his staff vertically with its base set upon the ground. He began to quietly say an enchantment. Moving his free hand in a few articulate motions, he brought it over and grasped the staff with both hands as a blue light encircled it. He picked it up, raised it with extended arms, then forcefully struck its base on the ground. A jet of water was emitted by the ground, glowing and radiating a mystical light blue. It rose and covered the training grounds but held its shape and didn't flow outwards as regular water would have. The glowing liquid kept rising over the bodies of the trainees lying on the ground. Once the entire training grounds were covered and you could not see the fallen any longer, Master Fry lifted his staff once more and brought it back down on the ground. The water receded back into the earth, re-exposing the bodies. Slowly, one by one, they came to and eventually got to their feet. Master Fry and Master DC went to each one and quietly gave them instructions. The only body that remained dead was that of the soldier who had questioned Master DC. His body was still purging itself of its blood, and his head rested on its side, the eyes remaining open and gazing at the other students.

"I hope you enjoyed this valuable lesson today," Master DC said and walked off into the inner sanctum of the fort. Codgarak and Master Jack were slightly behind her.

"The next group who wants to fight will get me! Better think that through before you open your mouth!" Codgarak said as he passed the students, glaring down at them as if they were gnomes to a cave troll.

"Make ready for training! Fall in!" Master Fry commanded, and the group on the outskirts jumped back up and rushed with haste to their positions. No one dared to challenge him. "Everyone grab your bow and a quiver of arrows! We'll do marksmanship training for the rest of the day."

The sun had long set by the time Liam was able to return to his tent. He practically collapsed on his cot, exhausted. He had hunted game for miles through the hills, chopped wood all day long, and explored the woods, rivers, and hills around his old home … but this training just seemed to hit a bit differently. There was no let-up! Everything was taught through action, learning on the go, thinking fast on your feet.

He certainly felt alone. The only time he had seen Codgarak was when Master DC and Master Fry had slaughtered the group of trainees and soldiers. A straight-up massacre! He replayed the battle in his mind, reliving the motions of the masters, and his hands waved over his body as he lay in bed, mimicking Master DC's slashes with her swords. The fort was as quiet as it could be, and as his exhaustion fell deeper upon him, so did the night fall upon the fort.

Ring-ring-ring-ring-ring-ring-ring-ring-ring.

The training bell was the worst in the early morning hours. "Let's go, boys!" came a voice from the first group jogging past Liam's tent. He slipped his boots on as fast as he could and sprang from his tent, merging with the next group that passed.

"I swear that bell is the worst sound there is," one of them said firmly.

"I'd much rather hear the sound of that bell than the horn announcing an invasion." A counter-argument brought reason to the early morning debate.

As they turned the corner and got closer to the training grounds, the first man said, "You say that, but let me tell you, when you hear your lady calling out his name instead of yours, that's the worst sound, lads … she got fucked in the ass and I got fucked in my heart." The troops laughed and chuckled. Liam couldn't hide his smirk. He had to admit it was pretty funny and a perfectly timed delivery.

"We want to tell jokes instead of train this morning, I see! Hit the dirt! Low crawl to your positions!" Master DC cracked her verbal whip upon their spirits and bodies. "Fuck!" came a long sigh as they all muttered under their breath.

The same voice that had told the joke said, "And now we get to be fucked in the ass!"

Semi-contained laughter came over the group, but it wasn't quite contained enough. "What was that? Add another hour to drills this morning? *Ab-so-fucking-lutely we will!*" They couldn't hide from the eagle eyes or the tiger ears of Master DC. This time they learned to keep their mouths shut and just grunt in frustration.

Liam quickly picked up the lessons from yesterday, and he did everything he could not to be noticed this morning. *"Let's go! Pick'm up, pick'm up!"* The drills and exercises wore everyone out, regardless of their strength and size, for the masters did not let up until everyone reached their breaking point. Only they, the masters themselves, determined what was acceptable. "*Re-cov-errr!* Fall out and get chow!"

Wasting no time, the trainees ran to the chow tent. Liam found the group he had sat with the day before and hesitantly stood a few soldiers back from them in line. One of them looked around and noticed him. "You going to join us, new guy, or is your tail still between your legs?" *Well, that's just my luck*, he thought. Grabbing the slop of white goo, he joined the group again at the table.

"Hey! You know why soldiers marry women in the lands they conquer?" The group shook their heads. "Because when they return home, he gets to keep the in-laws hundreds of miles away!" Everyone chuckled. They were of mixed ages. Some were older, some were extremely young. Liam learned quickly that no one was safe from harassment. You were grandfather if you were older, boy if you looked young, and an idiot if you didn't do something the way everyone else did.

The chow tent servant was walking through the area after emptying another bucket for the troops when he heard the joke and leaned over during a pause in the conversation, "Hey … what's the difference between being hungry and being horny?" The trainees listened in anticipation. "Where you stick the cucumber!"

The group laughed. "You fucking cooks and your distorted humor!"

Another chimed in. "Hey, did I ever tell the story of when I had a threesome?"

Another cut him off. "Jory, just because you had sex with your sister and she weighs as much as two people doesn't mean you had a threesome!" The group laughed at the mockery, but lo and behold, the training bell interrupted the break.

"Let's go, let's go, let's go! Move it!" The table all stood up together and began to run towards the training grounds. Jory took his bowl and threw it at his detractor as they began their departure, though he blatantly missed his target. His failure certainly amplified the laughter, as it was clear it had gotten under his skin.

The group returned to the training grounds to see the three masters standing in a line awaiting their arrival. "Red group with me!" Master DC pointed to the far end of the training grounds.

"Green group stay here!" Master Fry let out.

"Gray group! Fall out, head to Thunder Rock!" Master Jack yelled. "Liam! That includes you!"

The group of soldiers arrived at Thunder Rock and aligned in formation. "Relax!" They thought the master was setting them up in a trick. "I said relax! You know what—fall out, form a circle, and even take a seat if you like." The group hesitated, looking at each other to see who would act first. Master Jack looked at them during the long pause. "Okay … look, if y'all want to stand there, fine, but this is your last chance to fall out, because once I start instructing, that's it." One brave soul broke ranks, walked over to the left side, and sat down on the ground.

"All right …" Master Jack nodded in agreement as he turned his back to the group and walked over to the weapons rack. The rest of the group jolted into action and found seats upon the ground while his back was turned. He said over his shoulder, "That's the fastest I've ever seen you slugs move."

When he turned back to the group, he held a sword in his hand. "This is a sword … it is the primary weapon utilized in battle and warfare. There are many weapons that can be used. Spears, axes, pikes, lances, maces, bows, clubs, knives … you will face these and many more, and if you don't learn how each one operates, you will be defeated. The sword is our primary weapon. It is the most-used weapon, therefore we train to become experts in how to wield this tool."

A cadet raised his hand, giving a break to the lecture. "Yes?" The cadet got to his feet, placing his hands behind his back to show respect for the master's position of honor.

"Which weapon is the greatest?"

Master Jack waited for the soldier to return to his seat. "Your mind is the greatest weapon. Everything else is an accessory."

As he approached Liam he heard the familiar sounds of blades impacting the training mannequin. The thuds and cracks of the wood taking the impact was far more constant than the metal tings which were the desired effect students were suppose to work towards. A river of sweat ran down Liam's face and droplets went flying around him as he continued.Master Jack walked over to him. He didn't say anything but admired Liam's spirit, recollecting how he had once started—the same drills, the same exercises. *You have to admire the lad for truly dedicating what looks like everything he has.* The other soldiers and trainees had already gone to the fort for evening chow, but Liam remained and continued his efforts to excel in the sword training routine. The wooden training mannequin stood with six wooden arms, all positioned at different angles. Some arms had weapons affixed to the hands, but at specific locations on the body and limbs there were metal brackets.

Liam stopped for a brief moment, his arms dropping and shoulders slouching as the weight of the swords burdened him. He wiped his face with his shirt sleeve, and as he did so, he noticed the master standing behind him. He gave a final exhale as he continued his training sequencing and the returning sounds of the swords impact on the wood echoed out across the area, but with an increased speed.

Master Jack smiled. He admired Liam for trying to put on a performance for him, but he couldn't take it any longer. "Stop." Liam dropped his arms. His shoulders rolled in time with his deep breaths. "Well, let no one say you don't try hard and give what appears to be your best." A smile showed through the mountain man beard. The student returned the smile. Compliments weren't given often at the fort.

"What have I told you in training?" Master Jack watched a confused look come over Liam's face. His eyes danced from side to side as thoughts flashed through his mind. His eyes widened like those of a child when they know exactly the answer their parent is looking for.

"Pay now or pay later!"

Master Jack laughed gently. "That wasn't what I was looking for." Liam didn't have to say it out loud; his facial expression plainly said "dang it." He realized he needed to reassure the exhausted apprentice. "You're right—pay now or pay later is what I normally say … and you are doing exactly what you should be doing. The training you are paying for now with your sweat and blood will be worth it. What I also need you to remember right now is 'Slow is smooth, smooth is fast.' You are trying to be fast, but you're not being effective."

He watched the boy's eyes become lost to exhaustion as he started second-guessing all his efforts in training during the long afternoon. "Let me show you." Master Jack stretched out his hands and Liam passed the swords to him. Master Jack placed one of the blades on the metal sleeve of the training mannequin. He slowly went through the attack movement, striking the metal sleeve every time. The metal ringing out with a consistent tinging as his strike landed.

He paused to reinforce the instructions Liam had been given earlier in the day. "Remember, it is not just coming in to strike the arm—you need to hit directly on this point. If you are too far forward, you'll be fighting their full strength and energy. If you hit too high, you'll have to use more of your strength to force their movement off target. You need to hit exactly at this point. This will not only block their momentum but will enable you to conserve your energy."

He watched as Liam stared intently at the process and nodded slightly. The sweat continued to pour down his face. "Also, when we develop this attack sequence and add on to it, we will show you how you can move from this strike to a forward thrust." Master Jack placed the right sword into the crook of his left armpit and adjusted the limbs of the mannequin slightly before re-engaging both swords. "So I will come and hit here"—*ting*—"and once I get my second strike on that spot, I thrust forward with just a slight twist of my wrist and …" *Twang!* The sword pierced the rib cage of the wooden torso. "But you must first learn that flow will create the speed you're seeking. If you try for speed, you won't hit your mark." Master Jack began the sword movement again. Liam listening in as the metal clashed together began to create a rhythm.

As Master Jack speed up and the rhythm continued in unison, he projected his voice over the noise, as his arms never stopped. "Then you learn how to emphasize your attack within the movement." His training sequence changing with more significant strikes/ The battle rhythm being changed as the emphasized strikes added their impacts within the series.

"Then you develop that flow, because your target will never stay in the same spot like the mannequin, so you must learn to read their movements and adapt your pattern to find their weakness." Master Jack started to open up his strikes, hitting new parts of the exposed metal target, all the while adding speed and emphasis to his strikes.

Liam's mouth fell open. This was the first time he had seen Master Jack unleashing a full succession of these progressive striking movements. The entire time, he never hit the wood; in fact, he even took his gaze away from the training dummy and looked at Liam, still performing the onslaught with the swords. Making sure Liam didn't lose sight of the training movement and its purpose, he brought his speed back down to a crawl.

Ting—ting, ting, ting—ting—ting, ting, ting, whack.

Liam's eyes opened wide as he saw the sword's final strike land on the wood instead of the metal target. Master Jack tilted his head, a smile on his face. "Even masters require practice." He handed the swords back to Liam. "Slow is smooth, smooth is fast." He smiled and patted Liam's shoulder, then began walking back towards the entrance, where Master Fry had made an appearance, analyzing the sounds of Liam's strikes as they rang out in the training circle. A significant improvement from where he was at, but still only producing the intermixed sounds and rhythm of an apprentice.

Ting—ting—ting—ting—ting, whack.
Whack—ting—ting, whack.

Liam had finished for the night and was walking back towards his tent when he saw Codgarak in the distance sitting between Master DC and Master Jack. He wanted to go be with them but figured it was best not to. He just continued, and as he grew closer to the camp, he saw a group of soldiers sitting together. "Hey … look here … see this one … trying to be a master within his first three days."

"Two!" corrected another.

"Ahh yes, two days and he's putting in those hours to be amongst the ranks of masters. Gonna start teaching us his own lessons." Liam was used to their laughter by now. He wasn't the sole focal point as he had been yesterday, but he was still an easy target for most. He slowed his pace but didn't come to a stop until he saw Master Fry quietly appear and startle the others. They quickly closed their mouths and didn't continue their mockery.

As they quietened down, the master said, "Somewhere in this world there is an enemy who you do not know, nor have you met, who is training with the sole intent of killing you." No one dared interrupt. "They do not care about the hour or the conditions … they are solely committed to being ready to exploit that one moment of weakness. Therefore you must not be one who is interested but one who is committed, for you must train and prepare to be the hardest person they will ever try to kill."

After a brief pause, one of the soldiers let his arrogance and ignorance overcome him. "And Master Fry … how many of these enemy soldiers are there?" A slight smile appeared along with a glimmer in his eye.

Master Fry didn't even look at the fool but gazed out across the field next to the training grounds and appreciated the stars glistening overhead. "Have you ever met a Trapsnas soldier?" he asked plainly.

"No ... I can't even find it on a map."

He nodded slightly. "They would answer that question the best. Their army's motto was 'Do not tell me how many, but point to where they lie.'"

Another soldier attempted to rebuild the group's standing with the master. "Master, you are not just a master of war but also a master of wisdom."

Master Fry didn't waste any more time with the group. "Good night. I'll see you in the morning."

They echoed back "Good night" before they went their separate ways.

The morning bell rang in its usual routine, and the group fell into formation at the training grounds. Master DC already had her plan in place. *"For-ward ... march!"*

She marched the group for hours—pushed them right past their morning chow time, and the sun was heavy in the sky before she stopped them. *"Wedge for-mation!"*

The group responded: "Wedge formation."

She finished the command—*"Move!"*—and the entire group echoed each command to ensure they were in unison and executed them accordingly.

"Take a knee!" Everyone practically collapsed on the ground, their muscles exhausted to the point where they would have said whatever it took to earn a break. "The majority of you here today are men … but you are not going to be facing only men in battle … therefore you must understand that you cannot fight merely as an individual, for though you may stand equal to the person beside you, only you as a collective group can stand equal to whoever the enemy is. Your marching, formation, movements are all made so that each side can balance and support the other. Reptacrepts have very short legs and arms. They normally run on all fours over long distances because of how fast they are. They are extremely agile, and their strength comes from flanking motions or attacking you from the sides … their teeth can bite your head clean off and tear your limbs off, but that is also their weak point—once you compensate for their head strikes, their entire underbelly is exposed and can be slashed open."

She took a quick break, and though she actively watched the entire group like a hawk, she still paused and asked a trainee to repeat the last statement or two to ensure they were still paying attention. Satisfied with what she heard, she continued. "The reptacrepts will normally have very light armor on, because when they travel on all fours, it is more cumbersome with heavy armor and it can easily get snagged on the ground … it begins to eliminate their strength of their speed of movement. Orcs … those stupid frog bastards …" A slight chuckle came over the group; Master DC allowed it without hasty correction.

"Not all orcs are the same … just like men. Know your enemy and do not assume. However, most tribes and breeds of orcs do share one thing in common—their eyesight is drawn to reflections or shine coming off armor. Therefore find ways to conceal your force. If you can cover your armor in mud, paint, or fabric that can cloak you better … do so! Additionally, an orc's near sight is very bad, especially down low at their feet. That is why we teach you how to set up jungle wire traps … that is why we teach you to aim your arrows precisely at their lower limbs. If you can get the orcs off their feet or hinder their stride, you have countered their brute strength."

She stopped again and rescanned the group. A brave hand shot upward. "Yes?"

"Master DC," the trainee asked, "is it true orcs ran off a cliff in the Battle of Coff?"

She kept a straight face. "Yes, that is true." She smiled as a quiet chuckle rumbled across the group. "I guess y'all have earned a quick story. The Battle of Coff was won because the Trapsnas army created decoys and placed them at the edge of a cliff. The orcs, enraged, charged directly forward and in their blind bloodlust literally charged full force right off the cliff and to their deaths. Not a single Trapsnas soldier was lost." The chuckle became a light laughter. "Like I said … stupid frog bastards!" She motioned with her hand to tamp down the laughter. "All right, that's enough for today. *Recov-er!*" The group got to their feet and stood to attention. "*Fall out!* Go get your chow!"

The trainees greatly enjoyed the ability to finally have chow for the day. Everyone was too exhausted to harass one another, and the normal jokes and snarky comments were kept in as people gulped down their food and rested—or so they thought.

Ring-ring-ring-ring-ring.

"Let's go!"

"Get your asses moving!" Master DC and Master Jack came storming into the chow area and there began an eruption of chaos as trainees and soldiers sprinted out as quickly as they could and ran over to the training grounds. Master Jack and Master DC barked all along the way, "To battle! Prepare for war!"

The soldiers and trainees tried not to trip over one another as they rushed to the training grounds. Upon their arrival, there stood Codgarak with three female warriors clad in light armor with bows and light swords. The minotaur wielded his large battle-ax, which left the women looking like dwarves standing next to him.

"Red group, step forward!" Master DC instructed. The red group, on command, took one step forward. *"Red leader!"*

A trainee jogged over to the master and reported in. "Yes, master!" The other groups were instructed to fall out, and they returned to the edge of the training grounds. They were excited to get to experience something outside the norm but also nervous they may end up following red group if the red group didn't execute the exercise to the master's standards. Hell, at least their group didn't have to go first.

They all watched intently as Master DC provided the exercise information. "This minotaur and his three fighters have just raided a village. You have been dispatched from your garrison to meet them in the field and ordered to dispatch them from this life. *Begin!"*

The young leader was steadfast and took charge of his fear without letting it show. "Red group! Split formation!"

The group echoed, "Split formation!"

"Move!" the group split into two smaller formations. As they did so, the giant beast began to laugh.

"HAHAHAHA! DUSH-DA-BOO LO-HOO-KA!" As he finished, he raised his battle-ax up to the sky and brought its handle down upon the ground, sending down a shock wave of bright neon purple in a static line. The earth shook as the ground ripped open, creating a crevasse between the two groups.

The first group couldn't hide their fear now; they were taken completely by surprise and didn't know what to do. Their lines began to break from their disciplined formation and they looked at each other, hoping someone would know what to do. The other trainees, separated from them, dropped their guard, also looking baffled by what had taken place. Codgarak, laughing, started to walk toward the first group as the female fighters began launching volleys of arrows.

"Quick! Jump across!" the red leader yelled over to the separated group. Five of the young trainees attempted the feat but found they were unable to make it all the way across. Their screams echoed as their bodies continued to fall into the dark depths and were not seen again. The red group began to drop, as their reaction time was significantly lessoned by their panic. They were catching the arrows not with their shields but with their bodies; the archers being relentless with volleys. Codgarak closed the gap until he practically towered over the pitiful lot.

Taking a step and then pivoting, he didn't bring his ax crashing down but rather brought it round in a broad stroke that crashed into the far edge of the line, taking out the entire front line in one motion. The row of trainees collapsed like an accordion and fell straight into the crevasse. The arrows continued to cut down the troops surrounding Codgarak as he cleared row after row with his ax until he finally reached the red leader, who tripped over his own feet trying to back up and looked up at the beast from his backside. Terror filled his eyes as Codgarak reached down and grabbed him by the neck. Bringing him up to meet him face to face, he tightened his grip and crushed the poor bastard's throat. He released the body and the second group, paralyzed with fear, watched it fall to the ground.

The women turned their arrows upon the second group, and they easily hit their marks on the confused force. "Shell! Shell! Form a hardened shell!" one voice quivered. The few remnants of the second group raised their shields and huddled together. The rattle of the shields clanging together almost sounded like a drummer boy playing a battle pattern on a snare drum.

Codgarak leapt over the crevasse with ease and his ax split through the shields, leaving the blade embedded in the earth with two soldier's bodies pinned beneath it. He began to rip the shields away and claw each soldier to death. A few poor bastards tried to claim "surr-appa-door," which was their country's version of surrender, but it didn't stop the rage of war surging through his veins.

"Enough!" Master Jack called out and the onslaught stopped instantly. "Master Fry!" he called over to the far corner. A few of the spectating troops watched as Master Fry re-enacted his spell, which brought all the poor souls back up from the crevasse and restored the lives of those who had lost theirs as the bright blue healing waters filled the training grounds once again, then receded back to where they came.

The spectators chattered amongst themselves as they commented on the bloodbath they had just witnessed. Many of the onlookers, however, found themselves speechless. They doubted they'd ever be able to fight against the likes of the minotaur that stood upon the training ground.

However, that wasn't what was on the mind of one bastard as he leaned over to whisper his insult. "Like we'll actually see any bitches on the battlefield," he quipped, a smirk on his face.

"What?" Master DC sprang forward with her reply. *"What the ever-loving fuck did you just say?"* She moved so fast that it seemed she teleported, because the spectators didn't see where she started or how she got there; all they saw was her instantly face to face with the bastard.

"Nothing, master."

"You want to try and convince me you have a set of balls? You can't seem to find them when I ask you what you said!"

He looked back at the master, his eyes cold but filled with contempt as he finally admitted what he'd said. "I said ... not like we'll actually see any bitches on the battlefield!"

Hearing the voice more clearly allowed Liam to recognize who the individual was. Chino! He clenched his jaw but couldn't stop a smirk of delight. *You're going to get what's coming to you!* he thought. Throughout his time at Fort Patton, Chino had made every effort to let others know his thoughts and was the type who enjoyed asserting himself over others. The multiple accounts of harassment that other trainees within Fort Patton had suffered at his hands had finally reached a day of retribution.

Everyone around stood frozen as if made of stone. Liam swore to himself that he saw a small ray of light wrap itself around Master DC as she grabbed Chino's armor and, with an immediate spin, hurled him across the training grounds to land in the center. His body slid to a stop. *"Pre-pare yourself for death!"* she screamed.

The soldier's comrade interjected. "Master! You cannot kill this man. For we are soldiers of the Realm of RemaMortBrook." She slowly turned her head without turning her body, looking as if she was possessed by the devil himself.

"Well, soldier of RemaMortBrook ... tell me! What realm are we in?"

The soldier took a deep breath. "We are in the Realm of Cho'took, master."

"And tell me ... what does the realm's law state about Trapsnas soldiers?"

The soldier flinched. "Master ... I ... don't know ..."

Another trainee who had been sitting during the debacle stood and courageously interjected. "Master ... if my memory serves me correctly, the Realm of Cho'took's law regarding soldiers of Trapsnas is that they cannot be charged with the crime of murder."

"That is correct! It was Trapsnas soldiers that came to the aid of Cho'took and saved it from destruction … it was Trapsnas soldiers that preserved the peace between Cho'took and RemaMortBrook, and it was the Trapsnas army that gave their lives to defend both realms from the armies of the Realm of Delco during the Great War of Augustaross!"

The soldier who had made the insult had regained his feet and chose to support his comment with the follow-up, "That's all fine and dandy, but there are no Trapsnas left! These poor bastards," he waved towards the majority of the crowd, "should be happy that RemaMortBrook doesn't bring us back up here and take this pitiful realm for ourselves! We could easily claim every inch of this land."

Master DC turned once again to face Chino. *"I … am … Trapsnas."* She drew her swords and held them in her fighting stance with the blades resting on the backs of her arms. "I will not give you an inch of the ground upon which I stand … but I will happily take every inch of your body till I carve it free from your soul and bones!"

Chino drew his sword with a smirk, thinking he had a chance. Master DC charged forward and all the group heard was two clangs before they saw Master DC thrashing the flesh of the man away, exposing his bones. His body dropped to its knees but before his torso fell forward, she spun behind him, generating more energy just before, she cut his head off. As the severed head began to fall towards the ground, the master followed up with a punch square into the back of the severed head.

Liam saw the swirling light that was around Master DC surge down her arm as this was happening, and when she landed the punch, he could see the force culminating in the blow. The impact on the severed head was so powerful that it flew as straight as an arrow into the chest of Chino's fellow countryman who had challenged Master DC's decision to execute him.

Master Fry walked over to this soldier. "Grab your things. You are banned from this fort. Return to your leaders and report in." The man bowed his head, realizing that his choice of friendship had just caused him more than shame. Now he would be stuck serving in the worst jobs of the RemaMortBrook army.

"Yes, master." He nodded and departed the training grounds.

"That is enough for now. Go back to your areas and reflect on what you have seen here. We will return at sundown to discuss the lessons of the exercise then."

The fort was eerily quiet; some found humor in re-enacting the beheading, others found it shocking that a master had taken such action against a trainee, but almost everyone was reminded just how serious the training was. It certainly forced Liam to come to terms with the severity of what he should always be ready for—the future battle that he believed he would face some day.

As the sun set in the sky the groups slowly made their way back to the training grounds as they had been instructed earlier. They formed a makeshift circle as Master Fry and Master DC stood at its center.

"Many of you may be asking yourselves what was the purpose of the exercise today." Master DC observed the group. She watched everyone's body language, gauging their responses. "How many feel the fight was unfairly matched?" No one dared raise their hand. "Really? No one thinks the exercise was unfair?"

A few brave souls raised their hands on the second go. "All right, then! You!" She nodded to one of the hands. "Why do you think it was unfair?"

The trainee stood up. "The size and power of the minotaur was simply unmatched compared to their size."

Master DC nodded as she paced in front of the group. "I see ... how many strong was the group?"

The lad, still standing, said, "Fifty, Master DC."

"Correct. Thank you, soldier." The man sat back down. "But was it truly fifty against one?"

"No," came the response from several trainees.

"Ahh, and why do you say that?"

One voice was projected over a few other murmurs. "Because there were three archers to go along with the beast."

Still pacing in front of the group, she said, "That is a fair point. One could claim that the archers should be counted in the ratio..."

A voice interrupted. "The group was split in two!"

Her finger pointed immediately. "There it is! Say it again, soldier!"

"The group was split in two, so it wasn't really fifty to one."

She nodded in approval as she kept jabbing her pointing finger at him. "The group divided themselves! We've taught you over and over again, the power you have is in the unity of your formation, the collective body ..." She moved her hands in front of her face, as if their movement spoke for itself and helped draw a mental picture for the watching soldiers as she continued.

"Codgarak is not the only minotaur you may face. There are many out there, and they can turn the tide of a battle against those who don't remember how to counter their strength. What if your army faces a junteer? A giant the likes of which none of us have seen? A dark tree ent? An ifrit? A wyvern? It is too easy to get trapped in the thought that we can outwit or trick our enemy … the fact remains that when you march and fight in your armies, you *must* fight as one unit."

A soldier shot up his hand. "Yes?"

He stood up. "Master DC, the minotaur used magic to divide the group. How would we counter magic?" The trainee sat back down.

Master DC smiled as she replied, "Don't get hit by it!" A chuckle rolled amongst the group. "The world is full of magic, and good for those who know how to wield it. Many of your kingdoms, tribes, or mercenary outfits may have these users within them, but the fact remains that if you do not learn the basics of warfare, you will die by the hand of warfare."

Master Fry stepped forward. "Any questions?" The group remained silent. "That is all for tonight. See you in the morning."

The group dispersed, but Liam still had something on his mind. Reading the two masters, he finally approached. "Master DC … if I may?"

She turned to face him. "Speak." Master Fry slightly raised his eyebrows as he analyzed him.

"When you fought the trainees the other day and then the soldier today … I believe I saw something … something with you." She frowned at him, not appreciating a trainee judging her or her abilities. "I believe I saw a glowing light wrap around you during moments of your attack or as you were preparing for one. I didn't think I was seeing things correctly … but today … I know I saw it."

A smirk came across both masters' faces. "You witnessed Master DC conjure her magic, and then you saw how it can be combined with power in attacks. It appears your soul has been given the blessing of being connected to magic also," Master Fry said, a slight smile appearing on his face.

"It would appear so," Master DC agreed.

Master Fry placed his hand upon Liam's shoulder. "Go rest tonight. Tomorrow we will spend some time exploring how much your soul has aligned with the magic given to you."

Liam nodded in agreement and began walking back towards his tent. As he did so, he looked up at the stars shining down on him. *Perhaps it is my destiny to be a warrior. If my soul has been given the ability to receive magic and I have discovered it here at the fort ... this must mean I am right in pursuing this.*

The entire way back to his cot and for the remainder of the evening he felt as if it wasn't merely his soul but also his spirit that was speaking to him. As if there was something greater in the universe that was sending him a message and it was arriving from within. He let out a long sigh. *For what type of man would I be if I was given this gift and kept it all to myself?* He paused, thinking it was a clever phrase, but then Mala's voice came into his mind. *"Oh, goodie! Look at wise old Grandpa coming up with wisdom!"*

Fuck you, Mala! And with that, sleep befell him.

That morning, Liam found himself separated from the group and working directly with Master Fry and Master DC on his hand-to-hand combat skills and intermixed weapon-to-hand combat and transition skills. Master Fry worked extensively with him to ensure he knew the precise movements they wanted him to perform. Grabbing Liam's arms, he moved his limbs through the movements step by step.

After many hours and many movements, he said, "Okay, let's try Red Tree by the numbers ... one." Liam moved into position. "Two." He turned and adjusted. "Three." Again. "Four." And again. "Five." Another twist and turn of his body. "Six." Until finally, "Good. Okay ... Rising Crow by the numbers ... one." Liam changed his entire stance to match the next move. "Two." He moved his left arm across his body. "Three." Adjusting both arms outward, "Four." Turning his leg, "Incorrect. Again. Four." Tilting his head slightly, Liam realized his mistake and brought his arms down and lifted his left leg towards his chest, swaying slightly as he balanced. "Five." He kicked his leg out in a striking motion and did his best to hold it out there. "Six." He brought his leg back down to the ground and returned to his primary stance.

"Good. Stand aside ..." Master DC approached holding two bacca sticks, large wooden rods specifically carved and made for combat training. Master Fry grabbed the staff he normally carried with him. "Watch closely."

Both masters began their attack sequence, an orchestrated performance that played out excellently. As the two moved back and forth, Liam began to notice the yellow light that contoured around Master DC. The energy swirled and got slightly brighter as she continued; it began to move faster. He watched as the energy came surging together at the focal point of her arms while she completed her attack sequence. In the final movement of the sequence, she directed the energy into the attack, the strike landing on the other master. A loud *crack* and *pop* burst out, the shock wave radiating out as Master Fry slid backwards along the ground, though his feet remained perfectly in position, his body braced against the blow.

Liam's mouth hung open. "See. Your magic can be an energy that flows into your attacks," Master Fry said.

"But ... wait ... is magic ... magic ... or is it energy? Now I'm confused ... and it flows through you? But Codgarak and Mala have spoken about it being ..."

"Neither of us can give you a clear answer on that," said Master DC. "I honestly don't know anyone who can. We are still very young in our years for the Age of Magic. It appears that magic—or energy, whatever it is …" Master DC broke off and looked at Master Fry to validate her thoughts. "It is something very different for each person."

"To some, it comes very naturally from themselves … for others, they feel it is easier to use the language of the elves to speak it forth." Master Fry followed Master DC. "There are some who seem to be able to channel their magical energy in direct ways where it has to be connected to them, whereas some mages have been known to tether energy from the elements themselves." He added, "There was the War of Patastal … the story claims that magic was used to take control of deer and elk in the surrounding mountains and forced them to charge the lines and break through before the main force attacked."

Liam's eyes grew big as he received all this new information regarding magic and energy. He was excited to learn more about it all. He began to get lost in his imagination of the possibilities this created for him, the new opportunities, and the future that lay ahead.

Slap! came Master DC's hand across his shoulder. "Wake up, clown!"

Liam shook his head free of his imaginings. "Sorry … so you can't really tell me much about how my magic works, then, huh?"

Master Fry shook his head. "Sorry, Liam. We can do our best to train you and show you how we have come to use our abilities, but you'll have to discover it for yourself."

"But wait … I've been using a flame spell to light my fires, lanterns, see into caves and at night … many people know how to summon it as well."

Master DC raised her eyebrows. "Yes?"

"Well, the vast majority of people I know can produce it, so is magic really that special or selective?"

She was irritated now and cut to the chase. "Look, kid, some guys have a big dick, some guys have a little dick, some guys know how to use their dick, some clearly do not know how to use their dick. It doesn't matter how much magic you got, as long as you know how to use it … you feel me?" Master Fry couldn't help but laugh as Liam's jaw dropped to the ground. "That's it, I'm out. He's yours for the rest of the day." Master DC tossed the bacca sticks to Liam. He let them fall to the ground, not wanting to grab a rod-shaped item just after a master had gone on an epic dick rant.

The training continued for weeks on end. Liam stopped even trying to count how many days it had been. The masters never said when training would be finished, and he didn't ask. New groups of trainees and soldiers came in as the older groups eventually left. He came to learn that some were soldiers from other realms who were sent to be trained, others were there as a part of a guild or mercenary camp, and some attended training for purposes they did not say … which made him question even more why they chose to be there.

As the weeks continued, he was able to adapt and see the pattern of life in the training cycles, the routine within the chaos of it all, for when he had first arrived, the overwhelming sensations and his anxiety about the unknown had left him unable to grasp the small intricacies that were otherwise plainly visible for all to see.

His composure now allowed him to pick up on the subtleties of the rhythms of daily operations. He was able to identify the quitter's bell chime at the center of the fort. At first, he didn't think much of it. The training was pretty intensive—hell, people actually died at the hands of the masters! It was the most intense experience he had ever encountered in his life. His father had taught him the basics, but that training was done with the love and affection of a good father. Here you could have the ever-loving shit kicked out of you or even be cut to pieces in a battle exercise and, only out of the grace the masters showed, be brought back to life to do it all over again the next day.

Some people just couldn't handle that and found the ringing of the quitter's bell more to their liking. But, as he would find out, the new life that awaited someone back at home after quitting was a much slower hell then the one they were going through here. They would have to clean the bathroom troughs every day, gather all the rubbish by hand and burn it in the burn pit, or work in the mines or other labor camps. Exhausting work, but they were also treated like shit … if you weren't tough enough to defend yourself, let alone another, you weren't considered good enough to be worth a damn.

"Pay now … or pay later," Liam would remind himself as he reflected on such things. The famous Master Jack motto was imprinted on his mind. After weeks of training at the fort, he could understand the importance of it. As time went on, he saw how many of the trainees and soldiers simply didn't care about the importance of the training. For many of them, it was just a thing to do. They performed the actions asked of them in the day and forgot them that night as they joked, drank, and laughed until daybreak.

He did his best to stay focused. He felt as if the masters judged him quite harshly. There was certainly no slack given to him, as he noticed others received far more leniency for their errors.

Making his way to Thunder Rock one day, he noticed all the masters and Codgarak were standing within it. As he made his way closer, Codgarak instructed, "Choose your weapon." His eyes widened, then narrowed as he retrieved two gladius swords, perfectly made for close range combat. He knew there was no way to keep his distance from the minotaur. Though long-range weapons would be ideal, he would need a group to maintain the distance to maximize their effectiveness; with it being one on one, he was going to be forced up close. The gladius swords were the primary weapons that Master Jack had worked with him on—you couldn't say he was an expert on them, but proficient, absolutely.

The masters sat around the inner circle and watched the match begin. Liam charged straight ahead as fast as he could. Wielding his two swords in rapid succession, he did his best to keep Codgarak utilizing his battle-ax in a defensive posture rather than making the broad swings that could take out several soldiers at a time. His practice on the training dummies had been worth it. The majority of his strikes were landing right where they needed to. He was completely focused on his attack and used several different attack patterns that flowed in the artistic dance of combat. Right, right, left, right, right, slash-right, right, left, right, thrust-left—he repeated the patterns over and over in his head. Codgarak used his experience to see the gap in his mental focus and took him by surprise when he turned around and clobbered his face with a mighty backhanded strike. The force sent him flying backward and crashing into one of the rock pillars.

If this had been the first day of training, Liam would have been completely knocked out. His hardened defenses, though, allowed him to take such a mighty blow. He shook his head back and forth as he quickly stood back up. Wiping the sweat from his face, he spit on the ground. Codgarak and the other masters could see the faint glowing light of magic flowing around him.

Liam watched a slight smile form on Codgarak's face. *You ain't seen nothing yet!* he thought. Charging towards the minotaur, he switched his swords' positions to those of Master DC's Trapsnas fighting style and slid in close to Codgarak with quick slashes of the swords. Right up, left across, left counter-across, right across, spin, left across, right up … *Whack!* His right sword flew out of his hand as he missed his mark, and the minotaur's claw came bearing down upon him. Caught off guard and partially disarmed, he tried his best to recover and in his attempt to switch fighting styles discovered the *whack!* yet again.

Codgarak didn't hold back; he ferociously continued his attack, swinging the ax and trying to flay Liam with his claw. During the minotaur's salvo, Liam continued to generate more magic. The light swirled upwards and encircled his forearms as he redirected it and attempted to utilize the hand-to-hand combat skills Master Fry had taught him.

Throwing a volley of punches in succession at his target. He strained to focus and direct the magic as he fought, he finally found his opportunity and slammed his fist into Codgarak's gut. His mind raced as he worked to connect the magic within him to the physical force of his hit. The spark of connection ignited a surge of energy and he launched the built-up magic exactly in time with the hit. He did his best to channel everything he had conjured up at that moment, and the blow sent Codgarak sliding backwards about two feet. Liam's eyes grew wide—he'd surprised himself with finally being able to land a significant blow. It all occurred as if in slow motion. *And I used my magic on top of that!* The surprise distracted him, however, and the beast came back with a *whack-whack, smash!* His head was hammered into the ground with such force, his body bounced high enough for Codgarak to grab him in midair and spin him around before launching him into a pillar.

Fuck … me …

He awoke to see Master Fry and Master Jack standing over him. He had the eerie feeling he had been brought back to life as they helped him to his feet and brought him back over to the group. "You have significantly improved," Codgarak complimented.

"Not enough," Liam replied.

Master Fry took the lead. "Don't be too hard on yourself. We have all trained for many years, and we still train and learn to this day. You are a far better fighter now than you were when you first arrived."

Liam nodded at the reassurance. "All right, yo ... why did you try to switch your styles in mid combat?" Master DC asked with a slight sarcastic tone in her voice.

"I thought it would throw him off and allow me an opportunity to strike."

Master DC tilted her head down and moved it from side to side as she reminded him, "You definitely threw something off! Like your entire plan!"

"You're right" was all he could manage in response. He looked down in frustration and noticed his shirt was drenched from all his sweat and had a massive bloodstain on it as well. "Well, there goes another shirt!" He let out a long breath and smiled wryly. This seemed to be almost a daily occurrence with the training he had been through at the fort.

"Just think, if you hadn't been here and gone through training, you wouldn't have lasted anywhere near as long as you did today!" Master Fry encouraged him yet again.

He thought he had a good comeback. "It is everyone's destiny to die ..." A smirk crossed his face.

Master Jack looked at him and cut through the sarcasm that Liam had used. "That may be true, young Liam, but don't allow your arrogance to be your excuse for ignorance."

Liam was taken aback for a moment. "But ... I mean ... it is true. We are all destined to die. Soldiers, fighters, warriors ... we all know this to be true. We are here to die for our nations, realms, empires ... look at all the people who come through the fort to do so."

Liam was still in need of so much knowledge and experience. Master Jack, however, had wisdom, something that normally only comes to those who seek it, learning through hardships, and retaining it in their aging years. He had been through countless battles and wars and witnessed thousands of soldiers walk through the gates of the fort.

"Do you know who this fort is named after?" he asked. Liam shook his head. It had not come up until now. "He was a famous military strategist and brutal leader. His enemies feared and respected him. He performed on the battlefield with calculated strategies that others never truly comprehended, and even some who could understand thought his strategies were impossible." He watched as young Liam listened intently to the story. It was one of the qualities the masters had come to admire about him. He always listened intently to their instructions, and he certainly loved their stories.

"There was once the military campaign of Carthco." He smiled as he began to recall the story. "He led his army right into the heart of the Kingdom of Carthco … he had them wait there for days as the Carthco army closed in and encircled them." He could see Liam being drawn into the story. "He told his men, 'Boys, they've brought their entire army to us. They couldn't make it any easier for us. We will rob them of this victory … we will rob them of their kingdom … and this valley will forever be known as the valley of death!'" Master Jack paused for dramatic effect. "They slaughtered the entire Carthco army there that day … and to this day, they say the dirt in the valley has remained red, for their blood stained the earth as it dried upon it, and nothing has grown there since."

He read Liam's face and knew that even though he liked the story of the great military leader, he didn't quite understand the lesson he was trying to teach him. "Lord Patton would go on to say, 'No stupid bastard ever won a war by dying for his country. He won the war by ensuring the other stupid bastards died for theirs.'"

Liam's facial expression said everything that needed to be said. The wisdom had entered his ears and made its way from his head down into his spirit. Master Jack knew the young fighter would be reflecting upon the quote for a long while. "Yes, Liam ... it may be everyone's destiny to die, but I challenge you, focus more on how you live your life than on how your life will end."

MASTER DC

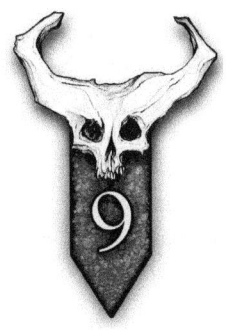

WHERE WE ARE CALLED

Jostled awake, Liam saw Codgarak peering at him. "Grab your things—we're leaving" was all the minotaur said before departing his tent.

His mind racing with questions as his heart began to pound deep inside his chest. The training he received had done its job to teach him to not question orders. Liam did as he was told and made his way towards the center of the fort. He joined the three masters and Codgarak where they stood in a circle. "What is this about?" he asked.

Master Jack replied to his question. "Last night we received two hundred trainees from Somopack, a nation within the Realm of Delco."

Liam shrugged. "Oh, okay. So, what's the big deal about that? The fort has received at least a thousand soldiers and trainees since I've been here."

Master Fry said, "They informed us that they were the first group." Master Fry glanced around the group as Master Jack continued the conversation.

"The next group is arriving at any moment. We were told by the first group that Somopack has called five thousand men to arms. Three thousand were to remain there and be trained; the other two thousand have been sent here." Liam began to digest the information as Master Jack continued. "It was only an hour later that five hundred trainees arrived from Ashfurgoth. They have also called three thousand men to arms but sent two thousand of their trainees to us and kept a thousand back."

Master Fry added, "They are also in the Realm of Delco."

"Why would they call up so many? Are they going to war with another realm or a kingdom within their realm?" Liam asked.

"It appears very unlikely. Delco has been one of the most peaceful realms in our history. They normally work very closely together to defend their realm. Going to war doesn't seem likely at all, but two kingdoms calling their citizens up for training does make it look like they are very afraid of something," Master Fry said.

"Additionally, these trainees were not told what they were training for or why they'd been called up for service. It is fairly normal for a standard citizen not to be given a lot of information. They are not told who the enemy is upon their order to activate. But they did mention rumors that the city of Lithram had fallen. That is on the far eastern edge of Delco and acts as the realm's first line of defense," said Master Jack.

"Not only that," said Codgarak solemnly, "I have tried to seek Mala's energy pulse to teleport to him. I cannot find his pulse, nor can I teleport out of this valley. And ... there has been no word from him either. Something is definitely off, and it's not just in Delco."

"So what are we going to do, then?"

Codgarak nodded to Liam after he asked the question, and then tilted his head towards the south. "We're going to work our way towards The Hunters Shrine. It is where we gather together."

"You are not coming with us?" Liam asked as he scanned the three masters. They shook their heads.

"We must all serve where we are called. We have been called to serve here at the fort. Our time here is not done," said Master Fry.

"You are all masters of your craft, and you could have a critical impact on whatever battles loom ahead. How can you not join us?"

Master Jack took a step forward and put his hand on Liam's shoulder. "Do you think this will be the last war? There will be many more wars, battles, and fights after this one. We must stay here to ensure these soldiers and trainees are trained to the best of our ability."

Liam sighed. "I understand. I just wish you'd join us on this journey."

Master DC finally added to the discussion. "You came to us wanting to be a warrior ... believing you were a warrior. And now that the challenge is on your doorstep, you have fear leering over your shoulder. Accept the challenge and face it head on." She stretched out her hand, palm upward with a ring sitting at its center. Liam went to grab it with his fingers. "No, clown! Shake my hand!" Startled and slightly embarrassed, he corrected himself and clasped her hand. As he did so, she rotated her hand from below to on top of his as they continued their handshake. "Take this with you, and may it remind you of the lessons you've learned and help you reflect on the lessons you will soon learn along the way."

She released her grip and the ring remained in Liam's hand. Gazing down at it, he appreciated the precise craftsmanship. It was scaly in appearance, like snakeskin. The color seemed to change; it wasn't one consistent color. "Imagine it as something else," Master DC said.

He did as she said and began to imagine what the ring would look like as a bracelet. As he did so, the ring began to morph within his hand, and it moved and wrapped itself around his wrist as a bracelet. "This is a special item made from my people. The few of us who remain. I believe it will help you when you need it most." She finished with a slight smile and a nod of her head. With humility, he simply said, "Thank you."

A faint echo could be heard in the distance. Soldiers and trainees being marched is a sound that stands out no matter where you are or what you are doing. "It is time we departed," Codgarak said. They all said their goodbyes and clasped hands as friends do.

Just as they were about to take their first steps away from the Fort, a deep pull came within Liam's soul. He looked over to what was known as the hero's row. A long line of weapons placed into the ground to honor the warriors who once wielded them. The area was near the main entrance of the forts gate. He looked up into the heavens and exhaled, believing his father was present with him at that moment. He walked to the end of the line of weapons, retrieving his father's sword, he drove it deep into the ground. Placing his hand upon the hilt of the sword he said a quite prayer for the souls of his family.

Completing the prayer, he then jogged over to the armory where the blacksmiths were always working throughout all hours of the day. He soon returned with two gladiolus swords strapped to him. Noticing the Masters' and Codgarak gazing upon him, "My father blessed me throughout my childhood, may his soul and spirit be a blessing to those who know train at the Fort as I also now have." To which the group just nodded in respect towards his decision without any further discussion needed.

Codgarak and Liam began to walk out of the fort. The brisk morning air had frosted the ground, and mist lofted throughout the area. Liam wrapped himself up tightly. His breath created clouds around him as he followed the minotaur. They passed groups of men and some women who were marching towards the fort.

The two pressed forward into the darkness of the morning. Torches illuminated the dirt road and glowed in the distance. There were a number of groups of trainees stretched out along the path. Whatever the Realm of Delco was experiencing, it was certainly enough to scare them into a reaction rather than pacifism.

The sun had risen, leaving some lofty mist rolling across the valley around the pair. They arrived at a small village and found an area to sit down to enjoy breakfast. Liam had quickly learned during his training not to ask how far they had traveled or were expected to travel. That was normally a question that led to the suffering of push-ups, planks, floater kicks, and any other demonic exercises the masters could think up.

Codgarak looked down at the young lad. Liam's face didn't show much happiness. He had found the comfort of a united team, but this was his first exposure to such a group. He knew what it was like to have a group of individuals saying words with meaning, but it was a vast contrast with those who lived out such a meaning. Young Liam had not experienced this difference. Codgarak looked at him as he slowly ate the eggs in front of him, a few pieces of bread, and a visvan fruit. Though Liam's posture was slightly glum, he appeared to be distracted by the ring Master DC had given him. He was intently focused on it as he manipulated it, forcing it to transition between a ring and a bracelet.

Codgarak enjoyed the silence but felt it was best to try and engage the lad. "That is quite the gift you were given."

Liam smiled briefly, barely making eye contact, and returned his gaze to the object as it turned back into a ring. "A gift that still remains a mystery to me."

Codgarak scratched an itch on his shoulder. "I have no doubt that you'll eventually unlock the mystery contained within such a small gift."

Liam withdrew his hand and tucked it underneath his garment in an attempt to warm it in the cool morning. "I would much rather have the company of the masters than a token of remembrance." He gazed out at the town square. His mind was clearly on the past and not the future.

Finding an opportunity to pass down a little insight, Codgarak said, "Liam ... would someone truly learn to stand on their own feet unless they were away from the ones who had taught them how to stand?" He watched as Liam wrinkled his brow in contemplation. He opened his mouth as if he planned to speak but remained silent. "In all aspects of life, children who are taught to walk by their parents are eventually let go and stumble with feeble steps to eventually grow towards a running stride. The tigers of the field who teach their young how to hunt eventually watch from afar as they learn the errors in their stalking and pouncing. A soldier who is instructed in war and may die by the sword comes close to death and learns new lessons. This is a part of the life cycle—failure and success." He took a brief pause to let the lesson sink in. "It is now time for you to decide what you will do with the lessons that have been passed on to you."

Though Codgarak's words were sincere and significant, the minotaur couldn't help the fact that he was irritated over not moving. He stood up without warning. "Time to go."

Liam worked to shove the last few bites of egg into his mouth, stuffing it full before grabbing the remaining pieces of bread and placing them in his pockets for later. Codgarak turned to see Liam struggling to get up; he had not a single ounce of grace and looked like a slobbering mess. "Move it!" The cup danced off the table and clanked onto the ground.

"Sorry!" Liam stumbled behind him.

By now it was much later in the day; the golden sun was just at the point where any time you tried to look ahead of you, it was directly in your eyes. Liam kept squinting and trying to cover his eyes with his hand, but all this did was amplify his frustration. "Stupid sun," he mumbled to himself. Letting out a sigh, he jogged around a bend that hugged close to the mountain. He made it around the corner ahead of Codgarak by quite a distance. He enjoyed the fact that he could turn and face the mountain, the freedom of not being blinded any longer. He chuckled out loud. "Codgarak! You are about to enjoy your favorite thing!"

The minotaur made his way around the bend and put his ax down, leaning it against a tree as he took a deep breath. "I forgot these were here." Liam's chuckle continued as he turned and looked at the massive staircase that awaited them. A brick wall followed the stairs as they proceeded high into the saddle of the mountain. He appreciated the uniqueness of the staircase. About every thirty feet there was a large rock base with a gargoyle sitting on top of it.

"These are cool!" Liam said in admiration. Jogging up to the first one, he ran his hand across the sculpted rock surface. Whoever had carved these figures looked like they had done them very fast. The first gargoyle looked like a demonic bird. It had a large birdlike beak and two horns protruded from its head, but it had arms and legs similar to those of an orangutan in addition to its feathered wings.

He trotted up the steps to the next carved gargoyle. Codgarak watched him and despised his youth. "I... hate... stairs..."

Liam looked back to see Codgarak glaring up at him. Well, maybe he was glaring at the stairs, maybe it was him, maybe he had to take a shit, anyways ... "Codgarak! What is this one?"

With a tilt of the head, he said, "That one is a goblin."

"So this is what they look like!" Liam turned, fixated on the gargoyle's broad shoulders and chiseled arm muscles, but it had a tiny waist and gimpy legs—a very top-heavy creature. Codgarak had made his way up the stairs and was closing the distance between them. "I thought goblins were bigger than this. Whenever people talked about orcs, they made them sound very large and powerful. This thing doesn't look anything like I pictured."

Codgarak tilted his head toward Liam. "Are all humans the same shape, size, color, and language?"

A blank stare came across his face. "Umm ... no."

Codgarak took a deep breath, partly from the exertion of the stairs and partly out of irritation. "Exactly. Not all goblins are the same, and similarly with their orc counterparts. They are classified within the same bloodline, but even that is shaky at best."

Liam was now even more curious. "Have you fought both in battle? What can I expect?"

Codgarak grabbed his chin and rubbed the side of his face. "That is a good question." He turned and saw a giant stump just off the trail by a few feet. He walked over and sat down on it; it turned out to be a perfect natural stool. He nodded towards the gargoyle. "That one appears to be carved in a similar design to that of gray goblins. Gray goblins is the common folk term because they normally live in low-lit environments. Caves, tunnels, thick forests ... I had a battle campaign where we had to root out a ton of those damn things from the Caverns of Siltadoor."

"Did they fight hard?"

"Yes."

The blank stare returned to Liam's face. "How so?" He had thought his meaning was clear, but he'd forgotten that Codgarak sometimes just answered questions without context.

"Many think goblins are dumb and stupid. Don't get me wrong, they are, but … They are cunning and clever and know how to exploit others' weaknesses. I was only able to fight a certain distance into the cavern before I couldn't fit any longer. That left the remaining soldiers to go fight them alone. Gray goblins' eyes have evolved over the generations to the point where they need practically no light at all to work, and they live in darkness. They normally target torchbearers with arrows, killing them and the light. As the soldiers fought further into the cavern, they were clobbered and overwhelmed as the goblins attacked their less-armored legs and brought them to the ground. It was a brilliant strategy that almost worked. Additionally, there was a tribe of goblins that I ran into many years back that we referred to as forest goblins. They were rather good scavengers and did very well at trading. The had a keen sense of where to find the best berries and mushrooms, so much so that they held a syndicate over the other traders in the region. They lived a peaceful life where they were content with what they had and embraced the beauty of simplicity—a race that viewed and interpreted the world through their hut windows and had no desire to cross their neighbor in spite. They were business savvy and knew how to make a quick profit, though their hearts were never influenced by greed. Because of this, you weren't able to trick them into a business deal that wouldn't be to their benefit. However, they had no concept of magic and could easily be scared, and they'd never deal with a kingdom they felt threatened by. Anything that threatened or worked to influence this cycle of life would be deemed evil and would forever close the door of opportunity to the outside world."

Liam smirked and looked at the carved stone figure, rubbing its bald head. "Well, look at you and your sophisticated cousins." He gave a slight chuckle.

"Orcs are much larger and are more commonly found in the open, not hiding and certainly not afraid of anything, though dragons and other creatures can bring fear to anyone else. As the masters probably taught you in training, orcs can become very disorganized in battle. Oftentimes they are so bloodthirsty that they forget what the plan was, charging straight at their enemies and trying to kill everything in their path. They're a very … unorthodox species for sure. I know that many say they are related in origin, but I don't see the connection in my experience. Goblins and orcs vary too much from each other, but you must certainly always be on guard when encountering them."

Liam looked up at the next gargoyle. "And what of this one?" he asked as he started to make his way towards it. Unbeknownst to the two, the gargoyle's rune, which was etched into the back of it, began to glow as they walked closer. As he stretched out his arm, pointing to the carved rock, and looked back at Codgarak, the sound of splitting rock ripped across the hillside and all he felt was a *thump* on his head, sending him face first down the steps. He rolled down until Codgarak stopped his fall with his foot.

"Time to fight!"

THE DEPARTED

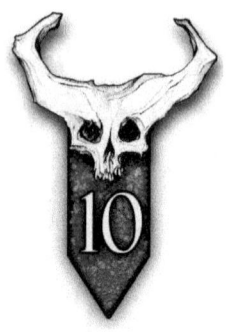

STICKS AND STONES

"Down!" Liam heard and immediately dropped to one knee as the ax blade went flying, cleaving two of the gargoyles that had come up behind him. He and Codgarak stood back to back and rotated as new threats emerged. The gargoyles were too many to count; all Liam could do was focus on whichever one was closing in fastest.

"Incoming left!" he warned Codgarak as he kept his focus on the pittazook monster that had just taken a swing at him with its claws. Codgarak turned to see a griffin gargoyle swooping in, and he landed an impressive and perfectly timed uppercut that shattered the head of the living statue. Liam was able to catch a glimpse of the badass hit in his peripheral vision as he finished slicing the head off the pittazook.

You never get a break in battle. The fight raged on as Liam saw this giant spider-like… arm … coming right for him. "Cut off the arms of the alphagad!" Codgarak yelled to him. The moment seemed to pass in slow motion as he watched the eight-limbed creature. It stood on its two hind legs but crouched down as it walked towards him and leapt back up to showcase its six arms, continuing this pattern as it went. They looked like the giant arms of a mantis, and the bobbing of its body as it moved made it appear large and intimidating as it came closer. He was able to see past the threat and pictured the moving training dummy that Master Jack had used with him. Seeing wooden arms and a wooden figure bearing down on him, he started the attack sequence of the Cano-8.

Right, counter-cross left, counter-cross right, left, counter-cross right, left, right, left.

The sensation of slow motion disappeared as fast as it had arrived, but now he felt overwhelmed to see three new monsters crashing in around him as the rocky pieces of the alphagad crumbled around him and dust lofted into the air.

Left, left, left, right block, left block, thrust, right-spinning slash, left-spinning slash.

"MOVE!"

He leapt up. Seeing a large tree branch directly above him, he fantasized an awesome battle move and without thinking tossed one of his swords above him into the air. He then jumped up and clasped the tree, brought his legs up, wrapping them around the branch. He glanced down and saw Codgarak making a sweeping slash across the place where he had just been standing, taking out the three gargoyles. The split-second strike ended as he refocused on his sword, which glimmered in the air as it began its descent from his toss. His legs gripping the tree branch tightly, he shot out his hand to grab it in midair and—*clapppp!*—the sword hilt slapped into the palm of his hand and continued its fall to the ground.

"Ahhh!" He dropped from the branch as the minotaur adjusted his footing and stepped towards the next threat. Not having time to beat himself up over his failed attempt of an epic battle move he reached down and grabbing his sword. He looked up the hill, not realizing the threat was behind him. A harpy swooped in and speared him from behind with its talons, knocking him face first onto the ground, dragging him up the hill as it maintained its momentum.

Thump!

Light began to pierce his vision as he started to open his eyes. There was a tree trunk in front of him and the cool sensation of liquid running down his face. He wiped his head and could just focus enough on his hand through his blurred vision to see red covering it. "Oww!" His head throbbed heavily for a moment until he realized his swords were nowhere to be found. He immediately began to search around him, and in his distracted state of panic, it struck again.

Thump!

The harpy smashed into his back, driving him into the tree. He felt the beak-shaped rock pierce his back. After a quick second for the pain to reset his panicked mind, he placed his fists on the ground. Magical light swirled around them as he pushed upward and enhanced his force with magical energy, which propelled him upward and knocked the harpy from his back—but only for a second. It regained its balance and came charging at him again.

He cocked his hand back and, without thinking, magical energy began to swirl again, but this time when he went to swing, the harpy dodged his blow and the energy extinguished itself. His mistimed hit cost him; the harpy spun quickly and knocked him hard in the stomach with its rock wing, sending him tumbling to the ground and knocking the wind out of him. He panicked again as he strained to inhale fresh air. The harpy launched itself and lifted over him, ready to pounce once again.

He looked left and right in haste and spotted a large branch that was shaped just right to be a makeshift staff. As the harpy came soaring down, he set the staff in place just in time to plunge it into the chest of the rock bird. The kinetic energy of the bird meeting the steadfast brace of the wood made a splitting crack through the bird's chest right to its outer edges. Liam braced himself against the ground, still holding the staff firmly. Getting to his feet, he utilized the sawmill strike Master Fry had taught him and finished splitting the harpy's upper torso, sending rocks crumbling to the ground.

Standing with his staff in hand, Liam noticed the cloud of dust that filled the area around the smashed rock corpses. It was finally quiet for a moment, and the only thing he could hear was the ringing in his head from being driven into the tree ... *A tree!* he thought as he clasped his head with his hand.

He was soon distracted, though, when a bright light appeared on the ground and a magical portal began to form. He brought his staff forward ready for whatever would come forth. The portal that formed was larger than the one he'd seen before in Codgarak's cave. In a flash, it spit out a massive lion, who stood clasping two kukris in his hands. A large mane wrapped around his head and massive shoulders protruded atop his chiseled arms. Though the lion wasn't as tall as Codgarak, he was broad enough to the point where you could say he was somewhat comparable in stature.

Liam didn't spend much time in admiration, as Mala quickly appeared out of the portal, which then disappeared. Turning towards Liam, the tiger said, "Well, well, well ... sticks and stones may break my bones, but Liam's still a cunt!" A broad smile spread across his face. "Ohh ... wait, maybe I mean runt!" He laughed loudly and grabbed his stomach as his mocking landed its verbal blow. "Nope, I meant cunt!"

Liam threw the stick down on the ground and went to find his swords. "Cashmes," Codgarak said as he approached, clasping the lion's hand in greeting.

"It would appear we're a tad bit late," Cashmes replied.

"Oh, don't bother; we didn't miss anything of importance! These ... well, whatever they are were nothing more than the blink of an eye," Mala chimed in sarcastically.

Codgarak raised an eyebrow. "It at least gave Liam a chance to put his skills into practice."

"Oh, Cod, you're too generous! There are no skills required to be a fuck-up cunt … it is natural with that one." Mala bared his teeth in a wide smile.

"I honestly don't know why we keep you around," Cashmes countered.

Liam found his swords and placed them back in their scabbards. He walked back to the group dreading the fact that Mala had arrived. "That was unexpected," he said as he arrived at the circle that formed amongst them. Codgarak nodded Liam arrived.

"It must have been your foul—"

"Enough, Mala!" Cashmes cut him off.

"But I am—"

"Enough!"

Mala hissed at Cashmes and wandered over to the rock wall where the gargoyles used to be set. "It appears you have already met my brother. I am Cashmes." A large paw was stretched out towards him.

"Liam." Completing the gesture, he shook the lion's hand. "Yes … I've … met him."

"No need to explain. I understand." Letting go of the lion's hand, Liam adjusted his clothes to a more comfortable fit. Cashmes turned his attention back to Codgarak. "We've been trying to get to you. It appears the dark magic is influencing its way even to here."

"I thought it was odd not to hear from Mala for so long."

"Trust me, old friend, it wasn't for lack of trying. The magic has distorted many things. We haven't been able to sense one another as we once could. Our teleportation has been blocked in many areas, including this one. It's as if there are small windows of opportunity, but they always fluctuate, and we can't seem to figure out if there is a pattern or not."

Codgarak nodded. "Seen anything like this?" He tilted his head at the crumbled pile of statue pieces. "Well, this is certainly a first for me. I mean, we've seen rock giants and other monsters, but I can't recall a tale of living gargoyles."

Liam chimed in. "They didn't come to life until after we had made our way up past a few of them. Almost as if it were a trap."

"Almost as if it were a trap," Mala echoed sarcastically from afar. "That damn cat always needs to be the center of attention."

"I heard that, Cash!"

"What about the Isles of Rayna-ox? Was there not a stone statue that was brought to life there?" Codgarak inquired of Cashmes's vast memory. Cashmes scratched his head as he looked down, his eyes scrolling back and forth on the ground as if he were flipping through and reading invisible pages of historical text.

He returned his gaze to Codgarak. "I think there was … but, old friend, we are living in the Age of Magic. I am rarely surprised at anything these days. Anything is possible when magic is involved."

"True." Codgarak turned his head and watched as Mala approached the circle, holding a piece from one of the many shattered gargoyles.

He watched Mala get closer and closer, thinking it was odd. He kept walking right up to where Liam was standing. Gritting his teeth, Liam turned away. *Why does he have to come over—*

He hadn't finished the thought before he was shoved on the shoulder. Caught off balance, he went crashing to the ground. "Your guard wasn't up" was all he heard as he braced himself on the ground and stood back up. He gripped his swords tightly but knew it wasn't worth it and just brushed off the dirt and dust. Cashmes backhanded his brother's shoulder. "What? It's not my fault humans are pathetic creatures!"

Cashmes and Mala stared each other down, and the tension seemed to rise until the two massive cats were about to have their own joust. The stare-down ended when Cashmes broke his gaze to check on Liam. "That's what I thought," Mala mocked. "Anyways! It looks like we have our culprit."

He tossed the rock over to Codgarak, who glanced at it and then passed it to Cashmes, who informed them, "I haven't seen any other runes like this one before. The looks of it, they appear to be made in haste. Whoever made these was in so much of a hurry that they didn't impart a significant amount of magic in them, and ... or ... they were not powerful enough in their magical abilities to impart a larger amount."

"That would explain why we can't sense one another, though, and our teleportation being limited and actively blocked. Someone doesn't want magic users communicating to one another and is delaying them from responding to whatever, or whoever is at the root cause of all this." Cashmes looking between Mala and Codgarak.

Liam walked back up to the group. "So if there is one, then—"

Mala reached his paw up, smothering Liam's face. The tigers mutated paw which resembled half a tiger paw shape and the other half that of a human hand, and shoved him back to the ground. "Still a bitch!" He glanced down at the human with an arrogant, devious smile, conscious of his superior strength, before returning to the adult conversation.

"As I was saying," said Cashmes, "whoever this magic user is was clearly given the task of placing these all around the realms. This spot will at least allow us to come and go from the area. We should get back to Dhather and inform him of what we've discovered."

The sound of Liam getting back to his feet drew Mala's attention as Mala saw the anger flowing over him. Liam began pulling his dagger from his belt as he glared into his eyes. "Ohh, look! He has serious face!" Mala taunted as Liam shortened the distance between them. As Liam took his final step towards him, Mala whipped his tail around and wrapped it quickly round the leg that carried all Liam's weight. A quick yank and the human went crashing to the ground and rolled a few times down the hill. "Okay, seriously … what are they teaching people at that fort? Because this isn't even funny anymore."

"Enough," Codgarak finally declared.

"Fine!" Mala replied. "Well, let's get out of this litter box of a realm and get back to Dhather." He turned to begin forming his portal.

"No. You two return. Liam and I need to stay a bit longer," said Codgarak.

"Do you need us to remain with you? Who knows what else could be lurking here?" Cashmes asked.

"We'll be all right. Besides, if there is another evil nearby, Golgoth will surely know of it."

Cashmes and Mala quickly looked at one another. Cashmes tilted his head at Codgarak. "You're sure this is the path you wish to pursue, old friend? Nothing good has ever been said of that name."

The minotaur crossed his arms in front of his chest, lowering his head and rocking it slowly from side to side as he weighed the options. "I have questioned my judgment on this decision myself, but when dealing with evil, especially that of magic, it may be best to speak to one who knows it best."

CASHMES

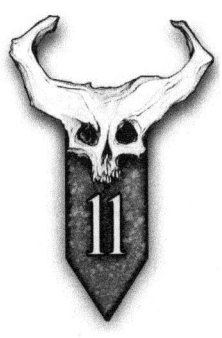

I AM EVIL

Liam barely heard the exchange between Cashmes and Codgarak as he returned to the group, but the little bit that he did hear caused the hair on the back of his neck to stand on end. His mind raced with questions over the legendary figure he had thought was of a genuine nature, a warrior who rooted out evil within the world—yet what did Codgarak mean? *Who is this person we are heading for?*

"It has been many years since I have seen him, and I can only hope that time has healed his soul." Mala looked at Codgarak as he finished his thought and added, "Well! You have *fun* with that! Feel free to leave your pet there too!" Mala nodded towards Liam before he turned and began forming his portal.

Cashmes's departing words were, "Be quick, my friend. Who knows how long this window will allow us to teleport to you. The realm is growing darker and filled with more chaos." The two large cats entered the portal and disappeared as the rays of magical light enveloped them.

Liam brushed off his clothes after once again being forced into the dirt. "You oka—"

"I don't want to talk about it." Liam walked off before Codgarak had even had the chance to start the conversation.

The half bull, half man shrugged and shook his head at his failed attempt to bring peace. He watched Liam march his way up the rest of the hill and crest over its top. Youthful pride didn't mix well with a seasoned ego; he had seen it all before played out amongst many warriors and armies. It was something that could only be fixed over time, and unfortunately, he knew the rest of the trip to Golgoth was going to be a quiet one. That aspect normally wouldn't have bothered him, but his failed attempt to help the young fighter gain more understanding of his old friend weighed heavily on him. He looked around the vast debris of destroyed statues. "What a mess."

Liam took his final steps, bringing him to the top of the hill, and slowed to a stop as he took in the sight of the rolling hills ahead of them. The forest stretched for miles until it faded into the distant rise of the next mountain range. He crouched down and took in the depth and vastness of the forest; it made the journey they had already undertaken seem so small in comparison to what remained ahead.

Liam enjoyed some time at the top of the hill before Codgarak finally arrived. "You could have just teleported here." He smirked in judgment.

The minotaur huffed for a few moments before he answered. "I tried … seven times! The window of opportunity appears to have passed yet again."

Liam's smirk got bigger. He was still bitter about his suffering at the hands of Mala, and he therefore found pleasure in another's suffering. He realized he had rested a significant amount and still desired to be alone. "In which direction will we find this Golgoth?" He stood up and glanced between the horizon and Codgarak.

The minotaur finally caught his breath enough to stand and gazed out. "There … if I recall."

Liam looked at the small knoll Codgarak was pointing to. "Sounds good. No time to waste!" He slapped the minotaur's arm before walking off in haste.

"Damn your youth," said Codgarak.

As the two left the mountainside, they drove deeper into the forest. As they did so, a dense fog rolled into the valley and shrouded the woods from the sun's gaze. It was hard to focus on aspects of the environment; the slight glow within the tree line made objects appear as if they were alive and not what they seemed.

As they continued their walk, Liam could hear the snapping of twigs. The hair on the back of his neck stood up and he fought off a slight tremble in his steps. He knew what it was like to spend vast amounts of time deep in the woods when he was hunting, but that had been when he was growing up in the forests of Artho. Here … he had no idea what the thick brush contained.

He watched Codgarak veer over towards a large tree. Grabbing it with his claw, he tore free a section of its bark, exposing a rune. Turning his head towards Liam and locking eyes with him, he commented, "Golgoth placed this here." He said it quietly, as if the darkness that had been creeping into the realm had ears that could overhear their conversation. "It is to keep any dark magical entity from entering. We're in the right area."

The guide of few words didn't waste any more time. He placed the bark back upon the tree and, lifting his other hand, he summoned a small flame spell that flowed from it and brought the flame towards the piece of bark. Liam moved closer to see. The sap from the tree began to extract itself when introduced to the heat. Codgarak moved the flame away from it and drew a deep breath, which cooled the bark as he exhaled upon it. The sap hardened and reattached the bark to the tree. "Come," was all he said as he brushed past the dense foliage on the forest floor.

Liam constantly checked his pacing with Codgarak. The fog wrapping itself around him felt as if it was trying to cling to him in an uncomfortable and eerie way. He cringed slightly as he was reminded of the wraith attack he'd experienced on the cliffs outside Codgarak's cave. Though he felt more confident now in his combat skills, especially after the surprise attack by the gargoyles, he still felt fear gripping hold of him when it came to the things he could not see. But he had to walk by faith and not by sight.

He glanced around the area and thought he caught sight of something in the distance. Grabbing the hilt of one of his swords, he did his best to focus on the shape, but he couldn't make out if there was something there or not. Turning his attention back to his guide, he discovered that Codgarak had continued his march through the woods and hadn't noticed he'd taken a pause. Not seeing the minotaur, he acted in a panic and jolted forward, trying to bridge the gap between them. His vision was impaired by the environment, and he floundered through the brush, branches reaching out towards him as if they were alive and trying to grab at him. He brought his arms up to clear away the hindrance. Picking up his pace, he didn't see the exposed tree roots below him. He caught his foot and was hurled to the ground, landing with a thud.

The floor was damp from the droplets of moisture in the fog. The thick tree canopy left the forest floor without much sunlight, and this area was covered with briar bushes that had small thorny branches that seemed to take hold of everything that passed by. Lying on the ground, he felt as if the briar bushes were clasping him tighter with every twist and turn he made. Struggling to get back to his feet, he brought his hand up to brush the dirt from his face. He turned and with instant terror noticed a pair of feet standing just off to his left.

He clambered to his feet in haste and drew his swords from their scabbards. His heart raced. The body before him didn't move. He swallowed heavily and caught his breath when he realized that fear had left him frozen for half a second, but the body stayed as silent as the dead, for life had left it long ago and only the shell of the person remained.

Investigating the situation, he took in the remaining details. The body was held up by a wooden brace that had been stuck into the ground. It was that of a man who had once worn a tunic, but it was ripped down the center, and a large cut across his stomach exposed the entrails. They had been pulled out and were dangling between the two outstretched arms, which held them in their hands. Blood had once filled the mouth that now lay open; dark red bloodstains showed where it had run down the man's face before it had dried. The eyes were pure glossy white with no pupils. It appeared that some form of magic had been involved with the poor soul's death.

Liam returned his swords to their scabbards and slowly took a few steps backwards. His stomach was in knots as his eyes took in the torturous scene, his mind wondering about the different things that might have happened to this victim.

A break in the fog rolled through and allowed him to look further through the trees, where he saw another body standing, horns curling out around its head. Surveying the land, he noticed a faint pathway leading from the nearest body towards the next. His perception of danger subsided somewhat, though his mind was still filled with fear as he walked over to the next figure.

As he grew closer, he saw that it was the body of a woman. She was wearing a flowing dress and had been placed in a standing position. Her dark hair covered the majority of her face, but half a skull had been put on her head as if it were a helmet. Ram's horns were affixed to the skull and wrapped around where her ears would be. The helmet also sported goat horns, which protruded from the lower jaw portion of the skull and wrapped around the front of the woman's face.

The lifeless body, though not a threat to anyone, left him feeling uneasy. The discomfort didn't leave him but was amplified when he saw that the woman's hands were tensed in place, as if they had tried to claw at something prior to her death. He couldn't explain it, but there was a feeling in his gut that this woman was a witch or had some association with dark magic. Though he had felt bad for the previous victim, he was actually happy this woman remained dead. He could swear that he could still feel hatred seeping out of her.

Peering past the preserved corpses, he watched as the figure of a minotaur stepped through the mist, remaining in the shadows. Its eyes glowed a dense yellow in the fog and its breath steamed in front of it. "Codgarak?" he asked. The figure stepped out of the shadows and was faintly illuminated by the glow of the dim fog, confirming Liam's suspicions. He breathed a sigh of relief. *Thank the Ancient One*, he thought.

The minotaur eventually made his way over to him. "Decided to go on your own adventure, I see."

Liam shook his head in response to the implied question. "I fell, and by the time I'd recovered, you were gone."

Codgarak gestured towards the corpse. "You made a new friend."

Liam looked back at her. "I believe a night with Lorelaylee is better than a hundred years with … this."

Codgarak snorted. "You might have a point there." A smirk came over Liam's face as he pictured Lorelaylee's gorgeous breasts pressing against the fabric of her dress. "Save it for later. We're close." Codgarak turned and looked further into the woods.

"How can you tell?" They didn't believe it was just happenstance, but as soon as Liam posed the question, they faintly heard a tortured scream in the distance. A chill ran down Liam's spine. "That doesn't sound good."

He watched as the dim glow of Codgarak's eyes turned to meet his. "There is nothing good in these woods." Codgarak took a deep breath. "Perhaps the only good is the fact that these woods have hidden Golgoth for many years. Come on."

The two continued, allowing the screams to act as a beacon to their destination. The volume increased slowly but surely as they narrowed in, closing the distance to the source. Along the way were more scattered corpses, each one contorted in its own way and adorned with accessories that amplified the darkness they were preserved with. *Certainly, a dark mind and soul was behind the creation of these… art pieces.*

The further they went, the easier it was to see the path, which had been matted down by the back and forth of who he could only assume was Golgoth. The path wound its way through the thick foliage and the trees.

Both travelers were brought to a halt as two large figures startled them. The trees no longer concealed their previously hidden placement. The two figures stood on either side of the path, both holding spears pointed towards it.

Codgarak lifted his arm and summoned a flame. Black, red, and white swirling magic flowed around his arm and poured into the flame, which grew from a small flicker to a burning torch. The light illuminated the figures so that they could see the embellishments on their armor in fine detail. It was obsidian plated with emerald-green engraved designs. The green glowed in the light, and the shine of the obsidian complemented the dark world of the forest in which their bodies were forever entombed. The spears were forged in a dark gray material, and the weapons were adorned with the same emerald-colored engraving, which swirled all the way down their shafts.

The two protectors were sleek and tall. Liam figured that if they stood upright, they'd be a full head taller than the minotaur, but they were slender to the point that both standing next to one another would not even cover Codgarak's shoulder width. Gazing upon their faces, he admired the hleorberg armor plating of the helmets that covered their cheeks. Silver hair protruded and sharp, pointed ears stuck out and flowed backwards.

"So these are elves," Liam proclaimed in admiration. "I've never set my sights on an elf before, but their description in the stories certainly does match."

Codgarak walked over and pointed to the obsidian armor that protected the left leg of one of the elves. Directing Liam's attention to an emblem, he said, "This crest etched in the armor ... they are Icelightal elves. None that I know have ever gazed upon them, and many thought they were all dead ... that is, until now."

"Based on your words from before, I assume these elves are vastly different from their fellow bloodlines?"

Nodding in agreement, Codgarak continued. "Icelightals were outsiders to many, even other elves, and their origins are unknown.

Many questions to ask Golgoth about how these two became part of his collection."

The bellows of the tortured soul crying out again interrupted the moment. "From the sounds of it, we're getting closer," said Liam. Codgarak, in agreement, nodded, turned, and continued down the path, but both still took a final glance at the two rare fighters standing guard over the pathway before they left their presence.

It was only a little further past the preserved elf guards that they saw a hut with a flickering glow coming from it. The screams had been silent for some time. Approaching the door, Liam made sure his swords were ready for combat, but he utilized the minotaur's size as his own personal shield, barely tilting his head enough to see the doorway.

Bang, bang, bang!

"Golgoth!"

He heard what sounded like glass breaking inside, as if the individual within was startled by the announcement of their arrival. Footsteps began inside, and without warning, the door was ripped open and slammed against the wall.

The first thing that captivated Liam was the skull of a demon glaring down at him. Paralyzed, he gazed at the skull, which was beige with the jawbone missing at the bottom. Two horns jutted out of the top and curved upward in a twisted fashion, with sharp points at the ends. The eyes, however, blazed with the intensity of hell itself, and wisps of red and blood-orange light flared out of them.

"*Himph!* Codgarak!" the high-pitched, curdling voice declared. "The Ancient One has brought you to me when I least expected it." Liam was able to break free of his enchanting fear of the demon skull, and he saw that the man standing before them was quite slender in appearance. He wore a dirty cloak and pants, but both his sleeves and the bottoms of his pants appeared to be torn off.

As Golgoth stood in the doorway, he was face to face with Codgarak. Liam assessed him as splitting the difference between himself and Codgarak in height. He watched as Golgoth shifted his weight and, reaching behind him, produced a hand, brought it up to his mouth, and took a bite of it with a jerking motion. *Wait ... that's an actual hand he's holding!* Liam thought. His stomach instantly tied in knots and, unable to hold back, he puked at his feet. Wiping his mouth, he stood back upright but found Golgoth's demon skull directly in his face. "What is wrong? Is there ... something ... wrong? *Himph!*"

Raising the hand to his mouth again, he chomped down on another finger, the crunching of bones audible in his chewing. Liam couldn't help it and vomited again. Golgoth's high-pitched curdling laugh haunted him as he worked to focus on keeping his stomach at ease. "You must have come a long way if you want to see old Golgoth ... *himph! Himph, himph.* Come inside so you can rest your old ... bones! *Himph!*"

The crunching of bones as he chewed after this statement didn't sit well with Liam at all, but seeing Codgarak accept the invitation and walk in left him feeling uneasy about *everything* going on at the moment.

"Come! Come ..." Golgoth waved him on, and he snapped round and began to clamber in behind Codgarak. His spirit screamed *"No!"* but his mind told him not to let the minotaur out of his sight. His instinct warned him "Do not be left alone with this thing!" His legs were shaking as he forced them to begin moving forward. He walked through the doorway with Golgoth on his left, who then slammed the door immediately after Liam cleared it. He jumped, startled. *"Himph! He-he-he."*

Looking around the hut, he saw a pile of glass bottles in the corner next to a large wooden chair. Most of them were broken. Around the edges of the hut was more broken glass. In the center was a fireplace with a mantel, and on the wall were numerous skulls of different types. Three of them, however, were demon skulls like the one Golgoth currently wore. He could hear a slight whimpering coming from what he assumed was a back room. The roof was old and leaky; there were signs of water running down the walls and damp spots on the floor.

As he slowly made his way further into the hut, he noticed a gray stone bench. On top was an assortment of items—bladed items, some that appeared to be tools, and other things he could never have imagined on his own. There was a splattering of dried blood on them, and some were still dripping wet with the life source. Liam figured that whoever was in the back must have been the source of the screams and the blood, and the one who was their tormentor now stood behind him. He gradually slipped his hand down and grabbed the hilt of one of his swords, slowly turning and mentally preparing to engage in combat, until …

His head turned before his body had completed the action, and he met the gaze of Golgoth's demon skull. It stared down at him. His head was slightly tilted, and his eyes continued to glow a heinous red and orange. Golgoth inched his way closer to Liam's face, and smoke seeped out from behind the skull.

The tension within Liam built. Taken off guard by the intimacy of Golgoth's position, he knew he would not be able to pull his sword out without Golgoth preventing it. He'd let his guard down when he shouldn't have. *Stupid move, Liam*, he thought.

Golgoth, still holding the human hand, reached his free hand behind his back again. This time he produced two sharp blades. Bringing them forward, he dropped them on the rock table. "*Himph!* You appear to have seen a wraith, boy!" A high pitched laugh following his statement. A chill running down his spine as his comment didn't sit well with him given the screams they had heard on their approach. "I can assure you there are no wraiths here!" As soon as the words had left him, he snapped around again, took two steps, and then snapped back towards Liam as if he'd forgotten. "There in the corner. You may place your weapons on the weapons rack. *Himph, hehe, himph.*"

Golgoth and his demonic head resumed their path towards his intended destination—the wooden chair in the corner by the broken bottles. Arriving at it, the slender figure plopped down as if a ruthless court jester had taken over the throne of a kingdom and chosen to rule as a sick joke over humanity, which would suffer the consequences.

A brief pause filled the room. Liam dared not move but still had a tight grip on his sword. Codgarak had already sat down on a large chair adjacent to the makeshift wooden throne on which Golgoth lounged. "*Himph.*" The pause continued.

"*Himph, himph* ... How long has it been now, Codgarak?"

The minotaur turned his large head and gazed up at the demon skull mounted above the mantel. "Ten years, if I recall."

Golgoth raised his hand and scratched the skull as if it would cure the itch below, or maybe he wanted to feel its coarseness as he reflected. "That cannot be true, but ... perhaps! *Himph, hehehe.* So much has happened, and yet ... nothing has changed! Golgoth is still the same today as he always has been! *Himph, himph, himph!*"

Liam interjected. "Something has changed! There is an evil in the land."

Golgoth snapped his gaze towards him, and the fire in his eyes pulsated with a new intensity. "I know there is, boy ... and do you know how I know?" Golgoth paused. He brought up his free hand, took hold of the demon skull, and lifted it off to expose his face.

Golgoth's face was thin; protruding cheekbones made him appear sickly. His skin was dark with charred ash, as if he had covered his hands in charcoal and rubbed them all over his face and neck. He had a grim and dirty appearance, as if he bathed in filth rather than water. His cheekbones were lighter than the rest of his face, which enhanced the impression that his face itself was a skull. His hair was wild and greasy. Both sides stood up, as if it had been growing upward inside the demonic horns of the skull. His eyes still burned with hellish intensity, and his gaze never left Liam's the entire time. "I am evil!"

Fear took hold of Liam, but his courage grew stronger. *Is this the evil that placed the runes that attacked me and Codgarak on the stone steps? He is clearly the evil that tortured the souls in the woods. He is torturing another victim within these walls as we speak! Evil shall be vanquished!* he told himself as he drew his sword and began walking towards Golgoth. *Evil will meet its death this night!* he internally motivated himself until Codgarak's hand grabbed the wrist of his sword arm. "Put it away, Liam."

"Hehehe, himph himph himph, hahaha!"

Golgoth tossed the human hand he had been holding directly at him. Liam leaned to one side, allowing the hand to fly past him. "Come, boy! End my suffering once and for all! Vanquish my evil from this land!" Golgoth brought his hands up and tore at his garment, exposing a shrunken chest that matched his face's charred, sooty appearance. A smile of wickedness and vile pleasure spread across his face as he proclaimed, *"End me now, boy!"*

Liam tried to move forward but was held tightly by Codgarak. The minotaur had finally had enough and slammed his battle-ax down on the ground with a ferocious *"Enough!"* A sonic blast exploded as he said it, knocking everything backward and shaking the small house. A few items fell from the walls, and more bottles broke as they landed on the ground.

Liam didn't want to obey the command, but the force of Codgarak's grip made him feel like the giant beast was about to snap his arm in two. The seriousness of the instruction that had ended with a sonic boom also brought forth the small whisper of a voice inside him reminding him that he had chosen to trust the minotaur many weeks ago. He needed to honor the legend and trust him yet again. He looked at the bull's eyes and saw a dim yellow glow growing within them. Slowly, but with an internal feeling of resistance within his soul, truly believing his actions were justified, he conceded and put his sword away.

"Sit!" was the only follow-up instruction he was given by the minotaur. Walking around the room, he found a small wooden crate lying on its side that could act as a makeshift chair. He glared at the withered, whimpering, rotten shell of a living corpse that sat before him. *"Himph! Himph ..."* Tears streaked down Golgoth's face. "I am tired, my old friend. How much longer must I suffer? *Himph!* These"—he pointed to the broken bottles that lay on the floor—"are just the constant reminders of who I am ... and what I've done." Another stream of tears fell from both eyes. He blinked quickly. The blazing red and orange glow left them and the weary old eyes of torment came into view. The same eyes that Liam had seen on roadside beggars. Eyes like those of his dying father when hope had left long ago ... when sorrow, grief, and pain were all that remained.

Though he could clearly see the agony within the eyes of Golgoth, he dared not give him any sympathy. He turned his gaze away, towards the skulls on the wall. The demon skulls took center stage. They were each different in nature, unique and mysterious. He was entranced by the horns, to see how they— Something flashed before his eyes.

He was mentally teleported back to when Mala, Cashmes, and Codgarak had all stood on the hillside with the shattered gargoyles around them. It was as if he were there, stuck within his previous body, but focusing on Mala's armor, he now saw it as clear as day. An ivory-etched demonic skull formed a crest. Wrapped around and intertwined with the skull was a beautiful flower. Though he had never seen it before, there was a tug within his spirit and an inner whisper that informed him it was an orchid. The flower was beautiful and was meticulously placed in union with the demonic skull. Its teal and blue color had just a slight shine and complemented the ivory of the skull.

His near sight faded as he refocused on Cashmes. The large lion had a medallion dangling from his massive neck. It was made of coarse black onyx with beige veins interlaced in the stone. Upon the black onyx was a gold crest edged with a silver demon skull with gold accents. Cashmes's skull was a completely different rendition, just like each skull above the fireplace. Instead of flowers, Cashmes's had the etching of purple smoke wrapping all around, turning bright red where it ran underneath the skull and down, as though blood were draining from the skull.

Flashing out of the memory, Liam peered over to see that Codgarak's shoulder armor bore an engraving of a demon skull. The minotaur's version was very simple compared to those of the brother cats. His was an inlay of dark metal that was very rigid and edged with straight lines. The two curved horns were the only curved lines in the engraving. Everything else was plain and, honestly, kind of boring. Liam looked up at the minotaur and thought, *Well, it makes sense, since he is kind of a square himself.*

But what was the connection between him and Golgoth? Why demon skulls? What were they supposed to represent? More questions filled his mind until he was interrupted by the distraction of Golgoth. "*Himph!* I tell you, my old friend …" More tears rolled down his face; he had grabbed hold of a bottle of amber liquid and took a large swig from it. "The mind does not forget what your eyes have seen, your ears have heard, and your hands have done. *Himph! He-hehe-heh.*" He took another drink from the bottle as another stream of tears flowed down. He paused slightly after the last drink, as if his mind were drowning in fog from the memories he suppressed.

"So … what brings my old friend to see Golgoth this night? *Himph, himph* … What terrors have bumped you in the night?" He placed the bottle on the floor next to the other empties and, leaning forward in his chair, wiped the streaked tears, smearing the ash and soot around his face and making him look even more deplorable than he already was.

"When was the last time you saw, heard, or felt any energy from your old master?" Codgarak didn't hesitate in his question. Liam looked back and forth, watching them both. Codgarak sat stoic as ever, whereas Golgoth sat back in his chair. His eyes began to water again, but his lips pressed together and his cheek appeared as if he was biting down on it from within.

"I have not done anything! I swear it!" His defensiveness grew stronger. "I swore I would never return to such darkness, and yes, I am evil, but I swear it, Codgarak, I have not sought him out since I left!"

Codgarak raised his hand, not changing his demeanor. "It is but a question, not an accusation."

Golgoth shifted and adjusted himself as if his body were crawling with the kind of insects that made one flinch all over. "I have enchanted these woods with the most powerful runes I could conjure so that his magic could never find me, nor I feel him."

The minotaur nodded. "I know … I found one on our way here."

The twitching continued as Golgoth carried on. "These woods have protected me from him … yet have contained me within them as well. I have done my best to atone, Codgarak … I have …" He reached down, grabbed the bottle, and finished off the rest of what little remained. "It has only been me and my own demons these days."

The minotaur waved his hand toward the back room. "And the tortured soul behind this wall?"

Golgoth leaned his head back in defense. "That bastard? *Himph, himph!* He found pleasure in the butchering of women …" Golgoth leaned forward in his chair. "Their spirits visited me in the night asking for justice … I happily sought him out and brought him forth to receive such justice." He stood up from his wooden throne and walked over to another corner of the room, retrieving a fresh bottle, popping the cork free, and taking the first sip. He smacked his lips together after it went down. "*Himph* … Once it hits my lips, my mind knows it will be over soon."

He returned to his seat, teetering all the way. He sat down, leaned forward, and nodded towards the back room. "Trust me, Codgarak—*himph*—that evil has received what it has earned." He turned his gaze back to Liam, who was still questioning who Golgoth truly was. "It takes evil to know evil, and I assure you, boy, though you question who I am, you may set your mind at ease, for the world is free of one more evil, for I am the one who takes the actions to fight it! *Himph, himph, ha-haha-hahahaha.*"

GOLGOTH

TO RESTORE

She lay on the floor. Her body was damp with sweat and stained with feces, and the fragrance of urine loomed over her. The lower cells were kept hot and humid, the preferred conditions of the prison guards. By this point, she didn't even notice the trembling of her body. It was her new normal. The little remnant of her strength was so small now that she couldn't comprehend it. A lifeless body waiting for its end was all she was. Her body was numb. Her spirit was gone. She was so dehydrated that she didn't even produce tears anymore. The castle was constantly glowing with light from the flames, for everything that bore the old mark of Lithram was being destroyed to proclaim the new reign of Emmanuel, "the God Amongst Us."

Her once-beautiful jet-black silky hair was now rough and frazzled. She had noticed when the first few hairs began to turn white, but now she paid no attention to it. Her life of enslavement meant she was no longer valued as a person but only seen as meat for devouring whenever her captors saw fit. This wasn't her specific fate but that of everyone who fell to the conquerors.

A clanging down the hallway and a quick scream set her staring at the wall. The names of the others who had once been in the cell with her were carved into the stone walls. The only lasting memory she had was watching as they accepted their fates, but she hoped that one day their memories would live on for any liberator who discovered the inscriptions. Where had they been taken? What had happened to them? It was a mystery, and she had given up wondering long ago. She accepted her destiny. The only thing she longed for was death … the sweet taste and relief of death.

The clanging and dragging of chains echoed down the hall as a cell at the end was opened, and the screaming of a woman could be heard as she was ripped out of it. It sounded as if the others with her were trying their best to cling on to her, attempting to keep her for just a moment longer. They tried to beg and plead with the guards, who yelped and laughed in their native language.

The gnolls were a vicious bastard hybrid of hyenas and humans. Their high-pitched communication was mostly barks and yips and that laugh … the type of laugh that reaches into your mind and almost drives you mad. When Emmanuel's machine army marched inside Lithram and launched their attack, the gnoll's had not yet arrived but were further back in the military convoy. Now however, they were unleashed and running rampant. Searching and scouring for new and hidden victims. It was easy to see that they were lowly fouder for Emmanuel to preserve his main force.

The gnolls ripped the poor woman free. Whether it was her clawing at the stone floor or the nails of the gnolls' feet, the prisoner couldn't tell, but the cries for mercy were a daily occurrence, part of the routine. Nothing they tried stopped the suffering from taking place. Yet for some, like the poor souls down the hallway … they must still be clinging on to some hope at this point. They at least still had the energy to try to resist.

The door at the end of the hallway shut with a loud metallic slam and the gnolls yelped in glee as they found pleasure in accomplishing yet another task. The woman cried out, but all she received in return were swift kicks to her body or gobs of spittle as she was dragged past the guards.

Finally arriving at the chambers of Emmanuel, the guards opened the doors and the two gnolls delivered the requested spoils of war. "Ahh ... splendid. You two arrived just on time. I believe I have finally drained the little bit of life left out of this one." Standing from his imposing chair, Emmanuel pointed to the lifeless body that was draped across the large imperial bed in the center of the room.

The gnoll guard looked down at the newly secured prize. Holding the chain that detained the victim towards Emmanuel, he gestured with his head towards the corpse. "Yick-yik, yak, yik, mmrrhhhh?"

Emmanuel glanced over at the body and back at the guard. "Yes ... you may, and enjoy your spoils! Be sure to share, now!" A heinous grin came over his face as the two gnolls jumped over to the body, licking its limbs and savoring the taste of their next meal. They grabbed hold of it and began dragging it out, yipping all the way. Their calls faded at the closing of the chamber doors, and all that remained was Emmanuel and his next devouring.

"Please!" The woman whimpered and pleaded for the lord not to take part in the same actions as previously.

"Please?" Letting out a sinister laugh, "Oh, don't worry, I will satisfy your begging for pleasure."

"No! Stop! That is not what I—" He grabbed her throat and began choking the voice right out of her, dragging her and lifting her onto the bed with one hand. He loomed over her as tears poured out of her eyes.

Bang, bang, bang.

"Let me in! You steaming pots of tea!" Set burst through the door, striding past the guards attempting to bar his way. He grabbed hold of one of the guard's hoses and pulled it out of its coupling, sending hot steam spraying out. The guard began to cough and labor in an attempt to breathe. "Sorry to intrude upon your feast, but we need to discuss a few things." Set walked in and sat down upon the chair that Emmanuel had just vacated.

"What is it, Set?" Emmanuel straddled the poor woman on the bed as she began to tremble. His grip on her throat practically left her on the verge of choking.

"Who did you send out to conjure the runes in Cho'took and RemaMortBrook?"

Turning back to the captive, Emmanuel dropped his head. "This is why you interrupt me?" Whipping his head back around, he released the woman from his grip and turned towards Set. "What difference does it make?"

Set pressed his lips together as he smiled and tilted his head. "Well, darling, the reason it matters is because … they did a piss-poor job of it! That's why!"

Emmanuel scoffed. "This is not a pressing matter, Set! It could have waited!"

Turning his head and flaring his hand out in front of him, Set said, "Ohh, isn't it now? Not pressing? Well, let's put it this way … a good number of the runes have been discovered, and the other realms are already taking notice. You said you'd have this covered, Emmanuel, and I thought I was dealing with a professional here! If I had known you were going to assign the task to halfwits, I would have assigned it to Bast or Azazel. They at least know what they're doing!"

Turning towards the door, Emmanuel yelled, "Bring me Sarpo-Gast! *And close the door!*" When the guards had closed the door, he turned his attention back to his visitor. "And what of the centaurs?"

Set stood up hastily, pointing his finger at Emmanuel. "Don't question me on expectations after I inform you of your soldiers' incompetence! Marduk has been priming them for over a hundred years, and trust me, darling, they've already been hard at work quietly for years. Those poor bastards won't know what hit them! Now I've upheld my end of the agreement, I suggest you do the same, dear boy!" Set began to walk towards the doors.

"And where are you going now?"

Turning back, he looked around the room. "I'm sorry, but do you think you are the only one requesting my assistance? I depart to attend to other matters, and seeing how behind schedule you are, 'Lord Emmanuel,' I don't think you'll miss my absence." Feeling the anger rise within him, he reached up and adjusted a dial on his armor. Steam shot out of a valve on his back and green goo pumped rapidly through the tubing, which was slightly exposed underneath the armor plating. Emmanuel making sure to emphasize his position, "My army will march on to the next city once we've restored ourselves. It's not simply a matter of wanting to win the battles; dominance in all matters is what we'll need for the other realms to come kneeling before me!" As he adjusted the dial once more, the armor calibrated itself according to the new instruction. "Besides … it's not like your demons aren't enjoying themselves either."

Set bounced his head back and forth. "The demons … all they need is to devour something and they'll be fine! They've been doing it since the dawn of time and they'll continue doing it once time has come to its end." He took another few steps to the door and placed his hand on it before he turned again with his final reminder. "Don't forget, though—my legions of the damned will grow tired if you keep them lying about for too long. My direct soldiers are not the same as the horde you were given. Best start moving to the next city soon, or they'll start turning on the gnolls and the other … ridiculous species you've recruited on your campaign of carnage … or whatever. Fuck off now, piss pat later!" He spun and ripped the door open, slamming it shut with Emmanuel cussing behind him as the guards stood frozen in place.

SET

LET US BEGIN

The morning arrived much faster than Liam's body liked. The hard floor had left him stiff, his muscles tight, and he did his best to stretch and ease the pain. The warmth emitted by the fire was nice; walking over, he sat by it and soaked up its heat. The crackling of the flames was the instrument of travelers, the music forever changing its tone, but the symphony always brought solace to the soul.

He turned over Golgoth's words in his mind. He had seemed defensive when his "previous master" was brought up, and Codgarak certainly hadn't shared this information with him prior to their arrival at Golgoth's hut. Who was the master of evil that made even a self-proclaimed man of evil shudder at the thought of him? He stayed there for quite some time, asking himself a multitude of questions developing theories based off of what he had seen and heard the previous night.

"Golgoth make an appearance yet?" Codgarak said as he awakened.

Liam shook his head. "Perhaps he has found peace within his dreams."

Stumbling out of the back room, Golgoth leaned on the wall. "There is no such thing as peace … well, perhaps when you're finally dead. *Himph!*" He made his way over to his chair and collapsed down on it. Tilting his head backwards and then dropping it forward, he said, "Tell me, Codgarak … what makes you bring up Emmanuel? Why allow that falsehood to enter your thoughts?" He reached over and grabbed the same bottle from last night, which he hadn't finished off. He swished the liquid around and looked at the amber color, then pressed the bottle to his lips and swigged away.

"There are reports coming out that Lithram was sacked."

"*Himph! Himph* … Was it now?" He took another swig from the bottle.

"Aibek is missing."

Golgoth's eyes had a thousand-yard stare. They began to gloss over from being filled with water, and his face flared in a sign he was fighting back a new round of tears. There was a slight tremble in his voice. "When did Aibek go missing? Where, exactly… did he go missing?"

"Have you ever met Mala?"

Golgoth shook his head slightly as he continued to stare into nowhere. "This name I have not met, only heard mention of briefly in the past."

"Mala felt a darkness growing in the Realm of Delco. He told me Aibek went to investigate its source but has not returned—no sign of him or any sense of his magic or energy. It's as if he has been erased completely."

The first tear fell down Golgoth's face. "Well … Aibek can defend himself. I am sure there is a perfectly good explanation."

"You spent quite a significant amount of your time under your old master in Lithram and Delco."

"*Himph!* You could say that … I have spent the vast majority of my time in many of these realms. Pieces of my soul are scattered all about them. *Himph, ha-hahaha-haaaa.*"

"Mala has not outright said it, but he is disturbed by the evil presence he has felt. I could use you, my friend."

Golgoth finally returned his gaze to the minotaur. "I am not a hunter."

Codgarak snorted. "You are certainly a hunter. You don't need the emblem to know you are just as much a hunter as the rest of us." A slight pause filled the room until Codgarak began to say a spell. A purple flame was conjured in the air. It wrapped itself around and formed into the rune that Mala had found on the gargoyles. "This rune looks very similar to yours."

Golgoth squinted at it intently. "I did not create that, Codgarak! I swear it!" He took a long deep breath, quelling his instinctive defensiveness. "Where did you find this?"

Codgarak nodded. "You know the gargoyle steps on the other side of the mountain?"

Golgoth burst into laughter. "*Himph!* What a clever and perfect placement for such a thing! I would have thought of that myself! *Himph, himph* … A perfect trap for an unearthly traveler."

"They attacked us on our way to find you."

Golgoth slouched back in his chair "*Himmph* … What a pity. I would have loved to play with such a toy."

Standing up, he finished the bottle in his hand. Looking down at it, he turned towards the corner of the room and threw the bottle. It shattered against the wall. He stretched out his arms in glee. "*Himph!* Come! Let us begin this journey to hunt the evil that plagues this land in the company of my old friend! *Himph! Himph, hahaha!*"

Golgoth departed the room, and the scrambling Liam heard led him to believe that he was gathering things for the trek. Standing up, he approached Codgarak. "Are you sure this is what's best?"

The bull's eyes met his. "Better to be an open sinner than live as a false saint." The minotaur stood and made his way to the door. Opening it, he twisted to best fit into the hallway, but once he found himself outside, his head reappeared through the door and peered at Liam in all seriousness. "Don't forget, Liam, you asked to join me on this journey, not the other way around." He disappeared as Liam stood in the middle of the room, the demon skulls peering down at him from the fireplace.

Golgoth reappeared. "Come, Liam. It would appear that there is some unfinished business that needs attending to. *Himph!*"

Codgarak and Golgoth stood outside Golgoth's home, sheltered within the woods. Liam was the last to leave. "Take your time." Codgarak gave a frustrated flare of his eyebrows and followed this up with, "Let's go. We have a long way ahead of us."

Liam paused and pointed back over his shoulder. "Wait ... isn't there a ... uhh ... thing in the ... you know?"

Golgoth was looking up at the tree branches above him. "You have no need to worry about him." Liam didn't know what to say next, but Golgoth answered his unspoken question. "His soul finally left his body early this morning. He now faces a more terrifying judge. *Himph! Himmph hmm.*" He lowered his head and made eye contact with Liam.

Golgoth's eyes looked as if he had had the perfect morning. He seemed completely at peace with the fact that there was a corpse in his home. "Time for us to see if our death awaits us."

Liam thought he had the perfect addition. "It is everyone's destiny to die."

Golgoth smiled from ear to ear, slapped his hand on his leg, and pointed at him. "Exactly! That's the spirit! *Himph!*" He turned to Codgarak. "This Liam you have found doesn't seem to be too bad after all! *Hehehe.*"

Liam was taken aback and now wondered if he shouldn't have said anything, as Codgarak reiterated. "We're wasting time. Let's go."

Liam began to file in behind his leader when Golgoth stopped them both. "No, no, no! Not that way. This way. It will bring us out closer to Explorto, and we can take the steel traders' road from there." They redirected themselves to a tiny animal path. Watching Codgarak swat tree limbs and bushes out of his massive way brought a smile to Liam's face. He compared the minotaur with the thin frame of Golgoth, who was taking the lead, and couldn't help but chuckle at the contrast between the two.

Marduk's dark robes and the accentuated sashes that adorned them were a stark contrast to Set's white and light-gray robes and shirt. They both stood out amongst the small crowd of townsfolk.

Walking through the town center and people moved out of their way due to their air of nobility; they looked like businessmen of an elite class. Set's condescension towards everyone else made him perfectly fine about openly discussing matters with Marduk. A child running by turned quickly and startled a small dog, which stepped on Set's robe and left a smear of dirt. "Aye! Tame your beast, you nitwit!" Turning back towards Marduk and flaring his robe, he continued. "As I was saying! Now that the centaurs—"

"Centeth," Marduk interrupted him.

Set turned his head, his teeth exposed. "Whatever! Those bloody horse freaks can change their name all they want. As long as they do their jobs, that's all that matters." Marduk sighed. Having spent so much time amongst the breed, he was quite fond of all the work he had put into the accomplishment. Set continued. "As I was saying! Now that you're done with the half-breeds, start working to infiltrate and influence Excelsem."

Marduk lifted his head in disdain. "We've tried to influence the Kingdom of Excelsem for hundreds of years. It's a lost cause at this point." He could see that Set was not amused by his response, but the last thing he wanted was his time wasted.

"Darling, just because it's nice and tight doesn't mean they don't want it. Get in there and impregnate that pig and let's make us a baby!" He clapped his hands with a laugh.

Marduk rolled his eyes at him. "Answer me this. Why are we still pretending with this pathetic Emmanuel? I'm sick of his shit."

Set reached up and clapped his hand on Marduk's shoulder. "Ohh, come on now! Isn't it the greatest of fun to manipulate even those who are so infused with their own evil intentions?" Set chuckled as he turned and looked at him with a raised eyebrow. "I swear some of the ideas they come up with surprise even me some days." A slight chuckle followed this statement. He flared his hands in front of him as he spoke. "Look ... we'll just let them run their course and eventually you'll see the grand plan." The smile on Set's face was one that mankind couldn't trust, but Marduk knew that he spoke the truth.

"I can only play their games for so long until I despise the bullshit," Marduk told him.

Set shook his head in response. "Don't worry, my dear Marduk. Emmanuel has provided the sweet carnage of mankind, and all we must do is reap the reward. Our own plan still lies in wait."

Marduk turned away from Set as they made their way to a table, which just so happened to have two cups and a cask already on it. He picked up the cask and twirled it in his hand. The alcohol swirling inside released the aromatic scent of the ushu berries used to brew the beverage. He poured the drink into the two cups and handed one to Set as he continued. "I hate these rural towns who pitifully attempt to make a proper drink."

He took a large swig as Set swirled the solution and responded before trying it, "Oh, come on now! You must give them credit for trying." It took less than a second for Set to spit it right out. "Disregard! That's not a beverage! That's horse piss!" Looking around, Set met the gaze of the poor tavern owner. He pointed. "You! Is this your concoction?"

The man normally didn't take criticism from customers, but their clothing, portraying as it did an elite status, left him feeling bashful. "Yes."

Set shook his head and waved his hand in a "no" gesture. "I would say go kill yourself for this pathetic excuse for a drink, but I don't want you filling up the halls of hell with your failure, so instead I recommend you go fuck off before you destroy anything else in the path of your miserable existence." The man turned and walked back into the tavern, his pride destroyed.

Marduk shook his head, bearing the terrible taste. "Told you."

Set gave a sarcastic smart-ass smile, not wanting to admit he'd been right. "Whatever!" He took another sip—not like there was much choice. But his attention was distracted, and he glanced across the courtyard. "Well, well, well … rare to see a minotaur these days."

Marduk swallowed the foul drink and gazed over to see for himself. "And in the presence of two humans. That minotaur certainly doesn't look like the ones I use to fight. A pathetic example of one for sure. They *use* to be formidable."

"Mmm, yes ... they look like a bunch of drunken halfwits if you ask me ... which I know you didn't, honey buns, but you know I can't help but share my opinion, especially when it's accurate."

Marduk snorted. "I bet that cow doesn't even know how to swing that ax properly. Probably just carries it to terrify the humans into giving him whatever he wants."

Set laughed. "Yes, you're probably right. That slender one looks familiar, though."

Marduk tilted his head. "You fuck a new slave every night and you want me to believe you can remember a random-ass motherfucker who happens to be in the middle of nowhere?"

Set raised his eyebrows, smirking at whatever thought was running through his head as it bobbed from side to side. "You're right. Can't argue with that." A smile appeared, his perfect teeth shining. "That slave from two nights back, though, let me tell you!"

Marduk put his cup down and wiped his mouth. "Though I despise the assignment, I'd much rather go begin it than stay here listening to your stories of indulgence."

He watched as Set frowned sarcastically and snickered. "Such a downer."

Marduk walked off and found a small alleyway that led behind the tavern. He glanced around to ensure nobody was watching before he formed his magic portal and left.

Set had now found a new set of curves walking in the area and began daydreaming of all the delights he wanted to treat himself to. She passed in front of him, and though he desired to gaze upon her further, his vision refocused back to the travelers. *What an odd group of deplorables if ever I have seen some.* He watched the minotaur and

177

the gangly, frail man separate from the younger lad and disappear down the road. *A bunch of worthless specimens.* He figured they were mercenaries from a guild in the outer regions. *Two pathetic humans have found themselves a rare beast to befriend and now they prance around as if they are of some importance.*

The lad lingered in the area and looked around, taking in all the sights and sounds. He seemed inquisitive, and to be fair, he stood upright and moved with a sense of confidence that left the impression that he was aware of his own personal purpose in life. Maybe there was more to this human than there seemed at first glance. Set's attention was distracted again, though, when the woman returned to the area. "Darling, seriously, you don't have to play these games. I'll happily take you away from here and show you all the greatness that you're missing."

Liam noticed the man's accent. It was certainly not from the area, and it wasn't one he'd heard before. He was well dressed in his white and gray robes, with highlights of what appeared to be gold interlaced in the fabric. His attire was not like the stories of royalty he had heard before, which were all about large gold chains and jewels—this man had no crown or scepter. Yet he could have been called clean-cut. His complexion was without blemish, there was a shine to his pitch-black hair, and though Liam had no desire for men, he could at least admit that whoever this was, he certainly had charisma. Though he was loud and seemed to purposely draw attention to himself, Liam could feel the pull of his circle of influence. He remembered what it had been like in his old village among his fellow youths. Everyone had wanted to be like Jason or Tommy. They were the popular kids, and everyone admired them. This man had the same aura around him.

Liam watched him intently as he continued to flirt with the young woman. He knew nothing about either of them, but they certainly seemed out of place. He didn't blame him for flirting with the woman, though, because, analyzing her from the backside, he appreciated the view, and—

"Aye, chap! I'm talking to you!"

He bashfully realized that the man was calling to him and he had blanked out for a quick moment.

"Are you bloody deaf or just plain stupid?"

He cleared his throat. "I'm neither."

The man tilted his head at him with a raised eyebrow. "Are you sure? Because last time I checked, when someone asks you to fix yourself, you don't just stare off into vandy-land. Seems like you certainly have a problem, mate."

A voice calling "Sharra!" could be heard in the distance. "I must go!" The woman bowed slightly and brushed her hair away from her face, tucking it behind her ear.

"Darling, no, wait—seriously, you don't really have to go. You can just stay—"

"I'm sorry, I must go now!" The man reached out and grabbed her arm, trying to prevent her departure.

"But honey, I beg you!"

Liam grabbed the hilt of his sword and detached it enough for the grinding of the sharp metal to be heard. "Who is the one with the problem now?"

The woman reached over and undid Set's grip on her arm. "I'm sorry" was all she said before leaving in haste.

Set held his hands palms upward to show he was unarmed. There was a smile on his face but sarcasm in his voice. "Calm down there, merc ... I don't want to stain my clothes with my own blood from you having an itchy trigger finger, so to speak." He lowered his hands and grabbed his cup, shaking his head in irritation. "Besides, a country girl like that is not worth the trouble. But what's it to you? You been trying to slide into her barn doors for a while now?"

Liam resecured his sword. "Merc? Why would you call me that?"

"You're certainly not a soldier, and your outcast group of friends there certainly screams merc to anyone who's ever seen one before."

Liam frowned. "I'm sorry, sir, but I still don't understand. What exactly is a merc?"

"Oh, bloody hell! Merc … short for mercenary! One who fights in wars for the highest bidder … or should I say normally marches with the army and runs away scared when it appears that their side will lose."

"I apologize, sir. I didn't know mercenaries were also known as mercs." Liam was bashful now. Though the man had upset him with his behavior towards the young woman, he simply couldn't help the fact that his blend of sarcasm, good looks, and humor left him with the feeling that he didn't want to disappoint him. He tried to recover. "I realize I didn't introduce myself. I am Liam."

The man shifted his head with a snarky smile. "But of course you are!" He seemed to read Liam's body language, because he retreated before continuing. "All right, fine! Hello, Sir Liam. I am Set."

Shifting his weight from one foot to another, Liam said, "I'm not a sir …" He read the heavy stare and fast blinking of Set's eyes and it dawned on him. "Oh, that was also a joke."

Set adjusted his posture. "There's clearly not enough intoxication within me for this. Beer! Wine! Dragon's Breath! Sour Serpent! Whatever is your best, bring it to me!" He shook his head and wiped his hand across his face. "Right … well, clearly you are not from a city with a population of more than Mom and Dad."

Liam stood slightly straighter. "I'm from Artho."

Set didn't even look at him. "Never heard of it, so clearly my statement still stands."

"I'm not a mercenary, though! Let me be clear on that. I follow the path of a warrior and hope to one day obtain such prestige." He was proud of that answer.

"Really now! How adorable … I had no idea there was a path one could take. Travelers being brought to the end of the magical rainbow with an achievement of such a reward. I would assume this path is crowded these days during the nice weather. Well, be sure not to let the word get out, now. It will become overcrowded with all us 'common folk.'"

Liam couldn't help it; he rolled his eyes. "And what are you?"

"Now that is a question I haven't heard in a long time. What is it that I do?" He shifted his head back and forth and then smiled as if a clever thought had entered his mind. "I'm a businessman of the innermost depths of opportunity and desire." His smile seemed to gleam in the sun. "Too little will people tell you what they truly desire, but for me … it's within the whole truth that I find the opportunity to provide." Liam felt the man must be very attuned to his facial expressions, because he continued, "You say you want to be a warrior … well, young Liam, I can provide that to you if that is what you truly want."

Liam smirked in judgment, questioning whether the man could fulfill such an order. "You can provide that to me?"

Set squinted back at him. "Again, if that is what you truly want, then yes … I can make that happen."

Liam looked at Set again. "You have no sword. How many battles have you fought? Where do you prefer to train and in what style?"

Set waved his hand, stopping the myriad of questions. "I didn't say I would teach you to be a warrior; I said I can provide it to you." Liam watched as Set let out a long sigh and continued. "If that is what you truthfully desire, you can come with me and join my army. They have quite a busy schedule ahead of them, and you seem to be a potential candidate. I don't think you'll have any trouble with the process."

Liam felt his eyes grow wide. "You have an army?"

"Of course! I wouldn't be a good businessman if I didn't have one. Lots to make in the war business, young Liam. And let me tell you, business is quite good these days." Liam glanced down at the ground but was asked once again, "Well … it is time I left for my next endeavor. Would you like me to bring you to my military commander so you can start your process towards warriorhood?"

As Set asked the question, Liam lifted his head and caught a quick glimpse of Codgarak in the distance. The journey up to that point flashed through his mind, and though there was a part of him that shouted in excitement at the possibility of achieving his goal, there was also part of his soul that clung on to something … something within him. At the same time, his ring from Master DC seemed to emit a heat that called out to him physically. Though Set promised a path to achieve his desire, he couldn't see this opportunity being the answer, though the temptation was so sweet. He shook his head. "No, thank you."

Set slapped the table as he nearly bounced out of his seat. "No worries, young Liam. As I said, maybe it's not your true desire." He patted him on the shoulder as he left.

Liam reflected quickly on what he had said. "No … I know this is what I want," he told himself. Looking around, he tried to regain sight of Set, but to his surprise, he was gone already. He had only looked away for a few seconds; Set should have easily stood out, but sure enough, he was nowhere to be found.

Liam begrudgingly sat down at the table Set had been using. He poured the alcohol into one of the glasses and took a sip but instantly spat it out onto the ground and looked to see if anyone had noticed. The tavern owner came over. "How is everything?" The man was a bit sheepish after his scolding from Set, but he still tried to maintain his establishment.

"Oh, everything is fine. Do you have anything else besides the … drink?"

"Well … I do have some pear juice I could bring you."

"Yes!" Liam paused, concerned that the reply had come out almost as a panicked cry for help after the torment of the current option. "I mean, that would be fine, thank you." The fruit juice didn't take long to arrive and was a far better choice than whatever it was the owner tried to poison others with.

A sharp, high-pitched whistle sounded over the area. Liam turned to look out of curiosity, as did a few others. Golgoth was on the other side of the square and waving for him to go over to them. He got up from the table and dropped a few coins down for the beverage he'd enjoyed while reflecting and daydreaming as he awaited his companions return. Trotting over to Golgoth and Codgarak, he was greeted by Golgoth's slight smile.

"Himph! Himph … hmmmfff RRfff … " Golgoth's demeanor changed as he lurched forward, grabbed Liam's face, and leaned in uncomfortably close. "You've …" His eyes squinted and his face began to flare and flinch with whatever was affecting him. "You've come face to face with the enemy!"

Liam's eyes widened as the news took hold. "I … I didn't."

"Himph … rrrr … You are covered in the darkness of evil's energy … you cannot deny it."

"I didn't!" He reached up and peeled Golgoth's hand off his face. "There hasn't been any evil here. There was a businessman, the tavern owner, a man who tried to sell me some healing potion ..." Liam went on to list everyone he could recall that had interacted with him while he waited for them to return. "Seriously! I've been keeping watch over the town square this whole time. There's no enemy amongst us."

Golgoth turned his head from side to side like a hawk looking for its next victim to pounce on, except he was glaring at the town square and the villagers within it. Twisting his head back, he said, "It is best we leave, Codgarak. Whatever it was, it appears to have left, but I swear it ... evil has been here this day. Best to get to the others." Codgarak nodded and took the lead as they made their departure.

MARDUK

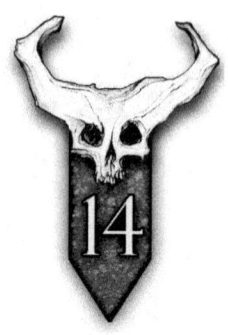

DEFENDER GRIFFIN

"Why must there always be stairs?" Liam complained to himself. They weren't as bad as the ones by the gargoyles, but still … too many stairs and no clear reason why they had to be here. Everywhere they went, there seemed to be mountains or trees or both. He had concluded the entire world must be covered in those two things; though he found great pleasure in sitting and gazing out on these aspects of nature, he couldn't care less at that exact moment. He was tired, hungry, and annoyed by the random high-pitched whines and noises that came from Golgoth. *"Himph!"*

He rolled his eyes. Golgoth was certainly unique in his own way. Mala was one who could never keep his mouth shut, Codgarak was one who rarely opened his, and Golgoth was a combination of the two; one moment he could be as quiet as the dead, the next moment he was wailing like a grief-stricken woman.

The two warriors were quite a way down the pathway, having found a small platform that gave a break from the intermittent stairs on the trail. Liam found a downed tree and sat upon it. Redirecting his mind, he focused on the ring given to him by Master DC. He mentally worked to create a link between his mind, his will, and the magic he felt was trapped within the ring. He could feel the connection take hold as the magic infused itself into his mental construct. He mentally practiced controlling it, intently focused in directing energy into it, then made it flow. He watched as the physical shape morphing back and forth between the ring and the bracelet shape he imagined it as.

As he continued the exercise in repetition, it became easier for his mind to manipulate the magic and control it. A spark of curiosity furrowed his brow as he attempted—and succeeded—to form a long metal nail. The confidence within him growing, he embarked on the formation of an arrow. As he imagined the shape and how it should be fashioned, his mind began to hear a high, piercing ringing. He fought it but felt a ripple tremble within his mind. The metallic nail began to take the shape of an arrowhead and then started to form its shaft, but as the rumbling within his mind grew, so did the vibration of the metal in the palm of his hand. Beads of sweat ran down his forehead and dripped off his face as he finally gave in to the resistance and quit his attempt. He panted from exhaustion, but a smile still spread across his face as he admired the arrow's incomplete form. It was already four inches long, and that was enough to keep his motivation going to continue his training.

Once he regained some stamina, he brought the arrow back to the form of a bracelet on his left wrist. As it finished its form, he grabbed it with his right hand and felt its edged, embossed scales. He was gratified by his new accomplishment and felt the texture of the bracelet; a cool mountain breeze swept over him, and everything seemed to be in harmony. He embraced the moment and felt peace within his spirit as his mind wandered back to Fort Patton. He relived the moment he had watched Master DC walking in front of his formation. Seeing her tailored armor and the garment that accentuated her tight, firm muscles and seemingly perfectly proportioned curves was all he needed to keep the cheesy smile on his face. He basked in the memory and enjoyed the … creative ways his imagination roamed as it deviated from the original moment.

"Liam …"

In his charmed state, he didn't hear the first call for him; the second, however … *"Liam!"*

He shook his head and broke free from the daydream. "Hah-huhh, wha …?" He looked down the pathway but didn't see anything, looking from side to side in confusion until he was hit on the back of the head by a tiny pebble. Snapping his head round to look up the pathway, he saw Golgoth at the top, waving him upward.

"Let's go!" He was unsure how long he had been zoned out, but there was certainly a new pep in his stride as he went bounding up the trail and, after a few short moments, caught up with Golgoth. "And what exactly has captured young Liam's mind this day?"

Not wanting to make eye contact with the strange new addition to the team, Liam said, "Oh, nothing particular."

"Himph! I see …" The devious smile broadened across Golgoth's face. *"Himph."*

To Liam's slight surprise, Codgarak had passed them and was no longer in view. He felt uneasy at being left alone with … Golgoth. Though he recognized the beast within Codgarak that could be unleashed at any moment, he felt a strong connection to the core of who the minotaur was. He trusted him, at least with his life and safety, for the time being. He respected and admired Master Fry, Master Jack, and Master DC. The hours of training and instruction, culminating in his final match with Codgarak at Thunder Rock. He had nothing but admiration towards them, and he still longed to have them accompanying the group on this campaign. He was still hesitant about Cashmes, the brother of Mala—"The apple doesn't fall far from the tree," as his mother used to say. Cashmes at least was far more pleasant than Mala and did stand up for Liam. "I guess I can give him a chance."

"What was that?" Golgoth piped up. "You said something? I couldn't quite hear it."

Liam was startled, not realizing that his thoughts had actually slipped out in a whisper. "Oh, nothing of value. I was talking to myself, and it must have slipped out." He tried to recover but made sure his thoughts of *Way to go, Liam! Now the crazy one thinks you're crazy!* did not slip out this time.

Golgoth just smiled. "Don't worry, young Liam. I talk to myself too! *Himph.*"

I bet you do, Liam said in his head, double checking to make sure his mouth remained shut.

The pathway finally crested the ridge and he could see it led to what appeared to be an enclosed shrine set upon a mountainside balcony. As they drew closer, he noticed the right-hand side merged into a solid sheet of granite, forming a wall alongside the path. The closer they got to the rock archway, the higher the granite climbed, a supporting wall which held back the mountain itself. The top of the archway had a carving of a demon skull upon it.

Liam slowed his pace; he could hear a collection of voices. They were soft, gentle, but deep in their bellowing cries as they sang a song in a language he didn't know. The melody left the impression that they were sorrowful, meaningful in intent, and the lyrics were about a lineage of honor.

He hesitated as he was about to enter, though; he realized that Golgoth was standing behind him, not saying a word. As he surveyed his expression, he couldn't help but see the thousand-yard stare in Golgoth's eyes again. A severity towards the homage of the shrine before them. "Are you okay?" he asked him.

At first, Golgoth didn't look at him. "I have known of this place for many years. I am unworthy to enter such a hall." He was steadfast and unwavering in his answer, but Liam did notice that he had clenched his fists, as if he were trying to conjure strength from his physical body and transfer the strength to his spirit.

Liam looked past the archway and listened to the chorus being sung. "Master Jack told me before I left Fort Patton"—he turned his head and looked at Golgoth—"to focus more on how I live my life than on how my life will end."

The pause lasted for a few seconds, but those seconds felt more like weeks, months, and years within Golgoth's mind as Liam noticed the slight gathering of tears in Golgoth's left eye. A single streak ran down his cheek. "I know that all too well, young Liam. *Himph.*" A slight smile crossed his face as he pressed his lips together, trying to regain his composure. "The life I have lived ... it cannot compare to those who have come before me and to whom this shrine is dedicated." A fresh tear falling down his face.

"That may be ... but is it not a fact that part of living a good life is coming to know and accept the fact that we have not done so? And also how we choose to honor those who have gone before us by remembering their example and working to live a better life with each day we have been given?"

Liam watched as Golgoth's vision seemed to hold the thousand-yard stare even though they were looking straight at each other. Another tear ran down his face for a moment before he blinked and appeared to return to the moment they shared. He lifted his arm and wiped the tear from his face. "*Himph.* I believe you are right, young Liam." He turned and looked into the shrine. "You have helped me realize I should have done this long ago."

Golgoth slowly took his first steps towards the shrine. The room appeared dark at first, but there was actually significant light inside. Immediately to the right inside the entrance was a massive stone griffin that had been carved out of the mountainside. The statue stood three times larger than Codgarak, who was kneeling in front of it, his head bowed in reverence, his right claw upon the left claw of the statue. The statue's right claw was raised in an aggressive manner, as if it was warning that it was ready to strike and engage in battle. The wings of the griffin were flared outward but wrapped around in the middle and curved forwards at the ends—the defender who shielded all those under its watch from the hell attempting to rain down upon the weak. Though the head of the griffin was slightly tilted down, it portrayed ferocity, strength, and the will to defend those it protected to the death.

Liam heard Codgarak whispering some words and dared not interrupt. Looking to the left, he saw that there were thirteen swords arranged in a circle. The hilts of the swords were facing up, and a warrior's battle helmet sat upon them. A medallion dangled down, suspended in front of the sword's blade, and metallic wings identical to the griffin's were behind each display. Below each of the displays was a circular cutout in the mountain where people could sit facing inward towards one another, and the swords would always be visible, watching over each guest from behind them, the griffin as the focal point at the front of the room.

High up on the walls were lantern cut-outs, but there appeared to be magical flames illuminating the great room, because Liam couldn't see the actual source of the light.

Liam leaned over to Golgoth. "What is the meaning of the swords, helmets, and wings?"

Golgoth's thousand-yard stare had returned, but he leaned over and quietly replied, "They are known as combat crosses—an honor which is only given to a warrior we have lost in battle." There was a slight pause before he continued. "Go … read their names and spend time amongst them." Liam felt Golgoth's hand softly land upon his back and, though he didn't force him, this compelled him to do as Golgoth instructed.

He walked over to the first combat cross, read the name, clasped the medallion in his hand, and said a prayer. He hoped that the

Ancient One was listening, that the person's family or descendants would somehow know that at that moment their loved one was being thought of, their name not lost to time. One by one he went to each cross and softly spoke their names to himself.

"Defender Elizabeth, of house Jacobson. Killed by explosion while on combat patrol."

"Defender Jason, of house Norton. Killed by explosion while on combat patrol."

"Defender Brian, of house McElroy. Killed by explosion while on combat patrol."

"Defender Leebernard, of house Chavis. Killed by archer while defending a post."

"Defender John, of house Self. Killed by explosion while on combat patrol."

"Defender Jason, of house Nathan. Killed by explosion while on combat patrol."

"Defender Joseph, of house Helton. Killed by explosion while on combat patrol."

"Defender Nicholas, of house Alden. Killed by rogue attack."

"Defender Todd, of house Lobraico. Killed by archer while on combat patrol."

"Defender Nathan, of house Sartain. Killed in convoy accident."

"Defender Kcey, of house Ruiz. Killed in convoy accident."

"Defender Joseph, of house Lemm. Killed by explosion while on combat patrol."

"Defender Louis, of house Bonacasa. Killed by explosion while on combat patrol."

By the time he had gone around the chamber, Codgarak had returned to his feet and taken a seat within the circle. Liam looked at the griffin statue and approached it. A fourteenth combat cross was set directly in front of the statue.

"Defender Travis, of house Griffin. Killed by explosion while on combat patrol."

He turned to see Codgarak looking at him. He had noticed a small puddle at the base of the combat cross, which he assumed was caused by the tears shed by the warrior when he knelt in front of the statue and said his prayer.

The low voice of the minotaur proclaimed, "Heroes will be remembered for what they did; legends are remembered for who they were." Looking back at Codgarak, Liam saw him lift his head to look at the statue. "We speak their name, share their story, and carry their light within us for the remainder of our days." He then looked Liam directly in the eyes. "They are legends, and we will never let them be lost to time."

Liam shifted his weight and let Codgarak's words resonate within him. The bellowing song of the choir echoed within the chamber walls: calm, peaceful, melodic vocals. The clouds must have passed overhead, for there was enough light for him to notice that the domed roof was studded with royal blue and golden yellow gems. He watched as colored light shone down in beams that rested upon the combat crosses. The helmets, swords, and wings glistened with vibrance and beauty.

"So you are Defender Codgarak, then?" he asked in curiosity.

"No."

Liam waited a while, thinking this was just a pause, but … nope. "And why is that?" he asked, searching for more information.

"For a long time, we all called ourselves defenders. Defenders of our realm, defenders of our people, defenders of the weak. For when evil came to our door, we were the ones who chose to stand up and stop it." Codgarak turned and nodded towards the two set of combat crosses to his left. "When Defenders Lemm and Bonacasa departed this world, we laid them in the Valley of Haivan. We then chose not to be defenders anymore. We are now hunters. We hunt the evil that preys on the weak, we hunt the darkness that forever tries to extinguish light, we hunt the wicked and bring justice upon them, we hunt the vile and provide punishment for their actions. We are the Hunters of Demons."

Liam lowered his head and walked over to the carved bench. Sitting down, he let the serenity of the room saturate his spirit and soul. The gravity of what the room represented made him feel small and insignificant in comparison to these warriors who had sacrificed their lives for others. He was humbled and asked himself, *How could anyone ever equal these men and women?*

As he let the question settle within his mind, he saw Golgoth approach him and lean over. "If you let fear conquer you, you'll be defeated before the first arrow is launched, but if you conquer your fear, you'll triumph over the evil standing before you. *Himph.*"

He smiled and nodded in appreciation of this wisdom. Golgoth lingered nearby as they heard footsteps approaching the shrine entrance. Liam was surprised to see a honey badger walk in through the entrance. The honey badger wore light armor and a necklace with extremely large fangs dangling from it. He carried two hand axes strapped onto his back.

"Cod! My old friend!" He dropped down on all fours and scrambled over to Codgarak, who was still sitting down; he jumped up and twisted his body in midair, landing perfectly in a sitting position next to the minotaur. His tiny size made the two look almost humorous next to each other.

"Agos! How have you been?" Codgarak asked as he looked his friend over.

"I've been busy. Many things appear to be happening, and I've done my best to patrol the dark forest areas to see if there is a rebirth of old evils there. But so far, nothing."

"I had the same questions but found the same results as well." A new voice entered the room, but they couldn't see where or who it came from. The scanned the room, and then they saw her as she slowly made her way from behind the griffin statue. "I've been doing my best to track Aibek's trail, and I believe I have isolated it down to one area, but I can't be sure."

The wolf humanoid made her way forward. Her coat was gray with silver highlights. She had long hair that was tucked behind her wolf ears; her arms and chest were those of a human, but her slender body tapered to the lower half of a wolf. Her hands were both human and paw and clawish; a kind of mutated form. She was attractive and mysterious—a wolf that could rip your heart out or spend a wild night howling.

"I assume you are Lythya, sister of Aibek," Codgarak said. She nodded in response.

Nothing else was said for the moment. Lythya paced back and forth, assessing the others. Agos and Codgarak were whispering to each other, and Golgoth and Liam just … sat there. Liam was wondering exactly how Lythya had gotten behind the statue. Was there another entrance? A hidden entrance? Had she been there the whole time? Did she teleport in? So many questions that he—

An orange portal began to form in the middle of the room. It grew larger than the ones Liam had seen so far, and as it did so, a black leopard humanoid stepped out of it. Behind her was Cashmes. Immediately after Cashmes came a large white lion almost identical in stature, and if Cashmes was here, that must mean …

Walking through last came Mala. The portal closed, and as the four big cats looked around the room, Mala met Liam's gaze and declared, "Oh, how lovely. I see the cunt fairy has blessed us with her presence once again!"

Liam wasn't about to have any of it. "I'll never forget the first time we met, but trust me, I certainly do try to."

Mala whipped his tail back and forth as he placed his hand on his hip. "Shock me, please—say something intelligent."

Liam struggled to find a good insult to hit him back with, then he remembered one that he had overheard in Fort Patton. It was the only thing he could come up with on the spot. "There is no 'I' in team, but there is a 'U' in suck!"

Mala shook his head in what looked like disappointment. "Stupidity is not a crime, young Liam … therefore you are free to go, but I must insist that you do not return."

Damn it! That was a better one than his. He searched frantically, trying to think of any insult that was better than the last. "If I wanted to hear from an asshole, I would simply fart."

As soon as the words had left his mouth, he realized that these sounded like the insults they'd used as kids. *What the hell, Liam? You can do better than this!* he chastised himself.

The other big cats had started to make their way over to sit down, but Mala continued with the engagement. "You are proof that evolution can go in reverse. Here I stand, a symbol of excellence, and there you sit, a mere pile of shit."

"You know what? People clap when they see you—clap their hands over their eyes, that is." Liam didn't think this was a suitable insult, but he wasn't going to let Mala get the last word.

Mala snorted slightly before he responded. "I don't know exactly what the cause of your problems is, but I'm sure that whatever it is, it must be hard to pronounce."

The older white lion who had entered through the portal with the other cats had taken a seat next to Codgarak, but he finally interrupted the exchange. "Enough!" Mala looked over at him with his hands out in front of him like a child attempting to proclaim his innocence. "Stop being rude."

Mala took advantage of one final jab. "I'm not being rude, he's just insignifi*cunt*!" The tiger's giant smile appeared again as he slowly turned towards Liam to show him his bare teeth.

"Mala!" The tiger released his smile and walked over to take a seat on the opposite side of the room from Codgarak.

Golgoth leaned over again to Liam. "It may be wise in the future not to exchange words with the big cat." There was a smirk and a squint on Golgoth's face, but Liam just rolled his eyes. "You certainly got your ass handed to you. *Himph! Himph!*" Dark laughter could be heard within Golgoth as he tried to contain it. He tapped Liam's shoulder, and he appreciated it, feeling as if this was just another part of slowly growing stronger mentally as a fighter. He thought back to Fort Patton. *If you can't handle an insult, joke, or criticism, how are you supposed to handle warfare?*

The room settled as everyone scanned each other. Codgarak finally broke the silence. "It is hard to believe, but this is the first time we have all come together. We live by our creed and have all been scattered across this world, hunting, yet it has taken the birth of darkness and the vanishing of one of our members to bring us together. How we have failed one another up to this point."

"Oh, Cod, you are always too hard on yourself, my dear friend. This will all be over soon, and we'll go back to normal," Mala said.

The older white lion sitting next to Codgarak said, "No, the minotaur is right. We have failed one another, and it should not have gotten to this point for us to come together in fellowship. There used to be so many of us, and now look at what few remain."

Each of them reflected on the significance of the lion's wisdom before he continued. "I am Dhather, the eldest brother to Cashmes, Mala, and Edha. It was through Aibek that we chose to become hunters."

Lythya dropped down from the ledge on which the griffin rested while it towered over the room. "I am Lythya, sister of Aibek. My brother and I have been hunters for many years now and utilize our abilities to help preserve the earth and prevent evil from corrupting it any further than it already has. My brother told me he could feel the darkness seep into the earth and dance upon the wind. He told me if I didn't hear from him, to come here, and that eventually he or others would arrive. He mentioned a tiger or a minotaur would more than likely be the two I would see, and here you both are."

Mala stood up from his bench and performed a curtsey. "You're welcome." He sat back down.

The black leopard raised her hand. "Edha."

Cashmes stood up. "Cashmes, the older brother to the always inappropriate Mala, and I apologize now for anything he does in the near future. I can assure you he will offend you at some point."

Cashmes didn't look at Mala, but Liam glanced over and saw Mala quickly glance towards his older brother. "Piss off!"

A slight chuckle came over Golgoth. "*Himph.* I foresee us becoming good friends." That comment left Liam grinding his teeth. It was bad enough having a crazed lunatic next to him and an asshole who wouldn't leave him alone, but those two becoming friends … he knew no good would come of that.

"Agos. My good friend Codgarak and I have been in many battles together over the years, and when he told me of what this group stood for, I knew I had to be a part of it. It is my honor to stand with such fellow warriors."

Mala chimed in once again from across the room. "Thank you, fair badger! It is always nice to find someone else who recognizes and admires like-minded spirits." Cashmes turned his head and whatever the look was that he gave Mala caused a response. "What? That was a compliment!" A low growl could be heard, which Liam assumed was coming from Cashmes. "Again, piss off!" was Mala's follow-up.

The slender frame stood up. "*Himph.* I am Golgoth … it was many years ago that Aibek, Codgarak, and Judah of Artho saved me from the evil I served. I am certainly not worthy of being a hunter, for I was once one of those you hunted. Today I stand here, ready to fight alongside you all, to hunt this evil that has entered the land and taken some type of action against our beloved Aibek."

"So you're Golgoth …" Edha squinted and her face flickered with emotion. Her eyes said that she would have liked to immediately take aggressive action against Golgoth.

Cashmes followed in verbal pursuit. "Tell us now why we shouldn't kill you where you stand!" Edha stood and began to pace slowly towards the center of the room as Cashmes also stood, directing his stance towards Golgoth. The lion not taking his eyes off Golgoth.

"I have heard your name spoken before. It was always that of a man who thought of himself as a demon, and his every action was of such towards all he came in contact with." Edha brought her hands down, interlaced her fingers in the grips, and pulled forward, retrieving two trench knives, ready to engage in combat. The knives were each a foot long, with tanto blades and skull-crusher pommels.

"I assure you that I do not wish to fight any of you, but even some heroes are seen as villians. *Himph! Himph.* But … if you wish to see what a demon fights like …" Golgoth reached into the backpack that he had carried on their journey and retrieved the demon skull he had worn when he'd met Liam. Holding it in his hands, he looked down at the skull and then turned his gaze towards Edha. His eyes burst with a blood-orange glow and he began to lift the skull as if to wear it as a helmet, but Codgarak interrupted the turmoil.

"Enough!"

The minotaur stood and made his way to the center of the room. He stood next to Edha and peered down at her as she looked up and hissed, showing her teeth as she returned her knives to their scabbards.

"Who amongst us is perfect?" Codgarak demanded. Mala raised his hand. Dhather had finally had enough, and all Liam saw was a ball of energetic light flying across his field of view from left to right. He glanced over and saw that the energy had wrapped itself around Mala, who was now bound by cables of yellow light. He could see Mala was trying to speak, but though his mouth was moving, not a peep could be heard. *Can we just keep him like that?* he thought. At the same time, Golgoth lowered the demon skull and returned his eyes to their normal appearance.

Codgarak continued. "We have all done some wrong in our lives. We have all failed. We have all fallen short of living a good life. We are the bastards that society despises. We are the ones who are looked down upon by the elite, by the scholars, by the self-proclaimed righteous. Yet who do they call when the terrors grab hold of them in the night? Who do they cry to when their hope is lost? Who do they plead to, that they may be saved from the destruction about to befall them?"

He took a brief pause and looked at each one of them. "We are the few—the few who chose to devote ourselves to the fight against evil, and though we all have a past we may not be proud of, we have devoted ourselves to a future that so many know nothing about or have the strength and courage to walk towards. I can only wish that, of everything I have done in my past, my future actions weigh heavier than the words I have spoken, and that the Ancient One may accept my minuscule sacrifice as a worthy enough offering to grant me the blessings awaiting those in the Valley of Haivan."

Taking another brief pause, he turned and looked at the griffin statue. "I can only hope that I will be there someday. I will blaze my own pathway if only I have the strength to continue to go the distance That I not cower in the face of evil; I will fight fire with fire, and should I be defeated, I ask that each of you avenge me." He turned back towards the group. "We are hunters. We don't stop until we have vanquished evil in this world."

Codgarak let out a long breath and made his way back to his seat. With the quiet in the room, Liam felt it was his time. He took a breath, and just as he was about to proclaim who he was, a hand wrapped around his mouth and muffled his voice. Golgoth whispered in his ear, "Not now. *Himph* …" Golgoth turned and looked at Mala, still bound and steaming in anger, before he turned back to Liam. "I believe Mala would say something like 'Shut your cunt.' *Himph!* Trust me, tis best to let the beast have the last word." He let go of Liam's mouth, and though Liam was furious, he did as the deranged wayward drifter had suggested.

Lythya brought the moment back to where it should have been. "And what are we going to do about my brother?"

Agos said, "Clearly we must act. Whether I know him or not, hunters will not abandon another hunter."

Lythya continued. "I last felt him near the Forest of Stonevor, but his energy seemed to fade from me as if it were being choked, and then it left me altogether."

Dhather followed suit. "I felt the same as you. It appeared to me that Aibek was surrounded by a darkness, and I believe it has taken him captive."

Cashmes looked over at Mala, who was blazing red in fury, waiting to be released from his magical bindings. He turned back and addressed the group. "As my brother would say, 'Let us not waste the day when victory awaits.' As we know, whatever magical influence or interference is taking place, it is not consistent, and there are gaps in it. I believe if we channel our energy together, we may be able to open a portal close to Aibek's last-known presence in Stonevor, and we will all go together."

"Would that work?" Lythya asked. Cashmes turned towards Dhather. He respected his elder and recognized his wisdom in such things.

Dhather answered, "I don't see why it shouldn't work, and it is certainly worth an attempt."

"Then what are we waiting for? Let's do it!" Lythya said emphatically.

"Agreed—let's face this evil head on!" Agos stated. He stood and started to ready his gear and armor.

Codgarak chuckled. "The honey badger—always ready to take action." He stood as well, and the rest followed suit, standing and readying themselves, except for Mala. That was until Cashmes looked over and nodded to Dhather.

"Though I don't mind him like this and quite frankly prefer it, we're going to need him."

Dhather looked over at Mala, whose head was tilted in judgment upon all of them. "I agree … on both points." Dhather moved his hand in a pattern and the magical energy evaporated from around Mala; his voice returned as he cleared his throat. He was about to make a statement but was cut off by Dhather. "Don't. Don't make me regret releasing you."

Codgarak made his way over to Mala and placed his massive claw on the warrior's stout shoulder. "My friend, we need you now. Your ability to isolate portals accurately is the best."

Mala shrugged it off. "Don't worry, dear Cod. I already know." He walked to the center of the room. He began shrugging his shoulders and stretching as if loosening up in preparation, looking back at the group. "Let's go form up. Codgarak, take the center. Dhather and Lythya, behind me. Cashmes, Golgoth on the right side. Agos … why don't you stand in front of Cod? Not like he won't be able to see over you." Mala gave a slight chuckle, but Agos didn't take offense. It wasn't like he hadn't heard that joke before.

"And what about me?" Liam asked.

Mala didn't even look at him. "Did someone say something? Hmm! Must have just been the wind." *Asshole!* Liam thought, but Golgoth waved him over and motioned for Liam to stand behind him.

Mala turned his head slightly to his left to look at Dhather. "All right, dearest brother, whenever your geriatric bones are ready."

Dhather and Lythya began to chant incantations under their breathe, their arms moving left and right in front of them. Their hands formed shapes as if they were grabbing something in the air, turning right in a circular motion and continuing down. Teal blue light waves began to form, with light spreading from the main beam like snow slithering across frozen ground. Lythya's light was a dark burgundy, but her circular patterns looked like twisting tree branches and vines interwoven with each other. It was a very coarse pattern compared to Dhather's, which was smooth and sharp-edged.

When the circles had taken their full shape, Lythya stated, "Uhay mu." Though Dhather didn't say anything, both his and Lythya's gestures sent their colored light towards Mala—Lythya's red to his right hand and Dhather's teal to his left hand. Liam saw Mala take the magical energy in his grip and convert the light into a blazing bright orange. The portal he'd previously seen form on the ground was instead suspended in front of Codgarak. The burning lines formed their patterned design as the circle took shape. Once the circumference was complete, a shockwave pulsed out into the room. An internal shockwave, inside the portal, shot in the opposite direction, towards the location they were trying to isolate.

"I can feel a dark resistance, but we should be—" Mala didn't have a chance to finish his sentence. Two flaming claws from the other side of the portal grabbed the edge of the circle. A new shockwave burst out and a tearing sound could be heard as the claws forced the portal to open even wider.

Two flaming horns appeared first but were immediately followed by two blazing red eyes with fire dancing off them. A quick roar was heard before a cannon of flame shot out. It just missed Agos's head and flew directly over him. Codgarak took the full force of the blast, and the minotaur was launched back, crashing against the wall.

Liam didn't have any time to assess Codgarak's condition, for as soon as the flame was launched, laughing screams were mixed with the sound of the blast and gnolls came pouring through the portal as if a dam had ruptured and nothing could stop the flood. The flame had temporarily blinded Agos, and he hadn't yet recovered enough to see one of the first gnolls approach him and knock him to the ground.

Mala let go of his attempt to control the portal and called out, "What a fun way to start the day!" Though Liam hesitated, not knowing what to do, the others immediately began to take action, launching themselves into the chaos of battle. Their hardened spirits did not flinch at the threat. Liam had no time to admire their experience but leapt into the fight, attempting to prove his worth amongst legends.

Dhather let go of his first casting and conjured two swords of pure magic in his hands. The swords burned with teal flames as he began flaying the gnolls approaching him. Lythya began to leap from one side to another and spear gnolls one by one, protecting Dhather and Mala from the unseen gnolls trying to encircle them. Though they had never been in combat together before, the expert proficiency of each warrior showed in the precise execution of their movements. Lythya's and Agos's techniques complemented the fighting styles of the big cats.

Almost no words were spoken throughout the entire engagement except by Agos—at least, Liam heard through the chaos filling the shrine, "I will not accept defeat!" Though the honey badger was the smallest of them, all he saw was charging ahead as his courage was clearly larger than his stature, slashing his way through gnoll after gnoll. Along the way he yelled, "The ifrit is mine!" As he stormed towards it, the ifrit continued to make its way through the portal while countless gnolls surged into the room.

Cashmes and Golgoth were both engaged in battle as Liam held his gladius swords tightly in both hands. "Let's go!" he yelled, motivating himself. These were not gargoyles but creepily laughing and highly agile doglike monsters. He slashed and moved with purpose, working with his instilled techniques. His confidence was slowly growing, but at the same time he realized how much mental focus was required. Nothing else mattered at that moment— he didn't think about magical energy, only about whether his foot placement was accurate for his stance. He noticed the unique things that his senses narrowed in on. His outer vision became a blur, and as gnolls came in and out of his immediate area, he could see the saliva falling from their snouts; he could feel the warmth of their breath when they tried to bite his face; he could smell wet dog hair mixed with dirty water—all the weird sensations that his senses picked up on as he tried to survive his first true battle.

He slashed the closest gnoll in front of him, took a quick breath and tried to find his next target, taking in the sight of a gnoll flying across the room right into the fire spirit that had now made its way through the portal. Not even a second later, another gnoll went flying, landing another powerful blow on it.

He watched as the beast within Codgarak had awaken. The minotaur marching forcefully towards the front of the room, purple electrical energy sparking all around his ax blade. He grabbed the closest gnoll and hurled it like a projectile towards the spirit. The minotaur had a slightly charred appearance and what looked like smoke rose from him, but he was unfazed in his pace towards the ifrit.

Liam was able to snatch a quick glance at Mala before looking back at Codgarak's march forward. As the giant cat came into view, he noticed that Mala had one hand on his hip and was standing in a casual pose and actually yawning! *What the?!* he thought until a gnoll paw came slashing across his face, ripping open three fresh tears across his cheek. That was all it took for him to wake up, and everything came into focus around him in crystal-clear definition. He spun around and executed a perfect double slash technique, which chopped into the rib cage and back strap of the grotesque mutated dog.

The combat raged all around the room, gnoll bodies stacking up and making movement harder. Amidst the chaos, Lythya came in with a clutch, saving Liam more than once by spearing gnolls in his blind spot as he actively worked to slay the others around him. The musical chorus playing in the background, though melodic, brought with it an elemental feeling of being connected to a greater spiritual entity. Such a place was being protected by a celestial force, and no matter what happened, it would not allow them to be defeated.

Liam was finally able to feel like he'd found peace within the chaos, allowing the different sensations to work in harmony. He began to adjust to the feeling of time slowing down while his eyes and ears took in all the threats and sounds, processed each one, deciphered which was the greatest threat to him, and ignored the rest. This was the natural, rhythmic flow of animalistic survival that Master Fry had taught him about, but he had also told him that he wouldn't truly understand the principle until he was immersed in his first battle and the real sensation of danger overwhelmed him.

As the battle began to quieten down, he realized that the portal that had been ripped open and captured by the ifrit was now gone. He hadn't seen it happen, but Mala had regained control and destroyed it, giving them the ability to finish off the wave of gnolls without allowing the fire spirit to escape. The few remaining gnolls began to circle around together, realizing their fate was literally and figuratively sealed, with no chance of survival.

The ifrit had collapsed on the ground, laboring to maintain its breathing. Codgarak backhanded the fire spirit's face, which turned its body, allowing it to lean against the rock base of the griffin statue. The flames that had blazed from its body were all but snuffed out. The gnolls started to chirp and yelp even louder, provoking an interruption from Codgarak: "Stop wasting time and finish them off!" Cashmes, Edha, Golgoth, and Lythya quickly fulfilled the request.

Not a single person wasn't covered in blood. Liam looked around the room and noticed the hundreds of gnoll bodies strewn around. Adrenaline was rushing through his veins, the greatest feeling he had ever experienced. Death had approached him for the first time that day, and staring it in the face, fighting back with everything he had, had left him feeling more alive than ever before. His heightened senses made him see things in sharper contrast, hear in more precise detail, his touch processing the finer details of the textures woven into the very fabric of life. The euphoric high of this new sensation was short-lived, though. As soon as the danger was gone, his sympathetic nervous system began to release its hold on his body, and with that came the crash as the physical and psychological exhaustion, which had been suppressed by his nervous system, now opened the flood gates and began to overwhelm him.

Though he had no desire to sleep, no matter what he did to fight the sensation, his body pushed him towards it. His vision started to blacken and his breathing became heavy. A hand grabbed him from behind, bracing and supporting him as his body started to slump. His vision was blurry, but he could tell it was Dhather.

"Drink this." A small vial appeared and he grabbed it. A dark green liquid containing tiny bright blue balls swirled within it. He squinted at it and brought it closer to his nose to smell it; he picked up some fruity and earth-like tones but nothing too significant. The lion nodded at him, and with his energy depleted, he thought *What the hell. Can't make things worse.* He lifted the vial to his mouth and let the solution dance on his taste buds. The flavor burst with sweetness, yet it had a slight spicy bite. He swallowed it in delight, and Dhather shook him slightly, as if the jarring of the body would splash the solution around inside him and make it take effect quicker.

It was only a few seconds later that he felt as if his body was reawakening. The blackened fading of his vision slowly tapered back, and his senses were grounded back in the current situation. "Wow, that sure changes things," he said, looking up at Dhather.

"You'll struggle for the next few battles you endure, but soon you'll strengthen your ability to resist sleep. As your body's adrenaline slowly dissipates after a battle, you'll have to strengthen your will to resist the exhaustion."

The lion was intimidating, though Liam was able to accept the ferocity that dwelled within these warriors and appreciate the meekness they also displayed. They had the power to hurl enemies across a vast room but the tenderness to lift him gently from the ground. "You've done well today."

He looked at Dhather, a slight smile on his face at the compliment. "Thanks." He gazed around the room and added, "To be honest … it seems like a blur to me … the whole thing."

A gracious smile formed on the lion's face. "Don't worry. Though your memory may be a blur, you'll be reexperiencing it soon enough."

He didn't have a chance to ask Dhather to explain in more detail as Mala walked over to Codgarak. He couldn't hear the words that were said, but he watched Mala point to one side. Codgarak walked over to where Mala had pointed. Kneeling, he retrieved Agos's lifeless body. He held the badger in his hands, lifting his head. "Golgoth."

The slender man was crouched down on the far side of the room. "Yes, Codgarak?" The minotaur looked over at Golgoth and then turned and nodded towards the ifrit. "*Himph!* With pleasure …" Golgoth slowly stood and turned, retrieving the demon skull from his pack. Liam watched. A smile was on Golgoth's face; as he grabbed the skull, he looked down at it, the smile broadening even more. *"Himph! Himph … hahaha."* His eyes erupted with burnt orange flames. Placing the skull on his head like a helmet, he turned and began moving towards the spirit.

Everyone watched in anticipation, looks of judgment on their faces as they intently analyzed every move, word, and gesture Golgoth made. He stood over the spirit as it clung on to what little life it had, taking gasps of air in between its words. "There is nothing you can do to me … this physical realm … is but a vessel for your pathetic games … for I am but a visitor … and will return to my home once again … amongst the spirits that dwell there."

"Himph! Himph! HAHAHA! Himph!" The deranged mind of Golgoth received the words excitedly, his body animated with joy as the flames in his eyes flashed brighter. "I'd like to welcome you to my nightmare … *himph!* I hope you enjoy the monster which awaits inside it! *Himph! HAHAHA."* He put his hands out, his fingers in a clawed shape as magic began to spiral around them, "SKOL ROK TERMORQ!"

A black wave of energy flowed out of the ifrit's body and was absorbed by Golgoth's left hand. A tormented scream rang out and echoed within the shrine. The horror of its cries reverberated off the walls, mixing with the serene chorus that still subtly enveloped the room. Golgoth's right hand twisted and a multilayered portal opened. Liam was amazed, for the portal appeared to tear open a gateway through four separate planes of existence.

Golgoth released the darkness from his right hand and forced it through the portal into the final plane. Liam had to strain to see anything, but the slightly glimmering pieces he could see reminded him of a starry night, but with a vast array of colors and mist strewn across the vista.

Suddenly, Golgoth lurched forward. Something from within the fourth plane had taken hold of the ifrit's spirit and was pulling it with a force that Golgoth had to resist. The screams intensified and a sharp ringing entered Liam's ears. Without warning, a shockwave and thunderclap exploded, the black energetic light stopped coming forth from the ifrit, and the gateway slammed shut.

The room seemed as if it was silent, as the transition was so quick and the ringing in Liam's ears so loud that he could no longer hear the choir's song. A few seconds passed before Golgoth continued. "CITI-BAK!" An eruption of fire came over the ifrit's body and its physical form evaporated in the blazing flames, and then it was gone. A few sparks of charred flesh danced above it for a second or two, and with that, it was over.

Liam watched as Codgarak carried Agos's body over and placed it at the foot of the statue and the combat cross. "The honey badger is the most fearless in all life, and you have proved that once again, my dear friend."

DEFENDER GRIFFIN

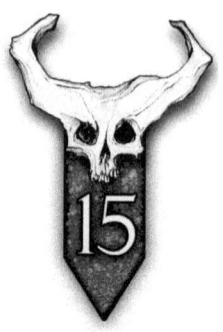

CONTINUE FORWARD

The ceremony was over. The body of Agos was buried within the shrine in the same fashion as Codgarak's family. The other warriors were upset that he could not be taken to the Valley of Haivan, where he should really be—where he belonged. Yet the shrine dedicated to their fellow warriors was a place of honor as well. They found peace in knowing that his soul was now amongst them within the Valley of Haivan.

Mala and a few of the others tried many times to form a portal and make another attempt to reach Aibek. Nothing worked. Even when they attempted to channel their magic and combine it—nothing. The feeling in the room was the same; everyone wanted to tackle this evil head-on. Bitter and enraged that their shrine was desecrated with such an attack. Golgoth shared with the group what he had learned from the ifrit's spirit, which he had consumed before sending it into the other plane. It was Odra, who had a twin known as Odry. Both fire spirits were typically summoned by an "Azazel" to protect an area and await further orders. There was a vision of Aibek within Odra's memories. Aibek was sitting cross-legged inside a prison cell with runes glowing around the room. Before the memories faded, Golgoth saw the crest above the main gate of the stone keep from which Odra had come forth before he'd taken over the portal. It was a shield with three swords upon its face.

The group finally decided it was best to begin their journey, and they would stop at Jerikako, which was the closest kingdom to where Aibek's energy had gone missing.

"Let us continue our hunt," Cashmes said as he led from the front of the line, and they all marched out of the shrine and down the path leading to Jerikako. Lythya and Edha worked together and often went off to scout further ahead. Lythya had amazing scent detection capabilities through her wolf lineage, and Edha would climb high into the tree tops and utilize her enhanced vision to scan the area. The two were a good and successful pairing.

Mala, Golgoth, and Codgarak were the next in formation. They moved at their own pace. Every so often a devious laugh would come from Golgoth or Mala. Liam's thoughts went in all different directions, imagining the vile and rude banter between them. He had no way of hearing them, but he certainly judged them without evidence or context regarding their conversation. There was a slight tension in the group towards Golgoth, though. No one truly trusted him yet. Well, except Codgarak, and still no one knew why that was. Though Liam had stood behind him at the portal and fought alongside him, he still felt a cringe crawling up his spine and a knot in his stomach whenever he got close.

Odra's memories had informed them that the ifrit had been brought to the location by this Azazel. It was this insight which led them to believe he was the one responsible for the scene of Aibek being held in his captivity. A captured warrior could be an easy bargaining chip, or perhaps there was some other dark intentions in Aibek's future. It was anyone's guess, but onward they went.

The trail took them up and down the ridges of the mountains. As the deep forest receded behind them, the countryside gave way to a lush green valley. The bright green contrasted with the black sandstone rock formations and made a beautiful view under the rolling white clouds against the blue sky. The valleys sloped away from the rocks, giving them the jagged appearance of what could be thought of as the ancient bones of the ferocious monsters or colossal dinosaurs that had once roamed the land. Finally finding their resting place amongst the hills. The patterns and shapes aligned just right to allow your imagination to run wild with what the beasts would have looked like if the rocks really were their bones.

Liam reflected on how life was pretty simple, yet its most common attributes were pieces of a grand fictional tale ready to be told. All too often you were reminded of the terrible and horrific aspects of life. Liam was taught at an early age by his father to always fight ones' instincts and look for the positive side of life. The few times

214

Liam did spend with his father, he always challenged him to accept things as they were and spend time within his own mind, spirit, and soul. He did his best to stop, block out the noise, and recenter himself in what he felt was true and present—the tiny details of hope and perspective that he felt few others took notice of.

They finally took a break on one of the ridges where there was just enough for them all to gather around. Chatter and conversation took place, but Liam remained quiet, pondering the day and taking everything into consideration. He retrieved a small scrap of parchment and a lead stick to write with. He worked everything through his mind until he felt his emotions and thoughts come forward.

Upon the mountain peaks I stare,
Looking up and curious I do dare,
Climbing until I reach its top,
The passion within does not allow me to stop.
Gazing down on life below,
I realize how few people know
The sacrifice it takes to walk this path,
To endure all of evil and nature's wrath.
Conquering my fears and doubts as I go,
I now stand champion, for only I am my own worst foe.

Liam's head was down as he wrote it out, not paying attention to what was going on around him. It took him a while to really gather his words, and he didn't want to be distracted to the point that he forgot how the pieces fell into place within the flow of the poem. Golgoth noticed him writing and made his way over. He looked down at the young lad and asked, "What is it you write? *Himph!* The historian amongst us to capture what evil deeds we do? *Himph!* Come! Tell us what you write."

Liam looked up to see the stare of the slender man standing over him like a mocking crow cawing down at an injured animal that only wants a merciful death. He tried to play it off. "It's nothing, I assure you."

The attempt to deflect the inquiry didn't work, though. Edha even amplified the pressure. "So you devote time to writing your thoughts down to remember them, but you don't have the courage to let them stand on their own?"

He was now regretting that he had pulled the parchment out and written anything at all. He was on a journey with a gathering of warriors. Cashmes, Lythya, Edha, Dhather, Codgarak ... so far he had nothing but respect for them and wanted to learn more, but Golgoth, Mala ... he despised practically every word that came out of their mouths. Those two chafed at him day and night and now, when he was trying to find relief and get lost in positive thoughts about his surroundings. Now his writing was to be exposed and brought out for all to hear. He read the poem out loud, doing his best to make it sound with the significance that he had felt within his spirit when he'd first written it.

They were at least silent as he read it out loud. The silence lasted for about a minute until Golgoth followed up with his critique. "You are your own worst foe? *Himph! Himph.* Just wait until you come face to face with your first demon, perhaps even a wyvern ... then we'll see what you think of foes! *Himph!* Tis a nice try, though, young Liam." Golgoth twisted and turned away, walking back to where he had been sitting, his high-pitched chuckle escorting him.

And, of course ... "Well, son of man, you've certainly given me inspiration to also become a composer of words! Tell me what you think." Mala cleared his throat, stood with a grand gesture as if he was on a pedestal in front of a large crowd, and declaimed,

"I realize how few people know
that Liam is a cunt

216

who wears a dress and a bow."

The tiger bowed, and when he came back up, his giant devious smile displayed his teeth, which was nothing but another way to mock Liam.

Motherf—! Lythya interrupted his thought. "Enough *rest and reflection* … let's get going." She looked at Edha and with a slight nod, the two women headed out first with the men in tow.

Liam hesitated and almost scribbled all over the poem, as if erasing it would somehow erase the event that had just taken place. He decided, however, to stuff it back into his small pack, and when he looked forward, he saw Dhather reaching down to give him a hand and help him back to his feet. He readied his pack on his back as the older lion placed his paw on his shoulder. "If the place is worth going, then there will be no shortcuts which you can take to get there, for only the wild can be tamed by those who have the courage to take each step required to travel its depths." The large lion's gaze spoke to his crushed spirit, bringing some relief from the mockery, and they soon followed in pursuit of the group ahead of them.

Liam did his best to put the comments behind him and move forward as he had been doing since the expedition began. The rock bones of the earth continued to showcase themselves in patterns that inspired his imagination even more. Corpses of the earth's layers were strewn about from when it had formed itself back at the beginning of time. The ridges turned with the mountains' crests as the valley curved its way around.

"It should just be around this bend a little further," Dhather said from behind him. A few steps further down the trail, the mountains peeled away and exposed the grandeur of Jerikako. Two mountain spines were cut out on either side, with a massive stone wall connecting the two. At its center was a statue of a knight, his sword held in front of him and pointed down into the ground. At the base of the sword, cut through the stone base, was the kingdom's main gate. Liam could see trade carts and sporadic travelers entering and exiting like tiny ants.

Their position high up on the mountain allowed him to see that the stone walls protected a large, developed city. The buildings looked as if they'd been built on top of one another, as the city was compressed against the mountain barriers, with no more room to flex the expanding infrastructure any further. The further they went along the trail, the better he could see that from the main walls all the way to the end of the narrowing mountain range, the city had not an inch to spare.

Arriving at the gate of Jerikako, Liam stood in amazement. He couldn't take his eyes off the wonder of the stone carved knight. He watched as the Sergeant of the Guard exchanged words with Mala and Lythya. The sergeant pointed forward and looked as if he was giving directions for them to follow. They continued through the gate, but the sergeant stopped Liam. "The tiger told me to inform you that access to the sewer was off to the right and that you'd feel more at home down there."

He balled up a fist and looked to see where Mala was, but he was pushed forward by Dhather. "Thank you, Sergeant. I'm sure we'll be comfortable together." Dhather didn't need Liam to say anything; his emotions were clear on his face and could be read from a mile away.

"Imagine living with him your whole life."

Liam looked up at the lion, his anger radiating. "He doesn't even know me!" He turned his head away and stared blankly ahead, not even taking in his surroundings, which only a moment ago he had taken such pleasure in admiring.

"Young Liam, you don't know him either." Liam kept looking straight ahead, as if Dhathers' words had entered his ears but passed right through his mind and out the other side. The lion kept his watch over the son of man, but the remainder of the walk held no more conversation, just the sounds of the townsfolk going about their daily lives around them.

Liam sulked the rest of the way until they arrived at a tavern with a massive wooden table outside it; the group commandeered it, but the massive sizes of the creatures made it a tight fit for everyone. Golgoth and Lythya retrieved another small table and brought it over to extend the space available. Liam, being the closest to their stature, sat with them, and size-wise it was a pretty comfortable fit for him, but Golgoth's company was certainly not comfortable, or preferred.

Drinks had already been brought for the main group when Dhather, having arrived late with Liam, walked around the table towards the seat they had saved for him. He purposely walked behind Mala, and with stealth, he snapped his tail up and knocked Mala's drink onto his lap. The tiger instantly roared in response and bared his teeth, extending his claws and digging them deep into the wooden tabletop. By that time Dhather had arrived at his seat, which was opposite Mala, the tiger had tensed his muscles, but the lion, watching his brother's reaction, leaned over the table. He placed both his paws on the table and blue flames burst out of them. A low, rumbling growl resonated from his chest and throat, but the stare-down lasted for only a few seconds. Mala left long scratches in the wood as he ripped his claws away, snapped around, and departed the group. *That's what I thought!* Liam thought to himself as a small feeling of justice lit within him.

He watched as Codgarak looked over at Dhather and their eyes met. "Sometimes we all need a reminder," Dhather said, and the minotaur just nodded in response. The group's energy calmed slightly as they all began to enjoy their drinks. Some jokes and stories were shared, and the mood became pleasant as the rest from the journey calmed their sore bodies.

After some time had passed, a soldier walked over to the group and plopped down in Mala's seat. Codgarak and Cashmes welcomed him and clasped his hands. Cashmes stood and addressed the group. "Hunters, let me introduce you to an old friend. We met this young lad many years ago when he was Sergeant Nealy, and now he stands amongst us as captain!" Cashmes then turned his attention to the captain and, one by one, introduced everyone to him.

"Thank you, old friend, you are too kind. I am surprised Mala is not with you. I would have bet that he would be amongst the group."

Cashmes coughed slightly. "He is around here somewhere ... he needed to dry off from an accident." Cashmes glanced at Dhather, who shrugged. A chuckle came from Captain Nealy.

"Well ... normally a wet pussy is not a bad thing, but in this case, that pussy is certainly not pleasant when it's wet." Chuckles rippled across the group, everyone enjoying a moment free of the resident asshole.

Codgarak then asked the captain, "So, what have you heard of Lithram? We were at Fort Patton when soldiers and young trainees entered from Somopack and Ashfurgoth."

Captain Nealy looked around, scanning the area as if checking that it was safe to speak openly. "The king is convinced that it was orcs that attacked and overthrew Lithram."

Faces outwardly displayed confusion, and the group glanced back and forth at each other. "And what do you think?" the minotaur asked.

"I don't buy it … and I honestly think it's bullshit. None of it makes any sense."

"How so?" Edha inquired.

"The most powerful orcs in the far east we know of are the Horde of Calgo-Kramok. But even they … the numbers that I've estimated couldn't have overthrown Lithram. They would have had to have received a magnitude of support in the form of additional troops from another clan, horde, or even another race brought into the war effort. They attacked Lithram five years ago and were slaughtered … just slaughtered … but now you're telling me that after five years, they've returned and overthrown Lithram in one attack? I don't buy it at all."

Codgarak lifted his hand in confusion. "How does the king not see this, then?"

The captain took a long drink and let the brew settle deep within him, and brought the mug down firmly on the table. "Because the king is influenced by Major Pelden. Pelden has the king convinced that the orcs overthrew Lithram and there is no real cause for concern … that Somopack and Ashfurgoth are overreacting and should just counterattack, reclaim it, and be done with the panic."

Codgarak snorted. "And they wonder why we refuse to officially follow such kingdoms."

The captain nodded in agreement. "Exactly! The major has been lying to the king for years and has convinced the royal court the army is ready and there is nothing to worry about." The captain took another drink and put his mug down again with the same firmness. "No the fuck we're not! The major hasn't been on the training grounds in years, doesn't spend any time amongst the soldiers, and whenever he is around them, all he does is tear them down and tell them how stupid they are compared to his intelligence, and yet he's the laziest leader we have in our entire military force. All he does is worry about influencing the king and staying in his good favor, and if you try to do anything to thwart that, you're immediately sent to the depths of the fallen chamber."

Edha interjected. "So why not come with us? Leave this behind you."

The look on the captain's face gave everyone the impression that he had asked himself that very same question many times; his pause before answering left them even more convinced that that was the case. "I've thought of doing that many times over. There are just too many good soldiers here. I can't bring myself to leave them alone under the major's leadership."

Cashmes raised his mug towards the captain. "Respect," he said and took a drink from it. Liam scanning the facing in his party and read their facial expressions. Though each one was different, all portrayed respect and appreciation towards the captain. Standing firm with conviction to not abandon his soldiers.

"Any idea of who it could be that sacked Lithram?" Dhather bringing conversation back on track.

The captain shook his head. "Truthfully, we've received mixed reports. We received a hawk from Somopack that claimed the army that marched outside Lithram's walls was wearing pure white armor. It claimed the army was seven thousand strong." Their faces filled with the thoughts racing through their memory banks—the knowledge of banners and kingdoms' colors. "Your faces say the same thing we all have. There is no nation we currently know of that wears all white armor. So the accuracy of the report has been thoroughly scrutinized."

"It appears we need to continue to rescue my brother and seek out this threat for ourselves." Lythya leading the conversation onto the next issue needing to be addressed.

"Waiter!"

A small boy approached the table and looked at Cashmes, who had made the call. "Yes?"

The lion turned and looked at the lad, who was standing slightly behind him. "Do you have paper and lead?"

The boy nodded. Returning a moment later, he delivered the requested items to the lion. Taking the items, Cashmes turned and looked at Golgoth, motioning with his head as the items were passed down to him. Golgoth scribbled the crest image he'd seen in Odra's memories. When he'd completed the sketch, he handed it over to Captain Nealy. "Do you know this crest?" Cashmes inquired.

It did not take the captain long to reply. "This is the keep within Stonevor Forest. It was a small settlement of Mystamight dwarves; they built the keep but were attacked and killed by the Pashro-Shaltok orcs over a thousand years ago. The RemaMortBrook region was in so much chaos back then that it was simply abandoned. Our scouts normally sneak over and use it when they go to spy on that region. But I don't believe we've sent any of our scouts over that way in months. We're planning on doing it again soon, with recent events." He handed the piece of paper back. "Wait—what does that keep mean to you, though? A connection with what's going on?"

Lythya brought the captain up to speed on her brother, the information they had, and the attack of the ifrit at the shrine when they'd tried to teleport into Aibek's last felt location.

"Yes … the few of our members who can teleport have been blocked as well. The ability to access magic is certainly being affected by whatever is going on. At least, that's what our mages tell us."

"And what do we have here?" A new voice interrupted the moment as a male figure approached the table.

Captain Nealy straightened his posture and stood tall as he answered. "Major Pelden, this is—"

He was cut off before he had the chance to answer. "The"—the major used his hands to quote and add emphasis—"hunters." He flicked his eyebrows upwards as he rolled his eyes. "I'm surprised to see the *hunters* in Jerikako. Begging for coin again?" An insulting smirk appeared on his face. "Well, let me be the one and only to inform you all, but Jerikako is in no need of the likes of you, nor will I allow us to waste our coin on a bunch of mercenaries whose glory days have long since passed."

Liam scanned the table and looked back and forth between Major Pelden and the others, doing his best to read their expressions. A movement caught his attention; if he hadn't been scanning the table, he would never have noticed it due to how subtle it was. As Major Pelden was hurling his insults, a small girl brought some new bottles over to the table and set them down. She did her best to avoid any disturbance but just slightly brushed Golgoth. He turned and, out of instinct, grabbed the little girl's arm and gazed down into her eyes. There was a look on his face as though the girl was an evil spirit visiting him through a curse. His eyes widened and a thousand-yard stare came over them. He maintained his composure, but Liam couldn't help but believe that his mind had been suddenly taken back to a certain moment in time that was ignited by the encounter.

Neither of the two said anything; they just stared at one another. Golgoth eventually gently released the girl's arm. She departed and Golgoth grabbed one of the bottles and took a long, long, long drink from it.

"Like I said, there's no need for you to be here. I suggest you finish your drinks and move along on your journey. I bid you fair trails." Major Pelden turned and looked straight at Captain Nealy. "Captain," he said in a stern voice before departing.

"I'm going to hear about this later," the captain remarked once the major was far enough away for the group to continue the conversation.

"I almost forgot what it felt like to be compared to a mercenary," Dhather said as he looked over at Codgarak, who replied, "I remember it being a daily occurrence."

Dhather shook his head. "And yet the mercs never seemed to accept my challenge when I dared them to combat." The lion chuckled.

It was easy to see that Captain Nealy was contemplating something. He finally made a statement.

"A warrior of Jerikako I stand,
Accepting my duties with pride.
I shall defend my country,
Charged with dignity while striving to earn nobility,
Integrity to oneself, honesty above all else.
I pursue excellence in the execution of these duties,
For if I fail, thy kingdom shall fall.
A warrior I stand, until the end of us all."

The table remained silent as he paused before continuing "Every nation, army, band … they come up with these phrases, these statements, these creeds. Telling each person how they must know the creeds and speak of them." He shook his head slightly. The months of frustration had finally come forth. "It is one thing for a man to recite a creed, but damned be the person who has the courage to attempt to live it daily." The captain swayed and looked around at the city's walls and watchtowers. "These men stand watch over the elites who don't care about them. They preach a message they themselves do not fulfill. When hell comes to our doorstep, may I at least have the courage to live in the moment of darkness, because I fear I will be the only one these soldiers will have standing beside them." Looking back at the table and meeting the gaze of the party, he said, "You may not carry a nation's banner with you, nor allegiance to a kingdom, but we live our lives dedicated to something so much greater than ourselves—a purpose the likes of those cowards will never know and never be able to achieve. So fuck them all, and when our day comes, we will be reunited in the Valley of Haivan!"

Liam was startled as the rest of the party rose to their feet. They cheered and raised their glasses in salute. *"Fuck them all!"*

DHATHER

THE KEEP

By the time Liam had made it to the front with Dhather, the others were already sprawled out on the ground. Utilizing a small embankment as concealment, he low crawled up to them. He took in the scene that had caused the sudden stop, setting his sights for the first time on orcs. He tried to count them but eventually gave up after the third attempt. His best estimate, though, was that the group was close to a thousand strong.

At the front were leaner-bodied orcs who carried bows and arrows on their backs and long thin spears in their hands. As the formation moved through the valley, these orcs used the spears as signaling devices to change the formation, pace, and direction of the main body. Most of the orcs were large in stature, carrying battle-axes and swords. They marched in two separate lines but lacked any sense of uniformity. The scouts in front attempted to signal and direct the formation, but the majority merely moved in a gaggle and ignored whatever commands were sent to them.

The scouts, finally getting frustrated with the lack of discipline and the lack of obedience to orders, brought the formation to a halt. Heading back towards the center, they slapped, yelled, and spit on some of the orcs as they went. Though Liam watched the commotion unfold and did his best to take in what was going on, his true focus remained on the center of the formation, where a mixture of humans and other creatures were chained together.

As the scouts proceeded towards the back of the formation, they slapped one of the main guards, following up with what appeared to be slanderous statements. As soon as the scout was further down the line, the guard who'd been insulted grabbed one of the enslaved humans. A swift slash with their ax broke the chains keeping them captive. The orc severed the metal links, reached down, and grabbed the human by the ankle. Twisting its hips in one fluid motion, the orc flung the frail human's body at the scout. It landed precisely on target. The human's screams were heard for a moment but were silenced on impact. The orcs reacted in turmoil, showing how fractured and segregated the group was.

"How should we attack?" Liam whispered to Codgarak. Though he thought he was quiet, he saw the heads of Mala, Golgoth, Edha, Cashmes, and Lythya appear around Codgarak with faces that said *What a moron!* He pressed his lips together, embarrassed and slightly pissed. There were prisoners in need of rescuing! This seemed like a simple, straightforward question about what they should do in this situation. He slouched back down on the embankment.

"We can't attack that," Dhather whispered to him.

He turned and leaned closer to the lion. "Why not?"

"There's over a thousand in that alliance force."

"Alliance force?"

The lion nodded. "An alliance force is what orcs call it. They're taking these prisoners to another tribe, nation, or horde and offering them as an alliance gift towards future war bands."

229

Liam looked back at the prisoners. "And what will happen to them?"

"They will more than likely be tortured and killed in ceremonial rituals." Liam had already assumed that, but he had still hoped that there would be something else besides that—slave labor, servants, maybe.

The thought of torture gave him the urge to compel his group to act. "We have to do something." He did his best to emphasize his point.

The lion shook his head in disagreement. "That is not our mission. We must find and get to Aibek."

It was Liam's turn now to shake his head. "We can't let these people just be tortured."

The lion raised his eyebrows in a counter-argument. "And how do you know that Aibek is not being tortured as we speak?"

Liam hadn't thought about that; his mind was so focused on the immediate issue in front of him that he hadn't stopped to think about what could be happening to their companion. "But this is for the greater good. We need to take action."

A smile appeared on Dhather's face. "Ahhh ... the greater good. It's always about the greater good, isn't it?" A confused look came across Liam's face as he attempted to understand Dhather's statement. "You still have a lot to learn about this world, young Liam. All too often, the compelling point focuses on the greater good, yet it doesn't actually help the greater good. It is a great feeling but never a promise fully fulfilled. A mindset that others will force upon you with guilt, yet they themselves are excused from it."

"So we're just to let them die?"

The lion leaned his head slightly towards the prisoners. "Since when have we been given authority over their fate?" Both paused, Liam taken aback by the question, but the lion continued. "You have taken on this burden of assuming that if you do not act, they are doomed to death. Yet that is the Ancient One's decision. It is upon Him to determine the fate that awaits them. There could be three thousand RemaMortBrook soldiers waiting for them in the next valley who will rescue them. LithoLaleth elves could come and place a sleep spell on the orcs and rescue the prisoners without a single arrow being fired."

The lion paused once again to allow the young man to reflect on the significance of what he was trying to convey. "Do you know what would happen if we tried to attack and bring freedom to them for 'the greater good'?" Liam shook his head before the lion continued. "Let's say we set up the perfect surprise attack and were able to gain the advantage, slaying every bastard frog throughout the valley that we could... even as victory drew near, they would ensure they killed the prisoners before we had the chance to save them. They would rather kill the prize and die than bear the humiliation of losing it. No matter what we try to do, young Liam, we must stay on our mission, and that is Aibek. Their destiny is in the hands of the Ancient One and we must accept that."

Liam closed his eyes. A long exhale followed as he tried to put his wandering thoughts to rest. A cold chill ran down his spine as he battled the feeling of betrayal. Those poor souls were to be offered to some frog deity, a stupid ritual the orcs believed would make them more powerful, and all he could do was turn a blind eye. "Do we know which clan they come from?"

"Their banner shows that of the TakaSkitt clan. They also dwell in the Realm of Delco."

He opened his eyes, engraving the appearance of the clan on his memory. "The next time I lay eyes upon the TakaSkitt, it will be from the destruction of my hands."

Dhather placed his hand on Liam's shoulder. "Just wait, young Liam. You have yet to see the evils of man firsthand; then you will be truly horrified."

Liam found it hard to focus on what lay ahead after having to leave the TakaSkitt prisoners behind. The group moved at a snail's pace, and he was straining to maintain focus and discipline. The others moved with perfect stealth, communicating through years of hand signals utilized in battle and similar situations. Everyone knew these except Liam. Though he could recall Master Fry teaching a class session on it while he was at Fort Patton; his exhaustion that day was at an all time high. He was barely awake during the class and now could not remember anything of value.

The slow pace and precise, calculated movements drove him crazy. He wanted to break the silence with a hundred questions about context, information, and reasoning. He had at least picked up on the fact that every time a cool breeze flowed through the woods, they would all lie prone on the ground. He thought it was quite bizarre the first couple of times they performed the act. Eventually, as they lay there, he found himself staring at a pile of dog shit within arm's reach. His eyes picked up on the slight impressions of what looked like dog paw prints upon the dirt floor of the forest. It then dawned on him that what he was seeing was the tracks of the gnolls, the disgusting creature that surprised attacked them within the hunters shrine.

He lay upon the dirt for a while and waited for the signal to rise, but it didn't come. He looked ahead at the minotaur's massive body as it lay flat on the earth. As minutes passed by, he would slowly, tempted by curiosity, begin to raise his head to look around, but every time, he'd be pelted in the head with a small pebble by Dhather. *MMMrrrruhhhhh He placed his index finger in the loose soil in front of his face and began to draw lines and shapes in the dirt.

A slight rustle sounded ahead of him; he glanced up but only saw Codgarak, still lying in front of him. He looked back at his dirt lines, but mere seconds later, the wolf paw of Lythya landed next to his face, "Seriously?" She stared down at him. Startled, he looked up to see that the group was beginning to circle around him. *How is that even poss*— He couldn't even finish his thought before he was being further scolded. "Move, cunt!" Mala chastised him.

They stayed crouching down but formed a circle in Dhather and Liam's area, where there was enough room for the group to meet. Lythya took the center and began her briefing. As she started, her mouth barely moved, looking as if she was whispering her words, but half a second later, her voice entered your ear and the whisper amplified within you as if she was speaking at a normal conversational level.

"The gnolls have been actively patrolling the local area. Drag marks up ahead look as if they're still actively hunting the local townships and villages for new prey. Their trail leads to the keep. It's still two miles ahead. A dark energy shield surrounds it. There are two demons at the main entrance and three more scattered within the clearing. We don't know how many may be within the keep, nor the gnolls' strength in numbers."

"Well, now we know for sure that it's not orcs we're facing. *Himph!*" Golgoth added.

Liam looked over at Dhather sitting next to him, who answered his curiosity. "Gnolls and orcs are practically mortal enemies. They would never align themselves with each other. Ever." Liam nodded in response. This was a lesson in historical context that would not normally reach the villages in the outer regions and that could be easily forgotten when telling a story around a campfire.

"How did gnolls come into alliance with demons, though?" Cashmes asked the group.

"I have the same question," Codgarak said.

Lythya began to draw a map in the dirt to show what her and Edha had seen on their scouting mission. Without any prompting, Mala intruded with the plan of attack he had prepared. "Dhather's swords should be able to penetrate their shield. As soon as he cuts open a slot, Golgoth and I will take care of the demons standing guard. Edha, Lythya, and Cashmes will take out whatever gnolls are in the area. Codgarak will breach the keep's door and then him and Dhather will get in and rescue Aibek."

"Sounds good."

"All right."

"No problem here," came the responses from the group.

"War is delicious, and time is wasting!" Mala swiped the dirt with his paw and erased the map. The group responded accordingly, filing back into line and beginning to move stealthily. All except Liam, who stood, his arms slightly at his sides and his hands out in perplexed questioning. "What am I supposed to do?" he almost called out but caught himself at the last second. he stood there, baffled, until he had accepted the fate of being left out again and trotted forward in the wake of the group.

The keep was rather large, but nothing like Liam had imagined. He'd assumed it would tower into the sky, covered with grand carvings of warriors and of a sheer volume to leave him in wonder. That was not the case, however; the keep was a simple four-sided building with a sheer vertical edge. Simple, plain, and straightforward. The tower no longer looked out over the trees but was more hidden since it had been abandoned so long ago. He easily saw why someone would want to use it as a hideout rather than an observation post; it was certainly out of the way and discreet.

The team repositioned themselves with Dhather at the front, Mala and Golgoth immediately behind him, Cashmes, Edha, and Lythya following, and Codgarak and Liam at the rear of the team, which was about to breach the shield. Liam could just make out the demon's standing at the Keep's main door. Leaning forward and whispering to Codgarak, "What is their armor made of?" He was actually surprised when he received his answer, "It is believed they construct their armor out of the bones of the damned within hell itself. Now focus!"

He watched Codgarak tap Edha's shoulder and saw the pattern repeat itself as each warrior tapped the person in front of them. As soon as Dhather had received his tap, he conjured his magical swords with his blue energy. There was no further warning or preparation; Dhather slashed downward, and as he did so, the blue swords cut through the air. You could clearly see a ripple effect exposing the dark energy barrier upon their impact. Purple and green hues faded in and out as the shield's exterior was breached and the energy redispersed itself across the zone. Just as suddenly as Dhather had drawn his swords and slashed, the group was surging into and past the just barely visible shield. Liam watched Mala and Golgoth move in ferocious haste towards the two demons, who were now clearly in his view.

The demons' armor was made of skeletons of the damned. Ribs had been crafted into chest plates that ran all the way down, protecting the demons' intestines. Red flesh and muscle fibers were still affixed to the bones, giving them a grisly and tattered appearance. Where shoulder plates would normally have been, they were instead adorned with two skulls. Liam didn't know which creature they came from, but they were certainly not human.

The demons' faces would have struck terror into any normal person facing their attack. They were humanoid in shape, but their mouths went further round the sides of their heads and had a torn appearance, with sharp teeth highlighted in front of their dark red throats. They were both bald; one had horns that jutted outward with a slight bend at the end, whereas the other's horns curved upwards from the beginning. As Liam moved, his vision was blurred, and he had not yet laid eyes on the other demons in the yard around the keep; he just assumed they would be similar in appearance to these two. The two demons held massive axes in their hands, each with a long shaft—the perfect picture of guards protecting a doorway.

Liam strained to remain aware of his surroundings as he moved forward, his ears picking up the sounds of yelping and screeching coming from all around. Mala and Golgoth successfully drew the guards away from the door, and Codgarak picked up his stride and, without stopping, lowered his shoulder and plowed through the keep's entrance. Liam was right behind him, and with the impact came a transition to slow motion. His senses heightened in awareness; wooden chunks of door and splinters floated in the air, and the dust particles created a slight cloud.

As quickly as the slow motion had started, it stopped as Liam's eyes adjusted to a dimly lit room. He noticed some doglike bodies lying near the threshold, looking like they'd been behind the door and received the full force of the minotaur's energy upon the breach.

Liam wasn't ready for it. He was taking in the scene when, without warning, Dhather came charging in behind him. A forceful shove in his back propelled him into the center of the room. *"Move!"* Dhather shouted, standing at the entrance and catching his breath.

A moment later, gnolls poured in from a side room as the commotion of the attack awoke them. Codgarak made his way to the stairs he found on the left side of the room, but after a quick assessment, he realized he wouldn't be able to navigate them due to his size. Liam readied himself to engage the wave of dogs along with Dhather, but the minotaur's command changed his course. "Liam! Work towards the top and seek out Aibek's whereabouts!" Dhather's blue swords engaged the dark metal blades of the gnolls. A smaller demon also appeared, and Codgarak, without hesitation, stepped forward to prevent it from hindering Liam's efforts.

The chaos of swords and battle reverberated within the enclosed room. The loud echo made Liam realize how difficult it was to communicate amongst the team, but he didn't hesitate to act. Turning towards the steps, he half jumped up two steps at a time. Adrenaline surged through his body as he made it to the second level of the keep.

Finding a closed wooden door, he reached out and began to open it. A loud creaking rang out as its heavy weight strained the metal hinges. Upon opening it, he was greated by a rasping spiteful voice, "What do you want?" Liam assumed it was Aibek challenging his captor and he leaned into the room, he noticed a startled creature sitting up from a bed in the far corner. He instantly realized he had no idea what Aibek actually looked like! Lythya was a wolf hybrid, and the thing standing before him looked like it could be a demon, but it wasn't like the guards at the main entrance. It basically matched his stature from what he could guess, "Aibek?" He asked.

"How do you know the prisoner's name! Who are you?" The creature then noticed his sword in Liam's hand, and heard the commotion of combat down stairs, "You're trying to rescue the prisoner!" The creature leapt up out of bed as Liam started to finish opening the door all the way. The creature flared out a set of wings as it hovered over and began to grab a spear propped up against the wall by its' bed.

Yup! Pretty sure that's a demon all right! He realized immediately that a threat was about to present itself. The door finally swung open wide enough for him to stand in the center of the doorway. The hairs on the back of his neck stood straight up as he saw the spearhead first, his body alerted to the danger long before his mind could process what he should do next.

The spear missed the right side of his head by inches as he as he now could more easily see the creature as it flew about the room. The small gray creature looked like one of the goblin statues that had come to life upon the hillside. Liam could now see a smaller set horns on its head and the charred wings protruding from its back left him reassured that this was some other type of demon.

The creature leapt upward and flapped its wings, taking flight. In its right hand it held another spear, and it began to swoop towards him. Liam darted to his right, adjusting his angle to counter the spear. He darted in a zigzag pattern, working to close the distance and get himself within a better striking range. The demon began to conjure a green ball of energy in its left hand as he did so, creating a dance of combat as they each tried to gain the upper hand.

The demon threw the green ball towards him, but it was such a bad throw that he could imagine Mala's insults at the poor performance. A memory of Master Fry flashed into his mind where he watched the master execute an attack sequence that launched him into the air. Liam had nothing to lose and without ever attempting the move before chose to just go for it. Taking another step, he crouched down and executed the tornado strike he had previously witnessed, his body spinning in the air as his left gladius sword struck the spear, the force knocking it away, exposing the demon's midsection. He continued his spin, the gladius sword in his right hand cutting straight into the demon's body. The sword sliced outward as he made a full rotation and delivered another round of slashes before he landed. The demon's wings flapped languidly twice before the body fell to the ground in two separate pieces. Blood and a gargling cough came from its mouth, but no words followed.

Liam ignored the immense amount of luck he had achieved and instead went with an dangerously over abundance of cockiness, "That's right fucker!" he said as he quickly looked down at the corps lying at his feet. Liam rescanned the room to ensure there were no other threats, but he found none. He instantly felt lightheaded and leaned over a small desk. It was then that he realized, *I held my breath the entire time!* Taking some long, deep breaths, he mentally reengaged his body. *Come on! Let's go!*

Though it took less than a minute, the seconds he had dedicated to gathering his composure left his anxiety feeding off the adrenaline and telling him *We have to go now!* His swords lying on the desk, he clenched his fists as he took a few more long, deep breaths, mentally fighting the anxiety and working to be present within the moment. *Okay ... we're good ... WE'RE REALLY GOOD!* He grabbed his swords and darted back out of the door and onto the staircase, leaping up several steps at a time, but this time reminding himself, *Breathe ... just fucking breathe.*

Continuing his climb up the staircase as it followed the edge of the square, he approached a corner and leapt for the next landing. He turned to round the corner and ran straight into two demons coming down the stairs with two gnolls behind them. The collision forced both groups backwards. The yelping and clamoring of the enemy blared out within the stairwell as Liam grunted and huffed, stumbling down a few steps before stopping and regaining his footing. The demons had gray skin similar to the others but wore cloaks and carried staffs made from bones. *There are wizard demons now?* He pounded back up the steps to the landing and readied himself to unleash his own personal hell upon them.

The gnolls had also regained their footing, and they jumped over the demons, not to be held back from their attack on Liam.

They barreled down towards him, their mass and speed enabling them to reach the corner first. Utilizing the height of the walls, they bounced off it and redirected themselves at him like missiles locked onto a target.

Liam, far more confident after his last encounter now focused intently on the moment. Analyzing the gnolls trajectory and instead of trying to block and counter their force, he used it as an advantage. He dropped down and turned until his back was against the stairs. Watching as the first gnoll approached, he waited for the perfect moment before he thrust his sword upwards, inserting it into the gnoll's lower chest. It cried out in agony, clamoring its way onto the steps, and rolled to a stop as it met death.

The second one, already in motion, was unable to change its course; Liam, however, had just enough time to roll to one side, creating a smaller target. The gnoll's sword, aimed at his previous location, missed him. He positioned his sword exactly where he intended and cut straight through the dog's face, carving down its throat and into its chest. The body, however, landed on top of him. The weight of it sent him falling backwards.

Taking a quick moment to breathe, he heaved the corpse off him. Looking up at the landing, he saw the two demons standing on the next landing, where they'd first collided. They began to speak in unison in garbled voices in a language unknown to him, and their staffs of bone began to emit an intertwined glow—one a red light, the other white.

The chanting continued as the light radiated outward and spirals of light shot down towards him. Though he instinctively put his hands up to block it, the light went through them and landed on his chest. Instantly he felt the pull within him come alive. There was no pain, yet he immediately felt a draining effect. His thoughts were slowed, as if his mind were trapped in a strong river and couldn't swim against its force. The more the red light pulsed into his chest, the faster his aggression, his burning motivation to defeat his enemy, left him. Likewise, the grayish-white light was ripping and tearing within him. His desire to live, the power of his will to win, all of it was being leached out of him the longer the evil magic did its work.

He could tell his physical body was fine, but his mind and spirit struggled to connect with it. He fought it and told his body, *Take the step! Move, move, move, move!* His body moved like that of a zombie, the muscles working, but the energy that drove the engine just wasn't there. He staggered more and more as he glared ahead, squinting as he continued to scream internally his commands to keep pursuing the demons.

He made some progress in closing the distance, but before he could reach them, the demon shining the grayish-white light on him stopped and summoned a barrier between them. Liam did what little he could to pound his fist through it, but it just bounced off as with each blow he saw a wave pulse outward as the shield sustained itself from his attempts.

He only glanced down for a split second, but that was all it took for him to remember: *My ring!* The magical ring that Master DC had given him.

He tried to connect his mind with its magical properties. In shock, he realized there was nothing blocking his mind from connecting to it. Yes, he was drained; yes, he felt as if death was soon to be a reality, but this unhindered connection to his ring, or whatever it truly is, now sparked a new hope!

How can I use this, though? The only thing he could think of at that moment was getting through the shield. Mustering every ounce of mental strength he had left, he focused and sent his magical connection to the ring, imagining it as a dagger. He watched the magenta shades of color come alive within the metal dragon-scale design. The ring beginning its transformation; the band stretched itself into a bracelet that wrapped around his wrist.

The light continued its glow as sweat formed on his forehead, droplets running down his face. His head shook ever so slightly. He felt like a mental barrier had broken free within him, and a new wave of magic poured downward into the metal band. A small flash of light flickered as a knife blade shot out over the back of his hand. With what little mental strength remained within him, he forced the magical blade down and watched as it sliced right through the shield just like Dhather's swords had done earlier. The demon's eyes widened in amazement and terror as he stepped through the shield wall.

They were barely out of his reach, but he still made every attempt to close the distance. The demon sending the red light into him also stopped once he'd broken through the shield, and both demons began to conjure balls of fire, launching them from such close range that Liam had no way of dodging them and had to take the blunt force head on. That was when he felt the physical pain come surging on top of him. A new crashing wave of pain pounded him hard against the cliffs of the internal damage he'd already sustained.

The demon on his right that had the red energy turned to run back up the stairs, and he reached out and sliced the throat of the other demon with his magical knife. The demonic chanting of its language ended in a gargled mess as blood poured out of its mouth.

"Liam!" Looking behind him, he saw the tattered, demented face of Golgoth looking up at him. "Here!" Golgoth threw a throwing knife towards him, Golgoth's skill ensuring that the handle was facing Liam as he released it into the air. Liam reached out and caught it with his free hand. Flipping it quickly, he threw it and caught the fleeing demon in the back, sending him crumpling forward onto the steps. Watching the body fall to its death, he didn't even notice the blurred darkness rushing in or the collapsing of his body upon the platform.

Golgoth watched Liam collapse as he leapt towards him. He wasn't able to reach him in time to catch him, but he immediately knelt down and checked his vitals. He was still breathing; his heart had a soft and slow pulse, but as Golgoth glanced over at the slain demon, he saw the remnants of the glow of the white and red energy from their bone staffs. "You've had quite the battle, young Liam! *Himph!*"

He checked once again to ensure there were no other injuries he had missed—no pooling of blood or anything else to be concerned about. "Do know, lad, I do not leave you because I want to … but I must in order to find Aibek." He placed his hand on Liam's chest. "Tusn op tusnatu." Though he could not see it, he could feel the energy transfer from himself to Liam. He had been the recipient of this spell himself and was aware of the peaceful, calming restoration it would bring the young lad.

Golgoth continued up the steps, leaping over the demon's body as he went. As he moved forward in haste, his memories came haunting upon him—flashbacks of a previous life that had ended with pure suffering for his victims. The narrow staircase, dimly lit by candles and torches, was a scene he had lived through countless times before. In the past, his primary concern had been stealth; now it was urgency to reach Aibek's location, wherever that may be.

Making his way to the next landing, he found an open door. Peeking his head in, he glanced around the room. "Aibek!" But only silence remained. "*Himph.* Where are you, my friend?" He had just turned around to continue when the demon that was hiding above the door swooped down and kicked him in the back, forcing him against the stone wall. The demon barely fit in the hallway itself; it was armed only with claws. The demon's power was limited by the confined space. Unable to generate powerful swipes with its claws, it grabbed Golgoth and attempted to choke him to death—something that would have worked on a lesser-skilled fighter but certainly not on a warrior. *"HIMPH! Himph, hehe hahahaha."*

A trickle of blood ran down Golgoth's face as his forehead smashed into the jagged stone wall. The demon turned him around so it could face him. Golgoth's eyes were glowing blood orange with rage. He sheathed his knives in their holsters on his belt and, bending his fingers into their commanding position, began the motion he needed. He finished with "SUOTONU!"

The demon's face distorted in bewilderment, the realization setting in a second before the audible cracking, popping, and tearing of its tendons, muscle fibers, and bones began. Its arms detached themselves from its torso and flew outward as if its shoulders had exploded.

The demon didn't even have the energy to cry out. Its mouth hung open. Demons rarely experienced pain themselves. This one simply stood there, paralyzed in disbelief.

"Don't worry, you are not the first demon to encounter me, nor will you be the last. *Himph!* And since you forced me to use so much energy on you, I will take what little of yours remains!" Golgoth reached up and grabbed the back of the demon's head. Bringing it closer to him, he opened his mouth and gave the command, "AP-SONP!" Red, gold, and black swirling energy poured out of the demon's mouth and eyes, and Golgoth consumed every ounce. The drained corpse crumpled to a heap, only blood left to pour from its wounds.

Golgoth's eyes returned to their natural state, a renewed strength within him from the demonic energy he had absorbed. Grabbing his knives, he pulled them out of their sheaths and dragged them along the rock wall. They ground and screeched, echoing throughout the stairwell. "Who else wants to come out and play? *HIMPH!*" To his disappointment, though, nothing else emerged to accept his invitation.

It wasn't long before the stairs opened once again onto another landing with yet another doorway. Breaching the door, he discovered what they had all been hoping for. "Aibek! *HIMPH!*"

The warrior sat patiently in a meditative cross-legged position surrounded by a purple swirling energy shield like a magical prison cell. Six stone pillars encircled the edge of the shield. On the inside, facing Aibek, Golgoth could see incantations etched into the pillars, which glowed purple. The dark ruins being utilized to maintain the shield around the warrior. Aibek didn't make eye contact. He remained perfectly still and seemed to have no inclination to care about anything outside his prison cell.

"This explains your absence! *Himph!*" Golgoth tilted his head at the closest stone pillar. "Unfortunately, this will take some time … *himph* … hmmm …" He plopped down, crossing his legs to gain a more comfortable position, and placed his hand at the back of the stone pillar, his fingers together as if holding a paint brush. His eyes glowed as he stated, "Odsatd doo molet htam yenhe, na tunuosu nhu tesaut na nhuet me." The ruin magnified in front of him, appearing like wool fibers that were interlaced and connected to form the engraving, only instead of wool, it was made of bands of magic. He began to make small strokes and precise corrective adjustments, slowly severing the magical fibers from their connection points, making sure to perform the critical deactivation in the correct order.

Thud! "Owww!"

Golgoth slowly turned his head, pearing over as his eyes burned in their orange glare. Seeing Liam land a faceplant just inside the chamber door, he shook his head and went back to deactivating the rune. "I tripped," Liam said. He walked sluggishly over to Golgoth. Struggling to keep his balance, he moved with bracing steps from side to side. "What was that chant you just said? I heard you say something as I was in the hallway."

"Absorb the magic from within, to release the prisoner to their kin." An old spell, but it is a very precise spell that works best when you need to untangle magical creations such as this." Golgoth glanced with his eyes in Liam's direction. "If I didn't know any better, I'd say you were drunk. *Himph …*"

"Well, you know what they say, Golgoth … alcohol does not make you fat, it makes you lean … against tables, chairs, walls, floors, and ugly people." A slight smirk came across Golgoth's face. "What exactly happened to me?" Liam asked as he knelt by Golgoth's side.

"You suffered a spirit and soul attack. You'll heal, but it will take some time before you feel normal again." Liam took a breath as he prepared his next question, but before he could answer, Golgoth's left hand lifted in a "no" gesture. "Not now, boy. Can't you see I'm busy working to free Aibek?" He turned his head slightly and glanced over at Liam. "Go tell Codgarak and the others that I will need them to buy me more time. I don't know how long this will take."

Liam got to his feet—barely, but he made it—and stumbled out of the room. It didn't take long before Golgoth heard a crashing sound. He assumed Liam had lost his footing and gone rolling down the steps. "Owww!"

The sun hit Liam's eyes as soon as he crossed the threshold. A stinging pain entered his mind. *I feel like shit and now I can't see and*

this dagger in my head … fucking fantastic. He clasped his face and exhaled. Spreading his fingers and slowly letting the light enter, he opened his eyes just a crack. Gnoll bodies were strewn all over the grounds. Clearly some patrols had heard the commotion and came back to defend the keep, but they'd had no idea of the force that awaited them.

"What the hell happened to you?" Moving his hand to cover the sun, he turned and saw Cashmes approaching him.

"I suffered a soul and spirit attack by two demons."

Cashmes nodded slightly. "Yeah, okay, but, umm, that doesn't explain all the blood."

He looked down and sure enough, he saw that he was covered in the red substance. "Oh, that must be from when a gnoll landed on top of me."

"As long as it's not yours, that's all that matters."

Liam continued to look around. "Golgoth wants us to buy him more time. He's working to undo some type of magical *thing* that's surrounding Aibek."

"So he is alive?"

Meeting the lion's gaze, Liam said, "It looks like it. He was just sitting there, but Golgoth didn't mention that he was not, so … it appears he is."

Cashmes turned and faced the open fields surrounding the Keep. "Hey! Bring it in!"

The group, hearing Cashmes's command, rallied around the two of them. "Oh, poor cunt. Is it that time of the month?" Mala said. Liam thought that he should have the will to fight, but he didn't and just thought *Screw it … it was fitting, and I just don't give a shit at the moment.*

"Aibek appears to be alive and well but is behind a magical field. Golgoth needs time to overcome it, and we need to ensure he has the time to do so," Cashmes informed the group.

Unbeknownst to the group, Golgoth had already defeated the first of the six runes within the keep. This immediately sent a magical beacon to Azazel informing him.

"Well, there doesn't appear to be any—" Just as Lythya was finishing her sentence, a white portal formed in the main field adjacent to the keep. The group watched as a man stepped forward, wearing prestigious-looking sleek black attire. His hair was slicked back, and a smooth, clean-shaven face, as he braced himself with a walking cane.

"Pardon my interruption. I am Azazel and I believe you may be interfering in business I have going on here."

The group rearranged themselves to face the new threat. "I have sensed you before, though ... some of you have magic within you ... and ..." He looked as if he was scanning the area and receiving information that he instantly analyzed. "It was you that destroyed Odra. How interesting." A pause filled the air. "Well ... there is certainly no reason to toil here any longer."

He spoke in his demonic language and the portal grew immensely larger. An ifrit identical to Odra appeared, followed by two demonic warriors, and gnolls began pouring out behind them, creating a circular formation. Turning to the ifrit, the man said, "Odry, it was these vermin that killed your brother Odra."

The fire spirit turned; the flames that burned from its arms, back, and head burst out with a blazing intensity. The yelping and yacking of the gnolls was followed by high-pitched cries for release as they poured through the portal. "Your efforts are noble ... but meaningless. Odry, destroy them!"

Without hesitation, the horde of gnolls streaked forward across the field and the ifrit and the demons charged towards them. "Mala, Dhather, take the demons! I have the ifrit! Everyone else, preserve the keep!" Codgarak shouted, and each member of the party immediately took action. The minotaur took a stride forward, his battle-ax in tow. He generated a massive amount of kinetic energy, met the ifrit's flaming spirit sword, and sent a shockwave across the newly formed battlefield.

Liam backpedaled, knowing his limitations, as he was still recovering from the previous attack. He stood in front of the keep's doorway and watched as Cashmes, Edha, and Lythya flawlessly dispatched gnoll after gnoll. Cashmes enjoyed grabbing them and throwing them across the battlefield, using their flailing bodies as projectiles. Liam now realized what the battle had looked like while he was inside the keep at the very beginning.

Dhather, slashing with his swords in a fury, exposed a demon's midsection. Taking advantage of this weak area, he landed a powerful side kick that propelled it backwards, tumbling over a cluster of gnolls. In this brief respite, Dhather discarded his magical swords. Extending his arms outward with his palms facing behind him, he roared with intensity. The same shade of blue light as his swords began to appear around his hands. As his roar continued, he brought his hands forward, slamming the backs of his hands together in front of his face. His roar ended, but the magic continued as a beam of blue light shot forward, scorching and eviscerating everything in its path. He moved the beam across the battlefield, and many gnolls didn't have a fast enough reaction. Liam watched as a dust cloud of evaporated gnolls wafted across the area.

Dhather finished his magical attack and returned to reengage the recovered demon and work to prevent their forward progress yet again. Mala seemed to be enjoying the battle—at least, it seemed that way, seeing how he was using gnoll corpses as his weapons, swinging them around by their hind legs as he laughed at the demon's failed attempt to overpower him. *Psychotic cat*, Liam thought, but he was quickly interrupted as a group of gnolls began to approach him. Having made it around the front line, they'd discovered what seemed to be an easy target. He counted at least twelve creeping closer to the keep's entrance.

Believing the attack was imminent, Liam gripped his gladius swords tightly and strained to connect his mind to what little of his will remained within his soul. With no more time to spare, Lythya came leaping in, landing between Liam and the gnolls. Growling and snarling with pure rage, she flexed her muscles, a slight tremble coming over her body, as if her body struggled to contain her anger. The wolf humanoid faced off against the hyena humanoids, baring their teeth at one another, until finally the first gnoll moved forward.

With a flash of energy, Lythya shot forward faster than an arrow but still slowly enough that you could just see her trajectory. She sent small shockwaves out with every gnoll she pounded, leaving only a spray of blood spatter floating in the air as she bounced from one to another. The gnolls were too slow to react, highlighting one of Lythya's greatest strengths in combat. The final count was seventeen bodies flat upon the ground when she had finished. She went off in search of her next victims, as Liam lowered his head, sighing in relief and grateful for the powerful warriors he had allied himself with. He thought how different this battle would be if they were just standard soldiers from one of the realms.

Codgarak had the upper hand against the ifrit, but that didn't last long—a green bolt of energy shot past him and pierced the ifrit's head. "An expert as always! *Himph!*" Liam turned to see a tall copper-skinned warrior standing behind him. His left arm was extended out in front of him, his right hand across his chest, pointing forward in the same direction as his left arm as if he were gripping a special king of invisible bow and arrow. Green energy still emanated from his left fingertips as he lowered his arms back to his sides. He wore a dark tan shirt and pants that appeared to be woven of soft wool, but Liam could tell that it was a different material entirely. There was a large black leather belt around his waist, but what really stood out was his face. It was painted pitch black with green streaks running down the front. On his head was a large mohawk, combed backwards and braided intricately.

"I have been conjuring a lot of magic waiting for this moment," Aibek said in a peaceful yet forceful tone. "And now it is time to—" He stopped as Liam turned to look at what Aibek had been focusing on.

Azazel appeared to be distracted from the battle, having turned his head hard to the right. It was clear by the sudden movements of his head that he had had a realization. He snapped his head to the left again with a fast jerking motion, appearing to sense something approaching fast. Without any further hesitation, he conjured his portal and began stepping through it.

"No!" Aibek shouted and raised his arms again, instantly conjuring the green magical energy and shooting beams towards Azazel. Azazel disappeared into the portal, but not without taking a hit to his right shoulder. Grabbing hold of it with his left hand, he looked back at Aibek, but he still gave the impression that he had no concern about the group that, up to that point, had defeated the evil force he had brought with him. Just as fast as he had appeared, he was gone.

Edha and Cashmes finished off the few remaining gnolls, although some had escaped to the safety of the woods. "The surrounding realms will have to finish them off," Edha said as the group began to come back together, reuniting with their rescued friend.

DEMON WARRIOR

AHAL THE TORMENTED

Large exhales could be heard from each of the members of the group. "Of course that pussy leaves right as Aibek and I show him what real warriors can do! What a cunt!" Mala said, walking up to Aibek. They clasped each other's right forearms, pulled each other close, and finished with an embrace. Mala followed up with, "It has been too long, my friend … I won't lie, you had me slightly worried that your time had come."

"I tried everything I could to get a message out to you all, but clearly they failed. The prison cell they conjured for me was stronger than I could overcome. I began to believe that perhaps my fate was finally sealed." A smile spread across Aibek's face as he finished.

"Out of the way! Out of the *wayyy*!" Lythya came up and embraced her brother in a long, tight hug. "I told you I should have come with you!"

A slight sigh left Aibek. "And you would have wound up sitting next to me in there. And yet here you are, my rescuer."

Liam squinted, his eyes moving from side to side. He was thoroughly confused. "Half wolf creature sister to human man …"

Golgoth leaned over and whispered in his ear, "Don't read too much into it. *Himph!* It will be explained in time." Liam shook his head but instantly regretted it, as everything now seemed to be spinning and his balance was far off kilter.

"Oh, shit," he whispered. Aibek nodded towards Liam and looked at Golgoth.

"He was attempting to reach you when he suffered a soul and spirit attack by two of the demons guarding your cell. He is still recovering. *Himph!* The boy has spirit." Realizing the irony of the phrase in relation to the attack Liam had just sustained, he added, "Well, what little remains of it, that is! *Himph! Himph! HAHAhahaha.*"

"Lythya, go fetch a chair from inside and bring it for the lad, and find a cup and water while you're in there." She did as Aibek instructed, and after a moment, she returned from the keep with the items. "I do not know your name." Aibek stretched out his hand in greeting.

"I'm Liam." He clasped the warrior's forearm just as Mala had done. Looking into Aibek's eyes at that moment, he realized that they were solid black. No iris or sclera at all, as if it was all just pupil. As soon as their skin made contact, however, he saw a flash of green pass over the solid blackness.

"He is the son of Judah of Artho," Codgarak interjected.

"Judah of Artho. That is a name I have not heard in a long time, nor …" The green flashed across his black eyes again, and there was a brief pause before he continued. "I'm sorry for your loss, Liam." Though Liam was taken aback by the fact that Aibek could know such information, he simply nodded in response.

"Here, take a seat." Aibek directed him to the chair that Lythya had retrieved. As he sat down, he directed him, "Focus on an object that is not moving." Following Aibek's guidance, he saw a tree in the distance and focused on it. "Mala, do you know what the bullticutt flower looks like?" The tiger nodded. "You should find some just over that knoll. Can you fetch some of its petals?" Aibek indicated with his head. Mala departed the area in search of the item while Aibek directed Edha in a different direction. "There." He pointed to a pine tree. "I will need pine needles from the tree and two of its cones." The leopard also did as directed. "Golgoth, go look for kliploo vines around those rocks."

The members of the group all returned a short while later holding the items Aibek had asked them to find. They handed them to the warrior, and he began to crumble and grind the ingredients into the cup. Finally, reaching inside a pouch attached to his leather belt, he retrieved a small orange. "What is the orange for?" Edha asked.

"Flavor … it is going to taste like absolute shit, but it will at least help with the potent taste." Liam watched from his chair, a melancholy expression on his face. He didn't care about anything.

"Should I add—"

"No." Aibek cut Golgoth off instantly, but he did it in a graceful and respectful manner. "Let the terpenes of nature be the healer. Magic does not always have to be met with magic. We are of the earth, and there are times when it is best to allow it to bring us back centered with it." Aibek swirled the solution together as he proclaimed his belief. Handing the cup to Liam, he said, "You must drink it all."

As soon as it entered his mouth and hit his taste buds, his instinct was to spit it out. He grimaced and snapped his head back and forth. Fighting the urge, he told himself to swallow and practically gulped the entire thing in one motion. Coughing and hacking up the remnants in his mouth, he spit out what small part remained, but it did nothing to ease the aftertaste.

Lythya had fetched more chairs from the keep, creating a small circle, and the group allowed themselves time to rest from the long day's events. Lythya shared with Aibek her efforts to find him while also informing him of the loss of Agos inside the Hunters' Shrine.

Aibek and Golgoth sat side by side upon the stone steps the led up to the shattered keep door. Aibek turned slightly towards the demented man. "I am surprised to see you amongst the hunters."

Golgoth had been looking at the ground. He glanced over at Aibek and then at the trees. "Tis a surprise to me as well, my friend. *Himph.* Never would I have imagined myself ... stuck ... inside a—"

Aibek cut him off. "Inside your own prison." Golgoth glanced at him again and nodded before he returned his gaze to the trees. "And why have you not released yourself from your prison?"

Gologth's head swayed from side by side as if he was watching a bird in flight gliding through the trees he was focused on. "*Himph.* Though I hold the key that could release me from this confinement, I simply cannot accept a new beginning when I still have so much to atone for from my past. *HIMPH, himph* ... How I have longed for this all to end ..."

Liam eavesdropped on their conversation. He began to feel compassion for Golgoth as he listened. It then dawned on him, *Holy shit! My spirit is being renewed!* It was subtle, but as the healing elements of nature were absorbed into his body, his soul and spirit were renewed with the original will to serve—the belief in who he was and why he'd originally started out on this journey towards being a warrior. Feeling his soul being renewed once again, his mind latched onto it, building a stronger connection between the three: body, soul, and spirit.

Liam noticed out of the corner of his eye that Mala had made his way towards the center of the battlefield outside the keep. "What's wrong with Mala?" he asked the group, who all turned their attention to the tiger.

The group went together to investigate, and as they walked, Dhather, said, "Something isn't right."

A split second later, Golgoth cried out, *"We are not saf—"* But before he could finish his sentence, a four-layered portal tore across the sky above them. Purple flames encircled them and beams of red light shot down onto the area where Mala was standing. He leapt out of the way just in time as the red light burned the ground.

Smoke began to fill the area, and the wind whipped into a small tornado. The smoke spun, forming a funnel that reached up and connected to the portal. The sun was veiled, with the purple hues and red highlights as the primary light source. The warriors began to draw their weapons and prepare for battle.

The black smoke pouring over them left some of them struggling to breathe and coughing profusely. The red light finished making its marks on the ground, and a purple flame and thick dark smoke appeared at its center. Before any of the warriors could react, glowing red molten chains shot out and wrapped around each of their throats, choking what little oxygen remained within the engulfing storm.

The blazing purple flame lifted itself into the sky and hovered over the group. As it did so, it pulled at each of the warriors and lifted them up along with it. Liam was gasping for air and could barely get enough oxygen to stay conscious. Their grips gave way and their weapons fell to the ground below, powerless to whatever entity enslaved them.

There was a hard tug around each of their necks as they gargled and strained for air. A giant human-like face appeared within the purple flames and dark smoke. The head was shaved clean, but Liam could see that twelve spiked horns protruded from its skull, and down the center of its head was a mohawk of jagged bones. Its forceful jawline protruded slightly forward, and its nose ring glowed purple with red inlays.

"WHERE IS AZAZEL?" The voice rang out with thunderous force, echoing as if encircled by mountains deep in a canyon. "I FELT HIS PRESENCE HERE MOMENTS AGO! WHERE IS HE?" Everyone struggled to speak. "ANSWER ME!"

Codgarak finally had enough strength to respond. "He fled."

The chain pulled the minotaur closer to the flame and the face protruding from it. "I KNOW OF YOU!"

"Yes … I helped free you after the Battle of Sent."

Just as quickly as the group had been enslaved in chains, they were thrown backwards and driven into the earth. Their chains fell off except for Golgoth's. "YOU!" Just as Codgarak had been pulled forward, it was Golgoth's turn, and he came face to face with what could easily be described as a deity. "WHERE IS YOUR MAS-TER?"

Golgoth struggled to answer but was able to squeak out, "I don't serve him."

"LIES!" In a split second, Golgoth was driven into the ground like a stake but was immediately pulled back up, hovering once again in the air. "YOU REEK OF HIS VILE STENCH!"

The smoke and flames raged around them and Liam held his hand up to shield his face, attempting to watch what was going on. "I KNOW HE IS NOT IN GRENSSOC. HE HAS WORKED TO HIDE FROM ME SINCE THE DAY I WAS SET FREE. I SENSE HIS PRESENCE HERE AND FIND YOU. YET YOU LIE AND SAY YOU ARE NOT ONE OF HIS? YOU ASSUME ME TO BE A FOOL!"

Golgoth looked as if he had passed out, barely holding his head up. In what Liam assumed was anger at the lack of an answer, the chain around his neck emitted more light and Golgoth appeared to come back to life. "I swear it." His voice trembled as if the shards of his memories were being dragged through the very fibers of his soul.

"I SHALL DEVOUR YOU FOR ALL THAT IT IS WORTH!"

Golgoth looked back at the flaming face. "Why would I send you the ifrit to devour if I still served Emmanuel?"

There was a slight pause until Golgoth continued. "It was me that gave you Odra to consume. Did you not enjoy feasting upon him?"

"WHAT TRICKS ARE YOU CONJURING NOW?"

Codgarak floating in the air with the others spoke over the clasped chains around his neck. *"It is not a trick. He speaks the truth!"*

Looking down at the minotaur for a brief moment, he drove Golgoth back into the ground once again, but this time the chain snapped back and returned to the cloud—and so did those of all the others. A loud thunderclap rang out with a shockwave, and the tower of purple flame dissipated. Floating in the air in front of the group was a large muscular entity with charcoal-gray skin and glowing red script all over its body. Protruding from each of its shoulders were two horns, similar to the horns around the outer rim of its head.

Liam, from his angle, could just see that there was a row of bones protruding down its back, continuing the line of the mohawk on its head. It wore metal forearm bracelets and a purple sash around its waist. Its massive legs were cut off where the knees should be; instead, the blazing purple flame remained.

Codgarak continued the discussion. "Ahal! Golgoth turned from Emmanuel just before the Battle of Sent when you were set free. He has never returned to his old master, nor will he ever. I swear this!"

Ahal looked straight at Codgarak. The purple flames flaring out of his eye sockets made it look like he wanted to obliterate every one of them just for the fun of it. Golgoth began to move and slowly got to his feet as Ahal turned his gaze to him. "Ahal … *himph* … you were the tormented one … *himph* …" Tears began to run down Golgoth's face. "I played my part in that, yes … but I swear to you

259

I turned from that evil long ago." He fell to his knees, his arms outstretched. "For once you were the tormented one, and now … it is me who is tormented … for the things I have done."

Codgarak followed up immediately. "Ahal … it appears we share the same desire, for Emmanuel has brought a great darkness and suffering upon this land, it seems. All the signs point towards him, and we … only desire to free the land from his evil, just as you are now Ahal the Free."

Ahal's face contorted with rage. He snapped his head between the two warriors, apparently fighting with whether or not to believe them. Finally, in his rage, another thunderclap shook from above; he roared ferociously as he forced his hands together, pointing them at the ground. Purple flames shot out, burrowing deep into the earth and consuming everything they touched. The entire time, Ahal was screaming in rage. His anger, emotions, energy were all channeled into the flames that carved their way into the earth.

Finally, after a brief moment of unleashing his fury upon the ground, Ahal seemed to snap out of existence. As fast as he had arrived, he shot back through the multilayered portal, and the purple flames and smoke that encircled them retreated with him.

It fell eerily quiet. No one said a word but just stayed where they were and took in everything that had happened.

Except Mala. The cynical cat stood up and went towards the crater in front of them. Standing at the edge, he peered down into its depths. "You know … we should probably put a rope around this … or perhaps a fence. Don't want cunts like Liam falling down there, now, do we? As you all know … I'm all about safety first!"

AHAL THE TORMENTED

A WASTE

A portal quickly appeared at the marble entrance to the celestial palace Set had constructed. White marble tiles stretched from the grand entrance all the way through the courtyard, past the fountains, gardens, and stone pillars adorned with statues. Beacons of light colored the walls and provided a grand spectacle no matter where you were. Angelic voices sang throughout the palace, which was surrounded by billowing clouds illuminated by aurora borealis energy waves.

Azazel made his way down the long entrance hall, his reflection gleaming off the marble and the ponds that lay on each side. He grabbed hold of his shoulder, but it was not enough to stop the bleeding; small droplets marked his trail as he went. He gritted his teeth, not wanting to report the news to his brother but knowing his blunder would eventually be discovered, and that would be far worse.

He arrived at the main corridor and continued until he reached the rear balcony. It jutted out of the house and overlooked what appeared to be the universe itself—a bottomless pit that continued into the depths of hell and a universe outstretched towards the heavens. Every single hue saturated the sky in a splendid mixture. But Azazel didn't have time to enjoy the view before—

"Are you bloody kidding me? Really? Really? Azazel!" He just shook his head in response to Set's barrage. "You're bleeding all over my palace!" Set pointed with his right hand, shocked that Azazel would be so inconsiderate. Set still gripped a stiff drink in his other hand. "You better clean that piss up before you leave!" He took a long swig of his drink before he continued. "If I wanted blood all over my floors, I would have built my palace amongst the damned way down below!" He walked over to Azazel and gave him a silk towel from the bar. "Pull yourself together, old boy!" Set slapped him on the right shoulder before he walked away, a grimace coming over him with a sharp inhale, Set turned his head as he continued his walk. "Oh, right! Bad form on me, but piss-poor performance on you, so ... oopsies!"

Marduk and Bast walked in from across the way. "What have you gotten yourself into now, little brother?" Marduk said in his smooth, flowing voice, continuing, "You're the pretty boy of us, not the warrior."

Set cut in with his arms outstretched. *"Hey!"*

Marduk turned his attention towards to Set, who smirked sarcastically and waved his arms up and down, drawing attention to his body. "I said pretty boy! We all know you're the handsome sex appeal and suave socialite!"

Set appreciated the compliment. "Ahh! *Right!* Thank you for clarifying that," he said with a charming smile.

Marduk added to the statement. "But I must say Bast almost has you beat on the sex appeal."

Set followed this with, "Oh, but absolutely, yes! It's practically impossible to turn her down now, isn't it! If there ever was someone who is twisted steel and sex appeal, it'd be you, darling!" He raised his glass to Bast, who had ignored everything up to that point, and sat down on the cushioned settee that faced the other three. She nodded her approval but didn't say a word.

"Pah! Where are my manners? Dearest sister, what shall I pour you to drink?" She just shrugged her shoulders and lifted her hand, a sly smirk on her face.

"The usual it is, darling!" Set poured a drink and began taking it to her.

Azazel chimed in. "So you get her a drink but not me?"

Set snapped back, "Look, baby boy, if you want to sit at the big kids' table, then give your balls a tug, start acting like a big boy, and get your own bloody drink! Everything isn't all about you, now, is it?" Bending over to Bast, he handed her the glass. "Kids these days! I swear!" She winked at him in appreciation.

Azazel walked over to the bar area and poured himself a drink. "What happened, little brother?" Marduk asked him.

"I captured a warrior who came investigating my activities at an abandoned keep at the edge of RemaMortBrook's border with Delco."

"Oh, right! I know that place!" Set intruded upon the conversation. "I fucked a ginger there right before I fed her to my pet Sarpath." Marduk looked at Set as he returned to behind the bar that he and Azazel were standing at. Set continued. "What? There was no point in keeping her around … gingers don't have souls!" Marduk dropped his head, having heard the same joke for thousands of years. "*Classic!* I know!" Set finished with a broad, charming smile.

Marduk returned to his previous conversation. "Azazel, why waste time with a prisoner? You should have just consumed his soul and spirit and fed him to the gnolls as a reward."

Azazel took a stiff drink before answering his brother. "I tried …" He placed the glass on the bar. "But everything I did didn't work. He was able to resist me in all attempts."

Marduk looked up at Set, who made a confused sarcastic face that proclaimed *The fuck do I care?* Turning back to Azazel, he said, "And then?"

Azazel had been gazing out into the cosmos for a second. "I figured eventually we'd figure out what was so special about him. So we imprisoned him within one of my rune shields and discovered that he wasn't powerful enough to overcome that—at least on his own."

Set, out of boredom, asked, "So you were with this prisoner the whole time ... you know! Up to his ... escape?"

Azazel grabbed his glass again, finished his drink, and went for a refill, knowing the harassment that was about to come his way. "No."

Set raised his eyebrows in frustration. "Hurry the fucking story along, Azazel!"

It was now Azazel's turn to raise his eyebrows at his older brother. "I was in Sun-Share-Co ... attending to business."

Marduk turned his head and looked over at Bast, who rolled her eyes with an "I'm not surprised" look. Set's mouth dropped open and remained there for a brief second until he responded, "You prancing little slut!" Azazel took another drink, letting out a long sigh as it went down, while Set continued to chastise him. "I told you to stop messing around with Princess Alsharra!" He bounced his head back and forth with his eyes rolling.

"Yeah, well ... fuck it."

Set pointed back at him. "If I wasn't the devil, then I would swear that she was!" He shook his head immediately after his statement, grabbed his glass, and polished it off. "I'm telling you, Azazel, your ego and that wench will be your downfall, just like Klipko-shek!"

Marduk sighed and worked to get the conversation back on track. "How did your prisoner escape?"

Azazel turned to him. "I felt the first rune be destroyed and immediately went to the keep. I took Odry, Engli, and Fortix with me and a few hundred gnolls I had lying about."

Marduk interrupted. "What about Odra, Pretox, Iud, Mat, Eadel, and Erch?"

Azazel had directed his gaze back towards the cosmos, having to admit his failure for not taking charge of the responsibility he'd been given. "One of my demons informed me that Odra apparently launched an attack through a portal. It was said he took a few hundred gnolls with him. Once the beacon alarmed, I went there as soon as I could, but by the time I arrived, everyone was already dead."

Again, Set's jaw dropped open. Extending his arm all the way above him and slapping his hand down onto the marble bar, he shouted, "*You don't say!* Shocking to think that the child himself left the stupid fire spirit and nonexistent-IQ dogs alone by themselves and hopped the twig while you got your jollies on!"

Marduk put his hand up in an effort to calm Set down. Bast tilted her head down slightly and motioned for Set to join her. Taking his glass with him, he made his way over and plopped down beside Bast as her arm wrapped around him. She brought her hand up and began stroking his hair and running her fingers through it as Marduk continued the conversation. "Do you know who it was at least?"

He shook his head. "They didn't carry any banners. Honestly, they just looked like a ragged group of fighters. A bunch of outcasts …"

"Outcasts that apparently c—"

Bast put her hand over Set's mouth and *shh*'d softly in his ear. The two looked back at the pair sitting on the couch before re-engaging. "A minotaur, two lions, some other animals intermixed with humans."

A smirk came across Marduk's face. "A minotaur! Now that's a fight I enjoy! I haven't fought one of them in a few hundred years. *Ha!* The good old days." He saluted the air with his glass, paying homage to "the good old days" before he continued with his next question. "And how many did you take down before you fled?"

Azazel looked down at his drink, swirling it around the glass before taking another sip. "I didn't engage."

Marduk shook his head. "You certainly aren't the warrior amongst us … it's all right, baby brother, you might as well leave that to us."

Azazel held his hand out to reaffirm some of his reasoning. "That isn't why I fled, though." Marduk returned his attention to him. "I could feel Ahal's presence, and he was aware of where I was and began quickly approaching the area. I left as soon as I realized that the … soul stone had been removed from the keep where I placed it."

Practically leaping off the couch, Set yelled, *"You stupid bloody bastard! Do you know how many souls we dedicated to powering that stone?"*

Azazel nodded and tried to calm him down. "Look, I—"

"That stone was powering the vast realms of RemaMortBrook as well as Cho'took and I-Rongoth-Hesgeth!"

"I know—"

"You better figure out a solution or else I'll disperse you into a new soul stone and replant it myself!"

Grinding his teeth as hard as he could, Azazel slammed his glass down on the bar and stormed off the balcony, proceeding through the palace the way he'd entered. Set shouted at him as he went, his words echoing throughout the area. "Your brother Marduk is doing his job with the centeth and Delco, your sister is doing her job in Showlay, I'm babysitting the walking dead, and you're over there fucking about! Do your job, Azazel!"

AZAZEL

THE CAPTIVE'S KNOWLEDGE

Golgoth sat far off to one side. Ashamed, he was afraid of the questions bound to come his way. Codgarak, Aibek, and Dhather had formed a small circle to discuss the immediate future of the group. "We certainly can't stay here." Dhather said.

Codgarak shook his head in a "no we can't" response. Aibek added his knowledge of the area. "It is a mile back, at the base of Red Mud Hill—there is a cave in-which I found shelter, two days before I was captured. I don't believe they discovered it."

"Can we all fit in it?" Dhather asked. Aibek nodded in response.

"We're heading out! The time to make ready is past. Let's go!" Dhather instructed. The group collected themselves and didn't hesitate to follow his order.

"Aibek will lead us out. Golgoth, me, and Codgarak will follow suit. Mala and Cashmes will follow. Lythya and Edha, rear security." Liam didn't even attempt to ask the question; he just dropped into the line wherever he saw fit, but certainly never anywhere near

Mala. Within a minute the group had formed a line and were heading away from the keep at a good pace.

The entrance to the cave had to be dug open more. Aibek barely fit in it himself as he contorted his body to get in. The others, with their broad shoulders and greater width, would not have managed. Codgarak used his battle-ax to drive deep into the rock face and loosen the earth around the entrance as the rest worked to claw the entrance wider. It took longer than they wanted, but eventually they were able to accomplish their task.

One by one they shimmied their way through the opening, immediately discovering they would have to drop down onto the next level to gain their footing. They all eventually made their way inside. Working together, they found boulders within the cave that they used to form a makeshift wall, blocking any light and sound they generated from escaping the cave.

Satisfied with their efforts, Aibek cast a spell that sent flames to each side of the cavern—a magical torch, as it were—and once the area was fully illuminated, they could take in the grandeur of the vast open space they occupied. It wasn't just any cave; it was an old lava tube that fed one of the many volcanos in the region.

For hundreds of years, during the Age of Survival and the Age of Discovery, Mount Shascus had raged with volcanic torment as the tectonic plates attempted to discover their proper resting places. The magma flowing from deep within the earth found its path of least resistance, melting the least-dense materials. Over time, as the magma flow lessoned, the sides hardened, leaving a smooth rock surface that formed a natural tunnel structure within the earth's layers. Liam could not believe the vastness of the network. They could have fit over a hundred of them down there and still have had plenty of space to rest.

The group made their way towards the center of the room. "Wait!" Golgoth stopped them. "Release some of your magic to me." They didn't question him, and everyone except Liam—who didn't know exactly how to do that—provided the requested resource. Golgoth began his conjuring. Dark green runes began to appear around him as his statements took shape.

"Rtanutn nhes sotu htam doo setens.

Rtanutn nhes sotu htam doo tattin sains.

Rtanutn nhes sotu htam doo uxens ah molet.

Rtanutn nhes sotu htam doo potmuss ah nhu tunusneons."

As soon as he had finished, he threw his arms out. Dark green runes, which had been hovering around him, shot out and hit the cave walls embedding themselves into the stones with a light pulsating glow to them. A dark green sheen appeared and moved in a wave over the entire cave surface, covering the area once the runes rested within the stone structure.

"*Himph* ... that should do the trick. Though I wouldn't mind finishing what we started with this ... Azazel? I would certainly prefer not to have Ahal intrude upon us again."

Dhather added, "Especially if he is actively seeking Azazel as well. With the likelihood of the demon returning, I would guess that Ahal will be more attuned to anything generated in this area."

"My thoughts exactly! *Himph!* Look at us being of the same mind. *Himph, himph.*" Golgoth gave a demented grin.

Codgarak took the lead. "Let us not waste the time we have been given. Mala, take Liam over there and begin combat training."

The white tiger drew his head back at an angle, his chin pointed down at his chest. "You sure you want me to train the c—?"

The minotaur cut him off before he could finish. "That's a good point. Cashmes, Lythya, take Liam over there and get some combat training in with him. Mala will oversee it, just... try to keep your mouth shut will you?"

Mala quickly chimed in, "No promises."

Cashmes nodded in agreement. "Come on, Liam. Let's see what you've learned so far."

"Edha, you have first watch at the entrance." She followed Codgarak's instructions and found a comfortable spot.

"Let the rest of us reflect on all we have seen and heard. Aibek … and Golgoth … it would appear your insight into the past will help us understand why this … Ahal is so interested in you." Without push-back, the remaining members respected the minotaur's direction. Aibek conjured a fire with his magic, and the four sat around it. The metallic *tang* of weapons engaging echoed slightly in the distance as the others went further into the tunnel to train.

Aibek started with the information he had obtained leading up to and after his capture. "The gnolls are from the Taka-Rok realm. But their genes have been altered. The more they feast on spirits, the faster they populate and the stronger they become. It appears that they have been strengthening their numbers for some time. I have seen hundreds come and go from the keep. They appear to be subservient, for I have never seen any of them give a command. The demons who managed the keep were the ones to issue the instructions."

"How do you know the gnolls are from Taka-Rok?" Golgoth asked. Twisting round and retrieving a small piece of plant from one of his pouches, Aibek held it up in front of him for the rest to see. "This is a piece of the littermacha bush. It only grows in the Cainten Valley, which is the historical home of all gnolls. I found this all over the area next to gnoll tracks and droppings. So even if the gnolls have expanded into a new area, these are from Taka-Rok. Additionally, though the demons spoke in their celestial tongue, I was able to decipher the names 'Emmanuel' and 'Lithram.'" Aibek threw the dried plant into the flames and looked around at his counterparts. "The demons you slayed certainly assisted in the overtaking of Lithram, and from what I could tell, they were quite disgruntled at having to leave it for this assignment."

A slight pause in the conversation spurred Dhather's realization. "I know exactly what this moment calls for." The rest watched, curious, as he reached into his travel bag and produced a pipe and a small container of Conocetico shade tobacco leaf. A chuckle rippled amongst them.

"That is exactly what I need," Codgarak chimed in with a sigh, and Aibek followed.

"It has been too long since we have shared leaf together."

Each of the four added the leaf to their pipes and the smoke wafted around them. They savored the slight tingling of vanilla, notes of almond, and a pinch of sweetness in every drag they inhaled.

Dhather brought the conversation back to the topic on hand. "So how did Emmanuel come into the alliance of demons, then?"

Codgarak and Aibek turned their attention to Golgoth. "Care to enlighten us?" Codgarak hinted.

"Emmanuel ... *himph!* He has always been evil ... *himph, himph* ... too long did I assist him towards the ... fruition of his desires to obtain more power and knowledge of such." Golgoth reached into his breast pocket and retrieved a small cask, drinking the solution to drown out his internal demons before he continued. "Emmanuel sent me to find Klipkoshek, a demon from the ancient times ... this demon thrived during the Age of Discovery."

Taking another long drag on his pipe, he quickly glanced at Codgarak, but seeing the minotaur's gaze looking back at him, he looked away, not wanting to make eye contact. "I sought the demon and found him, bringing him … introducing him to Emmanuel. I did as my master commanded, and then I saw how quickly Emmanuel advanced in his understanding of magic but also its corruption. *Himph …* "What a fool I was." His eyes began to water and he took another drink, letting his gaze get lost in the depths of the flames. "Back then I was so eager to serve my master … the things I … accomplished … performed … all of it for his enhancement and desire for destruction."

Codgarak worked to keep his companion focused on the topic. "And what of this Ahal?"

Golgoth pressed his lips together. "Have you ever heard of drakonmites?" Everyone scoured their memories, all of them making guesses from the fragmented information they recalled. Golgoth shook his head at their failed attempts. "Drakonmites' lineage comes from dragons. In our known history, they are the only bloodline directly connected to the ancient creature."

"No, you stupid cunt—not like that!" Mala's insult was loud enough to attract their attention. Codgarak rolled his eyes and looked at Dhather, who shrugged. Golgoth returned to his story.

"A tribe of trolls traveled deep into the heart of the Terrex Mountains. They discovered what they claimed to be the mother of all dragons. Captivated by the magnificence of the creature, they became entranced into serving it for the rest of their lives. Trolls do not connect to the spirit or soul planes as others do, but they are highly connected to the physical and magical planes, the same as dragons. In service to their deity, the trolls scoured the lands and captured tree ents, ifrits, sylphs, junteers … anything that had a strong soul or spirit connection.

"As the dragon feasted, it realized it could enhance its servants. Granting them a magical blessing, it provided the trolls with its blood. They eagerly consumed their master's gift. This went on for

274

many years, and over time they discovered that their bodies were changing. *Himph!* Their bone structure began to be enhanced and reinforced. The jagged bones protruding out of them acted as armor, as you witnessed with Ahal.

"Additionally, though, their connection to magic grew immensely stronger. They could wield it, create it, absorb others' magic and distort it to their will. The more they feasted on souls and spirits, the more powerful they became.

"It was after I brought Klipkoshek to Emmanuel that he dispatched me to … find these drakonmites. *Himph!* Oh, and what do you think old Golgoth did? Hmm? Hmm? Find them I did! Though … I never found their dragon mother. I captured Ahal and brought him to my master; it was then that Klipkoshek used his celestial powers to enslave Ahal and entrapped him to the magical plane. Mentoring Emmanuel, Klipkoshek taught him how to trap Ahal within the plane and to perform his bidding."

"And what of the other drakonmites?" Aibek inquired.

Golgoth looked over at his old friend. "When your master commands you to slaughter … *himph, himph* … you do as you are told. When we left the valley, nothing remained alive. *Himph!* I assure you of this."

"So it was after that when you left Emmanuel's service?" Dhather asked.

"No …" Golgoth's stared over the flames and met the lion's eyes gazing back at him; he knew, though justified, that the lion's judgment was not of ill intent but purely honest inquiry. "I served Emmanuel for much longer afterwards, watching as Ahal was tormented daily in his enslavement. I left Emmanuel's service just before the Battle of Sent. That is why when Ahal was freed, he still believed I was a servant to that bastard. *Himph, himph.* That is why I do my best to hide my tracks. Remaining hidden is one of the best tools of survival. *Himph!*"

"Then perhaps it is time you leave this venture," Dhather said.

"And why do you think that?" Codgarak enquired.

"Golgoth is a walking beacon for Emmanuel, demons, and apparently a rogue and reckless genie." Dhather's arms had been crossed until now, but, taking a new drag on his tobacco, he pointed towards Golgoth with his pipe in hand. "Is the risk of discovery really what we need?"

There was a slight pause before the lion continued. "I also…" Dhather paused and cleared his throat, "how is there no longer the temptation to return to your ways, Golgoth? In the presence of your old master, will you truly be able to resist returning?"

"*Himph! Himph* … There is only one temptation within me, my new friend, and—*himph!*—I assure you, it is never to return to the Golgoth of old."

"It is a risk that we need to consider and discuss later, at least," Dhather emphasized, to which Codgarak and Aibek nodded in respect.

"And what of the soul stone?" Aibek asked.

"What soul stone?" Codgarak replied.

Reaching into his bag, Aibek retrieved the purple-illuminating stone. "This had been set within the keep and appeared to be emitting an energy from within it."

"This is probably what has been sustaining and influencing the region," Dhather suggested.

"It is probably best we hide it. Surely this Azazel will come looking for it, possibly even Ahal if he realizes it is within reach," Codgarak said.

"His attention was certainly on Azazel, Golgoth, and Emmanuel. Clearly distracted from its presence, perhaps. But if this genie feasts on soul and spirit energy, it would certainly make him more powerful. We don't know Ahal's true long-term intentions, either," Dhather reminded them.

276

"Golgoth, any way you can encapsulate the stone?" Codgarak asked.

"*Himph* … I believe I have a binding spell that may work … but … *himph* … may not be best that I perform such." Curious about his logic, the minotaur urged him on with a hand gesture to continue. "Let us play the 'what if' game … *himph* … Should I be captured, if brought before Emmanuel … he will surely be able to identify the spell I cast and know there is something of importance we attempted to hide." Golgoth nodded towards Aibek. "Let the Originhaul utilize his people's magic to bind it. I do not believe Emmanuel, nor even Azazel, will be able to discover its source. *Himph.* Their influence on the physical plane is so vast that I don't even believe Ahal's magic could discover it."

Aibek nodded in appreciation at the positive affirmation towards his species. "I do not have a high enough skill to perform such a strong binding spell." He then pointed behind him with his tobacco pipe. "Mala does, though."

As if Mala himself knew how to time things perfectly, the group heard his voice clear as day. "If there was ever a moment I have lost all faith in your abilities … surely it is now, cunt!" The group around the fire all sighed in unison as the large cat continued. "Can you at least perform one attack sequence without fucking it up, son of man?"

"*Mala!*" Dhather called out.

"Oh, goodie … I am saved from the misery before me." The tiger appeared a moment later. "That son of man was shaken as a baby, wasn't he?"

"We need you to bind this soul stone to hide it from discovery." Aibek lifted the stone in an outstretched hand and gave it over to the tiger.

"Ohh, lookie! A glowing rock!" Mala began to juggle the rock in the air back and forth between his paws.

"Mala …" Codgarak tried to capture his attention, but the tiger continued. *"Mala!"*

"What, Cod?"

"Can you bind the stone?"

Mala still batted the stone in the air, not even looking at the beast talking to him. "Of course I can! You silly bull, you!"

Dhather turned and roared at the tiger, *"All right already!"*

Mala grabbed the rock in the midst of his juggling act and, without saying a word, began to produce layers of teal energy around the stone. Layer by layer the magical light was overlayed and intertwined meticulously. The stone and the encapsulating box of energy continued to float and rotate in the air until finally, a small clap of completion rang out. The box's teal color faded into a dark brown and it took on the appearance of a wooden trinket box.

"There you go. The stone is concealed so nobody will be able to sense its wareabouts." Mala tossed the box back to Aibek and began to walk off towards the cave entrance. The group didn't say anything but simply admired the skill of their companion. "You're welcome!" came the sarcastic statement from afar as the distance between them increased.

AIBEK

THE FIVE PLANES

Nudge

.

.

.

Nudge

.

.

.

WHACK!

Liam was jarred awake in the dimly lit cave. "Fucking titties ..." He twisted to see the white tiger standing over him.

"I bet you wish you had titties, you—"

He interrupted him. "I get it, I get it!" He grabbed his face and squished it to awaken himself more. "What is it, Mala?"

"It's your turn to take watch. Now get your ass up and do something semi-useful for once."

Liam exhaled. "Can't you just give me five more—" The cat reached down. Grabbing him by the ankle, he launched him towards the cave entrance. Surprisingly, out of sheer dumb luck, he landed on his feet.

"Guess it's not just cats who land on their feet! *Prick!*"

The tiger bared his teeth and hissed at the lad, who said, "I fucking hate you!"

The tiger bowed in return and stated, "The feeling is mutual, I assure you."

Liam made his way to the cave entrance, but instead of remaining inside, he chose to find a seat outside. The hillside had a slight slope to it, and though he was tempted to lie back and rest, he knew he would be chastised for eternity should he give in to his body's temptation to fall asleep again. Doing his best to sneak around in the dark, he finally found a fallen tree that he felt would make a good seat. He took a quick glance at the hillside contouring upward behind him and felt that there was no potential threat to concern himself over. It had been a while since he'd been able to take in the vastness of the universe surrounding them; gazing up at the heavens, he embraced the splendor that shone and sparkled down at him.

"You choose a good spot to star gaze." Liam was so startled that he physically jumped and fell off his seat into the dirt. Clambering back to his feet, he drew one of his swords. He couldn't see anything but knew that the voice had come from his left side. "You performed that move perfectly ... what would you call it?" A figure appeared slowly before him, a green glow coming from his hand, which he held close enough to his face for it to be illuminated in the darkness, and Liam was asked just to reassure his belief, "Aibek?"

"Who else would it be?" Aibek replied.

He bent over and placed his hands on his legs, gasping for air. He had yet again held his breath from the initial startling fear.

"I ... uhh ... yeah, that move there ... last I checked, it's called 'I shit myself.'"

Aibek chuckled in the darkness as he removed the green energy's glow from his hand. He made his way over and sat on the tree that Liam had picked out. Catching his breath, Liam secured his sword and sat back down next to Aibek. "Well, I was enjoying the view until the *night terror* showed up," he whispered with emphasis.

"Has anyone ever taught you the stars?"

"Uhh, well, there is the Malin Warrior, Hoag's Throne, and the Wolf River ..." Liam pointed out the three constellations he knew.

Aibek leaned forward slightly, stretching out his arm. "Coma Berenices, also known as the Black Eye Galaxy." Moving to the next one, he said, "Ursa. Circinus. Cygnus and Cepheus. Volans."

Liam took a minute to take in the scene. "So I overheard Golgoth refer to you and your people as Originhaul."

Aibek replied, "That I am."

Are all these people like Codgarak or something? What's with these short replies! Liam thought, but he said aloud, "Will you tell me of your people?"

"Mmm. Not this night but soon, I will share with you their story."

An owl called in the distance, while a running field mouse shuffled the vegetation just enough to hear. "Are you a hunter like the others?"

"Yes."

"How long?"

Aibek sighed. "I was amongst the first of us."

"No home or realm to serve instead?" Aibek shook his head and Liam continued his questions. "And why is that?"

Inhaling deeply, Aibek said, "My soul, it drives me to where I must roam. It tells me I belong to the wilderness; it begs and pleads with me to run. My spirit reminds me to turn away from the world, to leave it behind. My home is wherever the wild calls me to each night. Therefore I tear away the exterior so I may see what is on the inside and find solace in being one with my soul and spirit."

Liam didn't think Aibek could see it, but he rolled his eyes, still not awake enough to comprehend the complexity of this statement. "So what you're saying is …" He paused and left his sentence unfinished to see if Aibek would catch what he really wanted.

"What I am saying is the brave do not live forever, but the cautious do not live at all."

They all gathered in a circle around the morning campfire. Aibek had caught some rabbits in the early morning for them to enjoy. "What should we do?" Dhather asked the group, but the question seemed primarily directed towards Codgarak.

Cashmes stepped forward. "The last time I checked, we are hunters. That means we pursue evil when we find it, and we have found it. We know it lies in Lithram right now. We know that if we wait to act, Emmanuel will continue to leave a trail of destruction behind him. RemaMortBrook will certainly have their heads up their asses, be so disorganized I … I don't even want to think about what it would look like helping them fight that battle." The faces that had seen battle smiled, knowing all too well the situation Cashmes was referring to. "We could stay here and wait for Azazel to return, but we easily defeated him, and we know he is not too great a concern at the moment. We need to get into Delco and see what the kingdoms are doing to counter this threat. I say we head to Buuklingran and see how we can be of service to them and Delco. From there we can reassess the situation."

Everyone just nodded and looked at each other. "Come on, you slugs! No time to waste ..." Mala grabbed his traveler's pack and headed towards the cave entrance.

"*Himph!* I find great comfort in the pursuit of violence!"

They had traveled all day through the wooded areas. The magic wielders had tried multiple times to teleport but had come to stop trying after their failed attempts. It seemed to take forever, but now they had a greater understanding and knowledge of the evil threatening the realms. Aware that they were now prime targets for capture or retaliation, their movements were far more calculated. Remaining undiscovered was more crucial than ever before.

After traveling the entire day, they arrived at a location they all agreed upon as a suitable campsite. Each member began to attend to camp chores: gathering wood, hunting for a meal, setting up their lookout locations, and Golgoth placing enchantments around the area with magical runes to protect them from any late-night wanderers who might be ... curious.

The fire was started. Aibek made it look as easy as breathing. His people's ability to connect with the physical plane on such an immersive level made his abilities unparalleledAs Liam sat by the fire, he felt it was the perfect time to ask Dhather a question he had been pondering. It had been clawing away within his mind ever since his introduction to Ahal. "Dhather?"

The lion looked over. "Yes, son of man?"

"When we were at the Hunters Shrine ... Golgoth cast a spell which opened a ... portal. But there were layers to it."

"Yes."

"With the entrance of Ahal, there was that same layering effect, and Golgoth even said he fed Ahal the ifrit. So what exactly are those layers?"

"Ahhh. I see." The lion uncrossed his arms. "Do you know what this answer requires?" Liam shook his head before the lion continued. "Tobacco. Hold that thought." Dhather retrieved his pipe and tobacco from his pack and enjoyed some long drags from it before he began his answer.

"Our world is formed … as best we know … on five separate planes of existence. The physical plane, which we are in now. The spiritual plane, where the ifrit was formed and where it naturally lives. The soul plane. This is the plane that can be confusing, because not everything has a soul, such as dogs. But other creatures or animals can potentially have one, such as Mala, Cashmes, me …" Liam nodded, listening intently, and allowed his mind to imagine these planes of existence based on the little pieces of them he'd seen through the multilayered portals.

"The next plane is that of magic. As Golgoth said, Ahal was tormented and banished to this realm, given his strengthened abilities in magic. The final plane is the celestial. It is here we believe the Ancient One dwells, but also within that plane is the organic realm of angels, demons, and the other celestials." The lion took more long drags on his pipe, and the thick smoke danced around the fire and made its way towards Liam. The aroma of the smoke met with the chillness of the evening hour and left him feeling like autumn had fallen upon them.

"Some of us have the ability to span all the planes. For example, you are a man—"

"Baby back bitch is more accurate," came Mala's insult from behind him as Dhather continued.

"You have a physical body that connects you to the physical plane around you. You also have a spirit; it is this spirit that connects your physical body to your soul. Your physical body may be hurt, but your spirit is fine because it is influenced more greatly by your soul. However, one may be in a darkened state of depression—a soul that is lost and seeking out a will and purpose. This internal torment surges through one's spirit and can then infuse its dark nature into the physical body, practically crippling the person in the process."

As Dhather continued his master's course of education on the inner workings of the universe, Edha approached and handed them some fruit the others had found while foraging in the local area. "Cashmes has found some fish in a nearby stream, and Lythya caught us a deer. We'll have them prepared and ready for the fire soon. This should tide you over until then." They both thanked her, and Dhather continued his lecture.

"This connection in my opinion is one of the most crucial things that people need to understand, reflect on, and apply to their lives. But ... that is for another day. Another key aspect of this is demonic or angelic possession. Have you heard of this?" He pointed his pipe at Liam. Not wanting to assume Liam's knowledge on the matter.

"No ... I don't believe I–"

"All right ... there are times when people or beings can become demonically or angelically possessed. Additionally, creatures such as boars or deer can be controlled to make them act in certain ways."

It was Liam's turn to cut Dhather off. "Like in the War of Patastal?"

"*Ahh!* Yes! You know of this story?"

Liam smirked. "Yes. Master Fry told me briefly about it at Fort Patton when I was in training."

"Excellent! Yes … just like that. A soul cannot be possessed. It can be consumed, it can be influenced, it can be attacked, but it cannot be possessed. However, a spirit can be. That is why those animals were able to be used, through magic, against the opposition. Demonic possession, angelic possession, consumes the spirit and replaces it. The soul cannot connect with its physical shell, so to speak, while the spiritual possession is taking place. The soul is not harmed, but the physical body may be due to the spiritual possession forcing the physical form to act."

This is crazy! was all Liam thought. The wave of new insights was almost overwhelming to him. "So … have there been demonically possessed people, but then the demon departed them? And … if so … did the person die because their spirit was possessed?"

"Yes … there have been stories of such a thing happening. However, when the demonic presence leaves the body, it doesn't kill the soul of the person. The spirit is damaged or hurt. But the soul, which influences and fuels the spirit, from what I've been told, will regenerate and heal itself over time. Though that time is variable depending on the individual and the severity of the incident."

Edha brought over the items and began to place them over the fire to cook while they continued their lesson.

"The same goes for magical possession. The spirit may repair itself in time, but the spiritual possession can cause the person to die before the magic, demon, or angel departs."

The lion took another long and deep puff from his pipe, but he didn't slow in his efforts to impart his knowledge to Liam. "The magical plane … that is what connects the soul plane to the celestial. Just as the spirit is fueled by the soul, so is the magic fueled by the celestial. Though I must admit, neither I nor anyone else I've met knows exactly how this process works."

Liam tilted his head, eager to hear the reasoning behind this. "The current theory, I have concluded, is that it is actually the celestials themselves who give power to the magical plane, and those who know how to utilize or wield magic can benefit greatly from this, depending on who they've allied themselves with."

"So ... we know that Azazel is a demon ... theoretically, Azazel could be sending his power from the celestial plane into the magical plane for Emmanuel to harness and use for evil against the soul, spirit, and physical planes?"

The lion chuckled in a low voice, nodded his head, and exhaled another round of tobacco smoke. "Exactly ..."

"So what of the soul stone, then? Souls cannot be possessed."

The lion pointed his pipe at Liam. "Ahhh ... remember, the souls in a soul stone were not possessed; they were consumed. The soul stone is a good example to discuss, though. Dark magic was used to consume souls and spirits, which were infused into the physical plane, but it impacts, as far as we know, the physical and magical planes at the same time."

"This is fucking deep!" Liam reached up and ran his fingers through his hair, brushing and scratching it lightly.

Dhather laughed loudly. "*Exactly!* That does beg the question, *if* ... if souls and spirits can be consumed and utilized to empower and enhance magic, that would lead us to believe that the magical plane can be fed power from both sides—from the celestial plane and, on the other side, the soul and spirit planes." The lion slapped his knee. "I could talk about these theories and principles all night!"

Liam exhaled as Edha approached to turn their dinner to cook evenly. She whispered to him, "If you think this is bad, you should hear him talk about the lineage of the elves."

Liam shook his head and put his hand up. "I think this is good enough for this evening." She winked at him with a brief smile before departing.

"Wait!" his eyes narrowed at the lion, who was somewhat startled by the snappiness of his statement. "How is the ifrit a spirit, then? I mean … that doesn't make sense to me! It's a fire spirit but has a physical form. So how does … you know …?"

"You don't think that fire has a spirit?"

Liam pondered that thought. He tilted his head and looked back at the lion again, not sure exactly how to respond. "But … spirits are fueled by souls … but an ifrit doesn't have a soul … just a spirit and a physical form."

"Correct."

"I'm still confused."

"Have you ever seen a wildfire? Blazing upon a mountainside as it consumes everything it desires? I have seen many times where the entire world is on fire, yet it preserves a tiny house within the midst of its heart. At the same time, I have seen fire walk across water … nothing to stop it from devouring its victim on the other side of the void. Fire has a spirit. The ifrit is conjured within the spiritual plane for a single purpose, and whatever that purpose is, that is what the spirit is commanded to do. If an ifrit had a soul, it could change its spirit to, perhaps, not destroy … so whoever conjures a spiritual entity determines the course it's set upon."

Liam was still curious about what options there may be. "And there is no way to change it?"

"I have never heard of any other path."

The lion took a drag of his tobacco, and while he did so, Liam realized he had been converting his ring to a wristband and back into a ring throughout the entire discussion. "Wait …" Pausing everything, he looked down at the ring on his finger. His mind flashed back to the fight with the demons in the keep's stairwell. "Okay … the demons attacked me with a soul and spirit attack. They then conjured a shield with the white energy."

The lion nodded and interrupted. "That would have been the soul energy they drained from you."

289

Liam nodded in return, both traveling down the same mental pathway. "And my ring transformed into a wristband knife that cut through the shield."

"Yes …"

"Because it's formed in the physical plane but with magical properties."

"Yes …"

He tilted his head and looked down at it on his hand. "But … what power was used to infuse it? Was it a celestial power that placed the magic into the ring, or was it the consumed souls and spirits of others that powered the magic within the vessel?"

Now it was the lion's turn to nod and look down at the ring, but he quickly turned back to Liam. "Who said it is not your soul that is powering it?" That took Liam by surprise. "Could your soul not be powering the strength of the ring itself?"

Slightly shocked by the realization, Liam said, "I suppose it's possible, but I don't …"

"Perhaps it is both, young Liam. There is nothing that says both a celestial influence through magic and your soul could not be powering your gift at the same time." Liam looked at Dhather intently, grasping the simplicity yet seriousness of what the lion was suggesting. "The Ancient One works in mysterious ways, dear boy." A big smile crossed his face. "I have no doubt that in time you will discover the mysteries within it."

"Look, I don't know if y'all are done or not, but I know *I am hungry*, and I'm pretty sure the rest of us are too. So shut your munch boxes about the mysteries of the universe and let's eat!" Cashmes proclaimed as he intruded into the inner circle of the fire, and without further hesitation, the rest of the group joined them.

"You have been getting a grand lecture on the ways of the planes, I see," Aibek said to Liam as they sat around the fire. Side conversations, jokes, and stories of old were being shared amongst the group sporadically. Liam, with a mouth full of food, just shook his head in response. "The youth are eager to learn but are often arrogant about putting that knowledge into practice."

Liam swallowed his food. "And what knowledge will you teach me this night?"

"Ahhh, come on, kid!" Cashmes said as he got up from the fire. Mala, Edha, and Lythya all stood up as well, and they began to depart. "Way to ruin the mood." Lythya said.

Edha complimenting her, "Total turn-off for me."

As the four left, heading towards the dense woods, Liam turned to look at Golgoth. Though he still didn't care for the company of the demented warrior, he found reassurance in him not following the others. "Thanks for staying."

"*Himph!* Ohh, trust me, young Liam, I share in their sentiment ... I am just too drunk and too lazy to stand up and leave. *Himph!*"

Liam's head slouched in discouragement. "*Himph!* Oh, and Codgarak is asleep ... so the bull man would probably be bored with this too if he were awake. *Haha-hehehehe.*" Liam looked over and realized Golgoth was right. This whole time he had thought his first mentor was awake, but in reality, the minotaur just sat there, still as a board, with his arms crossed and his head slightly bowed. As he focused on him, he heard the faint sound of breathing coming from the bull.

Aibek looked down at some nuts that he was holding in his hand, sifting through them that he may select his favorites to enjoy first. He clumped some cashews together, dropped them into his mouth, and chomped down in delight. He didn't need to look at Liam; he could feel his spirit lower itself. The outcast ... the unwelcome ... the never worthy enough. He knew that Liam didn't realize it now, but this suffering would be something he would use later in his life. He would be the experienced one eventually; then he must be the one to bring the outcast into the fold.

Aibek kept his head down as he started to speak. "Suffering is never pleasant … that is why it is suffering. It doesn't matter what suffering it is either, but suffering has a purpose. Suffering is an instructor of life, just like many other things. Though you are suffering as the outsider, the outcast, the only way not to be that is to endure it."

Liam didn't want to admit it, but it was the truth. It was on that note that Aibek continued his lesson for the night. "Truth has become the most feared thing in our society. The truth is never pleasant. Because it places accountability and responsibility upon us. It exposes weaknesses, faults, and failures. People do not want to be seen as insufficient. So we always say we want the truth, but rarely do we ever actually want it."

Aibek grabbed the next cluster of nuts and consumed them, chewing as he continued. "The truth is, Liam … you are unwanted, you are unwelcome, you are unprepared for this." Liam did his best to have a poker face, to hide his emotions, because no matter what he did, the words came cutting through his spirit and landed directly on his soul. "It is not that you are not a good lad, young Liam … it is not that you don't have skills or abilities or potential … it is the fact that you are not ready for the level this journey requires.

"You are sitting here amongst some of the greatest warriors I have ever known. Hence why we vowed to be hunters. It is not that we are the masters of skills, but rather who we are as individuals. It is that which makes us the warriors we are today. The years of discipline, training, battles, wars."

Aibek let his last point hit home. Working the nuts around in his hand, he grabbed another cluster and indulged; the rest he placed back into a carrying pouch. "It was fate that brought you to Codgarak just before Mala brought him the message of my disappearance, and it was Codgarak's mercy that allowed you to join him up to this point."

Liam took his eyes off Aibek for a moment, glancing at Dhather, who just let their conversation unfold, but he met his gaze before he turned back to ask, "What if it wasn't fate? What if it was my destiny to be there and to be a part of this ... team?"

Aibek pondered his question for a moment before answering. "Then I would say you should be sure not to take any moment for granted, because the truth remains that your skills and abilities are more of a hindrance than an asset."

"Do not lose sight of the lesson, Liam. What Aibek says will help guide you in your many years to come. Truth is rarely sought after, and when someone comes and tells you they're seeking it, there is a good chance they may not actually desire it. You will see in life that the truth will make you even more of an outcast in comparison to a liar. Integrity is often a lonely road, similar to how you may feel now as a young apprentice," Dhather said.

Liam let the heavy conversation rest for a moment, but then ... felt the need. "I'll return shortly." Getting up, he looked for a good tree ... not too far away from the light of the fire, but not so close that there was no privacy ... it must be the right ... "Got it!" he said to himself as he spotted his target.

Walking over to his chosen spot, he began to undo his pants to christen the newly declared bathroom. You can't aim too high on the tree and get splashback ... but you don't want it too low either so you cover your boots; it has to be at the exact angle to ... his eyes caught sight of something just a little further ahead from where he stood. Squinting his eyes to get a clearly view, he saw the silhouette of a knight ... standing just at the edge line of the fires light and facing him. *"Oh, fuck!"*

His remaining piss sprayed around as he realized he'd left his gladius swords over at the fire. He stumbled through the tree line, ricocheting off trees as he went. *"We ... have ..."* CRASH! He hit the next tree head on, as his head was still turned towards the knight. *"OW! Comp-any!* Fuck, that last one!" He was still fumbling around as he went; he hadn't secured his pants all the way, and as he came thrashing back into camp, feeling like a colossal failure, he tripped over the log he'd been using as his seat and landed face first in the dirt with his pants barely covering his manhood.

"What the hell happened?" Dhather asked him in surprise. Liam had failed to communicate his sudden and incoherent message as he crashed through the woods.

"There was a knight stalking me in the woods as I p-p-p pissed!" Just as Liam ended his sentence, the dismal reflection of the knight's metal armor brightened as he stepped forward through the last thicket of bushes. Walking slowly and methodically, he approached the fire and stood at the edge of the camp. Liam squirmed vigorously as he secured his pants and retrieved his swords.

To the right of the knight, another figure appeared—a man with black and white paint covering his face. The sides of his head were shaved down to the skin, but he still had long black hair that was slicked down and hung around his face; it looked wet. To the right of him, a woman came through the thicket; she had a red horizontal line across her face, and feathers dangled from a band wrapped around her head. Looking from one figure to the other, Liam saw another figure appear, this time to the left of the knight. This slender figure wore metal armor as well, but it too had just a faint reflection coming off it. The helmet was metal and forged into a detailed replica of a human skull.

There was a tense pause as the two groups stared each other down with intensity, grips tightening upon each fighter's weapon of choice. Just when Liam thought the situation was about to explode into combat, a greeting came from the man with the black and white painted face. "We mean you lads no harm this night."

The man took a few more steps, the palms of his hands open and facing them to show he held no weapons and was not conjuring any magic. "We are but four weary travelers. We've been on a vast journey for many days now, keeping to the wilderness, and noticed the light of your fire from afar." He turned and looked at his three companions before turning back. "We humbly ask that you'd be so kind as to let us warm ourselves by your fire here ... and hopefully share with us whatever food remains you may have?"

Liam could hear the other four returning. They conversed openly, and he could hear a few chuckles. It only took a few seconds for them to arrive. They all stopped, not out of fear or concern, but as Cashmes put it best, "Who the hell are these guys?"

It was then that Codgarak broke the silence. No one had noticed if he was still asleep or not. "Which one of you four was supposed to be on watch?" The minotaur opened his eyes just enough to see as each of the four pointed in unison to one another. "Figures," was all Codgarak responded. They looked at one another as they each tried to place the blame upon another. Finally, shrugging off the error, they put their hands back down.

"Seriously, lads ... my lot and I mean you no harm. I am Crocontimont. But my crew here just calls me Cro for short." He pointed over to the woman with the feather headband and red-striped face. "This is Kimberonna." He then pointed to the knight who had originally terrified Liam—"Sneak"—and, making his way over to the last newcomer, "and finally, Ferra."

Aibek called out to his sister, "Lythya, have you seen any bastnaesite in the area? They should be—"

She cut her brother off. "There was one just back the way we came."

295

Aibek nodded. "Please bring it to me." She departed in haste as Aibek noticed Dhather looking at him. He knew what the lion was curious about, so he filled in the gap. "I need the neodymium from within the rock in order for the incantation to work." Dhather nodded.

"Sorry, fellas, but we've had some interesting encounters recently and … well … you could say we just want to trust you but verify what you're telling us," Cashmes said in the moment of tension.

"There's no need to apologize, friend. We would do the same given the circumstances," Cro replied.

Lythya returned with a small rock the size of a chicken's egg in her hand. Aibek stood up and clasped his hands over hers, encapsulating it between them both. In a soft voice, he began to speak.

"Mo shook, sha-hatta sep.

Mo shook, fema roto ma

Mo shook, sha-hatta sep

Ma rah, freeta roto sahh."

Lythya repeated the chant after Aibek, and once complete, she relinquished the rock to Aibek. He turned towards Cro and approached him. He did not seem concerned for his safety.

Motioning for Cro to stretch out his hands to receive the rock, he informed him, "If you are lying, we will certainly know it soon enough. Now … take the rock and tell us your name, where your origins lie, and what your intentions are." Cro nodded at the instructions. "Once you are done, hand it to each of your group members, for they will do the same."

Cro took possession of the rock. Holding it, he looked over it with curiosity before answering the questions posed to him. "As you wish … I am Crocontimont. My people are called Charohcha and we originate from Guttmaccafect, within the Realm of I-Rongoth-Hesgeth. In the twenty-third year of the Age of Expansion, my people were slaughtered by the orc horde of Pashro-Shaltok. My people fled, and the few who survived made their way to the Realm of Hoth-Raila-Mah. It was there on the island where my people wandered for many generations. I come to you now, dear friends, asking for your grace this night, seeking the warmth of a fire, the nourishment of some food, and the pleasure of company amongst new friends."

The tension grew within Liam, and he felt it amongst his group as well. He didn't know what to expect from the rock, as Cro's answer was now complete. He looked at Aibek and glanced at the others to see if there were any reactions or expressions he could interpret to give him a better idea of what to expect. Everyone remained cold, however, and kept a stony seriousness on their faces. All except Codgarak, who still looked like he was sleeping.

As Liam thought about it, he turned to look at Golgoth, who was the only one not looking serious. He had a drunken smile on his face. "*Himph!* I have known a Charohcha or two in my days. You can come to the fire with me, my new friend! Let me give you a tour of the city of hell within my head ... but don't you worry! *HIMPH!* All the streets are named, and I know them quite well!"

Though Liam couldn't see his own face, he could feel a confused look come across it. Turning back to Cro, he was amused to see an even more baffled and somewhat startled expression upon his face. His first encounter with Golgoth left Cro asking the group, "You know, lads ... I know we just met and all, but I just want to check and make sure that he's all right ... you know ... in the head and all."

Mala, having stayed relatively quiet up to this point, chimed in. "His ropes are more entangled than the rest of us, but he's a far better companion than the cunt, I assure you." He nodded towards Liam, at which Liam made a fist and held it in front of his face. His lips were pressed together, and he gritted his teeth. *Not now, hairball!* he screamed inside his head.

"Enough." Aibek asserted himself back into the leadership position. The rest of the group had to use more effort than him to see the stone's reaction—Aibek's vision was enhanced for a brief period when focusing on the rock due to its enchantment. He could see the rock glowing with a dark green illumination. "Hand it to the next one of your members."

Cro did as instructed and approached Kimberonna. Handing the rock to her, he then backed away.

She followed in a similar manner to Cro. "I am Kimberonna of the Amikkawa people. I lived in the Realm of Showlay and was sold into slavery as a girl to pay off my family's debts. The city was attacked by the Papapites during the War of a Thousand Roses. I took advantage of the chaos to murder my enslaver and escape the city. It was at the port of Phippotath that I met Cro. I mean no harm to you."

Aibek watched the rock intently and after a brief moment nodded for Kimberonna to pass the rock along. She made her way over, passing Sneak, and handed it to Ferra, who followed suit. "I'm Ferra … I don't know who my people are, and I don't care. I was raised in a farming community that served King Tor of Ozerre." She paused for a moment. "I left there … and … eventually found Sneak. Together we traveled and found Cro and Kimberonna. I don't plan to harm you as long as you don't try to harm me."

Ferra stretched out her hand with the rock in it, motioning to return it to Aibek. He approached her but was hesitant to retrieve the rock right away. "You didn't pass it to your final member." He turned his head towards Sneak.

Ferra had kept her helmet down up to that point, but she lifted it now, exposing her face to him. "Yeah, well … Sneak doesn't speak, so … good luck having him answer your questions." She tilted her head and put her hand on her hip as she shifted her weight to one side.

Lifting her hand in a defiant manner, she said, "So what do you want to do, super chief?"

Out of the corner of his eye, Liam saw Golgoth approaching Sneak. Lingering by the knight, he got what would have been uncomfortably close for most people; any sudden movement by either of the two would have caused them to touch one another. Golgoth pointed his finger and twirled it around in front of the helmet's face shield. "*Himph!* A knight of few words, are you?" Golgoth swayed slightly while his finger continued its dancing motion. "I bet old Golgoth here could … get a squeak or two out of you. *HIMPH, himph, himph …*"

Golgoth then placed his finger on the metal and ran it across the surface slightly before he gave the helmet a shove. "Perhaps you are a knight of secrets! *HAHAha …* Golgoth also likes secrets, he does! It's true! *Himph!* I do, I do … I promise this …" Sneak didn't move but remained perfectly still throughout the encounter, "Perhaps one day you will share your secrets with me, yes?"

The moment was getting more awkward by the second until Codgarak brought it back to reality. "Enough!" His low, forceful voice slammed down like a hammer driving an iron rod into the earth. "Come … sit by the fire and enjoy what remains of the dinner prepared." Liam looked back to see that the minotaur's eyes were open and his hand outstretched, motioning for the newcomers to join them around the fire. "And as for you four"—Codgarak turned his attention to Mala, Lythya, Cashmes, and Edha—"Mala, you will see to it that you four cover tonight's watch seeing how you allowed our new guests to surprise us with their arrival."

"I would jump for joy over another pleasant assignment, but my knees these days aren't doing too good, so you'll have to excuse me from the pleasantries," Mala replied.

A smile came over Liam's face. He was pleased knowing he wouldn't be awakened by the tiger and could get a whole night's rest.

LYTHYA

THE END OF FREEDOM

The group made their way over to the fire, though there was still some uneasy tension floating amongst them. Liam went back to his seat, and as he sat down, Lythya passed by and used her magical ability to whisper to him in such a way that you couldn't tell what she said until the message entered your ear. "Though they don't desire to harm us, it doesn't mean they don't desire the information and knowledge we possess." She continued past him and he let the warning stay active within him.

Mala took charge of his new assignment for the evening. "Lythya, Edha, take the first watch." Doing as instructed, they went their separate ways while Mala distanced himself just slightly from the inner circle around the fire and lay down to rest, knowing he and Cashmes would have second watch much later in the night.

Golgoth staggered back to his seat in the circle. He had taken another long drink of the alcohol he had been hiding within his pack. He went to plop down on the log he had picked out for himself earlier, but he failed to stick the landing, as his body couldn't adjust its balance in time. As soon as he hit the log, he fell backwards and slumped like a dreary sack of wet and dirty clothes tossed into the corner of a room. It took a few seconds for the group to realize that he wasn't getting up. Codgarak shook his head while Dhather and Aibek stared and shrugged their shoulders. "Is he okay?" Liam asked Codgarak, who was the closest to Golgoth.

"If he isn't, we'll hear about it in the morning when he awakens."

Cro and Kimberonna sat down opposite Liam. Sneak was on his left side, and to his right, Ferra sat down. Now that they were within the fire's circle, Liam could see the finer details of the new arrivals. Cro's face paint was mostly a white base, with four black wavy lines that ran vertically down his face but an all-black neck area. He wore a semi-leather armored chest piece, but it was more what one might find a hunter wearing for protection than an actual fighter's or soldier's armor. The leather was black but had some faded, weathered areas that told Liam that it had probably been either purchased at a market, stolen, or taken off a corpse somewhere along Cro's journey. He then felt guilty for passing judgment on a newly arrived guest and thought that it could have been handed down to him by a family member. He wore a woven shirt with two large tears in the chest. The part that threw him off was … *Is that a skirt he's wearing?* The thought continued: *Who goes through the wilderness wearing a skirt?*

The newly arrived guests helped themselves to the food still available. They appeared to be extremely grateful for the generosity shown to them. Liam couldn't help himself, though; he had a mental hand slapping the front of his mind as he pondered the question in his head. Without any grace or planning, it just came blurting out: "Are you wearing a skirt?"

Cro looked defensive, but not in an offended way. "Have you never seen a kilt before, lad?"

Now Liam was really baffled. The voice inside his head said, *Does he not know what a skirt is? Because I don't know what a kilt is, and at this point, I don't think there's any way I can make this not make me look like an idiot.* He decided to just be straightforward about it. "Umm … no … I suppose I haven't, since I have no idea what you just said."

Cro smiled. "I'm guessing you haven't traveled much of the world?"

Liam shook his head. "No … it was only a short while ago when I left the forest of Artho in the Realm of Cho'took. Now we are here in RemaMortBrook. That would be the extent of my travels."

"Aye …" Cro looked over at Kimberonna and then turned to his other companions before continuing. "Our lives are probably very similar to yours … I'm sorry, I don't think you told us your name."

He felt somewhat embarrassed at not having been cordial enough to introduce himself. "I am Liam." He pointed around the campfire. "Aibek, Codgarak, Dhather, Golgoth, Cashmes." The others followed as he went, and with each name shared, they gave a nod of greeting.

"Thank you for the introductions, Liam. As I was saying, I have done enough traveling in my short life to believe that creatures throughout this world all have very similar core beliefs. We could be swapped at birth and both have the same experiences, so I hold nothing against you for living most of your life in this … Artho. If I had the choice, I would have preferred not to have traveled so much, but … not all of us have lives handed down on platters of silver or gold. We must make the best of the opportunities that are presented to us."

Aibek raised his glass. "Well said."

Cro just nodded in return and took a quick bite of his meal before continuing. "The garment I am wearing … my people call

303

it a kilt. There are a few other nations that wear them as well. For Charohcha's, we sew our family history into the side of the kilt."

Cro adjusted his seat to help display his kilt better. Grabbing hold of the side, he pulled it across so that Liam could see a narrow red stripe that ran from the waistline down to the bottom trim of the garment. Within the red stripe were symbols sewn vertically with black stitching. Next to the red stripe was a similar dark gray stripe with white symbols. "What do the symbols mean?"

"Each symbol represents a family member." Cro pointed at one and began to name his family members until he reached the bottom.

"And what of the stripe next to it?"

"Ahh yes, this stripe is our life events. Many of mine have been fights or battles I have aided in, so the swords, axes, and arrows represent those."

"Which one of those events means the most to you?"

A smile came across Cro's face. "Oooh, that one is an easy question to answer ... there's no comparison there." His finger made its way towards the top area closest to his waist. "Here ..." He pointed to a simple white circle stitched into the gray stripe. "This is when we built this family." He lifted his arm and motioned towards the other three in their group.

"There are people in this world who are born, yet do not have the blessing of being raised in a family. Abandoned ... or their family taken away from them ... does that mean they should be cursed to never know the love of a family?" He looked at Liam with an intensity that made Liam believe Cro was ready to fight the vilest of hell to defend his beliefs. "Destiny tried to keep me from having the love of a family ... I told it to hell with that shit! The three sitting alongside you ... we have been together through the worst of times, and we have embraced the glory of heaven together in the comfort of each other's arms over the simplest of things ... such as a shared meal." He took his gaze off Liam and took another bite of the food before continuing. "You see, my new friend, there is no comparison when it comes to family, even if it is the family you choose rather than the one you have been given. So that is an easy question."

Aibek, Dhather, and to Liam's surprise even Codgarak all nodded and raised their glasses. "That is something we'll drink to." Liam didn't fail to notice, though, that fixed to the far side of Cro's belt was a skull.

"And what of your skull?"

"Ohh … that little guy! That was my first kill in combat, a goblin I slayed during the War of Nonons."

Cashmes chimed in. "You fought in the War of Nonons? What part, precisely?"

Finishing the sip of his drink, Cro answered, "We fought alongside Lord Frix and his Raritan dwarves at the Battle of Wilcus and then marched onward and fought at the Battle for the Black Lightning Cliffs, and finally …" He turned and looked at Kimberonna. "Kimber, what was the last place in that series?"

She kept her head down as if she didn't need any jarring of her memory. "The Siege of Hugithmurta."

As soon as the words left her mouth, Cro began nodding at Cashmes. "That's the one! The war seemed pretty much wrapped up at that point, so we headed off shortly after that."

Cashmes smiled. "Okay … yeah, that would make sense. My sister Edha and I also fought in that war, but we were in the campaign for Lord Madderhatch and the Sagetillith dwarves."

Cro was nodding along and pointing in the air as if a map was displayed in front of them. "Right, right. You were on the other side of those mountains there … the … the …"

Cashmes filled in the gap for him. "Red Naga Mountains. They had tunneled all the way underneath and across that valley to Hugithmurta, and that was how they kept reinforcing their numbers so easily."

305

Cro added, "Yup! I remember the old lot saying that now …"

Cashmes continued. "We were so confused about how they kept repelling our assault, but once we discovered the tunnels after the siege, we put two and two together."

Cashmes took a drink while Cro continued to relive the memory. "We had hoped you were going to launch the attack through the tunnels to help us take Hugithmurta. I remember the captains being just pissed, mate … completely pissed that you all didn't."

Cashmes protested, "There was no way we could have made it through there … they had the entire tunnels fortified and we couldn't have made it all the way across and to you guys … would have been suicide."

A smile was on Liam's face as he listened intently to the war stories of old. There was a brief pause amongst the group, and smiles were shared. Cro smiling and shaking his head, "Imagine us being at the same battle and aiding in the same war and only a few years later randomly running into each other deep in the middle of this shitty wilderness."

"Surprising how small this world truly can be at times." Cashmes agreed.

"Which does bring us to a good question. What exactly are you doing here … in the wilderness?" Aibek asked.

Cro looked at Aibek, a sarcastic gleam in his eye. "I suppose you wouldn't believe we were just out for an evening stroll, now, would yah?"

Kimberonna looked up at Aibek to answer his question once Cro finished his statement. "Word began to spread throughout HothRailaMah of a vast war on the cusp of breaking out. We found a ship that we were able to stow away on and came across the Killcath Sea and landed in the port of Boredstill. Once we got off the ship, we learned that the rumors appeared to be true about this … Realm of Delco. Some villagers pointed us in this direction and here we are."

Aibek looked over at Ferra, who could tell someone was watching her and caught his gaze. "Look … I'm just along for the ride."

"Fair enough," Aibek replied.

Liam chimed in with a response. "You travel towards what you believe to be the greatest war of our time and you're simply … along for the ride?"

Ferra's tongue appeared at the edge of her mouth, sliding partially across her front teeth. A devious smile crossed her face, and she gave the cold response of a woman who wasn't going to put up with shit from anybody. "Really, fuckface? And what exactly are *you* all doing out here?" She finished her pointed question with a tilted head and a smile that declared *checkmate*. Liam wanted to look her in the eyes but turned away, choosing not to say anything. "That's what I thought!" Ferra ended the conversation quicker than it had started.

Kimberonna tried to bring some peace and gratitude back to the center of the group. "Thank you yet again for sharing your meal with us. We have had very little to eat for the past three days on our travels. Tonight's meal was certainly a feast in comparison."

Aibek nodded. "We are happy to share with you that which nature has blessed us with. Besides, it is not like we would be able to finish—"

Before Aibek could finish his sentence, the campfire popped, snapped, and flared with intensity. Yet no one had touched it or added any new wood to the fire. "What was that?" Liam asked, but before anyone could answer, the fire sparked and came roaring to life with intensity. The flames leapt up towards the heavens as the base of the fire forced itself outward in a circular motion, spinning faster and faster.

Dhather and Aibek stood up as quickly as they could and attempted to conjure magic fields to contain and restrain the fire. Before they could enact their magic, however, the fire bellowed ferociously to life, shooting pillars of fire towards them as they worked. The only choice they had was to divert their magical attempt towards creating a quick shield, which succeeded in fending off the majority of the flames, but not until after they'd sustained some damage from the initial blast. *"To your feet!"* shouted Codgarak.

Dhather reached down and grabbed the living sack that was Golgoth. The lion roared with a surge of adrenaline flooding through his veins, and his face was grim as he opened his eyes wide. Suspended in the air as the lion held him above the ground, Golgoth's head turned and he tried to take in what exactly was happening. He began to squirm as he worked to get to his feet, and at the same time, the lion lifted him up further, which helped him achieve this feat a little quicker. By the time he had made it to his feet, most of the group were already on their guard and ready to engage however they could with the mysterious entity that had caused the flames to leap out in an attack.

The flames were now taller than Codgarak, the tallest member of their group, and as broad as Cashmes and Dhather standing side by side. The intensity of the heat forced them to take more steps backwards. Lythya and Edha charged in from their posts. The two groups were now forged into one from the threat of the moment; all stood in a circle around the fire.

Without warning, the flames shot out again, but this time they went in all directions and sprang past them. Each pillar of the flame ended with an explosion of fire, and giant flaming knights appeared out of the explosions. Shiny black armor covered their bodies, which had the appearance of burning flames themselves. Spikes and horns protruded out of their armor, and each one carried a massive metal shield. Finally, a final pillar flamed out of the fire, and from it sprang forth a figure of the same size. The group having formed around the center fire, found themselves completely surrounded as the fire knights created a large exterior perimeter around them. Liam focused his attention on the final individual who sprang from the flames. His armor also shone black, but had rose gold edging and jagged inlaid patterns. The man's skin was ash white, the color that wood turns when the intensity of a fire is at its peak. His face was sullen like Golgoth's; he had a pointed nose and narrow eyes. Spawning forth from the fire seemed fitting for him, as the glare in his eyes left Liam believing that all he desired was to consume. His voice, however, was not what Liam would have imagined from the figure.

"I am Lord Wairick. Azazel has informed me that someone within this party has slain my sons Odra and Odry!" Lord Wairick's voice was high-pitched and snappy, with the arrogance of a spoiled child that was not getting its way. "You shall know what true vengeance is this night! Now! Which one of you bastards was it who vanquished my sons?"

Codgarak, standing at the ready, said, "It was me! I banished your sons to an eternal darkness. And it is me who will send you to meet them now!"

"Insolent cow!"

Golgoth stepped forward slightly. "*Himph!* Did Azazel also inform you that we didn't just kill your sons ... but we fed their spirits to a djinn? *Himph! Himph ...*"

"What!"

"Sorry, Codgarak, but I can't let you have all the fun! *Himph! Himph!*"

"YOU WILL ALL BURN BEFORE GOD KING EMMANUEL!"

Liam looked around and saw that there were twenty-four of the giant fire knights surrounding them—a two-to-one ratio. If ever there was fear building up inside him, it was now. *The father of Odra and Odry … Codgarak handled both of those ifrits, but the warriors Wairick brought with him have to be at least as strong as the two ifrits … right?* he thought. He was ready, his grip tight on his gladius swords and only waiting for—*splowww!* The green laser beam of light shot across the area in a flash. Liam did not have time to look around and confirm it, but he believed it was Aibek's magical energy shot that launched the battle into motion.

"One down, twenty-three to go!" Aibek's voice rang out just before the rest screamed and yelled their own battle cries. They launched themselves towards the fire knights closest to them.

Liam's mind flashed back to when he faced Codgarak for the last time at Thunder Rock with Master Fry, Master DC, and Master Jack watching. The fire knights were almost the same size as Codgarak himself. But he didn't have time to watch the others, as Liam started his attack with a point to prove to Aibek and the others who questioned his potential. The battle order beginning as he and a fire knight exchanged attack sequences—offensive, defensive, etcetera. Aibek's statement entered Liam's mind as a solemn reminder. "You are unprepared for this … you do not have the skills or abilities or potential … you are not ready for the level that this journey requires."

Aibek's words clanged inside his head, reverberating like a church bell ringing across a town square for all to hear. The inferno blazed, but not the fire that had brought forth the evil they currently faced—the inferno that raged inside his soul. There was a new level of intensity within him, and he didn't try to stop it … he let it rage as he began to feel his soul's connection to his spirit, and the energy flowed into his veins with more ferocity. *"You'll need more than fire to destroy me!"*

Liam jumped upward. Planting his right foot on a tree immediately adjacent to the nearest fire knight, he propelled himself off it and launched a new offensive attack, forcing the knight backwards as both his gladius swords struck with precision. Liam felt the strong connection between his soul, spirit, and body, and he grabbed onto the sensation he now felt this connection reach out and begin to pull at magic. Conjuring the energy from the magical plane, he brough it into his leg as he spun his body around. He released the magic with a swift kick, which caught the knight off balance and sent him to the ground.

Immediately turning his attention to the second fire knight near him, he charged full speed ahead, leaping into the air towards him. The knight raised his shield to block him, but Liam still had control over his magic and landed a kick on the shield, and felt the kick landed with great force than his normal strength. The force knocked the knight backwards and he stumbled, off balance. Seeing this, Liam ran towards him again. The knight watched him coming and raised his shield, but this time it covered his helmet and he couldn't fully see Liam's approach.

Liam planned it perfectly. Seeing where he wanted to take his last step, he dropped down and slid across the ground just to the side of the shield. His momentum carried him past it; the knight was in shock as they came face to face, the knight with both hands on his shield, expecting an impact. But Liam's hands were on his swords. He did not waste any time: He thrust a sword directly into the knight's throat.

The knight's body stiffened for a second before he fell backwards, his face towards the night sky. Like a fire deprived of oxygen, his flames began to fizzle and fade away, eventually extinguishing themselves.

Liam turned to see that the other knight had recovered and was making his way towards him. *"I am your destiny this night, knight … your death awaits you by my sword!"* The fire knight threw his flaming sword at Liam. It turned end over end as it hurtled towards him. He dodged the attempt and the sword's trajectory continued until it drove itself into the trunk of a tree nearby. The fire knight reached behind his shield and produced another flaming sword.

They closed the distance between them, and the song of their swords clanged in their combative melody. They continued to exchange blows, but Liam deflected each of the strikes that the knight produced. Having unleashed another round of strikes during his next offensive volley, the knight crouched down behind his shield and shoved against Liam, sending him spinning off to the side. Realizing the situation, Liam adjusted his footing and continued the spin, working his way around and punching his sword straight into the gap in the armor that exposed the knight's armpit and obliques. The fire knight began to extinguish himself just like the first one.

Looking around, Liam noticed that Cashmes was, surprisingly, struggling and was still fighting off two knights. Without hesitation he began running towards Cashmes. Gaining speed and momentum, he redirected his angle of approach. He was facing Cashmes, the backs of the fire knights towards him. Coming up from behind, he timed his steps just right and leapt onto a tree stump, which he used to launch himself higher into the air. He judged it perfectly and came down exactly on top of one of the knights. Pointing his swords downward, he drove them straight into the knight's neck, slaying him instantly.

He rode the knight's body to the ground, retrieving his swords just in time, as the other fire knight was wielding a battle-ax and had begun to swing it at Cashmes, but he carried the stroke through towards Liam. He raised his swords and took the full impact of the force with his blocking maneuver. The power of the knight's swing sent Liam flying backwards. He landed on a tree, knocking the wind out of him, and was immediately stuck to the ground like a magnet.

Gasping for air with everything he had, he felt completely immobilized. Finally, the oxygen filling his lungs gave him instant relief of the mind, but his body also gave him an unwelcome report of massive pain from slamming against the tree. He braced himself with his elbows and tilted his head up enough to see the battle raging on. He was working to get to his feet when he saw her fall …

Kimberonna was fighting her best but was unable to overpower the knights facing her. As she unleashed slashes with her ax and sword combination, she wasn't able to guard behind her, and another knight severed her legs, sending her crashing to the ground. The second knight stood over her and snuffed her life out with his spear. Cro did everything he could to fight his way over to her, but no matter what he did … it was too late. Cashmes finished off his knight and went to assist Cro in his efforts to reach Kimberonna.

Edha and Mala, also realizing what had happened, worked their way over towards the pair, forcing the few remaining knights back and giving them enough room for Cro to reach Kimberonna's side. Liam got back to his feet and dashed towards Golgoth, who still had one knight remaining. They quickly dispatched this knight in a coordinated effort and, turning towards the rest of the group, saw the few knights who remained. It only took a few more moments for the group to finish them off.

The group encircled Wairick, and he began to realize that his fate was also sealed. In a last-ditch effort, he tried to summon a fire portal to retreat, but Mala and Dhather were ready for him and bound him in magical chains—appearing as the same tactic Ahal had used on them. "*Himph!* I have an idea just for you! *HIMPH, himph* … Your flame may burn out, but your spirit will burn with pain as you feel an eternity of suffocation. Golgoth slowly approached the captured fire lord, holding a small piece of wood in his hand. His free hand working an incantation as he spoke…

"Upon this wood I do bind

A fire lord's spirit intertwined

Only to be released in time

313

For the benefit to consume a choosing of mine."

The ash-white color drained from Wairick's face and it turned darker and darker gray as the lord bellowed out in agony. A deep orange and red light poured out of his eyes and mouth and streamed into the small piece of wood Golgoth held in his hands. The fire lord's spirit entered into the wood, which glowed like an orange ember until the light faded away with a few pulses that changed the wood's appearance to that of a piece of charcoal.

Liam turned his attention to Cro, who was sitting on the ground, Kimberonna cuddled in his grasp. Looking at Cro, he could see that he wasn't even attempting to fight the tears back; allowing them to run down his face like a river down a mountainside. "For so many years you suffered … for too long life was taken away from you …" Ferra walked over and knelt beside Cro, placing her arm around his shoulders to do what little she could to give him comfort. "We found our freedom together and lived every moment without the fear of chains." Cro paused briefly before he shared his final words of the night. "Tonight was the end of my freedom, for my soul will no longer be complete."

CRO

TO HUMMIT

No one in the group slept that night. Aibek and Sneak prepared Kimberonna's final resting place—a deep grave facing a small ledge on the hillside. It had just enough of a slope that you could look out at the valley and see the rolling hills and the trees adorning them. The best real estate the area had to offer—certainly not good enough, but it was the best they could do, given the circumstances.

Cro held on to her for as long as he possibly could. His tears had run out. Not because he was no longer sad, but because his sorrow had reached the point deep within his soul where you become numb to anything but just have to endure the pain dwelling within. Though death is a certainty in life, you always believe you'll have time to say your goodbyes, as if death greets you and grants you a few final moments to say what you'd like to say. The cold harshness of death has its own desires, though. All too often, the words we hope to say will never be heard, but will only be imagined in the dreams of the loved ones we leave behind.

The time came when they laid her down for the last time. Aibek, Sneak, Cashmes, and Liam slowly covered her with earth until her grave was filled. They collected large rocks and placed them over the site. "Will you say some final words?" Aibek asked Ferra and Cro; Ferra just shook her head "no." Cro paused for a moment but said, "How can a man say anything that would capture the meaning of his life and place it within a few mere sentences?" He looked at Aibek and then moved around the group, making eye contact with many of them. "We are no strangers to death. Everyone here has experienced it; I can see it in your eyes. The words which I will share will be for only her soul to hear, as I tell them to her in my dreams."

Cro said no more but turned and walked away, heading towards the main camp. Upon arriving, he sought out Codgarak, who was standing with Dhather. "That ... fire lord fucker last night made a mention of Azazel and Emmanuel. Who are they and how are they connected to us?"

"Us? It appears you and your family have been caught up in something that is slowly entangling all of us," Codgarak replied.

"It seems clear that you and your group are ... well, a group. Have you given yourselves a name or are you just making shit up as you go?" Cro had his arms crossed and swayed slightly while speaking. He looked as if the grief and sorrow had begun to boil faster and turn towards vengeance. His emotions were not allowing him to stay still; he had to move and turn this energy towards a future objective—revenge.

"We refer to ourselves as hunters. Many years back, there was a collection of us ... defenders. We finally decided it was our time to hunt the evil we defended against. We now find ourselves on a new quest doing precisely that."

Dhather following Codgaraks answer, "Azazel is a demon that held Aibek captive. We just recently rescued him from his imprisonment, and in doing so, we destroyed two ifrits ... whose father

317

obviously—" Cro and Dhather shook their heads in understanding, having no need for further details. Dhather continued, though. "Emmanuel has led a campaign into Delco, however. The great city of Lithram was the first to fall to him, but the more we investigate, the more we see evidence of him being connected to this demon, Azazel."

Codgarak added, "The guards protecting Aibek mentioned an Emmanuel, Azazel had the ifrits, and now Wairick also mentioned the 'God King Emmanuel.'"

Cro nodded as he received this information. "There is a different level of trust once you've gone into battle with someone. Aye?" He nodded, and the two others returned the nod. "Now … I and my lot may not be 'hunters' like you all, but, as your name implies … the only thought on my mind is hunting this Azazel and Emmanuel to give to them what they have given to me." He wiped his face briefly and then stretched out his hand as he asked, "We may not carry your name, but would you allow us to join you on this hunt?"

Dhather tilted his head slightly and glanced over at Codgarak to gauge his reaction. The minotaur met the outstretched hand with a handshake. "Who am I to stop someone who is compelled to act?"

The group gathered around as Aibek, Codgarak, and the few others with experience in Delco drew a makeshift map on the forest floor with sticks. After some discussion, they decided to head towards the nation of Hummit instead of Buuklingran as Cashmes had originally suggested. Their logic was that Hummit offered easier access to Lithram should they decide to remain on the southern route. Hummit also served as the western leader to the nations on the western side of Delco, similar to Lithram in the east. If any of the few nations in the west knew how the realm planned to respond, it would be Hummit.

They started to get into the traveling formation they had been utilizing. Along the way, each of the party members walked by and gave fist bumps to Ferra, Cro, and Sneak. Sneak would be rear security and remain significantly behind the group. Dhather and Codgarak would be the next two in front of Sneak, and they would be preceded by Ferra, Liam, Cashmes, and Cro. Golgoth, Mala, Lythya, Aibek, and Edha would remain at the front, in the deadly tip of their lance formation. Their aim would be to pierce the initial armor of any adversaries and let the beasts carry their momentum forward, tearing every bit apart and causing the most damage possible. As they took their first steps forward, Cro commented, "To us honored few who travel east … that we may give death an opportunity to feast."

SNEAK

FOR PRIDE AND EGO

The closer they got to Hummit, the more commotion they noticed. The group began to compress, keeping shorter distances between them. Along the pathway and throughout the surrounding hillsides they could see patrols of soldiers roaming the area. Approaching the main stone wall, they saw military tents being set up in a nearby field. The planning and preparation for war seemed well under way, and the military leaders in charge of the undertaking were clearly up to their necks with non-stop tasks.

Livestock were being hustled throughout the camp as orders were placed for the massive quantities of food needed. Merchants with fabrics to make more uniforms were carted through as the blacksmiths yelled and argued with the quarry masters over the low quality of the ore coming out of the mines. The freshly hammered armor was not up to the desired quality standard. The commotion was its own chaos; one had to keep on one's toes and be one step ahead of any crises just to ensure things did not collapse like a house of cards.

In the distance, Liam heard the clanging of metal upon metal. "One! Two! Three! *Thrust!* ... *Again!* One! Two! Three! *Thrust!*" Looking into the field, he saw a sergeant at arms commanding the training of a combat formation. Two sets of soldiers faced each other, each taking turns to practice their offensive and defensive movements.

A paw was placed upon his shoulder; he glanced up and saw Cashmes standing next to him. "Remind you of anything?"

He shook his head. "All too well. We've had so much happen since then ... it seems so long ago that I was at Fort Patton."

"Hmmm. The precision of training is something that every soldier remembers. No matter how long it has been, the cadence of instruction becomes a song to one's ears over the years."

"I don't know how much of a song it is—more like a living nightmare from what I remember." Liam raised his eyebrows in judgment of Cashmes's interpretation of his memories.

Cashmes chuckled at his humor. "You will come to appreciate it, I assure you," the lion said with a smile, to which Liam replied, "Doubt it."

As they stood looking at the training, Liam overheard Mala inquiring of the main gate guard, "Is there a sergeant in charge of the military planning we may speak to? Perhaps my friends and I can be of some assistance to them."

"Of course, Sir Cat! But I regret to inform you that Sergeant Erik is quite busy if you ... can gather from all the busy bodywork going on. I shall deliver your message to him. Stand by in the meantime." The guard disappeared into the fortress as the group lingered in the immediate vicinity.

"We're going to find a drink," Ferra said and turned to walk away, not waiting for a reply. Aibek and Edha left with her. Lythya approached Cashmes and Liam, informing them she would find a suitable spot for them to spend the night. The entire area was so full of activity that it was hard to move easily without running into some poor chap just trying to go about their business.

"Sounds good," Cashmes replied and turned back to Liam. "I hate crowds of people … it's not always a benefit to be larger than the vast majority of those around you."

It was a little time until the guard returned and found Mala wandering about the crowd of people. "Sir Cat, Sergeant Erik will see you midday tomorrow."

"Is there a specific place he prefers?" Mala asked.

The guard looked around. "I'd suggest over there in the market—there are some tables travelers usually dine at. That would most likely be best."

The tiger snapped his fingers in front of him. "Oh, bother! I had hoped you'd say an elephant graveyard."

The guard tilted his head back. "Pardon?"

Mala chuckled. "A misplaced joke, I'm afraid. Good day." He bowed slightly at the guard, who raised his staff in salute.

"To you as well."

Those of the group who had remained nearby rallied round, but folk still weaved constantly between and around them. Mala pointed towards the tables the guard had indicated—"This way"— and they quickly dispersed.

In the background came the shouts of the guard: "No, you nitwit! The royal wine goes to the North Gate for entry! You there! That is not where we dump the waste! Pick up your pathetic garbage!"

The shouting had blurred into the overall commotion by the time the group arrived at the tables. The sun had begun its tilt in the afternoon sky, its aim set towards the horizon. "We may as well eat now. The dinner hour will happen soon and we can get to our camp and away from this misery," Cro said, and no one argued with him.

Waving the server over, they placed their request for food and drink. Mala began to share the information the guard had provided,

323

and they conversed about what they had observed so far of the war preparations. The good, the bad, the ugly, the— *"You disgraced cow!"* came the bellowing insult across the marketplace. There were confused looks on everyone's faces as they turned to see a large minotaur standing on the other side of the marketplace, glaring at Codgarak.

"Friend of yours?" Mala asked as the minotaur began to approach their group, shoving and moving people out of his way.

"I have no quarrel with you," Codgarak said when he arrived within earshot, but without hesitation he retorted, "Oh, but you do! Codgarak, is it not?"

Codgarak turned back to the table and grabbed his drink, taking a sip. "Damn it!" He held on to the mug, keeping it in front of him.

"I have searched for you in the past but couldn't find you!"

Liam whispered under his breath, glancing at Cashmes, "Clearly not hard enough!" A smile broke out on both their faces while the minotaur continued his chastisement of Codgarak. "For years I thought I would never get revenge for what you did to my grandfather."

"And who exactly is that?"

"Minokrak of the Teskonok clan!"

"And who are you, precisely?"

"Sinotred!"

The group didn't notice until one of them coughed, but Sinotred had a small band of ruffians with him. Liam, coming off his newly claimed victory of three slain fire knights, felt like even he could take on these goons singlehanded.

Codgarak just nodded slightly. "Well … clearly you, your father, your grandfather, and your entire damn clan are worthless. I've never heard of any of you—or anyone from that clan, for that matter." As soon as Codgarak had finished, Mala unleashed a forceful spray of beer out of his mouth and laughed. His aim landed with perfect accuracy on the group of wannabe tough guys who were with Sinotred. Liam couldn't tell for sure if it was intentional or not, but seeing as how it was Mala, he was pretty sure it was planned. The tiger laughed in his devious bellowing tone, which stirred a dark joy within Liam.

"If you truly are a minotaur, you'd at least give me the honor of fulfilling the code of Trekka-nol-Trekka-nok!" Sinotred said with immense disdain in his voice. The tension was building in the air.

"If you're calling for the code of Trekka-nol-Trekka-nok, then please tell me where and when was it, exactly, that I supposedly ended your grandfather's life?"

Sinotred snorted with anger, not satisfied with the response. *"Are you going to honor it or not?"*

As quickly as Sinotred had challenged Codgarak, so did Codgarak snap back at him, but this time his eyes blazed with a golden yellow energy. His response came over Sinotred's next words: *"Answer my question, you heifer!"* Both minotaurs seemed to expand and contract in size, as every breath was deep and long. The anger and adrenaline rushing through their veins could be easily seen by everyone. More and more of a crowd began to gather to watch what would happen next.

"The Battle of Yumamock!" Sinotred finally said.

Codgarak's glowing yellow eyes faded. "That was a very long time ago," he said. "I was about your age when I fought in that battle ... that was one of the first true fights I encountered as I started my journey long ago." He could see that the anger within the young minotaur was boiling almost to the point of overflowing. He wanted blood—his blood—and that would be the only thing to quell the vengeance inside him. He glanced over briefly and saw Cro, a man who also had the same vengeance dormant inside him.

"You have challenged me to uphold the code of Trekka-nol-Trekka-nok. I will honor it. Be here tomorrow morning at dawn."

Codgarak began to turn, having no desire to continue the discussion any longer.

"Why must I wait another day when I have waited practically my whole life?"

Codgarak looked up at the sun briefly. "That battle was in the morning. Your grandfather was rested, ready … I faced him when he was in his prime. Do you not want the same? To fight me when I am in my prime? To truly prove your power and worth, to bring the greatest honor to your grandfather? I am but a weary traveler just arriving from a long day's hike … face me here tomorrow and allow me to grant you the duel you truly desire."

Sinotred spit at Codgarak's feet and stormed off through the marketplace with his pathetic henchmen in tow. "You seem surprised," Codgarak said to Liam, who was taking in everything that had just occurred.

"I guess … I'm a little surprised … and … just didn't expect all of that."

"It will be over soon. No need to fret over it."

Slightly curious, he asked the minotaur, "You're not worried at all about it?"

"Nope."

"And why is that, exactly?"

Codgarak put his mug down on the table with extra force to emphasize that the conversation was over. "Show up tomorrow and see why!"

The rest of the night was uneventful, and Liam was certainly thankful for it. They didn't post guards that night; the spot that Lythya found for them was next to the soldiers' temporary camp. They had posted their own guards, so they all felt relatively safe given the circumstances.

The next morning, the group awoke and made their way towards the marketplace. Not very many people showed up, but the few who did found comfortable spots or sat on the rooftops looking down on the area. Codgarak walked to the east side of the street which flowed through the center of the market place and waited. Just before dawn, Sinotred and his few lackeys arrived. Sinotred was rolling his shoulders as he swayed into the street the merchants temporarily surrendering the road to the event. Sinotred rolling his neck and stretching as best he could, while Codgarak just stood and waited.

"Are you ready to meet your fate, cow?" It seemed as if Sinotred was straining to get the whole sentence out.

Codgarak didn't respond right away, pausing for just a moment as the sun crested over the hillside in the east. Its golden rays beamed down on the small market, the fresh light of the morning slowly forcing the shadows back.

"What say—"

Codgarak didn't let him finish his sentence. "Tell your grandfather he's still a bitch even in the afterlife!" That was all it took. A roar came out of Sinotred as he motored forward in a dash. Giant thumps were felt in the earth as he ran towards his target. Codgarak stayed perfectly still. Sinotred picked up speed and mass. Codgarak remained perfectly still. Sinotred, getting closer now, began to raise his battle-ax on his right side, beginning the motion that would generate the most power when it came crashing down. He leaned ever so slightly to his right, and with only a second left, Codgarak sidestepped and leapt forward. He took two steps, braced himself hard with his right foot, and twisted around. As he did so, he jerked his ax up towards the heavens and brought it crashing down like a lightning strike.

The ax's blade hit the left side of Sinotred's neck, severing the collar bone, and carved its way inward until it hit his spine, which guided the blade straight down and into his pelvis, where it finally stopped. The minotaur screamed in gut-wrenching agony for a brief moment until there was no more air in its now-useless lungs. The severed sides of its body twitched and snapped, the muscles still flaring from the adrenaline that had been fueling them just seconds ago.

Liam's jaw was, like that of many of the other people in the market at that moment, completely on the floor. A quick shuffling and he turned to see that the four lowlife assholes that were with Sinotred had just realized they were prime targets for retaliation from the people they had treated like shit. They thrashed about trying to escape the area. He watched them turn their backs and run away until—*swwwooosh!* A throwing knife drove itself into one of their backs. The man cried out to the other three, but that didn't stop them in their efforts to flee. *Swwwooosh!* Another blade hit its target, sending the man hurtling onto the ground as Sneak walked past him, holding his next throwing knife in his hand.

Focusing on the third runaway, Liam watched a hand come out from behind a cart, catching the poor soul by the neck. Golgoth lifted the man just enough that his toes were scraping the dirt of the street. Liam could hear him pleading until finally his voice ended and his body went limp. Releasing his grip, Golgoth let the body drop in a heap on the ground.

The final member of the gang ran as fast as he could. Sweat was pouring down his face as he made it to the edge of the marketplace and believed he was home free. He turned and looked back at them, ensuring he had enough distance from them before proceeding. As he did so, Liam watched Mala appear from behind a tree that was just wide enough to conceal his stout frame. It didn't take long after that. The man turned, not realizing that the tiger had already sealed his fate and marked "express delivery" on his soul, headed straight for hell. A quick swipe of his claws and the man's throat flowed with a rolling river of blood from the four gashes the tiger had given him.

By the time the final body dropped to the ground, Codgarak had returned to where Liam was sitting. "I guess you really weren't worried," Liam said.

The minotaur smirked. "There's a very good chance he could—and potentially would—have beaten me had it been a straight-up fight."

"Why would you say that?" Liam asked.

"Because I'm old, damn it!" Codgarak snorted. "What do you think they did last night after they stormed off?"

Liam shrugged. "I don't know."

"They went drinking, Liam." He nodded slowly. Now it all made sense. "They went and fueled their anger and rage even further last night by drinking. Bolstering their egos and especially Sinotred's pride. He was young, strong, and could have easily finished me off yesterday. I worked to influence his pride. Who wouldn't want to defeat a warrior at their best? So while I had a chance to rest and recover, he stayed up the entire night drinking and awoke this morning dehydrated, which kept his muscles tense and tight. Did you see his bloodshot eyes? They were sensitive to every increase of light, and he could barely keep them open for more than a few seconds. So not only was he seeing three of me as he charged, but because I took the eastern side, he was forced to run straight into the morning sunlight. He never even saw me or knew that I had taken a step away from my spot. His pride, his ego, his stupidity is what caused his death today. Not his skills, strength, power, or lack thereof."

"But why slay the four fleeing members?" Liam asked, to which Codgarak replied, "It's part of the code of Trekka-nol-Trekka-nok."

"Hold on! What do you mean, it's 'part of the code'?"

"The code was written thousands of years ago, but it basically said minotaurs shouldn't fight each other, and to do so shows that your allegiance is to another and not your own kind. The fact that Sinotred was enacting the code means I must have killed his grandfather in a battle where we faced eachother. Therefore, if you are challenged to the code of Trekka-nol-Trekka-nok, everyone in your party is to be slain should you lose."

Liam didn't really want to scream, but all reasoning had just been blown out of his mind, and without any self-control, he yelled, *"What?"*

The minotaur looked at him and shrugged with a "what's the big deal?" look on his face. *"If you had lost, we would all have been killed!"* Codgarak nodded. *"And did you ever think to ... oh, I don't know ... tell us?"*

Codgarak tilted his head at Liam. "Wait—you didn't know that?"

"No! Of course I didn't fucking know that, Codgarak!"

"Well, that would explain why you're having a complete meltdown now."

"Meltdown!"

"Well, it's not that big of a deal."

Liam threw his arms out. *"And why is that not that big of a deal?"*

"Well, even if I lost, you outnumbered them basically three to one. You would easily have won that fight and then just had to worry about the Black Trekka Spirit Curse eventually coming for you ... but I honestly don't know if that part is really a thing or not."

Liam grabbed his head with both hands. *"What is happening?"* He started to breathe heavily and took a moment to calm himself down. "Okay ... so you're telling me that if you lost but we decided to just kill them anyways, we would have some dark spirit trekka thing coming after us to curse us until we die?"

Codgarak bobbed his head back and forth. "Basically."

Liam exhaled, his eyes wide with the sheer shock of it all. "Wait! Just ... hold on here! Didn't minotaurs have their— your own wars and battles where you fought each other?"

"Of course."

330

"Well then, that stupid code doesn't even make sense!"

Codgarak was now the one to hold up his hand in confusion. "I never said it made sense, Liam. Minotaurs have never been known for our intelligence. Most of us are quite dumb."

Liam took his hands off his head, held them up, and swung them downward to emphasize his point. "*Fine! Fine!* Fine! Well ... let's just put it this way! No more code of Trekka-Trekka-Shit! *Okay?*"

"The proper name is Trekka—"

Not even letting him finish, Liam snapped, *"I don't fucking care, Codgarak! No more!"* His voice cracked with a high pitch that left everyone else laughing internally.

Liam didn't know where he was going, but he walked off and wandered aimlessly around the marketplace, trying to get away from the others. Mala handed Codgarak some pipe tobacco. "If I had known it was that easy to get the son of man to snap, I would have taken him to the Cave of Larahvita and let him lose his shit over the gorgon in it." They smiled at one another, imagining a new level of "fun" they could have with Liam while on their travels.

The midday sun soon arrived and, as promised, the sergeant walked into the marketplace and found the "large white tiger" who was looking for him. "Sir Mala, I assume?" Mala furled his hand in front of himself with a slight bow. "Well, first let me thank you for the mess you've made this morning." The sergeant looked over at Codgarak, who just lifted his hands as if to say "What you gonna do, bro?" "My soldiers were telling me just how bored they were this morning and hoping for some extra work, and sure enough, here you are causing it for them. So grateful, truly ..."

Mala looked at Codgarak. "I like him ... can we switch him out for Liam?"

The minotaur shook his head in response as the sergeant continued. "Now ... let me introduce myself. I am Sergeant Erik of house Pena. Welcome to Hummit. I was told you wanted to inquire about our war effort—something about potentially helping us?"

"Yes, that's right. We were pleased to see your troops training and preparing for it. It's about time something is done. We would be happy to be at your service and assist in the retaking of Lithram. That cunt Emmanuel must be vanquished as soon as possible."

The sergeant gave a slight chuckle as he smiled and squinted. "Lithram? We're not marching to Lithram! Wait—you're not aiding Buuklingran and sent here to try and stop us from marching on them, are you?"

Mala and Codgarak looked at one another in amazement. "You're not marching to retake Lithram?"

The sergeant shook his head and lowered his eyebrows, believing they were crazy. "No ... we march to attack Buuklingran."

"But Emmanuel is at Lithram! Is he not?"

The sergeant rolled his shoulders. "I don't know anything about this Emmanuel you speak of. All I can tell you is that my captain informed me that once Lithram fell, it broke the alliances within Delco. We march to reclaim the west for the glory and honor of Hummit and King Tor II."

"But what of Lithram?" Mala emphasized.

"I would say that sounds more like Somopack and Ashfurgoth's problem right now."

"I cannot believe what I am hearing. This is by far the easiest military strategy decision I've ever heard of," Mala proclaimed.

"I apologize, Sir Mala. As the old saying goes, a soldier's duty is not to wonder why but to follow orders, live, and die."

Mala rolled his eyes. "That is by far the most accurate and also the most hideous phrase ever conceived."

The sergeant smirked, not agreeing but not disagreeing either. "Well, I assume you will travel further east to challenge your destiny against this ... Emmanuel?"

Codgarak chimed in. "It would appear so."

The sergeant nodded. "Well, I bid you safe travels and good luck in the future war you seek. Should you change your mind, we'd love to have you join our ranks. Goodbye." Sergeant Erik shook their hands and quickly departed, returning to his duties of preparing the army.

"Truly a bunch of imbeciles!"

Codgarak readjusted his arms, which were crossed in front of his chest. "The sergeant is just doing his job."

Mala tilted his head upwards towards his companion. "I don't mean him, but clearly his superiors need to stop stealing the fresh air I breathe." He reached up and began scratching his neck with his large paw. "That is why I could never serve a kingdom such as this." Mala shuttered and flourished himself. "I tremble at the thought of it, Codgarak ... I truly do!"

The minotaur smiled. There was always some type of theatrics to enjoy when the giant cat was around. Codgarak cut to the chase. "There is certainly no honor in this—to ignore one evil and choose to be the initiator of another."

"Mmm, yes ... just another dick-measuring contest for the feeble humans. They wish their dicks were as big as their prides and egos, but we all know that the only thing smaller than their manhood is their brains."

Codgarak gave a snort. "I won't disagree with you there."

Mala lurched forward away from the table he had been leaning against and turned to face Codgarak. "There is certainly no point in us remaining here … the human stench is already making me want to vomit a hairball. What do you think our next move should be?"

"We should wait until the rest have returned, but my immediate thoughts are to head north to Belshire and see what they plan to do."

"You really think you'll be welcomed there by the centaurs?"

"There's only one way to find out."

Liam had wandered the market and the town square for some time, blowing off steam and getting some fresh air. He found a small barrel midway down an alley at the side of a tavern and decided to sit down. He just wanted to escape, but walking through a crowd wasn't the same as being alone. Though the marketplace was still busy with activity and the chatter of commerce, the alleyway blocked out a good majority of the noise. He let the back of his head rest upon the tavern's brick wall, impacting with a slight thud, and let out a long exhale. It dawned on him that this was the first moment he had actually been alone in a long time. He had been on a journey where there was someone with him practically 24/7, whether it be Cashmes, Dhather, Codgarak, Golgoth … they were almost always together. Hell, the one night he had assumed he would be alone on night watch, Aibek was with him. They hadn't talked much, but he was still … there.

He smiled for a moment, enjoying the personal space to finally block out the troubles of the world … the future war against Emmanuel … the demented weirdness of Golgoth.

He closed his eyes as he continued to take long, deep breaths. He began to dream of his home in Artho. The trail through the woods he always took when he went on his hunts. The copper-brown bark of the pine trees; the blackened valleys separating the bark plates in their mixed patterns. The rich and smooth aroma of the pine oil that drifted on the breeze of the forest. The Quenick squirrels that ran up and down the white oak trees—the squirrels unique to the Artho region with their golden yellow fur. Normally their chatter was annoying, especially when he was trying to be quiet and wait for the deer to sweep through the small meadows, but now, in this moment, he missed it.

Life was so simple then. He rolled his head slightly from side to side against the brick wall. His mind began to drift away and imagine the horrors of Artho as if it were being raided by the gnolls they'd fought at the keep. How quickly they would have overrun the village. The screams that were normally of joy and happiness of the children playing were now ringing in his mind as screams of terror. A game of hide and seek was now imagined as hide and survive. He could hear the yacking of the gnolls, the high-pitched yelping and barking that stirred your mind towards madness. His peace was invaded by the thought of bloodshed. His breathing still heavy, he pressed his lips together. The more he tried to prevent the darkness from taking over his dream, the more it seemed impossible to stop it.

There were such good people in Artho … peaceful, only desiring a good life where they provided for one another. They had done nothing to deserve the slaughter his mind was currently projecting. It was then he thought of Lithram and the people within it. Though he had never been there, had no knowledge of what it looked like or of the people who dwelled within its walls or borders, he believed there had to be some who were just like his old neighbors. People who truly lived their lives in peace and harmony with their fellow men and fellow creatures. How could others ignore what was going on? There was evil in this world, and so few with the courage to look it in the eye and say, "I will not allow you to prevail!"

Taking his next long inhale, he slowly opened his eyes. He let out his breath with a thunderous pounding of his heart as he saw the reflection of the sun off a hammered nickel-plated skull helmet.

He brought his head forward and his eyes met those of the helmet's wearer. Ferra's face shield narrowed down to a point over the chest armor she wore, which was also made of hammered nickel. Under the armor was a tightly woven teal fabric that sat tight against her body. The color faded in and out as it wasn't one consistent shade but had been pieced together out of whatever material had been left over. The shirt collar covered her entire neck, and its long sleeves disappeared underneath the vambraces that protected her forearms and wrists. She wore black leather fingerless gloves and skeletal horned shoulder plating that contrasted with the teal fabric and nickel armor. But he didn't care about that.

A black leather belt was wrapped around her waist, securing a dark gray skirt. The bottom reached only halfway down her thighs, the edging heavily frayed and torn. The appearance was that of a longer dress which had been altered for the results she wanted. Suede leather boots with layered stitching and padding adorned her feet and calves, rising slightly past her knees.

She lifted her hand and grabbed the bottom of her face shield. He could have sworn she was moving in slow motion as she lifted it off her head, displaying her pale skin and deep purple lips. Around her right eye was a red scar, a line running down from her forehead, cutting through her eyebrow and continuing down the edge of her cheek. The scar went around her eye socket, and the eyebrow that remained was thinner than the other. Her eyes were pale green with tiny speckles of yellow and orange around the iris. Her dark hair was slightly frizzy, having seen the weathering of nature. She wore it wrapped, and it hung over her right shoulder and down her side.

She leaned towards him, placing her helmet on a barrel next to the one he was sitting on. Straightening up, she reached into a pouch that dangled from her belt and produced a pipe and small container; uncapping the small container and retrieving the tobacco leaf held inside it. She filled the pipe until it was full to capacity. She snapped her fingers and produced a small flame spell.

As she puffed at the mouthpiece, the embers burned and sank their way into the heart of the pipe. The exhalation of the smoke also surprised him, as it was a bright neon pink.

Her eyes left the pipe and returned to his. Her gaze gave him the feeling that she was looking past his stare, through his spirit, and seeing the core of his soul. They remained in the moment, looking through the veil of pink smoke produced between her drags at the pipe, not concerned about the world or the busyness of the villagers around them. Two souls present in a moment, and oh, how he didn't want that moment to end.

But, as is their destiny, all things must end. Ferra had almost finished her tobacco when they both noticed the figure standing at the entrance to the side street. Sneak looked down it towards them and motioned with his head for them to come along. Ferra had the sole of her foot flat against the wall, her knee sticking out in front of her; kicking herself away from the wall, she knocked the tobacco out of her pipe and blew out what little remnants remained within it. As she did so, Liam grabbed her helmet and held it out for her. Her attention was on securing the pipe in her pouch, and as she turned, she looked down at the helmet and her eyes drifted up to meet his.

They engaged in one final moment of connection before she reached out and grabbed the helmet from him. There was a slight pause before she led the way out of the side street and they followed Sneak. Not a word was spoken, but no words were required.

Returning to the tables in the marketplace, which the group had claimed as their own, Liam was surprised to see a table filled with food and drink—a feast he had not experienced before. Taken aback, he asked, "How did we pay for such a meal?"

Codgarak lifted a large coin purse, jostling it for him; he could hear the coins inside jingling freely. "Courtesy of our beloved Sinotred and his friends." A beaming smile came over Liam's face and he turned to Ferra, who was standing next to him; she allowed a smile to appear on her face. Liam quickly turned away, though. *"Eww, Liam and Ferra staring at each other!"*—he hoped no one had noticed. He cut Mala off abruptly with a pointed index finger. "No! Not now!"

Mala tried to speak in his defense but couldn't. He turned to Dhather, who was sitting across the table from him. Dhather looked at his little brother. "Promise?" Mala unable to speak from the magical spell Dhather used on him. Mala shook his head in agreement. Dhather slowly released the spell, and Mala let out a soft sigh, mostly to check that his brother had kept his side of the bargain. "I was just joking ..." Mala said and went back to enjoying his meal and ignoring Liam. Liam and Ferra sat down and began to enjoy the meal displayed before them.

Everyone ate well past their limits. Liam suspected he was having a very similar experience to the others when, for one of the few times in his life, his stomach hurt from consuming too much food. "This is what it must be like to eat like a king!" he proclaimed.

Cashmes was holding his stomach. "No wonder most of them are fat!" A chuckle rippled across the group, but only briefly, as many starting to mutter things like "ow" and "oh god, that's not good!"

They cleared the table and produced a large map that spanned its surface. Liam was amazed at its grand scale—another first for him, for he had never had the chance to experience the world in such grandeur. Codgarak shared with the group the information Sergeant Erik had provided, which generated scoffs and the shaking of heads around the table. A few people had side conversations in whispers as Codgarak and Mala continued.

"I believe we should head north and work our way to Belshire. See what the centaurs have chosen to do in these troubling times," Codgarak informed the group.

Mala had a counter-argument, though. "Giving this some thought, my friend, I believe it may be best to head further east. Make our way to Kline, or maybe even further towards Bisk, potentially as far as Ashfurgoth. They are the next great stronghold for Delco, and they would be best to meet Emmanuel in the field." Codgarak shook his head as he contemplated the suggestion.

"What if we were to do both?" Cashmes chimed in. The group looked at each other as he continued. "The centaurs could potentially take this threat head on … depending on the true numbers of both armies, which we still have no knowledge of."

Cashmes pointed to Belshire on the map, and Liam was grateful, because seeing all this information for the first time was overwhelming to him. Cashmes ran his finger down and around the mountain pass. "There is a good chance that if we can convince the centaurs to enter the war, they can march towards Ashfurgoth. If we can convince them in time, that is. *But!* There is even a chance we can then go to Serenyal, and bring the joint force of Belshire and

Serenyal together to meet at Ashfurgoth. At the same time a group of us can take the southern route and we can meet back together at Ashfurgoth."

Aibek said, "That is quite ambitious."

Cashmes nodded and asked, "What are your thoughts, Aibek?"

The ex-prisoner rubbed his chin, ran his hand up his jaw, and grabbed the back of his neck. "I think the southern route may be best." Aibek pointed to the map and drew his finger across. "We move to Kline. From there we head for Bisk and then Ashfurgoth. It is a shorter route and will allow us to get closer to Lithram, where we can get further insight."

Liam began to better grasp the whole map and asked, "I don't understand why we don't just head straight to Ashfurgoth now. Head straight towards the closest part of our enemy. Let's take him head on."

Mala was about to open his mouth but looked at Dhather, who shook his head. Mala returned to keeping his mouth shut. For about thirty seconds, that is, until he reopened it and provided some further experience. "Son of man … of all the warfare conducted in history, only ten percent is actually combat. The vast majority of war is spent moving troops, resupplying, making preparations for combat. Yes, we do want to attack and vanquish the bastard … but in reality, it will not happen overnight."

Mala paused, glancing at Dhather, who widened his eyes with a smirk and a nod. "Look at you being mature!"

Mala bared his teeth at his brother but continued after a slight delay. "We need an army to support this effort. We cannot just enter the field of battle thirteen against thirty thousand … we need to be strategic in how we approach this. You can't overthrow a king by just dropping him off a cliff and letting a herd of bison run over him."

Codgarak was not letting the group get off track. "Cashmes's plan could work and actually may be the best bet to bring the right force together to meet Emmanuel. If he really does have an army of demons in alliance with him, we'll need all the help we can get." Codgarak looked at each person around the table in turn, and everyone shook their heads in agreement and understanding. "A long journey awaits us come morning. Let us toast and embrace this moment together, for there is no guarantee when we will meet again!"

They all raised their glasses high and cheered the toast.

FERRA

DIVIDE AND CONQUER

The morning sun radiated golden yellow and orange hues against the scattered, billowing clouds as the piercing rays of light shot down from the heavens. The morning dew and mist was still rising as they awoke and began the day—a scene Liam did not take for granted that morning, as the moment did not last long before they began packing their items for the journey ahead.

They formed a gaggle together as they passed through the village outside the walls of Hummit. Liam gazed at it for a moment before looking ahead and asking himself what new wonders he would see. *Let no one say I didn't live life to its fullest!* he told himself. He called ahead to the group, "How will we know when our paths split?"

"There is a sign which will guide us," came Aibek's reply.

The majority of Liam's journey so far had not followed a trail but had consisted of the group navigating through woods and mountains. He felt out of place on this clear path that cut through the landscape. "Wait!" He stopped in the middle of the trail. "Why don't we have horses?"

The group came to stop at this question. "*Himph!* That's actually a good question. Why don't we have horses?" Golgoth asked.

Codgarak raised his hands to his head and gestured all down his massive frame. "Do I look like I would fit on a horse?" Liam tilted his head back as it immediately made sense. *Yeah, he would crush a horse*, he thought.

"Not everything is about you, Codgarak!" Mala quipped sarcastically.

"You would crush a horse just as easily as I would!" the minotaur shot back.

"That wouldn't be my problem, now, would it? That's for the horse to deal with!" Codgarak lifted his hands with a "what's the point?" sway in his stance. "The cunt actually has a good point for once. It would be nice to go on an adventure and have something else do the work for me for once in my nine lives!"

Dhather added his two cents. "Normally we just teleport into the area we need to get to. It's been quite a while since we were blocked from using that ability."

Mala raised a paw. "That's actually a good point. We haven't tried teleporting in a while." The large cat began his chant, but it didn't take long for him to give up and proclaim, "Nope! Still blocked."

Liam smiling at Mala's comments, seeing the humor in it and enjoying the banter for a moment. "But … it doesn't matter anyways. Emmanuel can probably smell the cunt all the way from here. So whether we teleport or not he gives our position away." And just like that, the smile departed his face. *Guess some things just don't end with this asshole cat.*

"Even if we could ride horses, there is no point. The first kingdom we would come to, like Hummit, would confiscate them for their war effort and give us a quarter of their worth," Cashmes said before Mala continued, "And that is a great point to remind us that all kings are *cunts too!*"

Aibek brought the group back to reality. "All right, enough. We're losing time. Back to it." He looked ahead and nodded to Lythya. "Go search for the split in the trail and wait for us there."

There was a slight pause as they went further through the small valley. Then Liam heard something. *"HIMPH! Himph, hehehe … "*

"What is it, Golgoth?" Liam asked.

Golgoth turned and waited for Cro to pass him on the trail before he answered. *"Himph! Himph!* It was what Aibek did say!"

Liam wrinkled his brow. "What about it?"

They started walking side by side as they continued the conversation. "He told Lythya to go search for the trail! *Himph!*"

Liam tilted his head. "And that's funny?"

"YES! *Haha.* And ironic, is it not?"

Liam was now even more confused. "How is it ironic?"

Golgoth leaned over, getting creepily close to his face, and pointed in the direction in which they were traveling. "She goes to search for the trail! *Himph!*"

"Yeah … and?"

Golgoth wiped his face quickly before he continued. *"And …* it is just like the old saying! *Himph!* If you search for good … you will find favor, but if you search for evil, it will find you! *HIMPH! Himph!*"

Liam was taken aback not only at what Golgoth said but how excited he was about it. "But we are literally marching towards an evil army now!"

A broad smile appeared on Golgoth's face. "Exactly! And find it we shall! *HIMPH! HIMPH! HAHAHAHA!*"

Liam finally saw Lythya lounging on the ground where the trail came to a fork. "Finally!" The group took a quick break, grabbing water out of their small carriers, and as they did so, they naturally created a circle. Liam barely noticed it out of the corner of his eye, but Codgarak and Mala returned from a side conversation by themselves. A slight nod between Codgarak and Dhather as they returned to the group.

Codgarak took a few steps back. "Dhather, Lythya, Edha, Aibek and Cro will travel with me to Belshire." Looking around the circle, he continued. "Cashmes, Golgoth, Liam, Ferra, Sneak, and Mala will travel east."

Liam's eyes widened in shock as the voice in his head cried out, *I'm supposed to stay with Codgarak!* He wanted to protest, to argue and declare how much he detested the idea. Just as he was about to take a stance and defend his case, he saw Mala watching him with great intensity. Though no words were said, he felt deep within him a voice that said, *You have trusted Codgarak this far; now you must trust him and his judgment.*

Codgarak's group began to depart, heading down their pathway, and as they passed the others, they clasped their forearms together. The reality was setting in, and though Liam was struggling to accept it, he now felt compelled to share a multitude of thoughts and feelings— the gratitude, the appreciation, the respect he had for the legendary warrior. His mind rushed with an overwhelming intensity until Ferra interrupted him abruptly. "Whatever … come, heroes! It is time to be *super*." And with that, Liam joined his newly formed group as they headed down the trail to seek the destiny that awaited them.

FAREWELL

TO BE CONTINUED...

GLOSSARY OF PRONUNCIATIONS

Agos (Ahh-gos)
Ahal (Ah-hall)
Aibek (A-beck)
Alavaro (Al-ah-var-o)
Alphagad (Al-fuh-gad)
Amikkawa (Ah-mick-awah)
Apraiuh (Uh-pray-uh)
Artho (Are-tho)
Asandee (Uhh-saun-dee)
Ashfurgoth (Ash-fur-goth)
Augustaross (Au-gusta-ross)
Azazel (Uhh-zay-zel)
Bacca (Bock-uh)
Bastnaesite (Bast-nuh-site)
Belshire (Bell-shire)
Boredstill (Bore-ed-still)
Bullticutt (Bull-tih-cutt)
Buuklingran (Buck-lin-gran)
Cainten (Cane-ten)
Calgo-Kramok (Call-go-Cram-ock)
Carthco (Carth-co)
Cashmes (Cash-mez)
Cello (Sell-oh)
Celtagoff (Celta-goff)
Centeth (Sen-teth)
Cepheus (See-fuss)
Charohcha (Char-oh-cha)
Cho'Took (Show-Took)

Circinus (Sir-sin-us)
Circolitch (Cir-co-litch)
Codgarak (Cod-gare-ack)
Conocetico (Cono-cet-ico)
Crocontimont (Crow-con-te-mont)
Cygnus (Sig-nus)
Delco (Dell-co)
Dhather (Dath-er)
Drakonmites (Drack-en-mites)
Eadel (Ee-dell)
Edha (Ed-ha)
Engli (En-glee)
Erch (Urch)
Excelsem (Ex-sell-sem)
Explorto (Ex-plor-toe)
Februe (Feb-rue)
Ferra (Fair-uh)
Fortix (For-ticks)
Gnoll (Nole)
GoGax (Go-Gax)
Golgoth (Gol-goth)
Grensocc (Gren-sock)
Guttmaccafect (Gutt-mocka-fect)
Haivan (Hay-von)
Happer (Happ-er)
Hematite (Hema-tight)
Hoag (Ho-agg)
Hoth-Raila-Mah (Hoth-Ray-lah-Mah)
Hua (Hue-ah)
Hugithmurta (Hue-gith-mer-tuh)
Hummit (Hum-it)
Icelightals (Ice-light-all)

Ifrit (Ee-frit)
I-Rongoth-Hesgeth (Eye-Ron-goth-Hez-geth)
Iud (Ee-uh-d)
Jardack (Jar-dack)
Jerikako (Jer-i-kako)
Junteer (June-tier)
Killcath (Kill-cath)
Kimberonna (Kimber-on-uh)
Klipkoshek (Clip-co-sheck)
Kliploo (Klip-lue)
Larahvita (Lar-uhh-vita)
LithoLaleth (Lith-oh-Lay-leth)
Lithram (Lith-ram)
Littermacha (Litter-mocka)
Lorelaylee (Lore-lay-lee)
Lythya (Lith-ee-uh)
Mala (Mall-la)
Malin (Mall-in)
Marduk (Mar-duke)
Mat (Mat)
Milguards (Mil-guards)
Minokrak (Minno-crack)
Misovaga (Miso-vaga)
Mortagolf (Morta-golf)
Mystamight (Mist-uh-might)
Nacoa (Na-co-uhh)
Neodymium (Neo-dim-eon)
Nonons (No-nuns)
Odra (Ohh-druh)
Odry (Ohh-dree)
Papapites (Pah-puh-pites)
Pashro-Shaltok (Pash-row-Shal-talk)

Patastal (Pat-ah-stal)
Phippotath (Fip-oh-tath)
Pittazook (Pit-ah-zook)
Pretox (Pree-tocks)
Quenick (Quin-ick)
Raritan (Rare-ih-tan)
Rayna-ox (Ray-nah-ox)
RemaMortBrook (Reema-Mort-Brook)
Reptacrepts (Repta-crepts)
Sagetillith (Sage-till-ith)
SarpoGast (Sar-po-Gast)
Serenyal (Sir-ain-yall)
Sharra (Shar-uh)
Showlay (Show-lay)
Sinotred (Sin-oh-tred)
Skilvage (Skill-vij)
Somopack (So-moh-pack)
Stonevor (Stone-vor)
Subalpine (Sub-uhl-pine)
Sun-Share-Co (Sun-Share-Coh)
Sylphs (Silffs)
Taka-Rok (Tah-kah-Rock)
Taka-Skit (Tah-kah-Skit)
Terrex (Tare-ex)
Teskonok (Tez-connock)
Thitra Kningol (Thee-tra Kin-goal)
Trapsnas (Trap-snaz)
Ursa (Ur-sa)
Ushu (Ew-shoe)
Visvan (Vizz-van)
Volans (Vole-ans)
Wairick (Ware-ick)

Wilpog (Wil-pog)
Wyvern (Why-vern)
Yumamock (You-muhh-mock)
Zareel (Zuh-reel)

THE REAL DEFENDERS

"Freedom is never more than one generation away from extinction. We didn't pass it to our children in the bloodstream. It must be fought for, protected, and handed on for them to do the same ... "

—*40th US President Ronald Reagan*

I joined the United States Air Force on July 10, 2007. As I went through the process and progression through the Basic Military Training (BMT), I found myself being asked multiple times, "What career field are you going into?"

"Security Forces! 3P0," I'd proclaim. As I progressed in my training through the Security Forces Academy, I couldn't help my natural desire to learn more about the history and heritage of this career field. I wanted to know where it started, what *we* stood for, and *who* came before me.

I was so eager and motivated in my youth. I knew I carried an intense desire that many others around me did not possess. To me, the Air Force core values of integrity, service, and excellence were a mantra that should be infused into all our daily lives. I was not just passionate, I was zealous. I gave a countless number of "love hours" to the military. I just didn't know of any other way to be.

I am honored and continually humbled to have accomplished a multitude of things within my military time. Yet one of the things that will forever be in my heart, within my mind, and carried inside my soul and spirit is the legacy of some special "defenders". I would like to introduce you to some truly incredible men and women. For they were a generation of warriors that defended freedom and liberty for so many. They are the true defenders, and they will never be gone or forgotten as long as we still speak their names and share their stories.

Airman First Class Elizabeth N. Jacobson

A1C Jacobson pleaded with her leadership for permission to perform convoy operations. Her passion to serve her country and make a difference was overwhelming. It has been said that A1C Jacobson always sought the hardest challenges and never quit or gave up. She was bright, intelligent, and cared deeply for her family, friends, country, and military. A1C Jacobson was the first female airman killed in the line of duty supporting Operation Iraqi Freedom. She was also the first female Security Forces defender to be killed in action.

While providing security support in a convoy movement, A1C Jacobson was killed in action as a result of her vehicle being struck by an improvised explosive device on September 28, 2005. Elizabeth was only 21 years old. The quote that she is most famous for, and one that many of us carry with us daily, is "I also believe in love and here is my quote: 'We're only on earth for a little while, so live life to the fullest and carry a smile.'"

**Technical Sergeant
Jason L. Norton**

**Staff Sergeant
Brian S. McElroy**

TSgt Jason Norton served as a patrol officer and military K9 handler at the 3rd Security Forces Squadron (SFS) in Elmendorf AFB, Alaska. Additionally, SSgt Brian McElroy also served and was stationed at the 3 SFS as the Information Security Officer. Both TSgt Norton and SSgt McElroy were deployed together in 2006 to Taji, Iraq (18 miles north of Baghdad).

On January 22, 2006, while on combat patrol, TSgt Norton and SSgt McElroy's vehicle was hit by a roadside bomb. TSgt Norton was 32 years old and SSgt McElroy was 28 years old.

Airman First Class LeeBernard E. Chavis

A1C LeeBernard Chavis did not start his military career in a positive light. A1C Chavis, after getting in trouble for a few events, was challenged by his leadership: "I challenge you to prove to everyone in this unit that you are the best there is!"

A1C Chavis accepted the challenge and would later be honored as the unit "Guide Bearer," where he carried the unit's flag on deployment and wherever the unit was represented in ceremonies—the highest honor a member of the unit could hold.

A1C Chavis became a shining example of the warrior spirit and carried the warrior ethos wherever he went, inspiring multiple airmen along the way. In 2006, A1C Chavis was assigned to the 732nd Expeditionary Security Forces Squadron in Baghdad, Iraq. A1C Chavis was killed by enemy gunfire on October 14, 2006. Due to A1C Chavis's story and his actions taken that day, the USAF responded with a newly desi>gned turret system with better security measures. The "Chavis" turret is still being utilized today.

Staff Sergeant John T. Self

Staff Sergeant John Self was a true servant warrior. Sergeant Self had just completed a six-month deployment to a war zone. He had returned home and begun wedding preparations with his fiancée when a volunteer opportunity presented itself. Sergeant Self convinced his fiancée to let him serve on a one-year deployment to Iraq, assisting the Iraqi Police and training them on how to conduct law enforcement operations.

Sergeant Self had only been home for a few months when he left once again for the "sand box." On May 14, 2007, Sergeant Self was serving on his 79th combat patrol on the streets of Baghdad, Iraq. His team was assisting the Iraqi police force in conducting operations when an improvised explosive device erupted, cutting through the vehicle, killing him instantly and wounding his three fellow Security Forces defenders. Staff Sergeant Self was 29 years old.

Senior Airman Jason D. Nathan

A1C Jason Nathan was from a military family that has served in both the Army and the Air Force. Following in his family's footsteps, A1C Nathan went to serve his country and instantly outshone his peers. He was awarded Security Forces Airmen of the Year while he was stationed at RAF

Lakenheath, England.

In 2007, A1C Nathan was selected to deploy to Iraq and serve in Detachment 6 of the 732nd Expeditionary Security Forces Squadron, Camp Speicher, Iraq. Their mission was to support the training and operations of the Iraqi Police Force.

On June 23, 2007, A1C Nathan was the gunner in the Humvee turret of his vehicle while on combat patrol. An improvised explosive device detonated near his vehicle, and he was taken from us. A1C Nathan was 22 years old and from Macon, Georgia.

Staff Sergeant Travis L. Griffin

Staff Sergeant Travis Griffin was raised in a military family. Both his mother and stepfather served in the United States Air Force, and he quickly joined the service once eligible.

Sergeant Griffin served four separate tours in Iraq as well as a total of eight deployments in his career. In 2008, Sergeant Griffin volunteered for another year-long deployment to Iraq. When asked why he must go again, he replied, "I am one of the few people who actually has combat experience, and I am going over there to do everything I can to make sure everyone comes back home."

On April 3, 2008, Sergeant Travis Griffin was killed in action when his vehicle was struck by an improvised explosive device.

First Lieutenant Joseph D. Helton

1Lt Joseph Helton was the leader that every airman looks up to and hopes to encounter in their career. 1Lt Helton was not just an officer leading troops but a dedicated team member who stood right beside his airmen at all times.

In 2009, 1Lt Helton was deployed and served an entire year with Detachment 3, of the 732nd Expeditionary Security Forces Squadron. 1Lt Helton completed his entire year in Iraq and saw his team members return home, but he volunteered to stay behind and assist the newly formed Detachment 2. His reasoning was that the lieutenant originally assigned was delayed in their arrival, and 1Lt Helton wanted to give his best in leading, preparing, and developing the newly formed detachment.

On September 8, 2009, while on patrol near Baghdad, Iraq, 1Lt Helton's vehicle was attacked by an improvised explosive device. He was 24 years old and always inspired his troops with his famous motto, "Don't be a weak sauce!"

Senior Airman Nicholas J. Alden

Senior Airman Nicholas Alden was murdered in cold blood while sitting unarmed on a bus at Frankfurt International Air Terminal, Germany.

Airman Alden was assigned to the 48th Security Forces Squadron, RAF Lakenheath, United Kingdom. Airman Alden had just completed his regional training center (RTC) and was en route to an overseas assignment. While in transit to his destination, a gunman entered the bus he and his fellow Security Forces team members were utilizing, screamed "God is great" in Arabic, and then shot Airman Alden dead, along with another airman serving as the bus driver, and wounded two others. The gunman attempted to flee but was chased down and captured by Senior Airman Alden's fellow team members. The gunman later confessed to the shooting.

Staff Sergeant Todd "TJ" Lobraico

Staff Sergeant T. J. Lobraico came from a military family where both his mother and father served in the Air Force.

Sergeant Lobraico had already served one combat tour, but as he headed for his second in Afghanistan, he did everything he could to volunteer to assist the K9 teams.

On September 5, 2013, Sergeant Lobraico was assisting the K9 teams and his fellow team members while on combat patrol just outside Bagram Airfield, Afghanistan. Sergeant Lobraico's patrol was attacked, and while defending his airmen and laying down suppressive fire and actively engaging the enemy, he was killed from wounds sustained by small arms fire while in the firefight.

**Senior Airman
Nathan C. Sartain**

**Airman First Class
Kcey E. Ruiz**

Senior Airman Nathan Sartain and Airman First Class Kcey Ruiz were both deployed to Afghanistan and were performing fly away security team (FAST) operations.

Their mission objectives were to protect the aircraft, crew, passengers, and cargo whenever the aircraft was land based between missions, normally in isolated locations throughout the theater of operations. Additionally, when not performing FAST missions, both airmen would conduct installation entry controller and armorer duties. On October 2, 2015, both airmen boarded a C-130J Super Hercules aircraft which took off from Jalalabad Airfield, Afghanistan but crashed shortly after takeoff. There were no survivors.

**Technical Sergeant
Joseph G. Lemm**

**Staff Sergeant
Louis Bonacasa**

Technical Sergeant Lemm and Staff Sergeant Bonacasa paid the ultimate price for their country on December 21, 2015. Four days before Christmas, both sergeants were tasked with providing security to Air Force OSI agents conducting operations outside the wire. Both sergeants were civilian law enforcement officers and utilized their skills to help protect other military members. As the team members were working their mission that day, a motorcyclist drove into their immediate area and detonated a suicide vest. The blast killed both sergeants along with four OSI agents.

TSgt Joseph Lemm's son salutes his father's casket at the memorial service in New York City.

At the beginning of this book, Edmund Burke's famous quote was highlighted: "The only thing necessary for the triumph of evil is for good men to do nothing." Though the characters in this book are fake, the men and women above are not.

This book is dedicated to these incredible men and women and all who stand on the front line and face evil every day. May God bless their families, and may we never forget the sacrifices they made by giving their lives for the cause of freedom and liberty and to ensure that evil does not triumph.

SPECIAL THANKS

This story originally started in 2009. It stayed within my heart, soul, and spirit for twelve years until finally one day I said, "Okay … it's time." Over the past year I have dedicated countless hours and resources to bringing this story to life, but there was no way I could have accomplished this without the help and support of many people.

Todd Benson

Todd, you were the first person who listened to me blab on and on about this epic story that had come to life inside my head. I cannot thank you enough for the long hours spent talking about the story, my ideas, where I wanted to see it go, and the goals I had for it. You were encouraging and supportive this entire time, and I cannot thank you enough for that.

Lucas Clark

Lucas, you have simply been by far the most important person to me and this book. From day one when I said I was working on this project, you simply volunteered to help, and you meant it in the most sincere and fervorous way. This book simply would not be what it is today without you. I simply cannot thank you enough for how much your friendship simply means to me.

Emmanuel Quinones

Q, you were the first person to become a beta reader for me, and you shocked me by actually reading the material and providing suggestions and recommendations to help me become a better author. I cannot thank you enough for your encouragement, and I am so blessed to have you as a part of my team helping me grow The Dying Breed series.

Elizabeth Gardner

My darling, you have been one of my biggest fans and supporters since day one. I cannot thank you enough for all your love and support over the years. You are amazing and I will forever love you.

Loren Leão

Loren, you are a blessing from God. I started out on this journey hoping to find an artist who could truly capture the spirit of the book and bring the characters in my head to life. You have exceeded my expectations, and I cannot thank you enough for your incredible work. You are an absolutely amazing artist, and I am forever blessed to have you on my team helping bring this story to life.

Mariam Yasser

Mariam, your talents are beyond measure, and I am amazed by every piece of art you color in. Thank you for becoming a part of this team and sharing your talents with not just us but the rest of the world. I am so excited to see where your future takes you.

Catherine Dunn

Catherine, I am so grateful for your grace and mercy in helping me edit my manuscript and fixing the countless mistakes I have made. You are a blessing, and I am so grateful to have found you and have your partnership in going forward. Thank you so much and cheers to the next manuscript!

Readers

I cannot thank you enough for taking the time to read this book. My three goals were:

1. For this book to be a blessing to at least one person on this crazy spinning rock we live on.
2. For this story to inspire at least one person.
3. For this book to motivate at least one person to make a positive change in their life.

I sincerely hope that one of these goals applies to you as you finish this story. We'd love to hear about it on our Facebook page: www.facebook.com/TDBseries

COMING SOON

Book 2: *The Dying Breed: Injustice* is currently being reviewed by the development editors' team. I hope to have *Injustice* complete by the middle of 2023.

Book 3: *The Dying Breed: Enslavement* (working title) is currently sitting at 20,555 words. I hope to have it in the hands of the development editors' team by the end of January 2023 and complete by the end of 2023.

Book 4: *The Dying Breed: The Warrior Arises* (working title) is currently in the concept design phase. I hope to start working on the manuscript in the fall of 2023 and complete it by spring 2024.

For the latest information, you can follow and like our page on Facebook.

www.facebook.com/TDBseries

Or.

Warriorpub.wordpress.com